# PROPHECY OF THOL

## BOOK 1

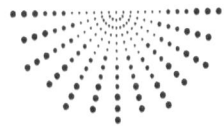

### DAWN GREENFIELD IRELAND

ARTISTIC
ORIGINS

# CONTENTS

Prophecy of Thol by Dawn Greenfield Ireland/D.E. Greenfield

Published by Artistic Origins

Copyright © 2017 - 2026 Dawn Greenfield Ireland

Paperback cover put together by Brandon White 6/22/2024 www.victorylaurel.com

Map of Thol: Cartography by Scott K. Leslie www.theadventurerspack.com

Glossary of Thol by https://www.fiverr.com/ayshaarias

Interior layout by Yours Truly (me) 11/10/2021 - 6/22/2024

Corrections made: 7/28/2024, 3/31/2026

ISBN 978-1-940385-06-8 (eBook)

ISBN 978-1-940385-08-2 (Paperback)

BISAC YAF056030

Please visit my website: www.degreenfield.com

Hey, leave a review on your favorite retailer. Reviews help sell books!

# ACKNOWLEDGMENTS, AWARDS & DEDICATION

I created the new cover with the Visionary on the front. He looks just like I pictured him when I introduced him.

Paperback cover put together by my eldest son, Brandon White www.victorylaurel.com

I wanted a map of Thol, but I'm not even capable of stick figures. Thank you Scott K. Leslie www.theadventurerspack.com the cartographer who tackled the Map of Thol.

Creatures, creatures, creatures... A hearty thanks to Alex Gravalis (Fiverr.com) for Ghury, the Egrom creature; AskOrbin (Fiverr.com) for my diwal dog; and my son George White for Jakla Bosakin. The borjo creature was created by me via an AI program. YAY me for figuring this out!

The glossary for the Thol book series was created by Ayshaarias from Canada. Man oh man, that gal had her work cut out for her. She did a fabulous job. Many thanks that I found her!

https://www.fiverr.com/ayshaarias

Many thanks to Cicely Wynne who proofed this book near the end of 2023.

Want to get to know me better? Read my newsletters, and check out my website www.degreenfield.com

Prophecy of Thol has the following achievements:

- Quarterfinalist ~ Geneva International Science in Fiction Script Competition 1/13/2024

- Finalist ∼ Sensei Film Fest 12/11/2023
- Quarterfinalist ∼ Filmmatic Sci-Fi/Fantasy Awards 12/15/2023
- Semifinalist ∼ CLIMAX Critics Awards 5/18/2023
- Finalist ∼ MAGMA Film Festival (Hawaii) script award 4/19/2023
- Quarterfinalist ∼ PageTurner Screenplay Competition 3/28/2023
- Readers Favorite ∼ 8/15/2018

## DEDICATION

*This book is dedicated to the blazing love of my two sons:*

*Brandon Clay White & George Thomas White*

*In Memory of*

*My parents, George and Dorothy (Daigle) Greenfield, my big sister, Robin, and Shasta Annie Ireland, my furry sidekick for 16-1/2 years and my muse during several drafts of this book. You are all missed so much!*

Quote from the Author:

*Kansas is nowhere in sight, and I can't find my ruby shoes.*
— D.E. Greenfield

# ALSO BY
# DAWN GREENFIELD IRELAND

| Nonfiction | |
|---|---|
| The Puppy Baby Book | Mastering Your Money (2022) |
| Puppy Adoption and Beyond | Writers Preparation Handbook |
| Mastering Your Money (2008) | What's Breaking Your Budget |
| **Online Classes** | |
| Writers Preparation Handbook | How to Format Word Docs Like A Pro |
| **Cozy Mysteries** | **Sci-Fi-Fantasy** |
| **The Alcott Family Adventures** | **The Thol Series** |
| Hot Chocolate | Prophecy of Thol |
| Bitter Chocolate | Gifts From Thol |
| Spicy Chocolate | Love of Thol |
| Nutty Chocolate | King of Thol |
| **Katz' Cat Series** | Earth Calling Thol |
| Katz' Cat | **Sci-Fi Romance Adventure** |
| Bill Hill's Pills | Forced Dreams |
| The Detectives | **Dystopian** |
| The Pact | The Last Dog |
| | Texmexzona |
| **Books by my Alter Ego ~ DG Ireland** | |
| **Bonded Shapeshifter Billionaire Series** | |
| Bonded | |
| Tothars | |
| Tilted | |
| Unforeseen | |
| Connected | |
| **Need A Notebook?** | |
| See my 54 themed notebooks on my website www.degreenfield.com/notebooks | |
| **Screenplays formatted as books** | |
| Plan B (Dark Comedy) | Where's Ralphie? (Family Comedy) |
| The God Child (Action Adventure) | Standing Dead (Drama/Tragedy) |
| The Far Corner ( Sci-Fi/Psychological/Creatures) | |
| **Screenplays as TV Episodes** | |
| Hot Chocolate ~ Episode 1 | Prophecy of Thol ~ Episode 1 |
| Bonded ~ Episode 1 | |
| See my screenplays and awards on my website: degreenfield.com Filmfreeway, ISA Network | |

# CHAPTER ONE

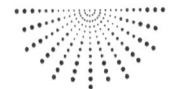

*T*he old leather high-backed chair squeaked as Victor Bennett settled down at his desk to read his current copy of the *Journal of Applied Physics*. Victor's home office was his sanctuary—peaceful, comfortable with a hint of lemon wood polish, and most of all, convenient—it beat the commute twice a week.

Buffy, a tan-and-white pit bull with a face of white hair showing her age, slept on a dog bed in front of the wall of over-flowing, floor-to-ceiling bookcases. Buffy had one ear pitched up; always in watchdog mode.

Certificates and awards adorned the walls, including a framed photo of Victor with famous British theoretical physicist, Stephen Hawking. Science prizes and exquisite images from space shuttle missions and the Hubble telescope completed the room.

Victor reached over to the dark cherrywood desk and grabbed a mechanical pencil. His eyes rested on a silver framed photograph on the corner of his desk. It was a reminder of a bygone time. If the house ever caught fire, he would rescue that picture before he would grab his cellphone or laptop.

The picture depicted a handsome man in his late forties, a striking blonde teenaged girl in an unusual silver-gray formed jumpsuit, two young towhead boys, and a nerdy looking dark-haired guy, about twenty-five, in sloppy clothes with cockeyed, black-rimmed glasses from being glued together so many times.

The girl's eyes haunted him.

He raked his thick sandy hair with both hands as he stared at the photo with a tenderness akin to longing.

Victor managed to pull his gaze back to the magazine. He let out a ragged breath, clicked the pencil to extend the lead, opened the cover and flipped to an article. He underlined a sentence and then turned the page and spied an advertisement for academic staff at The Whitting Institute in Los Angeles.

Clicking his mechanical pencil again, Victor perused the ad. None of the positions were for his department. He let out an annoyed huff. They were understaffed, but money was tight.

Both Victor and Stanley Daigle, another physicist, had surprised the Dean of Physics at MIT when they announced they were applying for a grant through Whitting to dig deeper into the many-worlds interpretation, the Anthropic Principle, superlaws, quantum gravity and wormholes. That had been over ten years ago.

The peace in Victor's office shattered. Buffy jumped to her feet as Victor's eight-year old son ran into the room.

"Dad! Dad!" Victor swiveled in his chair. Darren, his replica, crashed into his legs.

"Slow down, son. What's up?"

"Guess what, Dad!" Darren could barely contain his excitement.

"We're being attacked by Martians? We won the lottery?"

2

"Oh, Dad, get serious!" Darren said. "We can win five thousand dollars, and go to Disney World!"

"Whoa. Sounds like one of those Internet scams. Where'd you get that information?"

"Bobby sent me this email with all the details. Come on, I'll show you." Darren grabbed Victor's hand and tugged him out of his chair.

Victor allowed Darren to pull him away from his work. Buffy trotted down the hall, ahead of them, looking over her shoulder periodically to make sure they were following.

Two of Darren's walls were plastered with posters of rocks, bugs, planets and all things scientific. There were autographed pictures of NASA, Chinese, and Russian astronauts, and a collector print of Captain Kirk and Mr. Spock from the late sixties.

A built-in desk amid a wall of bookcases housed a laptop and micro-thin speakers, game controllers, an iPod stereo system and science toys.

Eager to plan his trip to Disney, Darren slipped into his chair and moved his mouse to show Victor the email. The outer-space screen-saver disappeared, and the email message was front and center on the screen.

Victor bent to read it. "Son, this email is called an urban legend. It's been circulating the web since way before you were born."

Totally defeated, Darren slumped in his chair. "You mean like that guy with the pet dinosaur that turned out to be a cockroach?"

"Exactly." Victor ruffled Darren's light brown hair. "It's a shame, but scams and stories are all over the Internet. You have to watch out that you don't get suckered into believing every-thing you read. You know what they say, 'If it sounds too good to be true...'"

"It probably is," Darren and Victor said together.

"Aw, Dad. Why do people do such mean things?" Darren's dreams of a trip to Disney World had just vaporized.

"I guess they don't have anything better to do with their time."

"So, all these things are lies?"

Victor crossed the floor to Darren's bed, sat down and scooted back. He leaned against the wall and stared at the posters on the opposite wall, not really focusing on anything in particular.

Models of space vehicles and satellites hung from the ceiling and swayed with the ocean breeze from the opened, screened window.

Buffy jumped on the bed, turned a half circle, flopped down and got comfortable. She lifted her brown nose to the air and sniffed then rested her chin on Victor's thigh.

"No, not all of them," he said. There was a faraway look on his face, and he appeared a little sad. He patted Buffy.

"Years ago, before you were born—actually, right about the time when I met your mother—something happened that changed my life."

"What happened, Dad?" Darren crawled onto the bed and sat cross-legged by his dad.

Victor sat quietly, thinking. "It all started when D'laine Jackson started having these recurring nightmares."

"Who's D'laine Jackson?" Darren asked.

"You know that special picture on my desk?" Victor asked.

"Uh-huh. The one you never let anyone touch?" He remembered when he was younger, his dad had moved the picture out of his reach. It had returned to the desk when

Darren was old enough to respect his father's prizes and to look, instead of touch.

"Yeah, that one. Go get it. It's time to talk about this," Victor said.

"You want me to pick it up?" Darren asked, surprised.

"Uh-huh," Victor said. "I know you'll be careful."

Like a tornado, Darren jumped off the bed and ran out of the room. Buffy launched off the bed and galloped after him, barking. Darren returned with the framed photo gripped in both hands, and handed it to Victor. He and Buffy leapt on the bed. Buffy wedged herself between Victor and Darren.

Victor pointed. "This is Brian, Jamie, and D'laine Jackson."

"Was she going to a Halloween party?" Darren asked.

"No," Victor said. He pondered. "She was wearing very special clothes, but they weren't a costume for a party."

Darren's forehead crinkled in thought, but he kept silent.

Victor pointed to a dark blond-haired man in his late forties next to D'laine. "This is their father, Lee, who was a leading NASA scientist, and this is my old pal, Stanley Daigle."

Darren waited patiently for the story to unfold.

"Brian was just a little older than you. He had a pitching arm that wouldn't quit," Victor said.

"He played Little League?" Darren asked.

"Yup, his coach had big plans for him, but all that changed when he didn't pay attention. D'laine had just graduated from high school and had a full scholarship to Texas A&M. She was a brilliant young woman. She'd already been in the Advanced Placement Program and the Texas Distinguished Achievement Program. MIT tried to get her, but she wanted to go to her father's alma mater."

"Wow. She sure sounds smart," Darren said. "Why don't you talk to these people anymore? If they're your friends, you should invite them over for bar-b-que."

Victor swallowed hard. He rubbed the top of Buffy's head. "They moved far, far away."

"Tell me the whole story," Darren begged. "Please."

Victor nudged Buffy to move. She curled up at the foot of the bed. Victor put his arm around Darren and pulled him to his side. "You have to promise you won't tell anyone, especially your mother."

"Does Mom know about this?" Darren asked in a whisper.

Victor nodded. "Oh, she knows all right. She just refuses to talk about it, so you can't tell her I told you."

"It'll be our secret, Dad."

# CHAPTER TWO

*M*oonlight winked in and out of the room. It illuminated a sacred space on an antique dresser. The delicate tinkle of chimes coursed through the otherwise quiet night as a warm breeze swayed the sheer curtains from the large windows.

A shrine sat atop a chunk of green marble on the dresser. It contained a small brass laughing Buddha, a plastic statue of Jesus, pictures of the Dalai Lama and Mother Teresa, along with a tiny brass elephant, a bronze bear and a candle. A small offering of rice in an aged brass goblet, and a vase of red carnations graced either side of the marble slab.

An indistinguishable noise nudged D'laine out of a deep sleep, but didn't wake the teenager completely.

Rhythmic.

Familiar.

Her subconscious worked to make a connection while she snuggled down into the bedcovers and chased a disturbing dream that eluded her.

A French-hook peace sign earring was tangled in her shoulder-length, honey-blonde wavy hair. D'laine's face was molded to the warmth of the mattress just off the edge of the low, latex pillow.

*What was that sound? Her brain nagged.*

*Not the ceiling fan.* It was silently operating on the low cycle.

The noise was right there in the center of her brain, waiting to be identified. Her mind sifted through the minutiae, scoring patterns until a match could be found.

Bingo!

Like a jack-in-the-box, D'laine sprang up, snapped on the bedside table lamp, grabbed her glasses and scuttled frantically toward the sound.

"Buffy! Buffy, off the bed!" She pushed against the dog's butt.

Too late.

Buffy, a two-year-old pit bull, barfed green and yellow Gummy Bears in the middle of the Ralph Lauren comforter.

"Jeez." D'laine, petite and curvaceous in a tank top and French-cut one hundred percent cotton Jockey panties, crawled out of the queen-sized bed. Her thighs sported deep, dark, strawberry-colored zigzag scars. Her feet automatically found the stool beside the bed. The TempurPedic mattress reminded her of *The Princess and the Pea* story. If she were any shorter than five-feet-two, she'd need a ladder, but the mattress was a crucial necessity to relieve her legs of the pain she carried every day.

In a snit, D'laine limped to the closet and snatched her thick terrycloth robe off the door hook. Grumbling, she whispered threats against her brothers, and marched determinedly out of the bedroom and downstairs to the kitchen. She grabbed a handful of paper towels, opened the utility closet and took the dustpan off the hook and headed back upstairs to clean up the mess.

Buffy wagged her tail apologetically as D'laine entered the bedroom.

"Who gave you the candy?"

Buffy wagged her tail. She wasn't about to snitch.

Stifling a gag, D'laine scooped the slime onto the dustpan with the paper towels and hurried to the adjoining bathroom. The toilet flushed. She returned with a little pink tablet.

"Come on, Buffy—let's settle your stomach so we can get some sleep, okay? I have a lot to do tomorrow." She glanced at the clock on the bedside table. "Today, actually."

She showed the tablet to the dog. Buffy sniffed and turned her head slightly.

"We're not going to play this game. It's two in the morning. Eat the pink stuff."

D'laine pushed the tablet into Buffy's mouth.

Buffy, spit it out.

D'laine retrieved the tablet and eased it back into Buffy's mouth while she rubbed the dog's tummy and crooned encouragement.

"Come on, Buffy, cooperate. It's for your own good."

Buffy chewed and swallowed.

"What a good girl." D'laine hugged Buffy. She grabbed the comforter and started to yank. Buffy jumped off the bed and watched as D'laine felt the sheets.

Dry.

Sighing thankfully, she wadded up the huge comforter and dumped it in the corner of her room. Then she went into the hallway and grabbed a blanket out of the linen closet. When she returned to the bedroom, Buffy was curled up between the pillows, snoozing.

"You're so helpful."

D'laine spread the blanket, crawled back in bed, removed her glasses and shut off the light. "No more junk food for you, little girl."

Buffy licked D'laine on the nose, hoping she'd forget the incident.

D'LAINE TIGHTENED THE FAN BELT ON THE CHEVY PICKUP truck. The detached four-car garage was set back from the sprawling two story house that sat on twenty acres on the edge of Katy, Texas, just west of Houston.

She finished up and wiped her hands on a rag, then walked around the open truck door and turned the key in the ignition. The Chevy purred to life, squeak-less.

"There you go. Quiet once again," she boasted. "Pretty soon I'll be driving you to Texas A&M." She shut the truck off and pocketed the keys.

Lee Jackson called out to D'laine as he approached the garage. His western shirt, jeans and comfortably worn cowboy boots belied his prestigious day job as a highly respected, highly paid scientist at NASA.

"I've got to get more oil. Let's go to the coin-op laundry, then we can stop at the auto parts store," Lee said.

D'laine closed the hood on the Chevy. She pressed the wall switch and scooted outside as the garage door rolled down.

"Let me go wash up, daddy."

D'LAINE WATCHED AS HER FATHER SHOVED THE comforter into the huge commercial washer. Lee stood aside, and D'laine tossed in a green globe. She shut the door, then fed quarters into the slots. She dumped a plastic cup of vinegar in the bleach compartment. As the machine began to fill with water, D'laine and Lee watched as the globe bounced around for a moment then they sat in white plastic chairs that were bolted to the floor.

"You really like using that thing?" Lee asked.

"It's one of the best environmental laundry products around, Dad," D'laine explained. "If everyone used a laundry ball instead of chemically hazardous detergents, our waters would be in remarkable condition."

Lee looked perplexed. "How can you tell if it's getting our clothes clean?"

"Honestly, daddy! How could someone with your background not have a clue? Smell your clothes! I've been using them in the wash for months. No one has had allergy problems in a long time, and your coveralls are brighter."

Lee checked out his coveralls and sniffed. "And you think it's all because of this ball?"

"Duh."

There was a moment of silence between them as they watched the washer.

"Have you had that dream again?" Lee asked.

"Second night in a row. I was right in the middle of it when Buffy got sick," D'laine said. "I'm going to burn some sage and do a clearing in my room when we get back home."

"Why don't you get that woman to come out and Feng Shui the place?" Lee suggested.

D'laine contemplated. "Nah. I'm leaving for A&M in two weeks." She adjusted her glasses, opened a magazine and scanned the page. The frustration built; she snapped the magazine closed and dropped it on the side table.

D'laine ranted. "This doesn't make sense, daddy. The same dream I had every night for what—six, eight weeks after I got out of the hospital? Why is it back? What does it all mean?"

"It's a little strange for you to have that same dream now. If you could remember anything new, we might be able to solve this puzzle," Lee suggested.

"Nothing's changed. Not one thing," D'laine explained.

"If you have it again, sleep longer. Try not to wake up," Lee suggested. "Or, if you do wake up, try to go back to sleep and see if it will pick up where it left off."

"I don't have any control over that. Something always triggers me to wake up."

"It's like a cue not to get any more information," Lee pondered.

D'laine grabbed up the magazine and flipped pages blindly. She stared through the magazine as the memory of that terrible day flashed in her head.

Lori, her mom, behind the wheel of the minivan, chatting and laughing with her while her brothers slept in their secured seats behind them.

The huge semi-truck, going more than twice the speed limit, jumped the median and barreled down on them—head on.

Within a split-second Lori's smile changed to a look of horror. She yanked the wheel and slammed her foot on the gas, but the driver must have tried to change his trajectory at the same time.

The screams echoed in her dreams. For the longest time, she didn't realize it was screams of her and her mother. And then the sickening crunching sounds of metal and exploding glass all around as the truck crashed through their windshield.

Then the memory of the horrific pain when D'laine thought she was being sliced in two.

When the police, wreckers and EMTs arrived, they worked

hard and fast to pry the truck loose so they could free them. The minivan's dashboard was embedded in D'laine's lap. She was soaked in blood.

An assessment determined that the only way to safely remove the truck from atop the minivan was by crane. D'laine, unconscious and barely breathing, waited with her mother for over two hours while the EMTs monitored her through her opened passenger door.

When the crane finally arrived and the truck was hoisted off the minivan, rescuers still faced the delicate task of lifting the dashboard off D'laine's lap.

Four-and-a-half hours after the fateful accident, D'laine was en route to Texas Children's Hospital where a surgical team awaited.

Doctors Vickers and Reynolds met with Lee after they had conducted a thorough exam and run a multitude of tests on D'laine.

"Both of your daughter's thigh bones are crushed, and both arms are broken," Dr. Vickers said.

Lee's eyes watered.

Dr. Reynolds, a middle-aged woman with huge black-framed eyeglasses, reached out and grasped Lee's hand. "The impact of the crash has caused traumatic brain injury (TBI). The prognosis isn't good right now, but I've seen many people pull out of a TBI state."

Lee was numb from hearing the news.

Many operations later, her arm bones were set and shrouded in casts, her legs contained steel rods, and her brain pressure was reduced. D'laine spent eight months in a coma.

Rachel and Brenda, D'laine's best friends since the third grade, snuck into her hospital room so often, the staff turned a blind eye to them being there. The girls talked to D'laine, telling her what was going on in school, how she was missed and urging her to come back.

When D'laine came out of the coma, it wasn't a twitching of eyes or fingers. Her eyes flew open and she screamed long and loud until her voice was hoarse. Hospital staff rushed into the room. Doctors, a child psychiatrist and Lee were contacted.

Dr. Reynolds practically flew into the room. She smiled brightly when she saw her patient awake and alert. She sat at the edge of D'laine's bed and took one of her hands.

"Hi, honey. I'm Dr. Reynolds. I'm so glad to see you awake. Do you know who you are?"

D'laine's face rushed through several expressions as she stared at the doctor. She nodded, slowly. "Uh-huh."

"What's your name?" Dr. Reynolds urged.

D'laine took in her surroundings, confused. "D'laine. Jackson."

"You sure are," Dr. Reynolds said.

Lee rushed into the room. "D'laine!" He couldn't stop the rush of emotions. His eyes welled with tears as he stood across the bed from Dr. Reynolds.

"Daddy?" D'laine asked. Her voice was raspy.

"Hi, Mr. Jackson. We'll be running tests and making assessments. This is a glorious day!" Dr. Reynolds proclaimed.

"Yes, it is," Lee agreed. He could hardly contain himself.

"I'll run along now and let you spend some time with your daughter. I know you have a lot to cover," Dr. Reynolds said. She left the room.

Lee pulled the side chair close to the bed. He brushed hair off D'laine's forehead. "It's good to see you awake, honey. Do you remember anything at all?"

D'laine's eyes darted all over the place then settled on Lee. "Accident."

Lee sucked in a big breath. "Yes, you were in a terrible accident. Brian and Jamie couldn't visit you because they're too young, but now that you're awake maybe the hospital will let them come up."

D'laine's eyes darted around the room once more. "Mom."

Tears welled in Lee's eyes as he met D'laine's questioning eyes.

THE DREAMS BEGAN WHEN SHE EMERGED FROM THE unconscious state. The psychiatrist disagreed with Lee's suggestion that the dreams were probably going through her mind while she was *in* the coma.

Brenda would never forget one of her visits after D'laine regained consciousness. She had been reading a paperback while D'laine slept. Suddenly, D'laine's eyes opened and she screamed up a storm.

Brenda talked her down from the nightmare, holding her hand until the moment passed and the sobbing began. She cried along with D'laine.

After almost a year in the hospital D'laine finally went home. The accident had changed her. Most of the time she was more like a thirty-year-old than a teenager. Once she recovered from her own physical and emotional trauma, D'laine shared the role of raising her two younger brothers along with her father, and Rosa, their housekeeper. Her small group of friends understood her, and helped to remind her she was seventeen.

THE BELL ON THE FRONT DOOR OF THE LAUNDROMAT jangled. Two screeching blond-haired boys raced inside.

"Slow down," D'laine said.

Jamie squealed and dove for Lee's lap as Brian closed the distance.

"What in the world are you screaming about?" Lee had to raise his voice to be heard over the racket. A middle-aged lady cringed as she folded clothes. Lee threw her an apologetic smile and a shrug. She smiled in return.

"Monsters, daddy!" Jamie boasted. He looked sheepishly at his sister. "Oops. Sorry, D'laine."

D'laine tsk-tsked at her brother's tacky apology. "Your monsters aren't the same as mine, so it's okay."

"Can we go next door and get ice cream?" Brian begged.

"Yeah, Melissa Jenkins and her friends just went inside the store," Jamie squealed in a taunting, sing-song voice. "Your friends are there, too."

Brian glared at his younger brother. Being ten years-old was tough when you had a six-year-old Velcroed to you all the time.

"Don't you think you should wait until after your game?" Lee asked.

The boys groaned, and shuffled around, downcast.

"Frozen yogurt?" D'laine suggested. She turned an imploring face to Lee. He sighed. He knew when he was outnumbered and dug into his pocket. He pulled out his wallet and gave Brian some money. "Bring me the receipt!"

"Okay, Dad!" Brian and Jamie raced out of the laundromat to the convenience store next door.

Rachel, Joey and Brenda came inside the laundromat. Brenda handed D'laine a cone with butter pecan ice cream. "Sorry, Mr. Jackson. I didn't know your flavor."

"Thanks," D'laine said.

"Hi, kids. It's okay, Brenda," Lee said "FYI, black cherry." He winked at Brenda.

A few minutes later, a tall, dark-haired boy joined the

group. He slid his arm around D'laine and kissed her cheek. "How's my favorite girl?"

She kissed him back and shoved her cone at his mouth. "Hey, Connor."

"Are we still going to the movies tonight," Rachel asked.

D'laine turned to Lee with a silent plea.

"It's okay with me," Lee said.

D'laine gave the thumbs up sign to Rachel. "You guys better not talk during the movie," she warned.

"For crying out loud, that was one time!" Joey said.

"Okay we've got to drop Brenda off at her mom's," Rachel said.

They all said their goodbyes.

"You've got great friends," Lee said.

FOUR IMAGES WERE BRANDED IN D'LAINE'S HEAD NIGHT after night: a dark-haired, handsome princely young man, a fierce reptilian monster, a white furry creature whose red eyes implored her with some unspoken message, and an ominous black robot.

# CHAPTER THREE

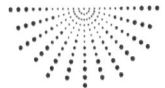

*T*he bleachers were crowded with parents and kids of all ages as the Katy American Little League game heated up in Katy Park. The Katy Bolt Cutters were playing their rivals, the Bellaire Wart Hogs. Each team had ten wins and four losses in the minors. Brian Jackson hoped to change that record.

Katy, a city of about three hundred ten thousand residents sprawled across one hundred eighty-one square miles west of Houston on I-10, and spanned three counties: Harris, Fort Bend and Waller. The towns motto was "Small Town Charm with Big City Conveniences."

It was a steamy eighty-eight degrees in the first week of May. People in the Houston area liked to joke about the seasons. Winter lasted about a month, spring was lucky to stretch out for two weeks, and fall didn't really happen until late October or mid-November. Summer dominated the rest of the year. Houston had an average daily humidity of seventy percent, which could be grueling in the summer with triple-digit temperatures.

D'laine's mother used to tease about how the humidity kept the age lines at bay and made hair appear to have more body and substance, since it frizzed wildly unless tamed with hair products.

An avid team supporter, D'laine wore her Katy Bolt Cutters T-shirt and ball cap proudly as she cheered for her brother and his team. Her cellphone rang. It was Brenda.

"Hey, I can't talk right now. We're at Brian's game. Yeah, my Dad helped him with his pitches all week. I'll call you when we get home." D'laine clicked the Bluetooth and ended the call.

Lee watched Brian, master of the mound, in rapt attention as the game played-out. Jamie, the hyper six-year-old, jumped and cheered for his brother down on the field.

BRIAN STOOD AT THE PITCHER'S MOUND. HE LOOKED across the field to the catcher, dipped the bill on his ball cap a skosh, then threw the ball like a pro.

The scrawny kid up at bat visibly flinched. He swung and missed. The umpire called. "Strike three."

"Yeesss! That's my brother." Jamie's face sported a huge grin as he looked at the crowd on the bleachers around him.

A small dent an inch under Jamie's right eye from a piece of glass from the shattered car window was the only reminder of the accident five years ago.

D'laine, Lee and Jamie hugged, shouted and jumped around. "Good work, Brian!" D'laine hollered.

"Knock 'em all out, son." Lee gave Brian the thumbs-up.

Brian took a moment and waved at his family. He could see Jamie and his sister jumping in the stands. People were high with team spirit.

The catcher, a beefy twelve-year-old boy, was showing off

as he threw a fast ball to Brian, who was not paying attention. The ball hit Brian squarely in the chest, knocking the wind out of him. He crumbled to the ground.

D'laine and Lee halted in mid-cheer from the edge of their seats as they watched Brian fall.

"Oohhh, I'll bet that hurt," D'laine said.

The coach and the umpire stopped their back-slapping and noticed that Brian didn't get right back up.

"Something's not right." Lee frowned. He stood and watched the field.

Jamie jumped in circles, unaware of anything wrong on the field.

The coach and the umpire rushed to Brian, followed by the Wart Hogs coach and players from both teams.

"Brian?" D'laine shouted, filled with panic. She sprang from her seat. They rushed down the bleachers.

"Jamie!" Lee called when he realized that his younger son was not following him.

Jamie spun around to face Lee then took off running to catch up with him and D'laine. He saw the two teams standing in a crowded circle on the field but didn't see his brother.

"Where's Brian?" he asked.

"Your brother's hurt." Lee yanked Jamie up into his arms and hurtled down the bleacher stairs.

D'laine was out of the bleachers and around the high fence with Lee and Jamie on her heels. She pushed her way through the crowd toward Brian, who was sprawled on the ground.

The bleachers started to empty as people swarmed the field.

The coach checked Brian's pulse. It was irregular, very rapid. He lifted each of Brian's eyelids. His eyeballs were rolled back in his head. "Call nine-one-one," he shouted to the umpire. The coach began CPR and mouth-to-mouth on Brian.

The Wart Hogs umpire was on his cellphone within seconds. He outlined the situation to the dispatcher.

D'laine pushed past the team and finally got to her brother. "Brian!" Panic froze her.

Lee was at her side seconds later. He settled Jamie on the ground beside him. Jamie clung to Lee's jeans, crying in fright at the sight of his brother lying so still on the ground. Within moments, the wail of an ambulance drew near.

D'laine knelt beside Brian and brushed the sandy hair off his forehead. She reached into her large canvas purse and pulled out a brilliantly clear quartz crystal, the size of a golf ball.

She closed her eyes and held the crystal above Brian's chest, then moved it slowly from his head to his toes without touching him. She flicked invisible lint off him as she focused internally.

"I pray to the Spirit and the Universe, for they are one. Guides, angels, Mom; gather near. Brian needs your help." She moved the crystal the length of Brian's body. "Heal him, guide him. Help him to release his pain."

The coaches, players and people gathered around Brian stared at her as if she were a nut case. She didn't care, nor did Lee.

D'laine worked around the coach. With her eyes closed, she said a silent prayer, then took two deep breaths and continued her routine, slowly passing the crystal over Brian's chest as the coach continued his ministrations.

"Bring him back—it's not his time. Guide him through his pain."

Brian shuddered with a deep, gasping breath.

Onlookers gawked. The coach appeared surprised. He stared at D'laine with an unspoken question.

The Emergency Medical Response Team arrived with

equipment and a gurney. The crowd parted and let them through. An EMT approached D'laine.

"Miss, move aside."

"All yours." D'laine stood and joined Lee and Jamie. Lee hugged her tightly.

The EMT team went to work on Brian.

BRIAN SLEPT AMID TUBES AND AN IV IN HIS HOSPITAL BED at the West Campus of the Texas Children's Pediatric Intensive Care Unit as a wall of equipment monitored his vital signs.

D'laine and Lee sat vigilant at Brian's bedside. Since the age limit for visitors was fourteen and older, Jamie was not permitted to visit his brother so Rosa, the family's housekeeper, had picked him up and brought him back to the house.

The memories associated with the hospital were painful for both Lee and D'laine. She feared for her brother, and the well-being of her father. He suffered so much the last time he had been here.

As they sat quietly beside Brian, a doctor entered the room. D'laine and Lee jumped to their feet.

The doctor shook Lee's hand first, then D'laine's.

"I'm Dr. Thompson," he said solemnly. "I'm afraid I have some bad news."

D'laine clutched Lee's arm. "Oh, no!"

"Brian has a tumor on his heart. It may be malignant. We are going to have to monitor it closely," Dr. Thompson explained. "The condition is called Leiomyosarcoma, or LMS. It's a very rare cancer of the soft tissues, and to be honest, most oncologists never treat an LMS patient in their entire career. It only strikes four in every one-million people."

"So, it's not his heart, per se?" D'laine asked.

"No," Dr. Thompson said.

Lee flinched. "How come this never showed up before? My son has played ball since he was six, and he's had all these physicals."

"Unfortunately, physicals for Little League and other types of children's sports activities don't include any type of scans," Dr. Thompson said.

Lee and D'laine were shell-shocked at this news.

"We'd like to keep Brian for observation for the next couple of days and run some additional tests," Dr. Thompson said. "I'll be prescribing several medications and he'll require bed rest. We're going to have to monitor the growth of the tumor so I would like to see him once a month."

Dr. Thompson concluded his report, shook their hands again, and left the room.

The beep on the monitor resonated loudly as Lee and D'laine were lost in thought.

# CHAPTER FOUR

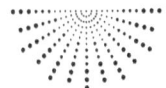

*B*uffy twitched in her sleep beside D'laine. She awoke and repositioned herself. She stared at D'laine for a few moments, concern clearly expressed in her warm brown eyes. After a little while she snorted then curled up. She watched D'laine, smacked her lips a couple of times, yawned, and attempted sleep.

D'laine was very still in the bed. The only apparent activity was in the REM phase of her dreaming. Behind her closed eyelids, her eyes moved rapidly in response to her dream, and periodically clenched tight with fear etched across her sleeping face.

The recurring dream never changed—even after the gap in the years. She had spent her twelfth birthday in a coma. When D'laine finally came out of the coma, the nightmares were relentless. Then one night, two months after going home, she slept soundly and they never returned.

Until now.

As soon as she was in a deep sleep, the dream began with the sensation of falling into a tunnel. The black void surrounding her dream-body contained no light whatsoever. She had never experienced such complete darkness in her entire life before these nightly occurrences began. The black was so dense it was claustrophobic, and crushing.

When the darkness passed, she was tormented by thick clusters of spider webs stretched out across the expanse of the tunnel. They clung to her face, hair, clothing, and fingers. As she dreamt, she pawed at the imaginary webs and made little spit sounds to remove them from her lips.

It was at this point every night that Buffy abandoned the bed and waited, curled up on the floor, exasperated.

Once the spider web stage of the dream passed, D'laine settled into a more peaceful state of sleep while thick fog rushed in all around her. It was like falling through the clouds in slow motion, and she gave in to it. The sensation was peaceful, euphoric, and calming, preparing her for the four nightly visitors.

The brooding warrior-prince appeared first. His unruly dark hair framed his face—a face so devastatingly handsome that D'laine sucked in her breath in her sleep. He was dressed in silver-gray leather-like armor molded to his muscular body.

He was about her age, eighteen at the most, but his presence suggested he was much older. His smoldering eyes bore into hers as he spoke. Night after night, all she heard was the same short, incomplete statement.

"Don't leave! We need you; I need you," the brooding prince said.

His stance made her think he had never known defeat in any form. Her hand reached out as if to touch his face.

Too soon, the prince's form dissolved and was replaced by an enormous reptilian monster, so fierce and threatening in appearance that D'laine's body jerked under the covers.

He stood eight feet tall in his battle helmet. A black and red tunic loosely covered his scaly body along with thigh-high black boots and fingerless gloves that flared above the wrist. A weapon hung at his hip— some type of pistol, she thought.

"I will hunt you down, D'laine," he roared.

She struggled to wake, trapped in the dream, unable to escape. Then, a large ominous, shiny, black robot with a human form, appeared. "Eliminate... replicate," the robot said in its machinelike voice. The robotic form disintegrated back into oblivion.

The last visitor calmed her. He was a white-furred creature with glowing red eyes and four arms. While as tall as the reptilian monster, this creature appeared to be gentle and concerned for her welfare. D'laine thought he was trying to teach her something.

"... your duty... your responsibility. You have the power... look within." He tapped her forehead. His words echoed as he vanished. Then she saw herself—dressed in the same molded silver-and-black outfit as the princely warrior. Her hair was longer, lighter and wavier. She looked like a warrior.

As D'laine reached out, her image dissolved. She searched in the void in front of her.

*There has to be a door here somewhere!*

She fell faster and faster, the breath sucked from her lungs. Suddenly, her body shuddered. She jolted to a sitting position, screaming the house down.

Lee, clad in pajamas, burst through her bedroom door. "D'laine! It's just a dream!"

Jamie ran into the room, dragging a small blanket. "Did the monsters come back? Are you all right, D'laine?"

Buffy raised her head off the floor, yawned at the disturbance, then lay back down. This was old news.

D'laine clutched Jamie to her. "Yeah, unwanted company." She kissed his head.

"Want me to sleep with you?" Jamie asked.

"It's okay, Jamie. You go back to bed. Buffy'll watch over me."

She ruffled Jamie's hair. He rubbed his sleepy eyes and walked to the door. Yawning, he stumbled back to his room dragging his blanket.

Lee sat on the edge of the bed. "You want to talk about it? There must be something new because it's been a long time since you've screamed like this."

D'laine raked her hand through her hair, then grabbed a medium-sized crystal off the night stand and clutched it to her chest.

"Daddy, I was actually in the dream this time. Remember the guy in the silver and black outfit I've told you about? He looks to be about my age. Anyway," she rushed, almost breathless with a hint of panic in her voice, "I wore an outfit just like his! I have the distinct feeling I was on another planet, even though I didn't see what it looked like. The big alligator monster called me by my name this time, and then this robot..."

Lee wrapped his arms around her. "Honey, it's probably the pressure from Brian's illness. It's a reminder from when you were in the hospital."

"No! No, daddy, this was... it was clearer somehow. I saw myself there. I looked different. And they knew me. I have a feeling that something bad's going to happen."

Lee stared straight ahead, his face a mask of stone.

# CHAPTER FIVE

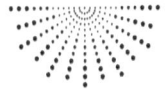

$\mathcal{D}$arren sat entranced, staring at his father. "Warriors, Dad? Wow. Were they good warriors or evil warriors?"

Victor smiled. "Trakon was a good warrior."

"You sound like you know him, Dad."

"Nope. I didn't get to meet Trakon, but I know the whole story, and it's true."

"Come on, Dad. Tell me!"

Victor picked up the picture frame, turned it over and pried off the back. He eased the easel backing away from the frame and carefully removed a piece of paper. He turned it over and Darren stared, mesmerized, as he saw the images of the four beings that haunted D'laine Jackson's nightmares.

"Are these really them?" Darren exclaimed.

"Yes." Victor swallowed hard. This was one experience he would never forget until the end of his days.

"Come on, daddy, hurry before Mom gets home!" Darren was keyed-up to hear the whole story."

"The whole thing started shortly after Brian was released

from the hospital. They were out getting D'laine things for her dorm room and they were just leaving a store at the mammoth Katy Mills Mall. You should see that place, Darren. It's too large to see every store in one trip."

"Wow!" Darren said.

Victor rubbed his chin for a moment. "Remember that part about D'laine being in a coma?"

"Uh huh," Darren said, waiting for more.

"Well, no one knows what goes on inside the brain when someone is in a deep coma," Victor explained. "They ran all sorts of tests on D'laine, including an fMRI."

Darren screwed up his face in question. "What's that?"

"A functional magnetic resonance imaging test," Victor said. "It's used to see what type of brain activity is going on. And D'laine's brain was racing, but in a different area than what would have typically been used if she had been awake, or say, just unconscious for a little while."

"Huh," Darren said.

"Her father and I both agree that her nightmares started while she was *in* the coma and that's why there was so much activity in her brain. But those doctors wouldn't have any part of that when Lee tried to talk to them a couple of weeks after she came out of the coma."

Buffy nudged Victor's arm. He stroked her head and scratched behind her ears.

"You know, son, my job is to discover what others toss away as ridiculous—those things they can't connect the dots to. I couldn't let go of this and I hope to be able to prove my hypothesis one day."

"So, what happened next, Dad?"

# CHAPTER SIX

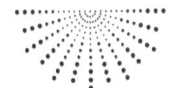

$\mathcal{T}$he glass doors slid open and Lee pushed Brian's wheelchair out of the mall into the blazing sun of the parking lot. Brian balanced several packages on his lap as Lee rolled the chair around oncoming people. Jamie walked beside Brian, swinging a shopping bag. D'laine pulled up the rear in crop pants, Game of Thrones T-shirt and glittery flip-flops. She was texting Rachel and Brenda, making plans for later.

Once she was around the crowd of shoppers, D'laine scooted around the wheelchair and trotted ahead. "Daddy, I'll open the van so it can cool down."

Lee reached into his pocket and pulled out the key. He pressed the unlock button on the fob twice. The rear lights flashed on the minivan.

"Watch for cars," Lee said.

The parking lot wasn't full but drivers stalked exiting visitors for their parking place closer to the store entrance. Bruce Miller was on his second round when he noticed the lights flashing on the minivan. He turned on his directional signal and stopped close by the minivan and waited.

D'laine looked both ways, then crossed the main entrance lane and hurried ahead toward the minivan.

A bag slipped from Brian's lap and wedged under the front right wheel of the chair. Lee stopped the wheelchair and backed up a couple of inches.

"Jamie, grab that bag," Lee said.

Jamie bounded over and retrieved the colorful bag from the ground. He tossed it haphazardly onto Brian's lap.

D'laine opened the hatch door on the minivan. A wave of heat hit her in the face as she raised the hatch over her head. "Take your time. The car is roasting."

Jamie pointed ahead to billows of white misty clouds that swirled and rolled to the ground. "Hey, daddy! Look at that!"

"Wow! Someone's got a fog machine!" Brian said. "Are they making a movie? Can we go see where they are?" Brian pleaded stretching his neck to find the source.

D'laine turned around to check out the fog. "Huh. It looks like a storm cloud falling to the ground! It's not a tornado, is it?"

Lee watched, eyeing the clouds with curiosity. "D'laine, watch for cars. They may not be able to see you."

"Don't worry, daddy." D'laine said. "I'll stay clear..."

The cloud of fog rolled up to where she stood. It engulfed her completely and then quickly rolled back and vanished into the bright, sunny day.

Bruce Miller, the man in the waiting car, rolled his window down. "What the heck was that?"

The space where D'laine had stood was vacant. The hatch door on the minivan stood open but the vehicle was empty.

"D'laine? D'laine!" Lee roared.

Alarmed, Brian lurched forward in the wheelchair as if to get up.

"No you don't." Lee grabbed his shoulder and settled him against the back of the chair. "Hold onto the wheelchair, Jamie."

Jamie, confused by the fog, joined Brian at his side. "Where'd D'laine go?"

Lee looked both ways and raced the wheelchair toward the minivan.

"D'laine!" Brian said.

Lee stopped short of the minivan. He engaged the brake on the wheelchair.

Bruce exited his car and jogged over to where Lee stood.

"Did you see my daughter?" Lee asked.

"Yeah, she was standing right here a minute ago. Where'd she go?" Bruce asked.

"I don't know," Lee said.

Other people in the parking lot started to wander over.

"D'laine!" Brian called.

Lee grabbed Jamie and pulled him to the side of the wheelchair. Brian got weaker from the stress of the moment and the heat. Lee gripped Brian's shoulder with one hand and Jamie's with the other.

"Stay put. Don't move an inch, understand?" Lee stared straight into their eyes, his face filled with fear. Frightened, Jamie gripped Brian's hand.

A small crowd formed.

"What happened?" A middle-aged woman looked from Brian and Jamie to Lee and Bruce.

"This man's daughter disappeared right before our eyes! One minute she's standing right there at the rear of the van. This fog rolls up and the next minute the fog is gone and so is the girl," Bruce said.

"I'm calling the cops." The woman whipped a cell-phone out of her purse and dialed nine-one-one. "This is

Trudy Weatherford. I'd like to report a possible child abduction."

Lee approached the open hatch on the minivan cautiously. He peered inside. He went around to the side door and opened it. He looked inside to the empty interior.

No D'laine.

He got on his hands and knees and looked under the minivan. He directed his search under the vehicles on both sides of the minivan. He got up, brushed off his hands and knees, returned to the boys and the small crowd.

"I don't know where she went," Lee said. "It's like she vanished into thin air."

Trudy rested her hand on Lee's shoulder. "Don't worry. We'll find her. The cops are on the way."

"Why don't we spread out and each take a row? Maybe she got disoriented or something," Bruce said.

"Good idea," Lee said. "I'll take that side of this row."

"I'll take this side. You stay with your boys," Trudy said. "What's your daughter's name?"

"D'laine."

Just as the crowd was set to disperse and begin their search, a faint scream sounded directly in front of everyone.

"Hhheeeelllppppp meeeeeee!"

Lee jerked around and faced the direction of the sound. "Sshhhh!" he warned the people. He strained to listen.

Another fainter scream sounded right in front of them.

"D'laine! Where are you?" Lee shouted. "D'laine! Can you hear me?"

Trudy's mouth hung open. Bruce looked shocked.

"D'laine!" Brian cried, scared for his sister.

Jamie clutched the wheelchair and cried.

# CHAPTER SEVEN

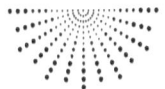

hree Katy Police Department vehicles screeched to a halt in the parking lot from different directions. One parked in front the minivan close to the crowd. The other two faced each other in the parking lane.

A Fox News truck stalked close behind the cruisers. Two men quickly exited the news truck and scrambled for equipment. They stood ready, recording as the story unfolded.

A middle-aged, fit and trim officer exited his car and approached the crowd, a serious look on his face as he scanned the group. "Did someone call in a possible child abduction?"

"I did," Trudy said. "This man's daughter is missing."

The officers from the other two vehicles got out of their cars and joined the first officer.

The first officer approached Lee, Brian and Jamie. Lee rested against the open hatch of the minivan, a dazed look on his face.

"I'm Officer Gary Davidson. What is your name?" he asked Lee.

Lee snapped out of his temporary bewilderment, held out

his hand and met the officer's stare. "Lee Jackson. These are my sons, Brian and Jamie. My daughter D'laine disappeared no more than twenty-five feet in front of us. Literally. In less than a minute."

Officer Davidson shook Lee's hand. His brow creased. "Tell me exactly what happened."

A young man in the crowd held up his cellphone and waved it at Officer Davidson. "I've got it on my phone."

He rushed forward and held his phone out. Using his thumbs, he made a couple of quick clicks and the video ran. Lee, the cops and others crowded around the young man and his phone.

The crisp footage showed a large roiling of clouds in the sky just over the tops of cars in the distance. Then the clouds dropped to the ground and rolled quickly forward. The video showed D'laine at the back of the minivan as she faced away from the clouds. Then she turned toward the clouds. The clouds engulfed her then pulled back and dissipated. D'laine was gone.

"What's your name?" Officer Davidson asked.

"Jimmy Shoemaker," the young man said.

"Don't accidentally delete that video," Officer Davidson said. "We're going to need it as evidence."

"I uploaded it to my cloud storage," Jimmy said.

Lee looked at the cellphone. "Can you email that to me?" He reached in his pocket and pulled out a business card and handed it to Jimmy.

Jimmy worked his thumbs and sent the email. "I just sent it to you, Mr. Jackson."

"Thanks," Lee said.

The Fox News guy holding the boom microphone approached Jimmy. "Can we upload your footage?"

"Fox will pay you," the cameraman enticed.

They walked back to the news truck and spoke for a moment. The cameraman opened a door and pulled out a laptop. He gave Jimmy his cellphone number. Jimmy texted him the video. Within moments, the footage was uploaded to the laptop. The guy holding the boom mic wrote Jimmy's contact information on a pad while the cameraman made a phone call and sent the video clip to the news station via email.

The news team returned to the scene and commenced recording.

Officer Davidson was talking to Lee. One of the other officers talked to Bruce Miller, and the third officer spoke with Trudy.

"She's five-foot-two. Blonde hair to just below her shoulders and blue eyes," Lee said. "You saw her in the video: crop pants, T-shirt, flip-flops."

"Would there be any reason for her to disappear?" Officer Davidson asked.

Lee unconsciously took a step back as he looked at Officer Davidson in disbelief. "Are you insinuating that she somehow fabricated these clouds, hopped into someone's car and took off?"

"I'm just trying to get the full picture as to what happened here," Officer Davidson said.

Bruce Miller stepped forward. "Look, officer, I know this sounds crazy, but I pulled up right there." He pointed to his silver Lexus GS Hybrid. "I was waiting for their parking place and I saw this man's daughter and the clouds with my own two eyes."

"What's your name?" Officer Davidson asked.

"Bruce Miller," the man said.

"It was some type of bizarre weather phenomenon. Not a kidnapping, or a girl running away. She had a full scholarship to Texas A&M and was all set to leave next week," Lee said. He was steamed at the stupid assumption the cop made and barely held his temper in check.

"We thought someone had a fog machine and was making a movie," Brian interjected.

"You think we're crazy, don't you?" Lee ran his hand through his hair, opened his mouth then snapped it shut.

"Mr. Jackson, no one thinks you're crazy. I'm just doing my job and I have to get the facts," Officer Davidson said. "Did your daughter have a disgruntled classmate or perhaps a breakup with a boyfriend recently?"

"Classmates? Boyfriends? Damn it, you just don't understand, do you? No one ran up and grabbed her! She was right at the tailgate of the minivan; this fog came out of the clear blue sky and then she was gone!" Lee hollered.

His face was crimson from the anger he was venting at the officer. "We're not talking UFOs and little green men, but this definitely was some type of an anomaly. I'm a NASA scientist. I know what I'm saying. No one grabbed her. She was not kidnapped."

"And we heard her scream right in front of us, but she wasn't there," Trudy said.

Jimmy Shoemaker kept recording.

# CHAPTER EIGHT

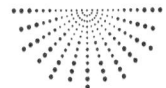

he familiar black void was no longer a dream. D'laine strained to open her eyes and focus her pupils.

There was nothing.

Only the pitch black in the free-fall of the tunnel where she was. The pressure crushed her clothing to her as if she were inside a vacuum-sucked storage bag.

An intense chill instantly engulfed her, making her teeth chatter like jackhammers. None of this was in the dream. She expected her teeth to shatter at any second. Then the pressure compressed the breath from her lungs. It could only have been seconds, but it felt as if time was suspended in the blackness.

A pinpoint of light appeared in the void. It grew exponentially until D'laine was engulfed in blinding light that penetrated her closed eyelids.

Her body slammed to a stop as she crashed onto a solid surface. She sounded like an asthmatic as she clutched her chest painfully refilling her lungs. She wheezed heavily, keeping her eyes closed against the blinding, ever-present light.

"Daddy..." she whispered.

And then she passed out.

Huge, colorful, dome-shaped tents littered the oasis for as far as the horizon stretched. The largest, and most ornate tent was fifteen feet high and twenty feet in diameter. A pond with undulating brilliant turquoise water stretched across a field of bluish-silver moss-like ground cover.

Large flowering plants with huge blossoms in vibrant shades of red, pink, orange and yellow clustered close to the water's edge between spiny land coral and wide, flat, smooth, black rocks.

Several giant trees stretched upward toward the double suns in the bright sky. White clouds with wisps of pink and blue streaks shaded part of the pond. The immense tree trunks were a deep purple bark and their branches held greenish-brown foliage that sparkled as if someone had flung glitter on them.

A tethered beast with an ornate saddle on its back rubbed its hairy side against an eight-foot-wide tree trunk. The ten-ton beast stood twenty-five-foot-high at its withers, supported by six thick legs and gigantic elephant-like feet.

The beast swished its back with a long, thin, cow-like tail, which seemed disproportionate to its mighty body. It munched on the spiny rocks at the base of the tree with its wide, flat teeth.

This creature, with long muddy brown hair, was of a size that made an elephant look like a pony. Its wide face, a cross between a cow and a goat, sported two fly-type eyes that looked in all directions simultaneously.

A tent flap opened, and a huge reptilian warrior in military garb emerged. His mottled green scales and skin the color of dirty mauve were covered with a long, ornate vest of a shimmering, colorful fabric with tribal symbols. Underneath he wore a red tunic. Yellow pupils were split in the middle by a streak of brown. He looked like a relative of an alligator but with a humanoid form. The top of his head had three inches of scales running from an inch above the middle of his eyes to the small of his back, like a mohawk haircut.

The monster-commander opened his long snout and yawned widely, showing rows of razor-sharp teeth. He stretched his powerfully muscled form and gazed up at the two suns. The pod on the end of his tail opened and closed lazily, exposing thick deadly barbs at least five inches long.

His vest swayed with the light breeze. An ornamental helmet with red beast-hair plumes rested on a post nearby. The monster-commander glanced around the quiet camp, satisfied with what he saw.

A distant crack, like thunder, shattered the moment. The monster-commander turned suddenly, nostrils flaring, as he faced the direction of the disturbance. He sniffed the air, raised his long snout toward the sky and bellowed a war cry. The pod on the end of his tail opened fully, and the sunlight glinted off the deadly barbs.

"Mount up!" he roared.

Tent flaps flew open. Thirty uniformed reptilian warriors emerged quickly from the tents and ran toward the beasts. The monster-commander grabbed his helmet and flipped it onto his head.

An aide rushed over and untethered the monster-commander's beast, then rapped the beast's front leg. The animal knelt. The monster-commander hurried to the beast and hoisted himself into the ornate saddle as the beast stood.

On the monster-commander's orders, the party headed out at a brisk pace.

SPRAWLED ON THE BLUISH-SILVER MOSS-COVERED GROUND, D'laine was out cold. Her glasses were three feet away with temples raised in the air, but her Bluetooth device still clung to her ear. Her canvas purse managed the trip through the tunnel without harm, but half its contents splayed across the ground.

Eight large, white-furred creatures with red glowing eyes, stood in a circle around D'laine, bent over, observing her. They chirped, grunted and nodded among themselves.

D'laine moved her head slightly. She opened her eyes slowly. The profuse blinding sunlight rocked her senses. She shaded her face with a hand as she squinted into the piercingly bright flashing sky.

"Did I faint?"

She breathed in, made a face. "What is that horrible smell? Buffy, did you roll in cow poop?" She pinched her nostrils closed with her thumb and forefinger.

The dazed feeling lingered for a few moments. She rolled to her side and sat up slowly, holding her head with one hand. She used the other to run her fingers across the ground.

"Not home."

The creatures moved back to give her space and to observe her.

"Where's my glasses?" She got on her hands and knees, crawled around and patted the ground with both hands moving in a tight circle, searching hopelessly. She bumped into a white, fur-covered leg. Looking down she saw blurry toes. She reached out and felt a very large toe. She giggled.

"Oh, that's so funny. A really big toe." She poked the toe a couple of times. "Not Buffy, that's for sure."

Eventually, the texture of the ground under her hands and knees caught her attention. She moved away from the foot, and a puzzled expression crossed her face. She knelt over and squinted to see the ground better, but without her glasses it was hopeless.

"Where's the parking lot? What is this stuff?"

The search left her dizzy; she clamped her hands on her head for a moment, groaned then laid back down curled up, overcome with exhaustion. She rolled onto her back, eyes closed tightly.

Two large, leathery, white-furred hands placed her glasses on her face. D'laine jerked her eyes open, focused on her surroundings, then screamed in horror at the eight pairs of red glowing eyes set deep in white fur that stared down at her.

A large, leathery furred finger touched her forehead. The white creature that bent over her seemed to have a compassionate face. It tried to communicate with her, but all D'laine heard was chirps, clicks and grunts. She opened her mouth to scream, a full-out panic and wild expression set on her face.

The white creature pressed one finger to the middle of her forehead again. Fear melted away. D'laine felt peaceful. She smiled a little goofily.

"Daddy? Did I get hit by a car? Faint? All I can remember is opening the minivan to cool it down," she said, all happy and relaxed.

After a minute of waiting for a response, she pulled herself together and pressed her Bluetooth.

No signal.

After a second try with the same results, she removed the Bluetooth device from her ear and examined it. "Huh. Do I have to re-sync this thing again?" She slipped the Bluetooth over her ear, sat up, grabbed her purse and looked at the scattered mess.

Then she focused on the ground. D'laine reached out and touched the moss. She pressed it and noticed that it left an imprint of her hand. "What the heck is this stuff?"

Mesmerized with the colorful ground cover, she took a moment and looked around her, then up. Her body jerked at what her mind registered. The sky was electric with flashing colors of a perpetual heat lightning. Two suns blazed large in the radiant sky and so close to the Earth.

"Huh. Will you look at that? Two suns. Maybe my vision is messed up." She closed her eyes and took a breath. "Nope. Don't remember this grass from any of our *National Geographic* magazines or any of the travel shows. Nope. Not on Google Earth either. This isn't right."

She sat quietly for a moment. Thoughts of books and movies flew through her mind. "Not the Amazon. It's not even this weird. Two suns? Definitely not home."

D'laine dug into her purse and pulled out her smartphone. She pressed buttons to no avail. It was dead.

"What a piece of crap. I've had it. I'm telling daddy to change service provider's tomorrow. Maybe it's time to get an iPhone." She slammed the phone back into her purse.

"I don't remember it being this hot in the parking lot a few minutes ago." She fanned the front of her shirt. It was dotted with sweat. She focused on her immediate area. Eight sets of white furry legs with enormous feet surrounded her. Those feet had big toes halfway around them.

A little eek escaped her mouth at the sight of the feet. D'laine caught a scream before it had a chance to voice itself. She had recalled reading an article that animals sensed fear. She stayed statue-still. She tried to control her breathing and her heart rate.

A thunderous noise in the distance got closer and closer. She felt the rumble through her body from the ground and looked around in search of the disturbance.

A large white, leathery, furred hand reached out and grasped one of her hands and tugged her to her feet.

Reality set in.

As her mind linked things together, she started to freak out. An animal-type hand was grasping hers. It was real. She could feel the leathery skin. She saw the white fur that met the skin of the creature's palm.

She looked from the hand to the leathery chest pads like an ape's, then up, and up, and up, maybe three or four feet above her eye level into the face of the white creature that held her hand.

There were four hands in all—two sets of arms. The second set was in back of and slightly below the front arms, almost doubled up. The creature's hands were large with a lot of fingers.

They stood upright like human beings, keeping their frames erect, not slouched like some of the early species of humans, the great apes or orangutans.

A different white creature tapped her on the shoulder. She looked up into the leathery face of that creature. He placed a finger to his lips.

D'laine stared at the creature for a moment. Her mouth formed a little o, dumbfounded, and understood she should be quiet.

The creatures formed a tight towering protective circle around her as the thundering noise grew closer. D'laine felt the reverberation on the ground through her feet. She parted the fur between two of the white creatures and peeked, horrified at what she saw.

The monster-commander led the reptilian warriors at a

breakneck speed on their beasts. The horde was heading straight for the white creatures.

It is known that fright does strange things to people. Testimonies of great courage or cowardly acts are common. Some people are robbed of all senses. D'laine discovered she was not an exception to the rule.

*Run!* Her brain screamed. But her body was frozen to the parcel of ground where she stood with the white creatures. Death was forthcoming and she watched with macabre fascination as the band of monsters and their beasts bore down on her and the white creatures.

"We're going to be killed," she whispered.

Large hands gently pulled her back to the protective circle. D'laine cowered in fright behind a white creature, then peeked between two of the creatures again.

"The dream monster!" she whispered.

Another white creature tapped her on the shoulder and placed a finger to his lips and shook his head. D'laine clapped her hands over her mouth to show she understood. She trembled by one of the white creature's feet, pushed aside some of its fur and watched.

The beasts stopped thirty feet away. The monster-commander bellowed and growled in rage at the white creatures as he tried to catch a glimpse of what they protected.

The monster-commander shouted something unintelligible at the white creatures.

One of the white creatures facing the monster-commander clicked and grunted and raised one right hand.

A trigger-happy reptilian warrior blasted the group of white creatures with his laser pistol. The beam dissolved inches in front of them.

The monster-commander turned his beast and rode fast to the warrior. He threw a mighty fist to the warrior's snout and flung his barbed tail at the warrior's back. The warrior howled in pain as blood spurt through his snout and blood ran down his pierced back.

D'laine made a strangled scream through her hands. She was petrified at the brutality she had witnessed.

Then the monster-commander rode to the front line of his troops and turned his beast to face the white creatures.

The white creatures held up each of their four palms. A wave of energy blasted the reptilian monster men and their beasts. The monster men roared in rage and pain. Their riding beasts shrieked in fright and stampeded out of control, carrying the reptilian monster men away in all directions.

D'laine jumped to her feet, shocked and amazed. The white creatures broke apart. She grabbed one by the hand and touched his lined palm in wonderment.

"That was incredible! You saved my life!" she said.

# CHAPTER NINE

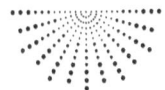

"*W*hat were those beasts?" D'laine asked the white creatures. "They reminded me of the wooly mammoths of the Pleistocene age, but much weirder with those eyes."

The white creatures responded with chirps and grunts, but she couldn't understand their language.

D'laine glanced across the expanse of the mossy plain. The silver-blue ground covering went on forever. Not a blade of normal grass in sight. A forest in the distance appeared as a typical Earth forest. She couldn't be sure due to the vast distance.

*Trees are trees, right?*

The two suns hung in the sky, but she was positive they were closer to the planet than Earth's sun. She rubbed her face then shook her head. "Doesn't make any sense."

A pen, credit card, hairbrush and notepad flew out of her canvas purse near one of the white creature's feet.

"What...?"

D'laine reached her foot out and nudged her bag. A spider-like creature, resembling a three-inch ball of pink cotton candy with little black eyes peeping out of its fluffy puff of a face, dangled from her purse. It was smeared with blusher and lipstick. Its tiny black spider legs clung to the fabric bag.

D'laine screamed for all it was worth.

The spider thing fell to the ground with a little thud and a squeak as D'laine kicked her purse away. The little creature disappeared under the spongy blanket of the ground cover.

"Oh my god! Giant spiders!" She hopped in a circle unevenly due to her damaged legs, screaming and shaking her hands.

A white creature tapped her on the back. Another one pressed a finger to her forehead during one of her spins. She stopped spinning, screaming and shaking her hands, and flopped down on the ground. After the tranquility settled from the creature's touch, she shook her head to clear her thoughts. She held the canvas bag at arm's length and shook it.

No more giant spiders came crawling out.

She looked around the ground at the scattered contents and tossed her stuff back into the purse. Two of her quartz crystals were half-buried in the moss. She dug them out and carefully placed them inside the bag. D'laine glanced around the ground. She spotted other crystals and grabbed one.

Sparks flew from her hand. She yelped with pain and dropped the crystal. She rubbed her hands together. "Definitely not one of mine!"

The white creatures watched her and nodded. Several of them conversed with chirps and grunts. Knowing it was about her, D'laine felt excluded from the conversation. Her mouth was set in a firm line.

One white creature bent down and took her hand. He

pulled her to her feet. She stared at the white creatures. The group nodded, chirped and grunted and D'laine figured that was their language. Another one pointed to the forest and tugged at her arm.

"You want me to go with you?" D'laine asked. She pointed to the forest.

The white creatures nodded as they appeared to understand her, and she thought she could make do with their gestures.

She decided there was nothing to lose. There was no familiar place for her to go in this bizarre land. She swallowed hard. She recalled the white creature in her dream. She always thought he was a guardian, or mentor who only wanted to help her.

"Not yet," she said. For as far as she could see, there was no hint of civilization. "I want to mark this spot. You know, make a permanent marker so I can find this exact place again."

D'laine spied the native crystals and thought. She dumped everything out of her canvas purse, took her purse and folded it over and picked up a crystal. It didn't shock her through the material. She held the crystal out to the white creatures.

"Can you find more of these so I can use them to mark this place?" She made a broad sweep of a circle about the ground.

The white creatures conferred then two of them hunted for crystals.

D'laine grabbed a handful of the spongy ground cover and pulled. It was an effortless task as it seemed barely rooted to the soil underneath. A couple of the spider creatures scooted away as they were uncovered. She soon had a circular area all but cleared. With the last handful of moss secured, she screamed in horror as a cluster of what looked like blue sod worms swarmed over the soil and moss and raced onto her hand.

She dropped the pastel vegetation, scooted backwards and wiped her hands in revulsion until all the sod worms dropped off. The nasty-looking insects curled up just like the pests in the garden back home when they were disturbed.

The two white creatures returned with a couple of dozen crystals and what looked like flat, black river rocks. They set them beside the circle on the ground.

"Thanks," she said as she returned to the task at hand. She used the canvas purse and rolled the crystals and rocks into place in the circle. Then she removed one of her flip flops and beat the crystals and rocks into the ground.

Grabbing the purse again, she placed the remaining rocks and crystals on top of the first layer.

"If the top layer is removed or disturbed in any way, the bottom layer will still be here, or at least an impression of it would remain so I can find this place again," she pointed to her work.

There was much discussion among her companions, which D'laine interpreted as approval. One of the creatures gestured toward the forest.

D'laine shrugged. "Guess there's not much choice."

She took a mental inventory of her meager possessions as she flung things back into the purse: dead phone, Kindle, Post It Notes, mechanical pencil, blue pen, wallet, eyeglass case, lens cleaning cloth, lip gloss, hairbrush, and a melted chocolate bar.

"Okay. I'm ready," she said. She extended her arm toward the forest.

They walked briskly across the field toward the immense forest keeping D'laine safely inside a tight circle of protection. A constant dialog went through her mind as they walked toward the trees.

*I wonder what's happening with daddy, Brian and Jamie.*

*Does anyone back home know what's happened to me?*
*Will I be able to go back home again?*
*Who's going to take care of everyone?*
*Will I get home in time for school?*
*Brenda's not going to believe this!*
*Rachel will think I went over the edge.*
*That back-stabbing Missy Childs better keep her hands off Connor!*

The white creature's long legs had D'laine trotting awkwardly to keep up with their lengthy strides. After fifteen minutes at the current pace in the intense heat she began to falter.

She finally stopped, out of breath, bent over and placed her hands on her scarred thighs and sucked in air. "I can't keep up in this heat."

D'laine sank to the ground. Two spider things peeked out from under the moss close by. One was a muted yellow and pink, the other a much brighter pink.

She stayed calm, not wanting to provoke the small creatures. *Male and female? The male of some species is more colorful... or is that just birds? Is the bright pink one the male then?*

The yellow and pink fluff-ball squeaked in fright and disappeared back into the mossy burrow. The other one moved forward and stopped a few inches from the burrow.

*I wonder if they spit poison like some spiders... or is it just snakes that do that? No, don't llama's spit?*

D'laine's mind raced with erratic thoughts as she watched the activity around her. More spider things scurried around the ground.

*Must be a colony.*

Little bitty rainbow-colored spider babies chased each

other, having a grand time. Some of the adults barely moved. Feeling brave, she reached out slowly to see what one would do if she touched it. As her hand approached one with faded coloring, it jumped and squeaked with fright.

D'laine yelped and yanked her hand back as it ran away. She watched it disappear under the spongy blanket of groundcover and peek out at her.

Frightened by the spider thing's reaction, she reasoned the situation out: It didn't attack her or show any aggressive behavior. It was probably just as scared as she was. The bright, colorful ones didn't seem to let anything upset them so she finally tried to touch one. It didn't mind the stroking of its fur.

D'laine stretched out on the ground to take a close look at the spider thing. She discovered the reason for its placidness: It was using two legs to stuff its mouth with the sponge, and he didn't let anything spoil his appetite.

After a five-minute rest, the white creatures coaxed her to her feet. They gestured to the forest, still quite far away. D'laine gathered her purse and her resolve and they trekked out in formation.

Ten minutes into their walk they came across a small water hole. The water was turquoise, and at first glance, as smooth as glass. Little ripples appeared around the edges as they approached.

The white creatures pointed from D'laine to the water, to her mouth.

"It's safe to drink?" she asked.

They all nodded.

"No monsters?"

Clicking and grunting ensued then one of the creatures shook his head.

*Okay. Maybe it's safe for them, but it could be poisonous for me. How can I possibly think of drinking this? I could die here, and no one would find me.*

After another moment of arguing with herself, logic won. She needed a drink and this was available and there wasn't a grocery store down the road. There weren't even any roads!

Tossing caution to the back of her mind, she sank down to her hands and knees, cupped her hands together and captured some water. She breathed it in. There were no odors that might be associated with scummy pond water. No chemical or mineral smells. Then, discarding all previous thoughts of safety, she sipped, holding the water in her mouth before swallowing.

It was cool and seemed pure. It tasted different than the water at her house, which she had always thought was the best, being from a deep water well and a whole-house water filter system. This water, however, tasted so good. *No humans to screw it up*, she thought pessimistically. Refreshing herself to the limit, she splashed some on her face and neck.

"Oh, daddy. I know I might not ever see you or the boys again, but I know you know that I love you. If I die here, my spirit will find its way back to you somehow," she said as she held her hands in prayer.

Glancing at her watch for the first time, she realized it had stopped. The glass was cracked and the wheel on the stem was bent. She was so fatigued she couldn't gauge how much time had passed since she stood in the parking lot at Katy Mills Mall. Her skin felt scorched from the hot suns; she didn't dare touch her scalp where the suns beat down on her fair hair.

A tap on the shoulder brought her back to the present. She took one more sip of water, gathered up her belongings and got to her feet. The troupe moved toward the forest in silence.

Not knowing how much time had elapsed, but feeling like it had been an hour of steadily trudging forward, when they finally arrived at the forest's edge, D'laine's jaw dropped in awe. She had been so engrossed with the trek across the colorful flat land, and surrounded by her tall travel companions, she couldn't see what was in front of them.

The forest was a magnificent colorful wonderland. D'laine glanced around, her mind boggled by the contrast of this forest and what she was accustomed to from *her* world. It was as if someone had chosen the color pallet with care then threw in a handful of glitter.

She reached out to one of the purple tree trunks. It felt rough. The bark crumbled at her touch and left a heady, musky odor on her hand. She brushed her hand on her capri pants, leaving a dark smudge on the material. She leaned back to see if she could gauge how high the trees were. A white fur-covered hand kept her from toppling backwards to the ground. The treetops disappeared into the clouds.

"These are bigger than the General Sherman tree!" D'laine said, mildly shocked. "I wish I could send a picture of these trees to my father. He wouldn't believe this unless he saw it right in front of him." She recalled the giant tree at Sequoia National Park in California. Her mind flew over the statistics of the General Sherman tree: The maximum diameter at the base of the tree was about thirty-six feet; circumference at the ground was one-hundred-two feet.

She studied the other trees that looked like monstrous ferns and yet others similar to palm trees but in an array of colors that would have delighted landscapers on Earth like the dyed daisies sold in bunches at the store. These trees were *all* larger than the giant sequoia!

Some trees had a substance hanging from the branches that looked like yellow Spanish moss with the same sparkling quality that colored the trees. The scene made her think of thousands of twinkling LED lights. She stared in awe at the colorful landscape, forgetting her dilemma, as she concentrated on the forest.

The beauty was sensational. Reds, pinks, orange, purple and every shade of blue were the colors of the plants, trees and flowers. If this were a dream, it was the very first one she'd ever experienced in such vivid color and description.

*Was nothing ugly in this place?* Even the sod worms had been in full living color.

D'laine finally decided she would never be able to accomplish spying a treetop unless she was flat on the ground with sunglasses secured in place. Since her prescription sunglasses were back in the minivan, the electric sky would make it impossible for her to locate the treetops. It was a battle lost before it began.

A small fern tree with a five-foot-wide trunk stood close by. She reached out and touched it and decided it felt like a rubber plant—smooth, solid, yet flexible to her touch. No smell was evident as she sniffed her fingers. Some of the fern trees looked like delicate plumosa ferns while others looked as though they had giant elephant ear foliage on their supple branches. None of the trees looked like oak, maple or pine.

The majestic giants on the edge of the forest were covered with vines that had woven many fingers in an intricate pattern of stems and leaves, from the base of the trees to as high as D'laine could see. The vines crossed from one tree to another, hung down, stretched out and climbed to the lost treetops, and across trunks further than she could see. She couldn't tell how many different varieties of vines there were.

As she stood looking from tree to tree, amazed at the vibrant colors that glittered in the full light, the sky flashed like heat lightning. There were places where the vines had been removed by either time or an unknown factor, leaving their past existence like a photograph, etched deeply into the surface of the trunks.

*How had they been removed?* She pushed the thought from her mind as it wasn't safe to dwell on. Whatever had removed those vines was either a giant, had a really long extension ladder handy, or climbed like a monkey.

In the overwhelming confusion of her situation, D'laine had to admit that if she were ever to travel the full surface of *her* Earth, she would never find this beauty. Pictures she had seen of beautiful gardens that everyone admired—gardens lit with tiny sparkling lights laced throughout trees and shrubberies that were a sampling of every color that was available in plant life on Earth. But none of those gardens could compare to this place.

The tap-tap on her shoulder drew her back to the present. The white creatures wanted to move on. Without warning, rain began pouring, beating her skin and clothes with a stinging force. Groping blindly and sputtering, D'laine shielded her face with one hand and pawed the air around her searching for her companions.

A large furred hand gently grasped her hand and led her to the shelter of the forest. Her face stung where the rain had hit like pellets from a toy gun. She gently wiped her face with the edge of her soaked shirt. She guessed that her skin was severely sunburned. It hurt immensely.

The white creatures visually examined her and must have determined that she was okay. There was a quorum of sorts with their noisy communication.

The pounding rain sounded like a waterfall crashing into a lake. Peering back around a huge tree trunk, D'laine witnessed the sudden disappearance of the hard rain. The torrential downpour ended as mysteriously as it had begun. The tightly woven trees had acted like a giant umbrella and protected her from the last of the onslaught.

The gloomy darkness of the crowded woodland provided a vast contrast to the overpowering, flashing sky. Curiosity piqued. D'laine eased around a huge tree trunk and stepped out of the forest. A white creature stood beside her, protectively. She cupped her hands around her eyes and looked up at the sky. Either another storm was brewing or the sky always looked like this. She was unsure.

Not wanting to take another painful drenching, she decided to continue with her white companions. They were taking her somewhere. She hoped it was to seek shelter and rest. She walked around one of the huge trunks into the forest and stopped to let her vision adjust to the darkness.

Everyone was waiting for her. She motioned with her hand to the white creatures to let them know she was ready. They moved forward. D'laine took a step and practically lost her balance. A root protruded from the ground like a gnarled arm stretching across her path. A white hand steadied her.

*Progress is going to be slow,* she thought.

She couldn't see well and the further in, the denser the forest. The pungent odors of the woodland took a few minutes to become accustomed to. But, *so far, so good—no allergy attack.*

The rough trunks had a very strong smell that clung to her hands and clothing, but she didn't sneeze, and her eyes didn't water. She fought to get her stomach under control; the overpowering damp animal stench caused several lurches inside her.

*This is not the time to become sick.*

After a few minutes, she noticed that there were no animal or bird noises. It just didn't seem possible that a forest this dense contained no flying, slithering or creeping life. Besides the tiny, fluffy spider creatures, she had come across in the field, which seemed harmless, nothing else presented itself.

*Huh. Why's it so quiet? You'd think there would be some kind of activity. All forests have rodents, snakes and insects. This one shouldn't be any different.*

The silence was unnerving, but she continued with her companions, slowly and carefully, putting all her listening skills to the test and feeling the ground in front of her with an outstretched foot. All she heard was the rustling of her own movements, her ragged breath and her pounding heart.

# CHAPTER TEN

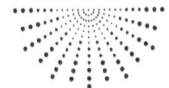

*D*'laine's vision adjusted to the deep shadows of her surroundings which made her progress easier, but small details were impossible to detect.

*It's just as well that the forest is dark.* She didn't want to see any insects or creatures that might live in the trees or on the ground. Her imagination conjured pictures, and she didn't have any way of knowing if a potential encounter with one of the silent and invisible things would prove fatal. Something as harmless as a caterpillar could turn out to be deadly.

Knowing intuitively that the white creatures would keep her safe, she tried to steer her mind away from guessing the identity of these hidden perils. The overwhelming size of the plant life suggested that insects and rodents would be monstrous. A bug on this world could very well be the size of a squirrel on Earth.

*Don't think about rats.*

Despite being carefully guided around huge tree trunks, and skirting extremely dense ground areas that wouldn't be wise to push through, D'laine was still compelled to continue.

There wasn't room enough to find any comfortable place to rest in this dense forest. She was hopeful that the further in they went, the foliage would thin out a bit. The plant life was thick in spots with vines and brambles growing up, hanging down and reaching out. The ground teemed with vines, roots, and small plants, making footing difficult. Flip-flops didn't help.

The white creatures moved effortlessly through the hazardous terrain. D'laine's weak vision adjusted more to the dim light. But the natural environment was just hard to get through unless you were a survivalist with ten years of experience. As a child, she had been more comfortable tinkering in her father's shop with pliers, wrenches and screwdrivers. She had never joined any type of team sports in school, and since the accident she had been more sedentary.

As the group trekked on, a great blob of water that had been captured by the huge canopy of leaves overhead bombarded her. Water dripped down her face and she swiped it away with her hands. The top of her head stung where she was water-bombed. Like a giant terrarium, the tall trees controlled the water filtering down through the dense foliage. The water that rolled from one giant leaf to another provided the balance of moisture necessary for the plants on the ground to survive.

The oppressive silence was shattered as something scurried behind her and the white creatures. Whirling around, she collided with one of her companions. He steadied her with his large hands and turned her in the right direction.

"What was that?" she asked. She cupped her ear to make her question understood.

The white creatures did not appear to be worried so she tried to relax while she only saw the shadows of the trees. With heart pounding, D'laine followed the creatures while she searched the area from ground level to as high as her head would allow her to bend back without impeding her progress. She was sure her heart could be heard for miles.

Emotions ran unleashed; there was no place to go for help, no soothing human companionship. Where was Connor when she needed him? She had to trust the white creatures explicitly.

D'laine stumbled onward, her senses alert for any sound or movement close by. After no encounter with anything more dangerous than the terrain, her nerves quieted and her heart rate slowed to a more normal beat.

Nothing had prepared her for the next sight. "Is that a... mushroom?" she asked loudly.

Forty feet ahead of her in a little clearing stood a mushroom that could easily be mistaken for a one-story house. Its size was mind-boggling, but taking the size away, the stem and cap were replicas of mushrooms from home. *My God, this thing would provide chopped mushrooms for the entire city for a month!* They circled the huge thing and continued on their way.

D'laine was so preoccupied with the large mushroom she almost missed a low growl nearby. She nervously glanced around.

"What was that?" She yanked on the white fur in front of her. She pointed to her ear and made a growling noise when the creature turned and looked down at her.

The white creatures chirped and grunted. The creature behind her nudged her back, urging her to keep going.

The bushes rustled. Ferocious growls grew closer. Suddenly, a large spiked, mottled green and tan hard-shelled animal emerged.

D'laine screamed. It echoed through the forest.

The creature looked like it came right out of the dinosaur age. D'laine darted between two of her companions.

Flashes of white rushed past her. A thunderous sound crackled in the air and the animal fell to the ground. After a long moment, the animal awkwardly rose to its feet, shook its head and stumbled away.

"Wow! You're walking weapons, but you don't kill." D'laine looked at her companions in awe and relaxed, feeling safe.

Once more they started up their little caravan. As she plodded forward, she spotted a clearing far away where the sunlight poured through. At the rate of her walking speed, and with all the obstructions, she figured it would take them another fifteen minutes to get there. Wiping the beads of perspiration from her forehead with the back of her hand, she tucked a wisp of hair behind her ear.

The flimsy canvas straps of her bag felt like lead over her shoulder. Her back ached. She wondered why she hadn't discarded the purse long ago. The answer popped into her mind. *The need for identification is a link to home.* She let her mind wander as they moved steadily forward.

THE BEASTS CARRIED THE REPTILIAN BRIGADE BACK TO the clearing where the conflict had occurred. The monster-commander slammed his boot against the beast's second front leg. It knelt to the ground, and the monster-commander dismounted. He walked to a mossy area that was trampled by large feet. He knelt and traced a tiny unknown footprint in the moss.

The monster-commander tilted his head from side-to-side like a confused dog. After a moment, he stood and looked around the area. Spotting a crumpled tissue, he walked a few paces and snatched it off the ground. He sniffed it, studied it then tucked it into a vest pocket and returned to his beast. He slapped the beast's front leg and mounted up.

Facing the forest, the reptilian monster-commander shook his fist in the air and bellowed in rage. He then led his troops in the opposite direction.

THE FEARSOME ROAR ECHOED THROUGH THE FOREST. D'laine came to a dead stop as she shuddered in fear.

"Oh my god... is that a T-Rex?"

A finger touched her forehead, releasing her from the paralysis of her fear. She smiled goofily then remembered to breathe; she snapped out of the momentary feeling of giddiness, then they moved in tandem once again.

Dead ahead was the clearing with bright sunlight pouring through. There was still a lot of forest between her and that area. It seemed denser toward the edge, making it more difficult to keep forward momentum. Making her way through the growth, she was almost strangled by a creeper vine of some unknown type. Squeaking out a cry, a large hand grabbed at the offending foliage and ripped it away from her.

"Thanks," she said.

The white creatures never had problems with the dense forest. They seemed to be able to navigate through anything in their path with ease.

Close to the perimeter of the clearing, the size of the tree trunks blocked much of the light. Progressing slowly, her soft blonde hair caught in the thick brambles of the dense growth where she tried to push her body through. Large hands forced her to stop while they pushed aside threatening ivy and stickers. D'laine didn't think she would ever get her snagged hair untangled, but she finally pried the last few strands from the rough branches of some unknown shrubbery.

They continued on, trying to avoid as much of the over and

undergrowth as possible. D'laine rubbed her sore scalp. It felt as if someone had attempted to pull her hair out by the roots. As she came around the circumference of the last tree, the light shone through in such brilliance it hurt her eyes.

She cupped her hands around her eyes to help her vision adjust to the contrast between the dark forest and the brilliant clearing. D'laine stared at a cluster of giant mushrooms. They were magnificent with their tall stems and wide caps stretching out proudly. D'laine could see that her first estimate was totally incorrect. They were more like forty or fifty feet tall. The one they had stumbled upon in the forest must have been new growth compared to this mushroom family. These were huge, like three-story houses!

As she stood gaping at the mushroom grove, she heard a lot of soft chirping, grunting and clicking noises.

"I guess we're here, right?" she said. "Is this your home?"

The white creatures chattered at her as if they understood her question. They led her through a maze of mushrooms. D'laine noticed that there was no debris in sight that would suggest a community lived here. The mushroom village was dead quiet and seemed abandoned. They stopped at a central mushroom with a carved-out doorway.

Inviting clicks and grunts sounded from inside. One of her companions nudged her forward.

# CHAPTER ELEVEN

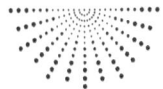

*B*ruce Miller shrugged in exasperation. "Okay, I guess you didn't see that kid's video. She was wearing a Game of Thrones T-shirt, crop pants, flip-flops and she had this floppy canvas handbag."

"What kind of flip-flops?" the officer asked.

"Just watch the video, man," Bruce said sarcastically. "I don't understand why you are being such a butt about this."

After the officers questioned several people they excused themselves and gathered at Officer Davidson's cruiser.

"I don't know what to make of this. Do you think this is a prank?" Officer Reidy asked.

"Jackson, the girl's father, is going to have a heart attack if he doesn't calm down some," Davidson said. "Something happened here, but I'll be darned if I know what. That man swears that his daughter just up and disappeared right in front of him. What does that other guy have to say?"

"Miller. Bruce Miller," Reidy explained, glancing down at his note pad. "Practically the same thing. No one kidnapped her, this fog just rolled in and she was gone. Let's call in and see what Lt. Brooks has to say."

Officer Davidson pulled his cellphone out of his shirt pocket, pressed a speed-dial button and made contact with the dispatcher. "Can you get me through to Brooks?"

"Sure thing, Gary. Line's free, I'd better put you through before he picks it up again. See you later," the dispatcher said, not waiting for a response.

"Brooks," a gruff voice boomed out of the silence.

"Lt. Brooks, this is Gary Davidson. Reidy, Holland and I were called out to Katy Mills Mall to investigate a possible child abduction. It's pretty weird. I'm not sure abduction is the right classification. I think your department might want to be involved."

The two men talked for several minutes then Davidson put his cellphone in his shirt pocket. He let out a sigh as he turned to Reidy and Holland. "He's sending Ferguson," Davidson told the other men his voice ringing with exasperation.

"Not that old fool! We'll be here forever," Reidy hissed. "When are they going to retire him?"

# CHAPTER TWELVE

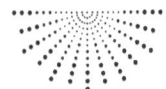

*D*'laine surveyed her appearance and came to the conclusion that flip flops might be great back home, but they weren't made for this place. *Why did I wear these shoes to the mall? Of all things! They aren't going to stay together much longer.*

Horrified, she noticed that her crop pants and T-shirt were covered with the crumbly residue of tree bark and were stained beyond recognition. She smelled terrible. Her hands, arms and legs were scratched and smudged.

Hand extended, she felt the surface of the large fungi house and decided it was exactly what it felt like—a mushroom. Thinking of all the mushrooms she had cleaned and eaten in her lifetime, she knew they couldn't add up to even a wedge out of one of these giants.

*Boy, mom, you would have loved one of these in your garden.*

D'laine laughed hysterically, tears streaming down her cheeks, then she felt foolish for having that thought pop into her mind in the middle of a crisis.

*Quit it!* She scolded herself.

Positive there was nothing she could do about her appearance or hygiene, she peered inside the mushroom house. Her eyes adjusted to the muted interior as she inched through the archway and stopped.

Then she saw him.

The white-furred creature sat on the floor of the mushroom house on some sort of mat. There were no furnishings except for three large boulders and an odd-looking nest in one area. She couldn't imagine why the huge rocks were there.

Two glowing red eyes and the large white furry body could clearly be seen in the dimly lit interior. Something was illuminating the room, but she couldn't see the light source. There were no windows, and only one doorway—right where she was standing, blocking the exterior light.

The creature stood, walked to the boulders then waved her forward with two of his four hands.

Feeling as if she were rooted to the spot, D'laine's heart hammered in her chest. Her body trembled with fright.

*Should I take a chance?*

*Will you walk into my parlor, said the spider to the fly?*

*What choice do I really have?*

*Where can I run that they couldn't find me?*

*I might as well get this over with.*

*Nothing like inviting myself to dinner and I'm the main course!*

*Think that he's friendly—the others were, she reminded herself.*

*He or she—whatever it is—has intelligence.*

*He could kill me with just one huge hand, and I'm sure he's well aware of that.*

*Maybe this isn't the main race of people here.*

*This is a dream. A bad, bad dream. Worse than those nightmares I've had.*

*Wake up and get out of here, quick!*

The creature impatiently shook his head and motioned her inside while chirping, clicking and grunting.

D'laine swallowed, fought back a surge of pure terror and entered the space.

It felt almost damp inside, but not uncomfortable. The musty animal smell almost overpowered her, but as she stood inside the mushroom, the odor became easier to bear. Perspiring heavily from raw nerves, she walked a few steps as her eyes adjusted to the light. Then she realized what those boulders were—a carved stone table and chairs.

Shocked, she sucked in a lungful of air and raised a hand to her chest. *Furniture?*

"Furniture!" she stated excitedly. She couldn't believe her eyes. *There must be civilization here somewhere!*

The creature waved her forward with two right hands as he chirped and grunted and motioned for D'laine to sit opposite him.

Taking a deep, brave breath, D'laine limped across the dirt floor. Her legs and feet ached from the exertion of the long walk across the field and the strenuous trek through the forest. Her limping was pronounced as she started across the floor of the hut. With difficulty, she pulled out a heavy stone chair opposite her host. She slung her purse over the back of the chair. Then she sat.

Forcing calm thoughts, she made herself stop fidgeting and looked up to make contact with her host.

And she outright stared. *They must be Yetis or Bigfoot,* she thought, able to reason once again.

He chirped, grunted and shook his head.

Bigfoot filled her head. It was covered with brown fur or hair, but D'laine remembered reading about the Yeti being white. These beings must be related to one of the earthbound creatures. The Bigfoot or Yetis could have two sets of arms—there weren't any crisp, clear digital or even 35 mm photos on file anywhere that she was aware of.

She could only recall vague sketches in various UFO magazines and books she had glanced through, and since no one had good film of either creature, how could she be sure they didn't have four arms?

As they sat staring at each other, D'laine noticed he had squinty eyes. Though the openings were wide and oval, the eyeball itself was tiny.

The creature gave the customary greeting to D'laine: a nod; she thought this must be a friendly gesture, like shaking hands.

"Your friends saved me."

The creature grunted an acknowledgment, then smiled, revealing two rows of gleaming teeth.

Reeling with fear, D'laine sucked in her breath and tried to distance herself from her host. The chair was too heavy to scoot back. She felt trapped.

He spoke in a language she couldn't decipher, almost grunts, but each sound was different with a distinct meaning she couldn't understand. She was sure he expected something from her in response so she took the initiative.

She began by placing her hand on her chest and saying her name, enunciating the syllables clearly, like many people did when talking to a foreigner, or trying to explain a point. He grunted in return so D'laine thought this was at least a start. She nervously talked to him.

"I know this is your territory and I'm trespassing, but I mean you no harm. I didn't ask to be here. I don't even know where "here" is, or how I got here, except for the fog and the tunnel I was yanked through. You don't know how much I appreciate you inviting me into your home—me, a total stranger and obviously not one of your own kind. We need to find a way to communicate, to understand each other so you can tell me where I am and how I can leave your world and return back home, to my world."

Silence engulfed the room as she finished her ranting. Not feeling any better for it, she felt that her outburst had released her tension somewhat. They sat across from each other, D'laine blushing brightly, feeling that she had made a fool of herself. The creature focused on her as if he understood everything she said.

He glanced at the Bluetooth device in her ear and reached across the table and pressed it. Then he crossed his two pairs of hands in front of him and chirped, clicked and grunted. With his face showing expectation, he stared at D'laine. She returned his stare with a questioning expression.

He reached across the table and removed her Bluetooth device and looked it over. Grumbling, he pushed his chair back and stood. The creature walked to a carved ledge in the mushroom wall and selected something, then returned to the table and sat.

He showed her a small device that rested in the palm of one of his hands. It resembled the metal clip on a ballpoint pen. D'laine stretched her neck to see the clip. The creature reached across the table, lifted the hair away from her right ear and gently pressed the clip into the skin behind her ear. The clip *settled* into her flesh.

"Oh!" she said. Her fingers played over the embedded clip. "That was weird."

The creature made soft noises, consoling in nature, and before she could guess what was about to happen, he spoke clearly. "That should be better. I am Ghury (Yur-e). Welcome to my home."

She jumped a little in the chair. Her jaw dropped and she

grasped her head as shock registered on her face at the communication.

His voice was strange, guttural in fact. She thought of an old man she had met months ago at a NASA function she went to with her father. The man had throat cancer, and he had spoken in a similar way, which resulted from a tracheotomy. She didn't see any opening in Ghury's neck or throat so she figured it was his normal voice.

"You are overwrought with fear and sadness; that is understandable. I will help you to adjust to this sudden change in your life to the best of my ability. Let me attend to your present needs and get you something to drink," he said sympathetically, concluding with a single nod of his head.

"Did you just speak English? I guess it's finally happened. I must truly be crazy. None of this is happening—I'm hallucinating, or I'm back in a coma. That's it. I wonder if Dr. Reynolds is observing me right now in Texas Children's Hospital," she blurted.

"You are not crazy and you are not seeing visions. I can find nothing out of place in your mind," Ghury stated with a hint of annoyance.

"Don't talk to me! I'll get totally convinced that you're real, and I'll never be able to leave the hospital. If only this vision would just go away and a regular sterile hospital room would appear! That's all I want. Is that too much to ask?"

"Accept the situation as it is and control your emotions. We have much to discuss," he scolded her.

"Poor daddy. To have to endure this breakdown on top of everything else that has happened."

She covered her face with her hands and spoke through her fingers, barely whispering. "You are real, aren't you? I'm living in my nightmare. How can you possibly understand my language? It would take me a million years to figure out what you were trying to say!"

"It's the translator," Ghury said.

Dumbstruck, D'laine touched the clip in her head again.

"I don't think you are, but if you're planning on killing me I wish you'd get it over with quickly. I'm not a brave person," she confessed.

A ferocious loud noise scared her, causing her to yelp and push against the table. Then she realized it was a laugh.

"It will be all right," Ghury assured her. He leaned forward and patted one of her hands gently. "You survived passage to our world. It would have been better if Jakla Bosakin had not found you so soon though."

After a few minutes D'laine recovered her composure. "The alligator man?"

"Plotal. Fierce, warring creatures. That's all they know," he said.

Another creature entered the hut with a jug, and offered it to D'laine.

"This is Kestrum," Ghury said.

"Would you like to quench your thirst?" Kestrum asked with a smile showing a mouthful of deadly-looking teeth.

Assessing the smaller newcomer, D'laine took the jug with shaking hands, almost bonking herself with the beautiful container. She overcompensated, thinking it would be much heavier than it was.

"Huh. That's strange." D'laine admired the container. It looked like marble. It was tan and smooth and looked like polished marble or granite, but she wasn't sure because it wasn't heavy at all.

D'laine peered inside and saw it contained a liquid she assumed was water because of the slight bluish tint. She sniffed then took a sip and coughed. She sipped more than guzzled the clean, cool water.

"Are you refreshed now?" Ghury asked.

She compared the two creatures. D'laine noted that Kestrum was similar to Ghury except this new creature had a slit across its belly like a marsupial pouch. Its features were more refined—smaller teeth, smaller body, not as fierce looking as her host. Continuing to compare the two, D'laine decided this new creature was a female, and the pouch was like a kangaroo's.

"Yes, similar to your Earth creature in that aspect only," Ghury said of the comparison that she had thought to herself. "The Yeti creature looks more akin to our kind, though neither the Yeti, nor Bigfoot has desirable life expectancy cycles, or the intelligence capacity."

"Oh, you Earth people, always getting us mixed up with your folklore," Kestrum said.

Shock registered across D'laine's face as she realized two things: *Others had been here before her, and the creatures could hear everything she thought.* D'laine wondered if she had thought anything embarrassing or insulting about him or his homeland. She remembered some pretty wild thoughts, but nothing unforgivable as far as she was concerned. With this ability, nothing was private; no secrets could be kept from them.

Finding this amusing, Ghury told her that he had already heard all her scattered thoughts as she walked through the forest. "Your brain is working overtime," he said.

*He has a definite advantage over me since I can't even remember everything that went through my head.*

She was dumbstruck with the concept of telepathy, or mind reading. She worried about any information she had about her father's work. Suddenly, the idea of an invasion of her world jumped into her mind. She tried clearing the onslaught of her brain chatter.

"Ease your anxieties. My people have no desire to travel to your world. Besides, we have had many opportunities, but we chose to wait for you to come to us instead," he explained.

"You waited for me?" D'laine asked. She tossed several scenarios around in her head, dismissing them all. She thought of her dreams and wondered if there was a connection between the dreams and her being here. She pushed that thought aside.

"How did you learn my language so easily?" she asked.

"Anyone can learn a language if they study it long enough," he stated. "My people learn instantly what other races would take years to accomplish. Be comforted that we have no interest in spying. It would take centuries for your greatest intellect to catch up with us. The inhabitants of your world are still in the barbaric stage of trying to slaughter themselves. That will pass."

Words failed her as she sputtered an attempt to respond.

He stared at her. "Your vessel is almost in complete failure for one so young!"

D'laine carefully set the jug on the table. "My—vessel?"

Ghury pushed his chair back and stood. He walked around the table and stood beside her chair. He placed two hands in front of her and two in back. He ran his hands up and down, about six inches from her body, as if scanning her.

D'laine felt a sensation as his hands lingered in front of her. Kestrum stood quietly by Ghury's chair.

Ghury walked to the middle of the hut. He urged her forward. "We will restore you," he said. "Your world will soon start to concentrate on evolved healing technologies. Come. Let's get started."

D'laine hesitated then turned sideways in the heavy chair, eased herself out from behind the table and stood. She limped over to Ghury. "I don't understand. What do you plan to do?"

"Just try to relax," he said. "Kestrum and I will restore you."

"Restore me? To what? I don't understand."

"To the original configuration of your species," Ghury explained.

"Your god-form," Kestrum said. "Were you not made in your god's image?"

D'laine stared hard at Kestrum and Ghury. "Yes, we were created in God's image." She looked down at herself. "But I'm all here."

"Your hearing is poor in one ear, you have failing eyesight, missing body parts, structural problems and potential organ failure," he said.

D'laine looked astounded. "What... how... I had my tonsils out when I was seven, and I was in a bad car accident when I was twelve."

Kestrum joined them in the middle of the hut and stood opposite Ghury. Their arms formed a circle around D'laine, but did not touch her or each other.

An energy field engulfed D'laine. Her head leaned back, her eyes rolled up and closed, and her mouth fell open as if in rapture. They levitated her to a horizontal position. She floated six feet off the floor with her hair spread out like a halo.

The hut vibrated with energy. Loud crunching noises emitted from D'laine's body as if bones were breaking. Pieces of metal clanged when they hit the dirt floor in a pile. Screws dropped to the floor.

Ghury communicated silently with Kestrum. D'laine's body rotated to a vertical position, and her feet touched the floor. Ghury and Kestrum's arms parted and D'laine stumbled. Her legs could not support her. Ghury held her up. She looked down at the floor in shock. She looked up at Ghury.

"How—my bones?"

Kestrum and Ghury each held one of her arms and led her back to the table. They eased her into the chair.

"Take a drink and sit quietly for a few minutes," Kestrum said.

D'laine drank from the jug. "I feel funny—like I'm buzzing inside. My bones..."

"Your system is rewiring and regenerating itself. You will be fine," Ghury said with a big smile on his face.

D'laine pointed to the metal on the ground. "I need that metal to function".

"Bones are much better inside your body than metal," Kestrum said.

"But the surgeon had to remove my crushed bones after the accident," D'laine said.

"Rest is called for," Ghury said. "We will continue our discussion later when you are fully rested."

Kestrum helped D'laine stand.

D'laine grabbed her bag off the chair and Kestrum ushered her outside, one large furry arm and hand around D'laine's waist.

# CHAPTER THIRTEEN

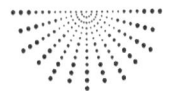

estrum and D'laine left Ghury and arrived at an identical dwelling just a few short steps away. D'laine's canvas bag dragged the ground as she tripped along on her weak legs with Kestrum.

They entered the dark mushroom house. Kestrum assisted D'laine to the table. She pulled out a chair and helped D'laine get settled. Then she lit a lantern. Moments later the interior was bathed in an ambient light.

The place was identical to Ghury's. Gauzy material was heaped in a corner like a huge dog bed. The table contained a carafe of water, a bowl, and several small pieces of gauzy cloth, like washcloths. Kestrum poured water in the bowl.

"Why don't you wash your face and hands? It will make you feel so much better," she said.

The illuminated lamp on the table was like an old-fashioned hurricane lamp. The holder was carved out of polished stone, smooth to the touch. It contained a trench that held the tube covering in place.

The tube was different from glass. It appeared to be made

from a mineral that reminded D'laine of mica, thin and translucent.

Marveling at the craftsmanship, D'laine ran her finger across the cool surface of the tube then rubbed the surface of the table, which was glossy, smooth and free of blemishes. The furniture and lantern would be the envy of a master craftsman from her world.

"Could you show me how this lantern works in case I need to relight it?" D'laine asked.

Kestrum walked over to a niche in the wall. She returned with another lantern and a couple of pieces of thick blue stalks from a plant. She held out a piece to D'laine. "This is the light stem."

The light stems looked like thick oily stalks of grass.

"Where does this come from? I didn't see anything that looked like this. All I saw was the mossy fields," D'laine said as she studied the stem.

"They grow in large clumps throughout the forest," Kestrum replied. "Mostly in shaded areas. One single stalk lasts several weeks; they are very slow to burn and also water resistant."

Kestrum pulled a light stem apart and handed it to D'laine. It was oily and sticky on the outside, which was probably why it was a slow-burning process, and the fibers on the inside seemed to be made of a raw cotton-like substance.

When Kestrum removed the tube from the base, D'laine saw a slit in the bottom of the stone that held the light stem in place.

D'laine rubbed the base of the lantern. "This is so beautiful."

"It comes from the same material as the table and chairs," Kestrum explained. She picked up two small rocks. "These make fire, but you must be very careful because it takes only a light touch to produce the flame. So, don't bang them together," Kestrum cautioned.

She tapped them together gently. Instantly, a low purplish flame sprang forth.

"Are those flint rocks?" D'laine asked.

"We call them lighting stones. They will light even when wet," Kestrum said.

"Wow! Better than our flint stones, or matches," D'laine said. She placed a hand on her forehead and tried to will away a headache of major proportions.

Kestrum walked across the interior of the mushroom and fluffed up the nesting material in a corner. "I will come help you after you are cleaned up."

"I feel so weak," D'laine said.

"You will be better soon. Right now, your body is slowing down to repair itself," Kestrum said. "Sleep is required for the healing process. I will be right back."

In the solitude of the mushroom house, exhausted and hot, D'laine kicked her flip flops off in the general direction of the chair where her canvas purse hung. She leaned on the table and slipped her crop pants over her slim hips and let them drop to the ground. She hooked a big toe under the waistband and lifted the pants off the floor.

D'laine snatched the crop pants, shook them, and placed them across the stone seat. She sat and looked down at her lap.

Ugly scars, like railroad tracks, crossed straight across both thighs. Even though five years had passed since the accident, the angry red lines and dots from the medical staples told a story.

She removed her glasses and set them on the table then picked up one of the cloths on the table, dipped it into the bowl and sponged off her face and arms.

After she was somewhat cleaned up, Kestrum entered the

hut and helped her over to the nest. D'laine reached up and placed her glasses on the ledge then sank down on the bedding.

"Sleep well," Kestrum said.

"Thank you, Kestrum," D'laine said.

Lying down, D'laine pulled one of the cloths about her. She was physically and mentally drained. Her teeth chattered and her body shook. D'laine closed her eyes and tried to think soothing thoughts. She felt as if she were nesting on a cloud. With that thought, she fell into a deep sleep.

MORE THAN A DOZEN WHITE CREATURES FORMED A CIRCLE around the mushroom house, facing it. They each held their four hands facing the mushroom, sending healing energy to D'laine.

HOURS LATER, KESTRUM ENTERED THE HUT. D'LAINE stirred in the nest.

"Feel better?" Kestrum asked.

D'laine turned to face the white-furred creature and took a mental inventory.

"I feel different, but I don't know how to explain it," D'laine said. She stretched her body. Her legs felt odd – strong, somehow. She reached for her glasses and put them on. She yanked them off and starred at the lenses in the frame. "I must have really hurt myself when I landed here. My glasses made me dizzy just now."

"Oh, you won't need those eye-balancing contraptions anymore," Kestrum said.

D'laine looked around the hut. Everything appeared sharp

and crisp, not hazy. "Huh. So, that healing you did corrected my vision? I've had to wear glasses since I was seven years old!"

"Yes. You will find many changes occurring in your body over the next few turns." Kestrum said. "But come now. Ghury has things to discuss with you."

D'laine wondered how she was going to stand without the metal braces inside, but she gave it a try. To her amazement, her legs supported her. She walked to the table without limping. She grabbed her pants, shook them slightly to get rid of some of the wrinkles then she raised one leg and slipped it into the waistband. She automatically looked down.

"My scars!" she shrieked.

Her hands flew over her flawless flesh. Gone were the deep markings that had haunted her every day of her life. Now she understood the metal at her feet in Ghury's hut.

D'laine cried as she sank into the chair and rested her head on her thighs.

Kestrum placed two hands on D'laine's back. "It is much better to be whole."

D'laine reached up and grasped Kestrum's hand. "I can't believe what you did. It's a miracle." She sobbed.

"Healing is easy," Kestrum said. She patted D'laine's back. "We must go to Ghury."

D'laine stood, stepped into her pants and slipped into her flip flops. She grabbed her canvas bag. Kestrum led the way to Ghury's mushroom.

"I'll be back for you later," Kestrum said.

D'laine stood outside of the mushroom. She pondered the protocol and social niceties of this place.

*Should I knock?*

She attempted to knock on the mushroom. It was like slapping a package of chicken from the grocery store. She shrugged and entered.

Ghury sat on the floor on a mat in a meditative pose. He opened his eyes as D'laine entered. "You feel much better, don't you?"

"Yes. My legs... I can see..."

He looked at her sympathetically, stood and walked to the table. "Come, sit."

D'laine approached the table, placed the canvas bag in front of her and sat. "I just realized that the ringing in my ears is no longer there."

"Some parts of the restoration will take longer than others," he said. He tapped her head. "Your brain has shifted and has settled into place."

She touched her head. "The doctors had to drill holes in my head after the accident."

"Not to worry. Everything's all there," Ghury said with a smile.

D'laine realized he made a joke, and she giggled. "That's good to know."

It was a strange experience, D'laine mused. The only thing that held her sanity together was the fact that she knew he was real and that the conversation was actually taking place. Her fear subsided. She didn't know what would become of her now that she was here, accepting his hospitality. A question loomed in her mind: *What are the odds of me surviving here on my own?* There weren't any odds as far as she was concerned.

"My people are of an ancient race, called Egroms. We are the most intelligent creatures of Thol, the oldest living race. We will watch over you and teach you everything that you will need to know to survive here. You have much to learn. You will also have many questions; all will be answered in time. We will only be able to communicate through the translator device until you learn our language."

"Why in the world should I learn your language? Besides,

you don't use words. You just make a bunch of sounds. That's not even talking. I don't plan on being here that long. I have to get back home!" she blurted.

"Home. Yes, you do have a home," he said.

She thought that perhaps something had gotten lost in the interpretation, but she waited for him to finish.

"The higher creatures of Thol communicate through a common language that all understand. Most species can communicate with each other, if they are intelligent. There are some that are of a low order, but they can make their wishes known," he explained.

*He ignored me!*

Deciding to see what common ground they could talk about, she interrupted him.

"What were those furry animals in the fields?" D'laine asked.

"You liked the hosks?" he asked, quite pleased. "Hosks live exclusively on the sponge, needing no water or other substance apart from air to breathe."

"They don't drink water?" D'laine asked, surprised. "How can that be?"

"The moss retains enough moisture for their needs," Ghury explained. "The female is flighty, but protective of her young; they are live bearers who live in burrows under the sponge."

"What incredible little creatures," D'laine said.

"Their purpose is to spin a web which is later woven into a material that is durable and used for bedding, clothing and many other things. The gauze is dyed into many colors from extracts of different plants," Ghury told her.

"What was that animal in the forest? It had a hard shell with spikes," D'laine asked.

"Augugal. They change color to blend into their environment," he explained. "It must have had a nest close by and felt threatened."

D'laine scrunched her face in thought.

"They are herbivores, so the attack was not to kill and eat you, but to scare you away from the nest."

"Oh!" D'laine said.

While it was all quite interesting, she had no idea where she was. "Is this Mars, the fourth planet from the sun?" D'laine asked, letting her imagination run amok while waiting to learn exactly where she was. All she could think of was John Carter of Mars.

"No, we are Thol, third from Volta and Astor—what you call suns," he explained.

Having been raised by a NASA engineer, D'laine became confused. *Surely, I couldn't have been thrust into another galaxy with the same layout as my own?*

Seeing her confusion and reading her thoughts, Ghury explained the situation. "Thol is the same planet as your Earth. We are but a lateral space from your world," he explained.

Continuing with his exposition, he told her that there were other planes, each called by a different name and having their own characteristics, people, and lifestyles. Everything was different, but all shared time.

"Accidents frequently happen. Life forms stumble across the hidden portals in these other planes and fall through them to places unknown to them," Ghury said.

"I didn't fall through. I was kidnapped! This fog rolled in and sucked me into this tunnel," she said, defensively.

"Yours is a special case that is difficult to explain," he said with secret knowledge.

"This doesn't usually happen to others, right?" she asked, hopeful.

"Precisely. The Egroms are the custodians of the portals of

Thol. We make sure unwanted visitors are returned to their places as soon as possible," he told her.

"Oh, thank God! I'm so glad to hear that! Let's get going so you can return me to Earth," she said, recovering her lost energy. She stood and grabbed her bag.

He shook his head. "The portals are forever floating over the surfaces of our shared planet in a very minute space of time, changing from plane to plane, forever drifting. You will have to wait until the portal you came through lines back up with your world again."

"You're telling me I may be here forever?" She paced frantically bordering on near-hysteria. "There must be something you can do!"

*I am not going to stay here,* she stated silently.

"You have no choice," he responded to her silent determination.

D'laine reeled with shock as she realized he answered her unspoken thought.

"If you were to return to the field right now and discovered a portal, you would have no way of knowing if it were aligned with your world. You might walk through to another world, much more hostile. There are many places that are ravaged by war. One place I have viewed is inhabited by cannibals. The perils outweigh the possibility that you would make a direct trip home."

"Why haven't you guarded these things better? This is sheer recklessness," she sputtered out.

"Nothing happens by chance," Ghury said. His face held a passive expression.

D'laine stopped her pacing, turned and stared him down. "Don't hand me that esoteric crap. I've been into crystals and metaphysics since I was a little girl, and all I've accomplished is the ability to see auras if I squint real hard," she said. "Face facts. You messed up!"

"You have mastered much more, but you do not have the training to recognize these new skills," Ghury said matter-of-factly.

"Oh, and I guess you're the teacher?" D'laine fumed. She slipped back into the chair. "I'm supposed to be heading out to Texas A&M next week with Connor, my boyfriend! What about all my scholarships?"

Ghury held up all four hands. "Arguing and worrying will not get you home any sooner. Would you like more rest?"

D'laine pounded the table. "No, I don't want to rest! I want to go home!" Hot angry tears spilled down her cheeks.

"Do you not understand your plight? We will continue this conversation later, when you are calm and rational," Ghury said, standing.

Kestrum entered the house and nodded to D'laine. She held out one of her hands.

Petulant, D'laine refused it.

"Kestrum will see to all your needs," Ghury said.

"Come now, D'laine. You're pretty overwrought from this whole experience, and Ghury has things on his mind," Kestrum said.

"I just want to go home," D'laine whispered.

"I understand how difficult this adjustment is," Kestrum said.

Dejected, D'laine's shoulders slumped and she cried silently as everything in her former life unraveled out of control. She hid behind her hands as the real crying started. After a few minutes, she regained control of her emotions and wiped her tear-stained face.

The canvas bag shimmied as it crawled a few inches across the table toward her.

"Now what?" D'laine asked, fearfully.

Her hands flew to the edge of the table as a baby hosk squeezed out of the canvas bag and dropped onto her lap.

D'laine screeched and launched sideways out of the stone chair as the hosk baby jumped to the floor with a grunt and scurried out the door. She slapped at her vacant lap, filled with fear.

"That was just a harmless hosk. Make sure you treat them with respect," Ghury grumbled.

The floodgates reopened. Kestrum came forward, grabbed D'laine's canvas bag and led her out of the hut. When they entered D'laine's mushroom, D'laine reached out and bravely touched one of Kestrum's arms.

"Do you have younger brothers and sisters? Or—children?" D'laine asked.

"Yes, I have both. My little one sleeps." Kestrum opened her pouch a few inches. A tiny Egrom baby slept curled in a ball. Its skin was pink with tufts of white fur.

"Oh, he's so cute." D'laine peeked into the pouch.

"My sisters and brothers are progressing." Kestrum used all four hands to show their different sizes.

"Please... Kestrum. Can you help me get back home? I have two brothers," D'laine explained. She used her hands to show their sizes. "Our mother died when they were very young, and I help take care of them."

Kestrum shook her head, sadly. "The portals are very dangerous. Many creatures have been killed trying to return home at the wrong time, or stepping into the wrong portal. It is best to wait."

Opening her arms, Kestrum drew D'laine to her and rocked her, purring like a cat. D'laine slumped against Kestrum for a moment of comfort.

# CHAPTER FOURTEEN

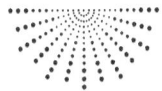

$\mathcal{S}$pellbound, Darren couldn't take his eyes off Victor. "Wow, Dad! Do you think we can visit there sometime?"

Victor ruffled Darren's hair. "Sorry, son. It doesn't work that way. Buffy would have been the first one on that train."

Victor patted Buffy. "Poor old girl. She tried digging her way into the portal to be with her family, but the timing just wasn't right."

Within twenty minutes of Officer Davidson's call for assistance from the detective squad, a late-model tan Hyundai, viciously keyed down the driver's side, pulled up and parked. Detective Ferguson, in a rumpled gray suit got out of the car and plopped a hat on his balding head.

Poking a cigar stub in his mouth, he worked it around with his tongue until he found a comfortable spot between his lips.

He looked around the parking lot then began walking toward the small crowd.

"Davidson, come here for a moment, will you?" he called.

Leaving the group, Officer Davidson walked toward the detective.

"Where's the body, Davidson? Is it in one of these cars? Has the morgue and ID already left? I just got the call so I can't be that late." Ferguson looked at his watch in exasperation.

"That's the problem, sir; there isn't a body." Davidson gave the details.

"No body! What am I doing here, for Pete's sake? I'm a body man, you know that."

The man smelled of cheap cologne and cigars. The stub in his mouth was disgusting. Officer Davidson averted his eyes, finding an intriguing pattern of concrete at his feet.

The detective turned to face the store and scanned the area. Everything seemed commonplace.

"Well, let's get this over with." Ferguson walked towards the crowd.

HOUSTON DAILY NEWS, THURSDAY, AUGUST 19, MORNING edition. Section 2, Page 7:

Police Seeking Clues

The seventeen-year-old daughter of a distinguished NASA scientist vanished from the Katy Mills Mall parking lot yesterday.

Police are trying to determine a possible motive. Detective Howard Ferguson said D'laine Jackson had been walking across the parking lot ahead of her father and brothers at approximately 1:10 p.m. The young woman had suddenly disappeared in what witnesses described as a "cloud of fog."

Ferguson said there were no signs of a struggle, and no physical evidence of Miss Jackson was in the immediate area.

WHAT GOOD IS THIS POLICE FORCE? LEE ASKED HIMSELF AS he watched the evening news for the umpteenth time. Little concealed the tension or the suppressed emotions of everyone in the room. Brian, Jamie, Brenda, Connor, Rachel, Joey and Lee were intently watching the news that showed the same story from earlier in the day.

Rosa Villarreal drifted in and out of the room. The housekeeper would listen to the news for a few minutes, shake her head, and drift back to the kitchen, only to return later for a few minutes more.

The television scene was what Lee and the boys had watched while at the parking lot. Police, along with lab personnel, scuttled around the area. Pictures were being taken from every angle.

One man was dusting the ground. Another was swinging his arms in the area that was now off-limits to the public. The detective in the droopy suit and loose tie was shaking his head and looking around while biting on his cigar. Lee chalked him up as a hard-nosed, thirty-year veteran.

Nothing would be learned from this newscast. It was a repeat of the earlier one and what they had experienced first-hand hours ago. Even so, Lee found himself glued to the TV as if in morbid curiosity.

Rosa entered the room again. She grabbed the remote and clicked off the TV. "That's enough. These kids don't need to see this anymore, and neither do you. It's just like OJ Simpson driving down the freeway over and over again."

Switching on the TV in his California apartment, a younger Victor Bennett went into the bathroom and inserted his contact lenses. He returned to the living room and lounged on the sofa in shorts and a T-shirt, flipping through channels. He landed on CNN and settled in.

Anderson Cooper was broadcasting live from Katy, Texas in front of the Katy Mills Mall shopping center. An Amber Alert had been issued for D'laine Jackson, daughter of Lee Jackson, acclaimed NASA scientist with more patents than M&Ms had colors. A photo of D'laine flashed onto the screen.

"Eyewitnesses said Miss Jackson disappeared right in front of them in this parking lot," Anderson said as he spread one arm wide, "at the gigantic Katy Mills Mall, west of Houston on Interstate 10, otherwise known as the Katy Freeway. All witnesses described *a blanket of fog rolling from the sky.* Moments later, when the fog rolled out again, D'laine Jackson was gone."

The film clip, captured by Jimmy Shoemaker on his cellphone, was on the screen.

Victor sat bolt upright. "Holy mackerel!"

The front door burst open. Stanley Daigle roared into the apartment, his energy high enough to power the entire building.

"Did you catch the news about that Houston girl?" Stanley flopped onto the couch and slapped a newspaper and several printed pages into Victor's open hand.

"Katy. She's from Katy, Texas. Anderson Cooper said it's just west of Houston on I-10," Victor corrected his friend.

Stanley brushed his hand through the air. "Semantics. A large suburb west of Houston."

Victor reached for a mechanical pencil and notepad on the end table. He started reading the newspaper and making notes.

"Got to act fast on this. It's all over the Internet," Stanley railed.

Stanley's industrial-looking black-rimmed glasses always slid down his long nose. He was sloppy and wrinkled—his typical "slept in" look. Victor assumed no one had taught Stanley the fundamentals of color coordination so his clothes never looked right together.

"Honestly, Stan. Are those your grandfather's clothes? All you need is suspenders," Victor said.

The big baggy pant legs were twice the size of normal slacks, and his loose short-sleeved shirt, which never stayed tucked inside the waistband, looked like a 2XX. On top of his general appearance, he was flat-footed, and always smelled like mouthwash.

Since Stanley never bothered knocking, Victor knew that someday he would either walk into a delicate situation, or smack into the locked door and break his prominent nose. *Stanley was Stanley.* You either accepted him at face value or you were a goner.

Born curious, Stanley never let the news go by him. He heard all the scoops, and with his retentive memory, he could repeat details others couldn't even remember seeing or hearing.

Victor and Stanley were two of the bright physics stars at California's Whitting Institute, where under the tutelage of world-renowned Dr. Joseph Paxton, they were working under a grant to investigate many-worlds interpretation, the anthropic principle, quantum gravity and wormholes.

Physicists in this branch of science thought some of the disappearances of people and things were associated with a vacuum that pulled them through a portal, by a negative energy density, to another world, parallel to the Earth. But so far, it had been like chasing a unicorn. No tangible evidence existed to be investigated except for some Bermuda Triangle incidents. No major activity had been accurately recorded by anyone.

Victor studied his notes. "This new disappearance is something else. It's new and fresh and might open up missing links in our theories regarding disappearances."

Experienced in *Daigleisms*—those *Stanley moments*, he should have known Stanley had seen the story. Victor knew that his friend could forget to stay focused while he was "onto something." Sometimes a simple thing such as driving from point A to point B was a challenge to stay in one piece.

When he was *in the zone*, he could be dangerous. Though Stanley was said to have the highest IQ ever recorded, Victor wondered how the man could tie his shoes and talk at the same time.

A natural speed reader, Stanley sped over details, analyzing theories beyond most scientists' reasoning. Remarkable discoveries paved his way into the scientific world and gained him high respect from all his peers. Yet, he was avoided like a social pariah.

Few understood Stanley. He was a thinker. People in their circles didn't understand his ways because he became so in-depth that he often lost his audience. Most could only take small doses of Stanley Daigle so his circle of friends was small.

On the other hand, Victor's looks kept the girls on his heels from early childhood to the present day. An intelligent man, dedicated to his profession, and Stanley's only true friend, Victor was well-published in the science community sharing credits with distinguished scientists twice his age and experience.

Moments after he finished reading the details of the articles, Victor noticed Stanley appeared more hyper than usual.

He wondered if it was a chemical reaction in his brain, some kind of stimulus overload.

"Did you take a bath in that stuff?" Victor asked. His friend smelled as if he had doused himself in mouthwash. Victor was almost overcome with the potent fumes.

Stanley pouted and grumbled.

"Okay, Stan, tell me what else the Internet carried. All I saw was what CNN showed just now."

"We need to track down that Jimmy kid and get a copy of his video," Stanley said.

Throwing in his own theories, among the news facts, Victor had to interrupt Stanley several times to get the *real* story before the theories. Picking up his notepad, Victor gave Stanley a synopsis of what the paper, TV and Internet had reported, including statistics, family, background—everything and anything. Sitting quietly, each was lost in thought.

Stanley jumped off the sofa and rushed to a blank wall. He whipped a whiteboard marker out of his pocket and diagrammed on the wall.

"We know curved space may have anywhere from five to ten dimensions. We just haven't had the right type of concrete evidence. And by evidence, I mean having someone *return* from somewhere and tell us about it. We also know there are curvature fluctuations that become so violent they're capable of ripping holes in space-time. We need more sophisticated equipment to measure the phenomena, or observe and reveal previously hidden facts."

Victor looked up from the notepad. "My wall!"

Stanley diagrammed frantically. "Fog convergences are one of the clearest telltale signs of physical dimensional activity on Earth."

Victor scanned the newspaper article again and outlined it

with a highlighter. He looked at the wall, got up and grabbed the marker from Stanley and made a correction to the diagram.

On a roll, Stanley paced the room. Victor just let him get it out of his system, knowing he would soon calm down and his thought process would smooth out and get back to normal.

"Do you think Dr. Paxton would let us investigate this? We would have to do a lot of fast talking and he'd probably make us carry some of the expenses on our own. He'd probably make us drive to Houston. He always complains about the budget, but he never tries to approach any of his influential friends for more money for any of our projects," Stanley whined. "I don't understand him!"

Not wanting to explain the basic facts of business regarding profit and loss for the umpteenth time, Victor just let Stanley go on with his feelings, not agreeing, and not contributing to the subject of Paxton's high-society friends.

"Stan, I hate to tell you this, but no one, other than scientists, or perhaps the military, would be wildly ecstatic about finding out a possible quantum world is right at our fingertips and could change the age-old theories about the planets, solar system and the universe," Victor lectured. "The general public would freak out with visions of monsters and *War of the Worlds* all over again."

"Not everyone would freak out. Think of all the science buffs, and the science fiction nuts that would really like to know," Stanley argued.

Victor and Stanley continued to discuss the details and angles they could approach, making notes and brooding about D'laine Jackson. The news media had shown a picture of the girl on TV. Thinking of how young she was, Victor knew her family and friends must be freaking out over her disappearance.

"Dr. Paxton is out of town at a scientific symposium, so the meeting has to wait until tomorrow morning when he gets back." Glancing at his watch, Victor was surprised to discover that it was eight-thirty. He was starving.

"Find out if Dr. Paxton will let us go to Houston," Stanley said once again.

"Okay. I'll talk to him when he gets back and let you know what happens. Want to get something to eat?" Victor asked.

"Eat? Who can eat at a time like this? I've got to go to the lab," Stanley said.

Victor grabbed his wallet off the end table and stuck it in his pocket then grabbed his keys.

"Time to leave. Are you sure you don't want to get something to eat?"

"I'll grab something from the gas station," Stanley said.

"That stuff is probably stale by now," Victor said.

He pushed Stanley ahead of him and locked the door. They walked to the parking lot and got in their cars. Victor locked his car door and kept the windows up so Stanley couldn't intercept him with another idea.

Stanley would never forget a thought or an idea so Victor wasn't worried about it. The problem was getting Stanley to understand that most human beings had to eat, and shut down their brains eventually to be able to sleep. People just can't stay awake to think every minute of the day without serious health consequences.

Sleeping more than two or three hours a night was wasted time for Stanley. He would rather spend his life at the lab, pounding away on the super computer, researching relativity and the Big Bang.

If the computer could talk, Victor was certain it would have told Stanley to take his brain and shove it. With an institute credit card, Stanley also haunted the online libraries to make requests for any periodicals or journals he couldn't find at his fingertips. He spent hours looking up esoteric articles that could only interest him; he knew it would all fit in somewhere, sometime. So, he spent hours downloading articles and storing them in his research folder on the computer.

With his last thoughts drifting to the image of the missing Houston girl, Victor backed out of his parking place and sought food.

Al Jordan chortled as he read the news clip again. "Is this for real or did someone plant a joke in the press that didn't get edited out?"

HE CALLED PRINCETON DALY, THE REPORTER WHO HAD written the story.

"Prince, are you writing for the scandal rags in your spare time? I've got a six-foot tall toddler you can put on tomorrow's front page."

"Funny, Jordan, try again," Princeton said. "Listen, I've been pulled from this to cover an arson case. I know you like this kind of stuff so if you're interested, I'll put in a good word for you."

"Yeah, do that. I couldn't write another birth announcement even if it was for the last baby to be born on this planet," Al joked.

"Well, it's better than the death squad, isn't it?" Princeton quipped.

"Not really. This isn't what I went to school for! I need something exciting, challenging," Al said.

An hour later the phone rang. Elated, Al pulled pad and pen toward him and began making notes before calling the witnesses. Two calls and forty-five minutes later, he had his own views on the occurrence.

Young and bright, Al had read enough *Science Digest* magazines to know that something wasn't quite right with this story. He was a junior staff member of the *Houston Daily News*, with just two years of work experience. *This could be my big break!*

Leaving his cubicle, Al headed over to Rice University to talk with Ben Joplin, the head of the Physics Department. Battling the congested traffic from downtown to the university, less than five miles away, was another matter in itself. What should normally take fifteen minutes could end up a half-hour ride, or longer.

"There's a lot more to this than what you're seeing. We're going to have to investigate with the proper equipment to determine if the act was a phenomenon, or if someone is playing a pretty bad joke," Dr. Joplin said. "I've got ideas about what occurred, but I'll hold my comments until I've got hard evidence."

"Dr. Joplin, does this have anything to do with a lateral plane of existence?" Al mentally crossed his fingers. A big science fiction buff, he constantly fantasized about new worlds and different life forms.

Frowning, the doctor rubbed his chin. "Strictly off the record, Mr. Jordan, yes, there is a good possibility of uncovering significant proof—if I can get the right people out there and get some equipment set up to take scans. I see you've done your homework, young man. It's nice to know that someone in the media doesn't think of us as a bunch of quacks chasing ghosts."

"I don't want any bad publicity," Dr. Joplin said. "I'll give you any information that looks genuine that the public can understand. Right now, I want to talk to a colleague in California about borrowing some people. He has two of the leading physicists on his staff who specialize in this type of thing. I'm going to beg, cry and plead to get them for this case."

# CHAPTER FIFTEEN

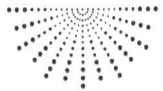

*B*renda stood. Rachel, Joey and Connor followed her lead.

"Sorry, we stayed so late," Rachel said.

"Do you want me to go back to the mall and look around?" Connor asked. "Maybe there's something that was overlooked with all the cars still parked."

Lee patted Connor on the back. "Go home, Connor. All of you need to go home and rest. No more TV or Internet searches. I mean it. All of this anxiety isn't healthy."

The four teenagers marched out the front door, got in Connor's SUV and drove off.

"Rosa's right," Lee said. "I've let you kids stay up way too late, and Brian, you're supposed to have complete bed rest."

"Aww Dad," Brian said, his voice weak. He stifled a yawn.

"You're seriously sick," Lee said. "You heard the doctor. It's very important for you to stay calm and get as much sleep as possible."

"Can Buffy sleep with me?" Jamie asked after D'laine's friends left.

"Sure," Lee said. "She's probably wondering what's going on."

Buffy eyed everyone from her dog cushion. She knew they were talking about her.

Lee scooped Brian up from the sofa. He carried him to the make-shift bedroom in the dining room. Rosa turned down the covers on the hospital bed and Lee gently slid Brian onto the sheets.

Buffy and Jamie hovered close by.

"No more news. The police will contact us when and if they have information," Lee said. "Jamie, you get to bed."

Everyone said goodnight and hugged. Jamie shuffled from the room and stomped up the stairs with Buffy on his heels.

Lee turned off the light in the dining room and stood under the archway between the dining and living rooms, lost in thought. Five years earlier, the dining room had been where D'laine had recovered after being discharged from the hospital.

It had taken two surgeries to repair her legs. The right femur had required a rod clamped into place where a portion of the severely crushed femur had been removed.

The left femur had snapped in two—a surprisingly clean break stabilized with another rod and clamps. It was close to eight months before the doctor deemed the bones healed.

Long months of agonizing physical therapy started in the hospital and continued at home in her dining room hospital bed. After almost one year of inactivity in the hospital, D'laine required extensive arm and hand exercises to even hold a spoon. It was hard work to strengthen her muscles to get her legs working again.

He didn't know what he would have done without Rosa and her husband, Eric. They took charge of the house and property while he slowly put his life back together. Lee recalled receiving the phone call from the doctor when D'laine awoke from the coma, screaming nonstop.

At first, she didn't know where she was, or why she was in the hospital. The doctor, child psychiatrist and the hospital staff assumed the screaming was from her last memory of the traffic accident.

He would never forget the pain of the conversation when he had to tell D'laine that her mother was dead. With two mending femurs and arms too weak to rise, all she could do was scream and cry, and that's what she did for three weeks.

When the crying stopped, the healing began. D'laine never mentioned the dream until she was discharged from the hospital and back home. That first week jarred Lee—he was helpless. All he could do was wake D'laine from the dream so the screaming stopped for the night.

Brian and Jamie had been scared. Buffy stayed close by with a concerned expression on her face. Jamie crept down the stairs dragging his sock monkey and slept on the floor by D'laine's bed so often that Rosa finally made a sleeping pallet for him. Brian's teacher had requested a parent/teacher conference to discuss Brian's drawings and his show-and-tell account of the accident.

Lee had talked to D'laine's child psychologist many times and had stood firm that it was the dream, not the accident that triggered D'laine's screaming when she emerged from the coma.

He sighed deeply and joined Rosa in the kitchen.

Lee sat across the desk from his boss, Mitch Lowenhaupt. There was a somber atmosphere in the room.

"I understand, Lee," Mitch said. "You've got way too much

on your plate with Brian's condition, and now with D'laine missing."

Lee rubbed his face with his hands. "I'm barely keeping it together, Mitch. This past five years has been torture. I can't even begin to get my head around D'laine's disappearance."

"Molly and I watched the news and read the papers, but it doesn't even make any sense," Mitch said. "Good thing that kid recorded the entire event."

"The cops asked the stupidest questions. Even after watching the video they concluded there must have been a disgruntled boyfriend, or she ran away! Can you believe it?" Lee shook his head.

"Go down to HR and fill out the paperwork. You've got plenty of accrued sick leave, but you shouldn't use that. Tell them you need an emergency leave of absence for the duration, until your daughter is returned," Mitch said.

Lee stood. "Thanks Mitch."

Mitch stood. "Take your laptop and all your passwords. You may be able to do some research."

"Good idea," Lee said. They shook hands and Mitch walked Lee to his office door.

"Keep in touch. I'd like to hear updates so I can pass them along to the group. Everyone is really worried for you."

LEE PARKED THE MINIVAN IN THE GARAGE AND BROUGHT the laptop case into the house. Buffy greeted him like a long-lost friend. Rosa peeked out of the kitchen.

"Everything go okay at work?" Rosa asked.

"Yeah. I'm one of the lucky ones due to my number of years at NASA and all the patents I've licensed. I don't think anyone else would have gotten paid time off for the next several weeks while this disappearance plays out," Lee said.

Rosa wiped her hands on a dishtowel. "I'm glad they're treating you right. You've given them a lot over the years."

Buffy leaned against Lee and looked up at him. Her face held a big smile with her lolling tongue hanging out.

"Want to go for a walk, Buffy?" Lee asked.

Buffy barked and nudged him with her snout.

"Okay, girl. Let me put this in my office and we'll go outside."

Rosa returned to the kitchen and Lee walked over to his office and set the laptop in his chair. He and Buffy went to the front door.

BUFFY RAN AHEAD OF LEE AS THEY WALKED PAST THE paddock where two horses pranced. Eric, Rosa's husband, was repairing a fence post. He stopped what he was doing and waved at Lee.

Lee and Buffy headed toward Eric.

"How are you doing, Mr. Lee?" Eric asked.

"Coping, Eric. Just coping," Lee said.

"I can't believe Miss D'laine is gone. Any word from the police?" Eric asked.

Lee shook his head. "I don't think it's a police matter, Eric. I think some strange other-worldly thing happened and I don't know if we'll ever find her."

"You mean like UFOs?" Eric asked.

Lee grimaced.

Eric looked helpless as he watched Lee's face crumble. He placed a gloved hand on Lee's arm. "Keep the faith. Pray for her."

Lee left Eric and continued walking with Buffy to a special place. He sadly acknowledged to himself that it had been five years since he set foot in Lori's sanctuary. He was thankful to see that Eric had kept it in pristine condition. Lori had worked diligently creating this meditative place. A koi pond with an overhanging tree and tall ornamental grasses, and a large wooden bench with the ranch logo carved into it, just waited for a visitor.

Lee stood at the pond's edge and watched several large koi fish swimming in the shade. Buffy walked into the water scaring the fish to the dark edges. She stomped around for a bit then climbed out and shook herself. She flopped down under the tree to dry off.

Lee sat on the bench, lost. He looked up at the sky. "Lori, your daughter needs you. Please find and help D'laine. Please help her get back home."

He lowered his head in his hands and sobbed.

# CHAPTER SIXTEEN

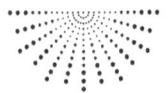

*S*he has much to learn quickly, Ghury mused. The Egroms, the highest order of life on Thol, knew that D'laine's destiny was already mapped out, although it was unknown to her. The prophecy was handed down to Akubel, the ancient Egrom leader, when Ghury was in his mother's pouch.

Deep in thought, Ghury headed toward the group of elders sitting around the fire in the center of the village. They would discuss her education and training, being careful about how much they let her know regarding her purpose and of the plan laid out neatly in their chronicles for the future of Thol. It wouldn't be deception, actually, just holding back some pieces of the puzzle. There was no reason to tell her things that she might not understand until she was ready to accept the inevitable.

The Egroms believed that life was pre-planned with little room for change. Many avenues and paths were open for a person to take, but unknown to the traveler of life's roads, the results were preconceived. Pondering this, Ghury couldn't understand why other beings, human and otherwise, didn't accept this. They usually believed that random things just happened to them, and they wouldn't be in the predicament they were experiencing if they had been more careful, or had planned better.

*Fools. Uneducated, closed-minded fools,* he thought, as he joined the others. *If they would take the time to look toward the universe, their answers would come forth.*

When the customary grunts, chirps, clicks and nods were dispensed with, they got down to business.

"The Plotals would pay dearly for her if they ever discovered her powers," Bensol said.

"She has no powers," Ghury said.

"She must stay hidden away until she is fully trained," Swezek said.

"She must be made to understand the difference between herself and the other races of Thol," Ditol said.

"Jakla would stop at nothing to get her if he knew of her existence," Adrum said, addressing Ghury and the others.

"Jakla already knows," Ghury said.

Noisy communication went around the circle as they all agreed.

"We have waited so long for her to come through the portal," Bensol said.

"Why did they send a *child*? They were supposed to send her as a full bloomed warrior woman," Trabet said.

"I don't know," Ghury said. "The prophecy has shifted. It will be our responsibility to bring forth her gifts."

"She is not aware at all," Adrum said, bewildered.

There was much agreement among them.

"She will awaken soon," Ghury said.

"Jakla almost beat us to her," Bensol said. "He will keep his senses alert."

They decided D'laine had to be hidden until she was trained to protect herself. Not only did she look different from all the other races of Thol, she *was* different. Adrum would be responsible for teaching her the history of Thol while the others would show her the life of the Egroms. Each would take turns, taking her out into the region to familiarize her with the area while analyzing her reactions and guiding her into responding correctly.

Unlike others of her race, she was special. Now it was up to them to guide her into her position of leadership. One day she would rule Thol; her powers would be greater than those of the Egroms.

Stirring awake, D'laine still held onto the lethargic feelings of sleep. She took in her surroundings: the hollowed out giant mushroom, the softly glowing lantern, and the wispy material she laid upon—it was no dream—she was IN the dream. She bolted upward in the middle of the nest. There was no escaping the reality of her situation.

"Are you awake?" Kestrum inquired as she entered the hut.

D'laine gazed up at the hollowed-out cap of the mushroom. She was momentarily frantic. "Doesn't look like this is a dream anymore," D'laine whispered. She cleared her throat. "It must have taken a lot of work to carve out one of these mushrooms."

"You will understand how it is done later," Kestrum said. "There is no difficulty. You will learn many things."

"Is someone going to check the portal things for me?" D'laine asked.

"The time is not right," Kestrum said.

"When will the time be right?" D'laine asked, her voice escalating.

"When it is," Kestrum said. "Come with me. We are ready to eat our evening meal, and you are to meet the village elders."

D'laine's shoulders slumped. She fell back on the nest and stared up into the hollow mushroom cap.

"Did those little hosk things make this bedding?" D'laine asked.

"Yes. They're industrious little creatures, always busy," Kestrum said. "This material and many other things are woven from their web."

She rubbed gauze between her fingers. "Wow, that's amazing. They're like silkworms." D'laine got up, studied her flawless legs which felt sturdy now, and dressed.

When she stepped from the hut after Kestrum, D'laine saw hundreds of Egroms, and a number of large cooking pots hanging over huge fires throughout the village. Only one sun remained low on the horizon. There were old Egroms and young, male and female. Some were in groups, others standing on the perimeter, facing the forest, swaying back and forth. She would later learn these were sentries scanning the forest to report any activity around nearby portals. This comforted her knowing someone was keeping watch for her.

The Egroms guarded the portals around the clock, seeing what others couldn't see, without missing a leaf turning. They had to be ready for any situation. If something came through a portal, they had to judge whether it should be allowed to stop at Thol, or be returned to the place from which it came, or sent on to another world.

Most creatures were returned before they knew what had happened to them. Small animals were constantly getting snatched up by the vacuum force of the portals and ended up in Thol. Rarely did anything ever sneak by unnoticed.

An Egrom child spotted D'laine. "Look! There's the human!"

Excitement ran through the community like a brush fire. They made a riot of noises.

"Chacoodi, where are your manners?" Kestrum scolded.

The young Egrom squirmed. "Sorry, Kestrum."

Alarmed at the chatter, D'laine backed up, bumping into Kestrum. She wondered what these creatures had in store for her. There were so many of them and only one of her. She knew she couldn't make a run for it. There wasn't anywhere to go to escape. Her fright transmitted to the Egroms. Being receptive to moods and able to read thoughts, they halted the noisy assault. One stepped forward, appearing to be very friendly.

"Welcome. We are honored that you are among us," the creature said.

Overwhelmed by their compassion, D'laine made an instant decision that she would come to no harm with these creatures. She was no longer frightened by them.

"Hi," D'laine said. She gave a little nervous finger wave.

Watching her response, Ghury motioned her to join him by the fire near the center of the village. Turning to Kestrum as if seeking permission, D'laine walked with her to the group. She was introduced to Adrum, Bensol, Ditol, Absadul, Trabet, Drusta and Swezek, the village elders.

"Hi. Nice to meet you," she said, shyly.

"Are there any necessities we might have overlooked?" Adrum asked.

D'laine fidgeted. *There's no bathrooms here!* "Everything is fine, considering the circumstances,"

Ghury motioned the group to sit. They made a circle placing D'laine in between Ghury and Adrum on the moss. The remaining sun set and darkness fell like ink being poured over a picture. The contrast was sudden, as if someone controlled a giant dimmer switch. D'laine looked around. She was thankful for the fires which kept the village illuminated.

The huge dwellings and strange creatures cast eerie shadows from the undulating fires in the inky blackness of the night. If it weren't for the fire under the cooking pot she would not have been able to see her hand in front of her own face.

For the first time, she understood how city lights masked the night sky and all its brilliance. D'laine took in everything. She looked up at the sky and was taken aback by the dazzling stars and constellations. Four large moons, each in a different phase, were spread across the night sky.

Bugs similar to lightning bugs started popping out across the dark and made a brilliant display. Their glow lamps shown in green, yellow and blue.

She forced her attention back to the circle. The Egroms' bodily characteristics were as diverse as humans, as far as weight and height were concerned. While they had the same coloring of fur and eyes, she could tell them apart the same way she could tell the difference in her neighbors or anyone else on Earth. Adrum disrupted her thoughts when he addressed her. The formalities were finished and the Egroms were eager for a discussion.

"Tell us of your life. We would like to understand the ways of your people and as much about you as you would like to learn about us," Adrum said.

"Well, I'm a female of my race, of course, and I'm known as a teenager because I'm seventeen years old. One of our years is three hundred sixty-five days consisting of twenty-four hours in each day, or fourteen hundred-forty minutes per day, or five hundred twenty-five thousand and six hundred minutes per year," she said, wondering if they were on the same time table as Earth. She didn't have any way of knowing if days were longer or shorter here.

"I have two younger brothers. Brian is ten, and we just found out that he has a tumor on his heart. My little brother

Jamie is six. They need me—they're little boys and our mom was killed in a car accident when I was twelve," she said. She looked at Ghury. "Remember, I told you..."

Ghury had a difficult time hiding his exasperation.

"Right now, my father, my boyfriend and my friends Brenda and Rachel are probably going crazy with worry. They don't know where I am or what's happened to me," she pleaded.

A male Egrom started serving the evening's meal in stone bowls and D'laine was handed the first bowl and a smooth spoon, since she was a guest.

"Oh, thank you!" D'laine said.

"I am honored," the Egrom said.

Swallowing, D'laine hoped the food was palatable. The heavy bowl held chunks of some type of vegetables or roots, and a thickened broth.

It looked pasty and smelled funny but she knew that she shouldn't insult these creatures, so she dipped her spoon, which reminded her of a porcelain spoon from her favorite Chinese restaurant, but larger, into the stew and sampled a small amount. Her eyebrows shot up in surprise as she discovered that it was spicy and delicious; she ate quickly.

"This is delicious," D'laine said between spoonfuls. "Tangy, like rutabagas."

"We're vegetarians," Ghury said.

"Oh," D'laine said.

"You were wondering if you were eating some unknown creature," he explained.

"You read minds, don't you?" D'laine asked, frowning as she weighed that knowledge in her head.

"You don't?" he responded.

D'laine shook her head.

Ghury grumbled.

D'laine looked around the village taking in the mushrooms, the cook-pot over the fire, the Egroms. "So... is mind-reading the only technology you have on this world?"

Ghury gave a loud harrumph and continued eating.

Adrum rescued her from Ghury's rude response. "You will discover the many technologies of the different species soon."

D'laine looked from Ghury to Adrum, perplexed. "Oookay."

"Describe your brothers for us," Bensol said.

There was excitement around the circle and she could feel the compassion.

"They look like me." She tried to describe their features.

Ghury shook his head. "Create a mental picture of them so we might see for ourselves."

"Oh!" she said. "Mind-reading comes in handy sometimes, doesn't it?"

Ghury grumbled.

D'laine thought of her brothers and her father, projecting a picture of them in her brain for the elders. Then she thought of her best friends. "These are my friends Brenda, Rachel, Joey and Connor."

A lot of their chatter ensued around the circle as the Egroms viewed her family and friends.

The discussions went into her life, ambitions, and feelings on the subjects of life and death, and morals. They talked on and on, seemingly for hours, but she sensed only a short span of time had passed.

THE OASIS WAS LIT WITH THE AMBIENT LIGHT FROM torches along the perimeter and throughout the vast encampment.

Plotal guards paced along the edge of the camp where the pakows were tethered for the night. The guards were always on the alert for an attack by the deadly diwal dogs, or an og sighting.

Warriors stood around campfires and glanced at a large mruck roasting on a spit over a fire. The mruck's little pig ears sizzled, and lidless eyes stared vacantly. The short trunk dangled into the fire. The warriors took turns cranking the handle that turned the spit.

Jakla stood at the fireside and speared a hunk of meat with his knife and devoured it, watchful of his hungry troops. The commander always ate his fill first. Anyone who crossed the line was eliminated quickly.

Two young warriors sat on a bench by one of the fires playing a board game similar to Cribbage, but not unlike Chinese checkers.

"Watch how a champion wins," the younger of the players boasted.

He threw a pair of octagonal dice, grabbed a thin dowel-stake and moved his piece around holes in the board. He passed his opponent's shorter marker and won the game. He stood, arms raised, fists clenched and bellowed in triumph.

The loser snorted aggressively and bashed the game board with a powerful punch. "Upstart!"

The players assumed battle poses, fangs bared, and the pods on the end of their tails fully opened. The barbs gleamed off the light from the fire.

"Poor loser," the champ said.

"You'll regret those words!" the loser threatened.

They roared and hissed while circling and swinging their barbed tails at each other. They grabbed each other by the shoulders in a wrestler's stance and fought savagely, biting and clawing each other. The champ lost his balance and the loser grabbed him in a lock hold and bit his shoulder.

"You may win at games but not at war!" the loser exclaimed.

The champ howled in pain.

"Enough!" Jakla said. He snapped his snout at the young warriors.

The youngsters returned to their seats and restored the game as if nothing happened.

Jakla ate his fill and moved away from the fire.

Loud squeals sounded from the pitch-black perimeter of the camp.

"Diwals! Detachment One to the pakows!" Jakla commanded.

The Plotals pulled their laser weapons from their holsters and joined the guards by the pakows. The entire camp stood ready. One warrior stood on each side of the roasting mruck. Diwal dogs always sounded an alert prior to an attack, using fear as a juggernaut to destabilize their quarry. Then the dogs silently spread out and came at their prey from all directions. The plotals nervously awaited the fight.

A large pack of diwal dogs bound into camp. Their gray oily skin, with tufts of hair on their frightful faces, shone from the glow of the camp fires.

One dog jumped for the young bleeding champ's wound. "You think you can beat me?"

Like land piranhas, the diwal's three layers of razor teeth clacked loudly in a hypnotic frenzy the closer the dog's mouth got to its victim.

The champ snatched the dog out of the air and clamped his large hands on the dog's shoulder and rump. He chomped down on its spinal cord ending the fight in an instant.

"I am the champion!" He bellowed in triumph and tossed

the dog aside. He wiped his bloody jaw with the back of his hand.

Two dogs leapt upon another warrior from different directions. He never stood a chance as he went down screaming. Within moments all that remained of the warrior was the metal from his uniform.

Jakla stood ready, laser in hand. He shot three dogs and then his gun misfired as another dog jumped straight for his throat. He smashed the dog with the laser gun. The stunned dog fell to the ground and shook its head. It leapt at Jakla again.

"Come meet your death," Jakla said.

He caught the dog inches from his face. The dog strained toward Jakla's neck. The clacking teeth made a deafening noise. Jakla's mighty jaws swiftly decapitated the diwal. He flung the body into the dark and kicked the head aside. He looked around the camp as his warriors dealt with the remaining dogs. With his appetite heightened by the carnage, Jakla turned toward the roasting mruck and sliced off a huge hunk of meat and devoured it. He moved away from the fire.

The Plotal warriors stampeded to the roasted mruck. They fought among themselves for the best position to get to the food.

Jakla growled and snapped his snout at the warriors. They calmed down and resumed their meal.

# CHAPTER SEVENTEEN

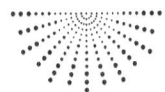

*T*he empty dining salon was lit with floating globes of soft light, and the enormous table was set for a dozen people. Staff members in knee-length brown, belted tunics, worked on food preparation in an adjoining room.

Jovial conversation drifted down the hallway and alerted the staff that the dinner party was about to begin.

The royal couple entered the room with their guests. At sixty-years-old, Jor-Dan looked every bit the stately leader, with shoulder-length black hair graying at his temples, and a trimmed beard more white than black. He wore his battle scars well, reminders of the barbed Plotal tails and the diwal dogs' steely claws. His broad shoulders and trim physique were displayed to advantage in an ankle-length white tunic with gold trim braiding.

It was hard to miss Kitry. She was a tall, dignified woman with beautiful bronze skin. She wore a sparkling sari-type dress, her black hair piled in a loose chignon at the top of her head. Five years her husband's junior, she was an elegant, classically beautiful hostess with flawless manners. She ran the palace with a precise goal: to make everyone feel welcome.

The guests, leaders from nearby kingdoms, accompanied their hosts into the dining salon. A soft murmur of conversation was underway as the party was seated. A few moments later, Trakon entered. He wore a short-sleeved leather-like suit of armor for working in the aviation hangar, and carried rolled plans under his arm. He set the plans on the sideboard against the wall and sat.

"There's your boy," Jubulon of Aveldon said. "When are we going to see a bride for Trakon? Didn't we just celebrate his eighteenth emerging day?"

"He has rejected everyone thus far, but I have hope that he will be more interested in Princess Yalalore, Emeric of Patrosym's daughter." Kitry tilted her head to Emeric across the table, and smiled wickedly at Trakon, who scowled. "We will be meeting her soon."

"If I recall correctly, Jubulon didn't marry until his thirty-third completed path." Trakon cast a hard glance at Jubulon, who laughed heartily. "Since I've only had eighteen completed paths, I'd say I have a way to go."

"Takes after his parents, I suppose," Jor-Dan said.

The oldest at the table, Youndon of Lansobar, roared with laughter. "You two were late bloomers, but yours was the best match of us all. Not only did you find true love, but you have a wonderful balance within Ebscalon. Your people respect you deeply."

Kitry smiled affectionately at Youndon. "Thank you, Youndon. That is what I desire for Trakon. A balanced relationship with his wife."

Trakon glowered deeply at the continued talk of marriage.

Staff members entered the dining salon, each carrying a platter, or bowl filled with various foodstuffs. There was an array of colorful fruits, steamed vegetables, and succulent meats. The guests selected what they wanted as each dish was presented. After everyone had filled their plates, the staff retreated from the room. As the meal completed and the dishes were removed from the table, discussions resumed.

"We are almost finished with the upgrade to the gravitational synchronizing beam in the new ships," Trakon announced.

"Show us what you have," Jor-Dan said.

Trakon spread the plans open. He took a device similar to a stylus and captured the first plan. A hologram of a blue ship appeared above the table. He touched the edge of the hologram with his fingers and rotated the image slowly.

The one-man ship resembled a speed boat with a high windshield. Large curved wings were paved with layers of sparkling crystals three inches thick. There was just enough floor space in the open area for one or two people to stand at the helm.

As Trakon touched a point on the plan with the stylus, the spot on the hologram brightened.

"The crystal collectors will have to be fully exposed to sunlight for a minimum of two hours before they will beam enough power to gravitate," Trakon said. "We need the beam strong enough to raise and stabilize the ship while skirting over buildings or trees."

Jor-Dan and the other leaders nodded in agreement.

"I will be ready to take a ship out for a test run soon," Trakon said.

"We certainly hope your trials are successful." Emeric's small city was two hours north of Ebscalon by pakow. They were eager for the technology.

"Let's do it," Jor-Dan said.

"Have the crystals been tested with the beam at all? How long will they stay fully charged?" Kitry asked.

"Just in the models," Trakon said. "They should hold throughout the night until first light. As the suns rise they will begin to automatically charge."

A murmur of conversation went around the table. Everyone was enthusiastic about the ship upgrades, except Kitry.

"You're going to get stranded," Kitry warned.

"Nonsense. There should be enough crystals onboard to last two nights," Jor-Dan said confidently.

Trakon and Jor-Dan appeared very sure of themselves, bordering on smug.

Kitry shook her head.

A patch on Trakon's chest glowed and vibrated. He pressed it. "Yes?"

"I've had the men layer two ships with crystals. They are ready to begin charging," a voice said.

"Good. You have a backup in case something should go wrong," Kitry said, knowingly.

# CHAPTER EIGHTEEN

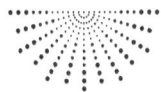

*T*he phone rang, jarring Victor out of sleep. Turning over, he squinted at the clock, trying to focus on the time since he did not wear his contacts to bed. Five-thirty in the morning? He had only been asleep for three hours and twenty minutes and felt dead. The phone was insistent. Sitting up quickly, he grabbed his iPhone, turned it right side up and pressed the green answer button. Before he had a chance to say "hello", he recognized the voice.

*What in hell was he doing calling at this time of the morning?* Victor thought to himself. *Doesn't he know what time it is?* Fumbling with the phone, Victor pressed the speaker button and set the phone down. As he reached for a pencil and pad of paper, he swung his feet over the edge of the bed and his face lit up with surprise. He couldn't believe what he was hearing.

Dr. Paxton had just heard about the disappearance of D'laine Jackson from a colleague of his in Houston.

"...I want you and Stanley to get on the first plane to Houston and investigate this disappearance business before a lot of nuts invade the area and the police do any more damage, you hear me Victor?" he asked.

"Well, yes, but..." Victor began.

Excitement ran through Dr. Paxton's voice as he told Victor that he had already made arrangements.

"No buts! Tickets will be waiting at the Southwest Airlines counter at LAX and you'll have to hurry because the plane is scheduled to leave at eight forty-five this morning. I figured you wouldn't want to wait until the eleven o'clock flight," Dr. Paxton said.

"Eight forty-five? I've got to find Stan...," he sputtered. Stunned, Victor couldn't believe his good fortune!

"Take the sensa-scan camera and the lens we received last week. Oh, and the bio-heat sensor. And Victor, you make darn sure you keep an eye on your buddy," Dr. Paxton warned. "Tell Stanley NO EXPERIMENTS! I don't have money in the budget to replace any of this stuff, and remember, that sensa-scan is a loaner!"

"Don't worry, we'll take care of everything. Stanley isn't that irresponsible," Victor said.

"Whatever, Victor. Ben Joplin from Rice University is going to meet you at the airport. He'll fill you in when you get there," Dr. Paxton concluded.

*Wait until Stanley hears this,* Victor thought as he hung up the phone. *What luck!* The university had just procured the sensa-scan camera to evaluate a new infrared process that would capture any significant detail not visible to the human eye. It was possible to scan the area through the lens and capture significant details on the USB.

The bio-heat sensor noted any variance in the temperatures of the surrounding area. Used in conjunction with the sensa-scan camera and two other pieces of specialized equipment, the camera would "shoot" anything that the bio-heat sensor "picked-up".

Victor hit the floor running. First, he would have to track down Stanley. Beginning with the logical place, he called his friend's apartment and let the phone ring sixteen times before finally giving up and dialing the lab. He thought about texting him, but Stanley wasn't a text expert. Three rings later, while Victor rubbed on deodorant, Stanley answered with his nasally "hello". Not wasting any time with lengthy details, Victor gave Stanley a synopsis of the doctor's phone call and instructed him to get together the equipment they would need.

"We'll stop by your place on the way to the airport to pack your stuff," Victor instructed.

He finally hung up on his friend who had started talking a mile a minute about their good luck. From years of experience, Victor knew that Stanley was on a roll and wouldn't shut up even after the phone was replaced. Half the time Stanley talked to himself because no one else would listen.

Scrambling, Victor threw open the closet door, grabbed his rolling suitcase, pulled open dresser drawers and yanked things out at random. Throwing underwear, socks, and polo shirts into the bag, he swung around, grabbed jeans, made a pretense of folding them, grabbed a pair of slacks and neatly placed them into the bag, along with a couple of long sleeved shirts, shorts, tank tops, and a lightweight jacket. He made a mad dash for the bathroom, brushed his teeth, put his contacts in, grabbed the case, cleaner and solutions, gathered his toiletries and stuffed things in a travel kit. He grabbed his tennis shoes, crammed them into the suitcase, then forced it closed.

He dressed in jeans and a brown knit shirt. *Probably won't need half of this stuff, but I'd better bring it all anyways.* Suitcase handle in hand, he shut the light off, rolled the suitcase out into the living room where he leaned it against the sofa. He crossed to the tiny kitchen and peered into the refrigerator. Almost empty. If he had time, he would get something to eat at the airport, he decided.

*The good doctor could have given them more notice!* Going back out to the living room, he pulled on his socks and then slipped on his loafers. Grabbing the suitcase, he shut off the light, turned the door lock and headed out the front door to his car. He fumbled with the keys in the dark. The outside light had burned out two nights ago and he never got around to replacing it. He finally located the Ford key. With a lot of luck and cussing, he finally got the car door unlocked.

Driving down half-deserted streets, he imagined what shape Stanley was in at the moment. Ecstasy was probably emitting from him like pheromones! Soon enough, he reached the lab and Stanley was waiting for him out front, hands in his pockets, pacing back and forth. Victor noticed that all boxes and crates were labeled with the university name, department code, address and phone number, along with their names as the receivers.

"Good deal with these labels, Stan."

"We have to make sure the university is covered for insurance purposes in case anything gets lost, stolen or damaged," Stanley said.

They loaded all the small things in the trunk of his car, and piled the crates in the back seat then headed for Stanley's place, just a five-minute drive.

Once there, the same procedures were followed as with Victor's packing. Too excited to think things out, Stanley grabbed at everything, stuffing his belongings into a duffel bag.

"You'd better take some dress slacks and shirts, and a jacket in case we have to go to any functions with Dr. Joplin," Victor suggested.

"A dinner jacket? I may have a sports jacket around here

somewhere," Stanley said as he tromped to the closet, perused the hanging clothes and made a grab for things.

Those were just crammed into the bag.

Shaking his head, Victor chose to ignore the state of Stanley's belongings until they landed in Houston. He helped him shove the clothes down into the tube and tie it. They would have to hurry and get to the airport to check in on time. Cussing under his breath, he remembered that he had forgotten to ask Dr. Paxton if the tickets were paid for, but he knew they must be because if Dr. Paxton wanted him in Houston, he would have to pay for him to get there! He would want to capture all research expenses for the project.

They made it to the airport and Victor swung the car into the passenger unloading area where he dropped Stanley off with the bags, crates and boxes. Then went in search of a parking place for long-term customers. He sure didn't want the car towed! It may look like a piece of crap, but he wasn't finished restoring it yet. Getting a ticket from the machine, he pulled into a parking space and locked the '65 Mustang. Crossing the parking lot to the elevators, he went down to the lobby where the ticket counters were. Looking around, he found Stanley at the correct counter.

A stickler for details, Stanley was probably driving the attendant crazy, Victor thought, smiling widely. Victor went around the people waiting in line and strode up to his buddy, patted him on the shoulder and asked if he had taken care of all the details.

"Yes, everything's checked in and on its way. I hope nothing gets lost. I verified the billing address and they had a digit wrong in Dr. Paxton's address. It's a good thing I checked it, Victor. Human error statistics are quite high as you well know," Stanley yapped.

"Everyone makes mistakes, Stan," Victor said. "You can't

judge someone for one digit. Remember when you overloaded the washer and flooded the laundromat?"

"That was an error in my judgment," Stanley said. "I used too much soap."

"Well, this guy typed one wrong digit," Victor said.

"Okay! I get it!" Stanley fumed.

Victor presented his driver's license to the attendant, got his boarding pass and asked the attendant if they were all set. Victor swung Stanley around to head him off in another direction, turned to the man behind the counter, gave him a thumbs-up and shrugged his shoulders in apology.

The man glared back and shook his head.

With only minutes to spare before people started boarding, Victor and Stanley made it through the security checkpoint, stopped at a food place and grabbed enough for their flight, then headed to the passenger waiting area. They approached the line of boarding passengers, handed the attendant their boarding passes, and boarded.

Houston, finally! While Victor was thankful for the direct flight to Hobby airport and was hoping he could rest a bit, Stanley didn't shut his eyes or his mouth for the entire flight. Victor still managed to doze off in the middle of a theory, only to wake up forty-five minutes later to find Stanley still going at it. As usual.

They were met by a gray-haired man holding a sign with their names.

"Dr. Ben Joplin," he said.

"I'm Victor Bennett," Victor said, "and this is Stanley Daigle."

Dr. Joplin shook each man's hand. "I had a hard time convincing Joe to let you two guys come out here. He's gotten stingy over the years, hasn't he?"

Stanley just huffed.

"Don't let Stanley get on one of his spiels about money and Dr. Paxton," Victor joked with the older man. "I have to listen to it all the time!"

Smiling his understanding, Victor told Dr. Joplin that he had watched the newscast last night, saw the short video and read the story in the newspaper, and what Stanley found on the Internet. They were raring to get into the field and study the site.

"I know there's much more to the incident than what the news carried, but they only give things like this a scandal sheet view, which is bad for people like us," Victor said, anxious to get the real scoop.

The group made their way towards the baggage console, then to the freight pickup area, collected their things, loaded up two carts and left the terminal.

"Wait here while I go get the car," Dr. Joplin said. He returned shortly with the large SUV and parked. He opened the back for the boxes, crates, and bags to be loaded inside.

"I see you've come prepared," Dr. Joplin said as he looked over the crates and boxes.

"Yup, we brought our department's most recent toy, the sensa-scan camera; that should give us a clue as to what happened, even though some valuable time had elapsed since the incident," Stanley replied.

"We've been waiting to get one of those babies, but the board won't approve it until we furnish proof of the accuracy of the instrument and our need for it," Ben said. "How do they expect us to prove anything if we don't have it? Things are tight in research these days. We only work with half of the resources that we need and our supporters expect miracles. When are they going to learn that you can't get miracles to work unless you go first class?"

"This device can pick up things that other cameras miss,"

Stanley began, going on to further explain the uses for the sensa-scan and the accessories that went with it.

"Rice's facilities will be open to you twenty-four hours a day for as long as you're here," Ben said. "We have some pretty sophisticated computers that will be at your disposal, plus a good team of people to work with you."

Talking nonstop, Stanley told Ben that he wanted to take shots of the entire site and he needed the clothes that the witnesses had been wearing.

"If there's something on those clothes, it should be intact unless they've washed them already. I'm sure I'll be able to find something with the equipment we brought. I want to sweep the entire area with shots to see if any other clues are evident," he said, holding onto theories of his own that he wanted to check out. He had tests to run on their computers, positive that something concrete would appear.

Victor explained to Ben that Stanley was tops in their field of research.

"Oh, I can assure you I already know Stanley's background. His credentials are amazing!" Ben stated. "You aren't exactly unheard of, you know. You've made some pretty valuable discoveries."

"I'm just trying to learn what's going on around us. I like to stay pretty low-keyed," Victor confessed. "Wait until you see Stanley in action. There are times when I can't stand being around him because his insight is unbelievable, and he can come up with things that will really surprise you. No one has a mind like his. He can also be the biggest pain in the ass that you have ever known!"

"Aw, Victor, stop making me look like some kind of savant," Stanley said. Victor smiled smugly at his friend, as if to say, *I dare you to deny it.*

Fumbling in his shirt pocket, Ben produced badges on

lanyards that would give them access to the university. He explained that the site was blocked-off by barricades the mall security had provided, as well as yellow police crime scene tape, to keep the public out. The university had been granted permission to conduct experiments, and the mall security officers wouldn't interfere with anything. They had been useful in keeping the weirdos at bay. People had swarmed all over the place that first day expecting to find God popping out of the concrete.

Everyone in the scientific community knew that this was bound to happen when a sensational story like this hit the news. Anytime something unusual occurred in the scientific world, the thrill seekers and weirdos converged like magnets drawn to metal, interfering with investigations. It was something they would have to live with, being in such specialized fields. The area of physics to which they were dedicated just seemed to attract nuts from the four corners of the planet.

"We had picketers late last night—you should have seen some of the signs. 'We are being punished for our sins against the environment', 'The Devil claims His own'; all sorts of nonsense. Today should be interesting," Dr. Joplin smiled.

"Have any of these people seemed dangerous or highly agitated?" Stanley asked.

"No, most of them are pretty calm—content to carry the signs," Dr. Joplin said.

The site was about thirty miles from the university via the Westpark Tollway West. The apartment where Victor and Stanley would be staying was less than two blocks from the university.

"We'll stop at your place first so you can unload your things. I rented university housing instead of getting you a hotel room since we don't know how long you'll be here. After we get you settled, we'll go by Rice and drop off the equipment and I'll introduce you to a few members of the team," he said. "I'm sure you'll like everyone, and you'll find that it's pretty easy getting around town compared to LA."

The apartment was just minutes away from the campus, a furnished two-bedroom that would suit their needs perfectly. They wouldn't be spending very much time there anyway, as most of their time would be at the university or at the site.

The lab at the university was larger and more elaborate than what they were used to, and Stanley flitted to and fro, completely enthralled with the equipment and computer facilities. They were introduced to several people that would be helping on the project.

After showing them around the physics research lab, they sat down at a conference table and went over details. There weren't any scientific details, actually, and the events could be considered criminal, as far as the police were concerned. The scientists were all convinced this was "the real thing." The small Houston group were ecstatic that it had happened in their own back yard, so to speak.

Wrapping up their meeting, they headed out the door for a bite to eat after their long day. They ended up at Vietopia on Westpark and Buffalo Speedway in the Kroger shopping center and had a feast on chicken mango rolls, shrimp avocado rolls, clay pots of soup, and beer before heading back to the apartment. Turning in early, Victor and Stanley were exhausted from the long flight and the busy day.

# CHAPTER NINETEEN

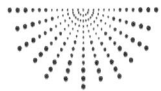

$\mathcal{T}$he cook approached D'laine. "Would you like more?"

"Oh, yes! Is that okay?"

"Of course, it is." The cook refilled D'laine's bowl. "I am happy that you find our food palatable."

"It's more than just palatable," she said. "This is delicious. My mother would have loved it and asked you for the recipe."

D'laine ate more slowly than before, relishing the flavor. She waited for the Egroms to finish their meal, watching them silently. Her head was filled with questions.

*How did they learn to eat with spoons?*

*Why don't their teeth get in the way?*

*How come they don't eat raw vegetables?*

*Where did they learn to cook?*

She decided to learn by watching. They were finishing the meal. Now it was the time for her to ask questions. She wanted to know about these people, their children, everything. Adrum answered her questions carefully.

"Our reproduction and birth are different, but the results

are the same: an offspring. The child is reared in the mother's pouch until it can get about on its own. No training is needed as all of our history and knowledge is genetically transferred, as an instinct," he explained.

D'laine's brows creased. "Do you mean the babies have adult intelligence?" she asked, confused. "Earth babies are helpless. It takes years to complete the growing process until they're responsible human beings. They have to be taught everything including walking, talking and eating."

The Egroms seemed very interested in this information. Silent conversation that D'laine wasn't privy to was ongoing around the circle.

"What is the human life span?" Absadul asked.

"Depending on lifestyles and what part of the world you are raised in, life spans can vary drastically. In my country, females average 86 years or better, and males average 79 years or better," D'laine explained.

The Egroms were dumbstruck.

"You are barely out of infancy." Swezek gestured to the circle of elders. "Our life cycle is 1,000 of your years. Those you see here are between 800 and 950 years. Our species depends on the knowledge from this small circle."

"Don't you have wars or get sick?" D'laine asked, disbelieving.

"Our people haven't changed at all in centuries. There is no one for us to fight, no sickness for us to overcome," Ditol said. "We are quite superior, and quite alone."

"Wow. We're all dead under 100 years old. Only a small percentage of the population lives over a hundred!" D'laine said. "With your advanced ages..."

The elders all seemed to know her next question before it was even formed. "We have understudies, so to speak," Ghury said.

It was D'laine's turn to contemplate their words. "Before, when you were talking about the intelligence of your species, did you mean that the Egroms are the people and the other races are just like animals?"

"No, what Ditol meant was that we are the intellectuals of the shared places you call Earth. Others are bright, intelligent, but not as smart as we are, and they don't have our advanced skills," Adrum defined.

There was a long moment of quiet around the circle. When the chatter began, D'laine assumed the discussion had come to a close. The Egroms rose to their feet.

"Your lessons will begin in the morning," Adrum explained.

"Lessons?" D'laine jumped to her feet.

The group broke up, the elders walking out into the darkness beyond the cook fire.

"Where's everyone going? What lessons?" D'laine asked to no avail.

Kestrum tugged D'laine's elbow and led her away to the door to the mushroom house where she had rested earlier.

"Would you like to bathe before you retire for the night?" Kestrum asked.

"You have hot water here?" D'laine was somewhat shocked.

Kestrum snickered a bit. "Wait here while I get you a lantern."

With a glowing lantern in hand, D'laine and Kestrum started off toward the woods, down a much-used path. The forest was spooky at night without the sunlight drifting through the branches. The huge tree trunks, vines, exposed roots and ground cover could endanger D'laine since her human vision was still inferior to that of the Egroms. That would change once the internal healing completed its cycle, Ghury had informed her earlier.

Kestrum walked slower so D'laine could keep close behind

her. After several minutes, D'laine was delighted by the sight at the path's end.

A hot pond, about the size of a skating rink, with rising steam above the bubbling water, greeted her. Almost giddy with delight, she stooped at the edge to test the temperature with her hand. At once, she was overcome with a desire to soak in the warmth of the pool.

"Is there any danger?" she asked.

"This pool has been unused for many years. No harm will come to you." Kestrum explained that the animals didn't like the warmth of the pool, preferring the cool springs and ponds for their drinking needs, so she shouldn't worry.

"Your people don't take baths here?" D'laine asked.

"No, we groom ourselves," Kestrum explained.

D'laine contemplated for a moment. "Oh... like cats."

"No, we're not like your pets."

"I'm sorry. That wasn't an insult, I meant it as a reference," D'laine said.

"I like those animal pictures in your head."

Shyly, D'laine removed her clothing and entered the pool, which was shallow at the edge.

"It is much deeper towards the center," Kestrum told her. "But you should be able to bathe in comfort where you are."

"Are you sure there aren't any dangerous creatures living in here?" D'laine asked, skeptical.

"Nothing that will harm you," Kestrum reassured.

The water was like liquid silk bubbling around her body. Unlike the hot sulphur pools of Earth, this water did not have any odor. Moving a few feet from the edge, she submerged more of herself in the steamy, delightful pond. It soothed her nerves and relaxed her muscles. D'laine leaned back and looked up into the night sky. Stars appeared brilliant in the dark sky, clearly visible because of the absence of civilization's lights. The four moons amid the stars and the dancing fireflies kept D'laine's attention.

After soaking for several minutes, she splashed water on her face, then ducked her head backwards, under the surface.

"Don't!" Kestrum shouted.

D'laine surfaced. "It's okay, I just needed to wet my hair."

Suddenly, she froze. A look of sheer terror crossed her face. "There's something on my leg!"

Kestrum approached the bank and bent toward the water. She let loose a series of shrieks that sounded like Morse code. A dragon-type creature bobbed through the water away from D'laine.

D'laine scurried out of the water as fast as she could. "Oh my god! What was that thing?"

"Quokins are harmless water creatures. Very curious. They like to touch," Kestrum explained.

"I don't want them touching me." D'laine shivered.

Another Egrom female approached with a handful of the gauzy cloth. She draped the material over D'laine's shoulders and giggled.

"When a quokin touches you, you will find your true love," the female said.

"I'd say that's not going to happen anytime soon," D'laine said. "My boyfriend is back on my world."

Kestrum nudged the female toward D'laine's discarded clothing on the ground. The Egrom scooped up the pitiful fabric and turned toward the path.

"Can my clothes be washed?" D'laine asked. "They're filthy, and I really don't want to put them back on now that I'm clean."

"All will be provided," Kestrum said. "It is time to sleep."

D'laine wrapped herself in the soft cloth and followed Kestrum back to the village. They parted at D'laine's new home. The solitude of her quarters was what she needed to sort out her mixed feelings. She doubted if she could sleep—her mind was a whirlwind of thoughts chasing around in her head. Looking around her, she compared the sparsely furnished room to the home she had left behind just a few hours ago. Would she ever see her father and brothers again? Would Connor wait for her? What were Brenda and Rachel doing?

Leaving those thoughts safely locked away, she decided to sleep in the cloth until her clothes were returned to her in the morning. She placed the lantern in the niche in the wall then crossed the room to the table, lost in thought. She sat, drumming her fingers on the edge of the table.

"No Internet. No books. No TV. Dead phone. Nonworking Kindle. What am I supposed to do?" D'laine sighed. She glanced at the nesting place and stood. She crossed the small space, blew out the flame in the lantern and sank down in the gauzy material of the nest. She bunched up a handful of material and fashioned a pillow of sorts then covered herself with the silky, shiny cloth.

She stared up at the hollowed-out mushroom cap. "Dear God. Please wake me from this nightmare and reunite me with my family and friends." She closed her eyes. "Brian, Jamie... daddy... I hope you are safe at home."

Expecting sleep to be long in coming, she drifted off with thoughts of the family she had left behind on another world. She longed for them fiercely.

# CHAPTER TWENTY

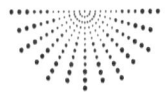

*T*he dream didn't care what dimension she was in. The familiar fall through a dark, bottomless well—through yards and yards of a spider's web with thick fog rushing past—was upon her once again. All the while she felt stretched tight, like some funhouse mirror image come to life. A face loomed before her.

Her brain sort of went on autopilot as it focused on the visitors. There he was, the handsome young man who made her heart flutter like a bird in flight. Another face sprang before her, blotting out her dream guy. She covered her eyes with her hands. This was the hideous monster that reeked of evil.

The reptilian face disappeared as she continued to fall, faster and faster. Waking with a jolt as if she had found a bottom to the pit, D'laine. knew this was a repeat of her journey to Thol. But she was sure the two faces she had seen were not of her own making. She had seen the monster in the field when she was among the white creatures in physical reality.

Two figures walked past D'laine's hut. Ghury and Ditol nudged each other; they were aware of the dream and its significance. Trakon, the Ciertron prince, and Jakla Bosakin, the Plotal, implanted in D'laine's mind from another time, were beginning to surface. They agreed: *tomorrow could not come soon enough for the lessons to begin.*

"We can only prepare her for what lies ahead," Ditol said. "She will have to awaken her powers from within."

Ghury grumbled. "Her abilities are primitive. This will be a challenge. These humans do not even communicate telepathically anymore. We have a lot of work ahead of us."

TRAKON SLEPT FITFULLY IN HIS ENORMOUS BED IN THE spacious suite inside the palace. He tossed and turned. His fist clenched his pillow. Sweat glistened on his naked, muscular chest as his dream launched.

He dreamt of fighting Jakla Bosakin in a field. Extraordinary loud thunder sounded. A breathtakingly beautiful girl appeared in warrior's clothing, ready for battle. Jakla struck her down. Trakon raged in battle.

He woke with a start and sprang to the edge of the bed. His heart thundered in his chest. He grabbed his hair with both hands as his face registered unanswered questions. He stood and walked to the window, his loose sleeping pantaloons moving gracefully. He peered into the night sky. After several calming breaths, Trakon returned to bed and settled back into sleep.

WITH HER PULSE THUMPING WILDLY, D'LAINE STARED UP into the black, seemingly topless mushroom hut. Having formed a quick plan, she quietly rose from the bed and wrapped several yards of gauzy cloth around her and tied the ends firmly. *I've got to stop these words in my head.*

Instant outfit complete, she slipped her feet into her flip-flops, grabbed her canvas bag and swung it over her shoulder and crept to the door, keeping to the inside edge, hiding in the darkness. The village looked deserted as she peered out. She tiptoed outside, keeping snug against the exterior wall of her house. She darted across the way to the rear of Ghury's house. Making a dash for the forest, she reached the edge, unnoticed. *I have got to get out of here! I have to get back home before something terrible happens.* She quit thinking so much to avoid alerting any Egroms that were awake.

Carefully, D'laine sidled around one of the huge tree trunks and stepped into the dark forest. Gingerly, taking small feeling steps, she inched her way forward into the night as her eyes adjusted to the dark. She could barely make out the tree shapes, and the ground cover and hanging vines made progress tedious.

Like earlier in the day, the forest was a silent menace. Waiting to hear the scurrying of nighttime animal life around her, she strained to hear over her galloping heart. As she made her way forward, groping inch-by-inch around the giant trunks, something moved above her in one of the trees.

"Oh, God. I hope it's not a snake," she whispered.

She stumbled over roots and ground cover, stretching out her hands to feel from tree to tree. D'laine felt something drop on her back. Then her shoulder. She brushed her back and shoulders with her hands. More things dropped. So many that she twisted and turned, slapping herself in total panic.

Thousands of tiny warriors swarmed her like an army of ants, all chattering in their tinny high-pitched voices. The sound was deafening. Large insects similar to dragonflies, but ten inches long, buzzed around her head, each carrying a tiny warrior.

Some unknown force within herself beckoned D'laine. She stood still with arms outstretched. For a split second, she appeared serene. Then she opened her mouth and said a single, forceful word.

"STOP!"

Her voice projected an energy wave that threw the tiny warriors off her body and flung them away. Others scurried back up the vines hanging from the enormous trees. The dragonflies tumbled end-over-end through the air then landed in the trees.

GHURY AND DITOL WERE DISCUSSING SERIOUS MATTERS with Bensol and Adrum when D'laine's energy wave hit them full force. It flattened them against the nearest mushroom. When the energy wave passed, Ghury and Adrum ran for the forest.

THE VISIONARY'S TEMPLE, SACRED TO THE PEOPLE OF Ebscalon, was strategically set in the center of the city. It was made of the same sandstone-type material as the palace and other buildings, but its sheer presence boasted serenity. Immense glassless windows with rounded arches and blue lights glowing softly, and the tall, carved double doors at the front were inviting.

The old Ciertron Visionary sat on an ornate mat in a meditative pose, eyes closed. His long, white beard reached mid-chest, and his thick, white, braided hair fell to the middle of his back. He and his two disciples, Ekal and Rettu, were the only inhabitants of the temple. The disciples were fast asleep in the inner chambers.

The energy wave hit the Visionary. His eyes sprang open as he struggled to keep upright. The wave passed. He rose and hurried toward the middle of the vast room where starlight shone down from the open, fluted top of the temple. A replica of Thol floated under a large glass dome surrounded by swirling clouds. The Visionary waved his hands across the surface of the glass. The clouds parted, and an image of D'laine appeared, in the forest.

"She has arrived," he said. "So be it."

He returned to his mat and his meditation.

D'LAINE STOOD QUIETLY, LISTENING. THE WARRIORS stared at her from trees and vines, talking among themselves. She stared back, studying their small forms. Suddenly, two white giants lumbered before her and she recognized Ghury and Adrum.

"You were so frightened by my people that you braved the unknown perils of the Cember forest?" Ghury asked, softly.

"I'm sorry. I'm so sorry. You just don't understand," she said. "I have a family, friends – and a boyfriend. I've helped raise my two younger brothers; we've struggled terribly since our mother died. I've got to get back. It's not as if I don't appreciate your kindness, I've just GOT to get back home!"

"You are unsettled—it is understandable. Everything will be all right if you let things *be*," Ghury said.

"I want to go home. I want to go to college next week. My father. My life." D'laine's words tumbled out.

"We understand. I only wish that I could make your world

line up with the portal," Adrum said. "We cannot do that; our powers are great, but even we don't have any power over dimensional space-time. Come. You are weary and need to rest from your healing."

"You are so patient. I'm sorry that I reacted like this," D'laine said, sniveling.

"It is only natural for a trapped animal to want to escape," Ghury said. "You are like such an animal."

D'laine looked up at Ghury, teary.

"It will be better in the morning," Adrum said. "You are still recovering."

D'laine took one more look at the tiny people before Ghury and Adrum led her back to the mushroom village. They stopped outside D'laine's hut.

"You've met the Kudaja and their borjos—their mounts are like your dragonflies, but more like an actual small dragon without the fire breathing. You should not have any more problems from them," Ghury said.

"What are they? I saw some flying on those borjos," D'laine said. "The others were all over me!"

"Tiny forest people," Adrum said. He raised one hand and spread his fingers five inches from his thumb.

"The Kudaja fear The Voice," Ghury said.

"I just wanted them to shut up and get off me," D'laine said.

"You accomplished that... and more," Ghury said.

"Go rest. No more outings on your own, please," Adrum said.

"I promise," D'laine said as she entered her hut. She crawled into bed and cried until she was drained, then dropped into a deep sleep.

Ghury and Adrum shook their heads.

"She does have abilities," Adrum said.

"Subduing the Kudaja is no simple feat, and using The Voice came naturally to her," Ghury said. "Let us hope her training in other areas is fruitful."

MORNING CAME TOO SOON FOR D'LAINE. SHE FELT completely depleted of energy from the healing and her crazy excursion into the forest. As she gazed about the mushroom house from her gauzy bed, she realized that it was not a good idea to wander around alone in this new world. The perils were too great.

Dreams filled with monsters, dragons, and tiny people attacking her, interrupted her sleep as well as flashing skies that made her head hurt. Wildly colored landscape surrounded and engulfed her.

Looking about her, she realized that part was true and part had been nightmare; the Egroms were gentle, hospitable creatures, not monsters. It could be a lot worse, she thought, cringing at the memory of the monster face she had dreamed about during the night and the brutality she had witnessed in the field. The Kudaja had alarmed her beyond reasoning, and her head and back felt the brunt of their tiny bodies dropping on her. D'laine looked at her red palms and arms where she had slapped herself silly in the night. She was so sunburnt.

D'laine wondered when Kestrum would return with her clothing, and as the thought left her head, the female Egrom appeared in the front opening of her hut. She was carrying silver-gray material in her hands, not the clothing D'laine expected.

"You may wear the garb of the Ciertrons. They have forms like yours," Kestrum explained.

D'laine clutched the gauzy material and sat bolt upright.

"You mean there are real people here, like me?" She scrambled to get up, wrapping the bedding material around her and tightening the knot.

"We have many different creatures and people here. The Ciertrons are the closest to your species," Kestrum said. She handed the material to D'laine.

D'laine took the material, paying no mind to it. "People? Will they be able to help me get back home?"

"The Ciertrons are unaware of the portals," Kestrum explained with a shake of her head.

D'laine held up the material—a flimsy jumpsuit and a pair of socks. "A jumpsuit? I can't wear these things in this climate! It's too hot. I'll roast! Just bring me my clothes and I'll see what I can do with them," she said angrily.

She handed the jumpsuit and socks back to Kestrum.

Kestrum pushed the clothing back at D'laine. "These are more functional than the clothing from your world, and they will last quite a long time," Kestrum explained.

"I should be able to remake my clothes into something reasonably comfortable," D'laine argued, passing the outfit back to Kestrum.

"This is the clothing that is worn here," Kestrum said on a closing note. "Do you need assistance with these garments?"

D'laine wondered what a Ciertron was, but restrained herself from asking any questions, knowing that she would find out from Adrum since he was going to be her teacher.

"No! I can figure it out by myself," she said with a slight hint of anger.

She wanted to be by herself to assess the situation. When Kestrum left, D'laine laid the garments on the table. Rubbing the main garment with her fingers, she decided that it was made of thin, gauzy material, but it didn't seem to be transparent. Slipping her hand in between the cloth and lifting it toward the bright light beyond the doorway, she couldn't see through it.

Sitting down on the curved stone chair, she rested her elbow on the table and supported her chin while studying the outfit. Shrugging, she stood, untied the makeshift covering she wore and threw the cloth aside and began dressing in the strange clothes.

D'laine stepped into the jumpsuit and eased each leg up like panty hose. She wiggled it all the way up to her chest and slipped her arms into the sleeves. It was baggy and sagged in some areas and tight in others.

"Definitely not my size. These people sure have weird bodies," she said, examining the fit of the suit.

She noticed a tiny round bulge on the cuff of one sleeve, about the size of an eraser on a mechanical pencil. Wondering what it was, she ran her index finger over the little bump. D'laine let out a muffled cry as the suit molded to her form without warning. She noticed other tiny bumps on the suit.

"I'm not touching anything else!" she exclaimed.

She glanced down at her bare feet and turned her gaze back to the table. The stockings were made from a two-toned black material, just as thin, but noticeably different. After pulling them on, she walked around briefly. They were very big and flopped on her feet.

"What about shoes?" she said.

She sat and stared at the stockings and noticed each had a tiny dot on the top of her foot.

"Hhmmm," she said.

She pressed one dot. It inflated the stocking into a boot. She pressed the dot on the other stocking and watched it inflate. She stared dumbfounded at her feet, then glanced around the hut.

"I'm sitting in a mushroom hut out of the stone age and I'm wearing a high-tech suit. What next?"

She stood and walked around. The soles felt like the soles of a shoe, but they were only millimeters thick and not like leather or a manmade material. She felt nothing uncomfortable under her feet, and she wondered how they could soften the impact of her foot meeting the ground.

Though she walked over rough spots she didn't even feel a pebble. Sitting down, she grabbed one of her feet to look at the bottom of the stocking. The material was a little thicker, conforming to her foot like a second skin. Curious, she wanted to know how they cushioned her feet the way they did, and was deliberating this mystery when Ghury entered and supplied the information.

"The material is a combination of the hosk webbing and the sap of the agrin trees. The resin protects the material from dirt and strengthens it," he explained. "The trees are almost perpetual, renewing their sap as quickly as it is tapped."

D'laine stared at him. "You're like a walking Google or Wikipedia," she said.

"All intelligent beings should be knowledgeable about their world," Ghury said.

"But it's not conversation. It's like showing off, or babbling statistics," she said.

Ignoring her, he went on to tell her that clothing could be dyed many colors from extracts of different plants. He said most of the races of Thol used the hosks webbing for bedding, clothing and other things. When combined with the resin, the material was excellent for footwear, tents and banners. Its uses seemed endless, and D'laine thought of many ways it could be utilized back home.

"Are you ready to eat?" Ghury asked.

"Slim chance of getting a cup of cafe´ mocha, right?" she asked, hopefully.

"My people do not pollute their bodies," he said.

D'laine appeared indignant. "Since when do you know about coffee?" she said. "Besides, I switched to decaf."

Ghury turned and exited the hut, grumbling. D'laine followed him outside. She had to trot to keep up with him.

"Who are the Ciertrons? Will you take me to them? Maybe they can help get me back home," she said as she jogged to keep up with him.

Ghury stopped abruptly and turned to face her. D'laine crashed into him and almost lost her footing. He extended two of his four hands and caught her before she hit the ground.

"Oops. Sorry," she said.

"No one can help you get back home," Ghury said, exasperated. He turned and continued to walk, grumbling to himself.

D'laine had to run to catch up with him. "Why are you so certain?" she nagged.

"Because the portals are not aligned with your world," he said.

"I have to get back for college, my brothers and my father," she argued.

"Your brothers are in good hands," he said.

D'laine ran hard and caught up with Ghury. She yanked one of his arms, making him stop. "How do you know that? You really read minds?"

"Your mind is a chatter box. The entire planet will soon know what you eat for breakfast," Ghury said.

D'laine let that sink in. Ghury continued walking to the eating place. Her mind ran a million miles an hour as she stood thinking of all sorts of implications. She focused on her thoughts and quieted her mind a bit.

Kestrum waved from the eating place. In a few short strides, for an Egrom, she was at D'laine's side.

"This clothing is comfortable?" Kestrum asked as she appraised D'laine in the jumpsuit and boots.

"I thought it would be too hot, but it's quite comfortable," D'laine said.

"It breathes," Kestrum said.

"Huh," D'laine said. She looked down at her covered body and appraised the material.

"Are you hungry?" Kestrum asked.

"Yes, but I would like to wash first before I join the others. Is that okay?" she said.

"Of course." Kestrum pointed her in the right direction, then joined Ghury.

D'laine was glad she had her hairbrush with her as her shoulder-length blonde locks would get unruly if left unattended. The golden, natural waves offset her bright green intelligent eyes. Her shapely figure was flattered by the unique clothing. It made her feel as if she were dressed for a costume party.

She followed the same path that Kestrum had taken her down the night before; the forest looked kinder in the daylight, but she still didn't trust it. She half expected those tiny forest people to plop down on her again. Looking from side-to-side and up to the treetops for unknown assailants, she cautiously made her way to the pool where she washed her face and attempted to brush her teeth with her fingers.

The quokin slithered up to within a yard of her face. D'laine froze. She stared back at the creature—black with green-tipped scales that made it appear iridescent. It inched closer. She recalled the conversation from the night before—the quokin liked to touch. Bravely, she held her hand out. The creature approached and rubbed the side of its face against her hand. She cupped her hand against one of its scaly cheeks. Then the quokin dove under the water and was gone.

D'laine let out her breath. She stared at the water. The rippling surface became smooth and appeared peaceful. The color of the water hypnotized her. The turquoise coloring was still evident when she cupped her hands and captured some for a quick study. It sparkled with a pureness that would be difficult to find on Earth. Industry would never taint these beautiful water sources, she thought. She reluctantly finished her grooming, then returned to the village.

# CHAPTER TWENTY-ONE

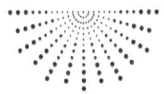

*L*ee sat at the kitchen table with a cup of coffee. He rested his head in his hands, worn out, contemplating. He wasn't a religious man. He considered himself spiritual. He talked to God continuously and wondered how these events could be part of a big plan.

First the accident. Losing his wife, best friend, lover and the mother of his children. Then D'laine's long recovery, a miracle in itself. Brian's illness seemed to be something he could understand, but D'laine's disappearance was so far out in left field he could not focus on the scientific implications of the event.

He took a sip of coffee as Rosa puttered around the kitchen. The dog door clattered as Buffy came through. She bumped Lee's leg with something. He looked down, surprised.

"What's that you've got there?" Lee reached down and took the bunched-up flowers from the dog's mouth. "Where did this come from, Buffy?"

Rosa came over to look at the flowers, and to clean up the trail of leaves and petals from the mini-roses Buffy had hauled in. "That's unusual."

Buffy barked. She shot out of the dog door and returned minutes later with a larger than average greeting card. Lee pried it away from her and he and Rosa read the card.

*We are so sorry for your loss. If there is anything we can do for you, please call.* Signed by all the students in D'laine's high school senior class with Ms. Marshall's phone number.

Lee stood abruptly and walked out the kitchen door. "Buffy, come on. Show me where you got these."

Buffy bounded after Lee and she raced down the long driveway to the edge of the road where a memorial had accumulated. Lee found stuffed animals, bouquets of flowers, potted plants, candles, greeting cards, photos and all manner of things. He kneeled down and read some of the cards, stopped, put his hands over his face and wept.

THE MINIVAN PULLED-UP ADJACENT TO THE ROPED-OFF parking place at the mall. Lee and Buffy exited the van and stood before a shrine to D'laine. The same type of memorial items were here, but these were mostly from total strangers.

Lee knelt beside Buffy. He took her head in his hands and looked into her eyes.

"Where's D'laine?" he asked the dog. "Find D'laine!"

He stood as Buffy rushed all around the parking place and sniffed the ground. She looked back at Lee as if to say, "she's not here." Lee looked sad, not knowing what he expected. Maybe he thought Buffy would find a trail that led away from the parking place.

Lee patted his leg. "Come on, Buffy. Let's go back home."

# CHAPTER TWENTY-TWO

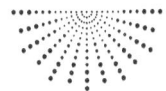

*S*ome of the Egrom tribe sat around the fire while others were going off into the forest to their posts where they would stay until dusk. The Egrom that had served the stew last night served breakfast. There wasn't very much difference between the two meals; they looked the same, but tasted different. Eating only one helping, D'laine felt satisfied.

The sky was ablaze with color and fascinated her. "I love the sky," she said.

The flashing light and subtle colors mesmerized her so much she almost got a crick in her neck from looking up. More aware of her surroundings, she noticed things that she didn't see yesterday.

Flying creatures that looked like parrots and bats combined in one body, were silent as they glided through the air. *Strange looking creatures,* she thought, as she wondered about their purpose. They had a head like a parrot, wings like a bat with little claw feet and bright coloring that could be — feathers?

"I wonder what other creatures were hiding that I didn't

see when we walked through the fields and the forest yesterday," D'laine said as she continued to stare up at the sky.

*Did the Egroms have power over these creatures to stop their
flight and noise?*

"A rainbow of color to glide through the remarkable sky,"
she said.

As she sat there, D'laine discovered several different types
of flying creatures passing overhead, squawking or chirping.

"Are those classified as birds or flying reptiles?" she asked.

"They are practically one and the same," Ghury said.
"Flying creatures were one of the first things created. There are
18,000 different types of flying creatures on Thol, and they are
the closest living relatives of the Plotals."

"No way!" D'laine said, stunned.

Ghury nodded. "Plotals are the largest species in the reptile
category."

As she pondered this, a yapping sounded overhead and
what looked like a flying cocker spaniel, although a third of the
size of the dog, flapped fluffy champagne-colored wings as it
chased a bat-bird.

"Oh, how cute!" She pointed to the dog-bird flying away.

"The floff does resemble the dog in your head, but the floff
is a meat eater and he chases the gagu for its next meal," Adrum
explained.

D'laine frowned. She was disconcerted that the dog-bird
was so different from the gentle dog of her world.

"It is time for your lessons to begin," Adrum said,
disrupting her thoughts.

D'laine looked at the Egrom. "What are the lessons about?"

"If you go, you will find out," Ghury grumbled as he shook
his head.

Exasperated, D'laine followed Adrum to his hut. "Is he
always so grumpy?" She could have sworn Adrum snickered.

The elders watched as D'laine and Adrum walked away.

"Stubborn," Ghury said.

The elders nodded in agreement.

"A good trait," Drusta said.

They all agreed again.

ADRUM'S MUSHROOM HUT WAS IDENTICAL TO THE OTHERS. D'laine didn't see any teaching tools anywhere, and wondered how she was going to learn.

"Am I supposed to just sit here and listen to you?" she asked, somewhat belligerent.

Knowing that her retention was terrible when she was stressed, she made up her mind that she couldn't learn from speeches.

"There is nothing wrong with your memory. As a matter of fact, your memory is better than two-thirds of your species on your world. Sit down and close your eyes and relax," he said. "You spend too much time worrying about the wrong things. You will learn to let those insignificant things go—to let things BE that are not in your immediate control."

"This is ridiculous!" Sputtering protests, D'laine was silenced as Adrum interrupted her.

"Think of this as an alignment, or integration of your brain," he said. "You are only using a tiny portion of your brain."

He pinched two fingers together with one hand. Then he held up two of his hands and formed a circle. "This is the size of your brain," he said and brought the two hands forming the circle forward. "See how little is being used?"

He adjusted his pinched fingers at different parts of the brain to show her the difference.

Despite her niggling doubts, D'laine found herself interested.

"When your brain is integrated, you will be able to call upon knowledge and power from all of these other areas of your brain that have been dormant. Humanity shut off these parts as they evolved. It was not a good thing," he said as he shook his head, sadly.

Concern passed over D'laine's face. "Will I lose memories?"

"You are storing too many insignificant things from as far back as your birth that no longer have any use. You will now apply much more of your brain power and your now dim memories will be crisp with details and you will be able to bring them forth as needed," he said softly.

She crinkled her forehead in thought. "What about the bad memories? I don't want to see the details of things like the car accident."

Adrum rested one hand on D'laine's hands on the table. "I promise you that these things will be able to be viewed objectively from this point forward. But first, I will explain some common terminology that is slightly different than what you are accustomed to. A full turn is one day. A notch is one week. A keld is a month and a complete path is one year."

"They seem similar," D'laine said.

"After a while these new terms will be automatically understood—your brain will swap your terms for these new terms, so to speak." He smiled at her.

D'laine worried some more, but finally made herself comfortable in the molded chair which fit her body perfectly. She closed her eyes, blocking out the light pouring in through the hut opening.

A vivid picture of Adrum came into view, with a detailed picture of Thol behind his image. D'laine's eyes flew open.

"I saw your face in my head!"

"A good start," Adrum said enthusiastically. "You will like this lesson."

She closed her eyes again and a smile softened her lovely face as she stared back at the furry teacher in her head. Her education was about to begin. As Adrum's face faded, D'laine's whole mind was filled with the beauty of Thol. It was overwhelming.

It was a motion picture going through her head, complete with narrator. D'laine felt her mind absorbing details as though a balloon was being blown up in her brain. The lecture began with the surface of Thol, exploring the fauna and flora in the terrain of each region of the planet. Seeing different creatures, she was told what they were, where they lived, how they survived, who their predators were and whether they were friendly or should be avoided.

Everything was explored. It was an experience for D'laine to sit through, forgetting misery and loneliness, focusing on this history and the detail of this world. There were mountains, rivers and other bodies of water. The sponge was everywhere and ranged in different colors throughout the surface of the planet. There were deserts and unique things, and mountains that held snow caps.

She learned that the normal temperature of this world ranged from eighty-six to two-hundred-ten degrees Fahrenheit in the lowlands, which were not desolate wastelands, but were home to many strange creatures and plant forms.

The mountain temperatures ranged from minus fifty to plus forty-five degrees Fahrenheit where the Raagor ice people and their saber-toothed chuns lived. Fear momentarily filled her as she observed the ice-white people with the coal black eyes. They wore no body coverings. Their hairless, white skin was veined in blue which gave off an eerie halo.

A high humidity rate accounted for the accelerated growth of the vegetation and its abundance, with the extreme opposite in the cold mountains where everything was frozen and no one ventured.

When D'laine saw the inhabitants of Thol, beginning with the Egroms, she could understand them better. They possessed powers of the mind that were staggering. They COULD walk on water and leap tall buildings!

The knowledge they possessed was enormous—more than any other creature here or in any of the other dimensional planes, even the most intelligent of her world. She couldn't imagine their IQs, if they could even be measured, but she was sure that they would overwhelm someone from her scientific world.

As Adrum showed her day-to-day things the Egroms did, she was positive that no one would believe these gentle creatures could possibly do the things she was seeing. She watched as an Egrom stood in front of an enormous solid rock boulder, ran his four hands over its surface and with the powers of his mind, possessing something like mental laser skills, he carved a chair, similar to what she sat in, with a precision and smoothness unknown on her world.

These beings had the ability to heal the body and the mind, and had a compassion for their brethren that was unequaled. They could also project themselves to another place a great distance away, and they moved at great speeds. She watched as an Egrom disappeared from in front of her, going from one place to another so fast her brain could not track the movement. Using more of their mental rather than physical skills, they could accomplish great tasks.

Their opposites were the Plotals.

Creatures of blood and greed, they craved domination and power. These bloodthirsty slavers welcomed travelers into their camps. At first, they showed great hospitality to guests who would then wake the next day to find themselves in slave shackles.

As cruel nomads, the Plotals wandered over the surface of Thol, fighting and taking captive any lower tribe or people that inhabited the area. They did no physical labor because slaves were used for everything. It seemed that their sole purpose was to plunder and do battle—like land pirates, leaving scars wherever they went.

The pictures went racing by in her mind. If learning was so easy back home, everyone would be knowledgeable on all subjects. Life, as we know it would be nonexistent. All lifestyles would change dramatically, D'laine thought. New talents and new ways of doing everything would evolve. Man would totally change, perhaps leaving behind their thirst for power to become more concerned with the environment, feeding the people of the world, and developing their minds.

As the tour of Thol progressed, she saw a lovely city with buildings of sandstone, or a similar material, with roofs that sparkled like diamonds. The buildings were two to ten stories high topped with turrets and towers, most of which held colorful flying banners that, she learned, denoted the rank of the family.

*The citizens of this city were like her!* Letting out a squeak of surprise, D'laine's hands flew to her heart.

"Humans?" She gaped at the tour stop.

There were real human people here! They had black silky hair and their skin ranged from a light copper color to a dark burnished bronze. They were like the Native Americans or perhaps Spanish or Italian people. *Maybe Moorish*, she thought. Such beautiful people!

Some of the women wore the same type of clothes that D'laine now wore. Others wore flowing cloths in shimmering colors of pastel meadows, draped over their shoulders, like the saris of India. Most had their hair held back with a colorful band that went around their heads and fastened in the back.

The entire population had black hair.

The men wore similar clothing to hers which seemed like a warrior's outfit from the Roman Empire. Some wore outfits with short sleeves and short pants; others wore the full-bodied outfit, like she wore. They were a healthy, good-looking people.

D'laine could hardly contain her excitement. "Are these people friendly?"

She didn't want to see any more pictures, anxious only to get information about this race and she didn't care about anything else, but she was trapped in the lesson until it ended.

Sensing her anxiety, Adrum paused his teachings in her mind.

"These people are called Ciertrons and this is their city, Ebscalon. The original city of Ciert had been destroyed fifty years ago in an extensive war," Adrum explained. "They rebuilt the city and renamed it Ebscalon, which means *knowledge*. They learned the lessons of war, but the expense had been staggering."

The mind-tour continued and another similar city appeared, inhabited by Plotals.

"Long ago, harmony among the species was blissful. Then a Ciertron rescued a cast-out Plotal—a strict taboo. Before long, squabbling began which escalated and erupted into a full-scale war," Adrum explained.

The Great War between humans and Plotals with lasers and other sophisticated weapons and warships flashed in D'laine's head. Cities and technology were destroyed. The different peoples slaughtered each other. Almost all the great minds of invention had been killed.

"Rebuilding was an effort with so few craftspeople left.

But, in time, the Ciertrons managed to build a new city," Adrum narrated. "The Plotals never rebuilt. They wandered the land and set up their tent cities."

Ciertrons, unlike the Plotals, were defenders of justice, a noble people with bonds of honor. The scenes of the city raced past her. As she settled down emotionally, a greater shock hit her than the previous jolt when she first saw the people of Ebscalon.

"Him! That's him!" she pointed.

Before her stood a very familiar boy, but unlike any that she had ever met on Earth. Her heart hammered as she recognized him from her dreams. Tall, muscular, with an incredibly hand-some face, with jet black hair, dark blue eyes and skin the color of rich bronze, he stood like a god, emanating authority. She could tell he knew what he wanted and would get it—not through a ruthless acquisition but through desire.

Her breathing was ragged and her emotions remained askew as his presence slowly diminished and disappeared alto-gether. She was confused about her emotions. It was almost like she was cheating on Connor. The scene moved on to show the outlying area surrounding the city, but her thoughts drifted back to the stranger. She wanted to know who he was and why he was picked out of all those people for her to see, and why he starred in her nightmares. No other person was singled out like that.

She wanted answers, but was suddenly seeing fields and pens that contained the beasts that Jakla and his horde of marauders rode. Studying the animals, she determined that they looked almost like an ancient woolly mammoth from Earth's past, but the resemblance in their huge bulk ended when she saw them up close in this projection.

Blessed with six legs, Pakows could run fast, Adrum narrated. Looking at one of them, D'laine decided that a whole zoo was represented in one body. In the distance, a man rode on the back of one of the beasts, herding the rest toward the pens.

"A roundup!" D'laine exclaimed to no one in particular.

"Pakows are used for many purposes including transportation and labor," Adrum explained. "They are gentle and quick to learn and can follow instructions quite well."

Enjoying the "film", D'laine was startled as she saw a ship pass through the air. These were civilized people! She was sure that they were more cultured and advanced than her own people.

The vessels, called crestriders, came in sizes ranging from a single man ship to the large vessels that could carry a whole fleet of men into battle. They were made of a material unknown to her, gun metal blue in color with large sparkling, curved wings. A glass-type windshield extended about one foot higher than the man standing behind the controls. She learned that they were invaluable as the air patrol to guard the city against intruders, such as Plotal attacks.

History, knowledge, everything passed through her brain.

Adrum passed one hand in front of D'laine's face. Her chin fell and she appeared to be in a deep sleep. He placed two fingers at each side of her temples and placed another hand on the top of her head. He stayed that way for a moment then removed his hands. He waved a hand before her face again.

She opened her eyes, perked up, unaware that she had blitzed out. They faced each other across the smooth, stone table.

"Your mind has absorbed many details; more than I thought you could grasp," Adrum said. "You are a fast learner. The next lesson will be much quicker."

"Why did you show me all of this?" D'laine asked.

"This is a time of change. Not only are you in a different environment, but you will have to relearn things that you have taken for granted, and things that your race has forgotten over the centuries."

"Relearn what?" she asked.

"The many mysteries your people have forgotten through your evolution," he explained.

D'laine sat star-struck, listening to her teacher.

"In the next few days, you will understand many new things. There will be more lessons later. You will become more in tune as to what is going on around you and more aware of life and its creatures."

When she looked around, she was surprised to see that it was dark outside. The evening meal was being prepared. She didn't feel tired, but was relieved that their way of learning was not an effort. The time went by without realizing it. She rose to her feet, leaving the hut to join the others.

# CHAPTER TWENTY-THREE

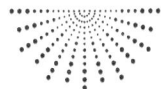

*D*'laine marveled at the unique way of learning here. She wished Brenda and Rachel could experience this type of mind education. It would be so much easier to get a degree! Her thoughts drifted. She wondered if all the intelligent species on Thol used this method, or if this was a mystic wonder of the Egroms. In the span of a few hours, she acquired enough of the history of Thol, information about its people, animals, cultures, religions and languages, to more than just get by. At least she could have an intelligent conversation without showing total ignorance.

The virile young man, singled out of a complete nation of people, kept her mind occupied. She didn't have to close her eyes to see his face—it was imprinted upon her brain from all her dreams. Not capable of analyzing her feelings on this subject, she felt that her life would be intertwined with his. She didn't think Connor would like this at all. The mystery was unsettling with the answers to those questions still forthcoming. She found herself impatient again, wanting to know everything immediately.

"Tomorrow I will take you on a short journey," Trabet said to D'laine as she joined the others for the evening meal. "There are many things for you to learn firsthand because you were not born with this knowledge in your genes. Each day one of us will show you a different area of our territory. You need to know where the main sentry posts are and how to detect the portals, even though you don't possess our keen eyesight yet."

"I can understand you teaching me everything, but why are you showing me where the portals are? Isn't it dangerous if that information falls into the wrong hands?" she asked, curiously.

A roar of Egrom laughter made the fine hairs stand up on her arms. Would she ever get used to that sound? It sounded more like a group of angry grizzly bears roaring! She wondered what she had said that was so funny.

"We do not look like those grizzled bears," Swazek said.

"*GRIZZLY* bears... not grizzled," D'laine giggled.

The group stared blankly at her, not understanding the difference, or her humor.

"Forget it," she said, shaking her head. She stared at the group, a hopeless expression covering her face. "The English language is too difficult to explain."

Swazek picked up where he had left off without pause. "Your mind is incredible, holding powers that even we don't possess. We will help you to find those dormant powers and use them to guide you and sharpen your instincts. It will take much self-discipline, patience and a strong will."

"How could that be possible. I'm nowhere near as smart as you," D'laine said.

Ghury tapped her forehead. "It is in there; in a locked-down state. We will teach you how to unlock the door."

D'laine ate in silence, scrunching her forehead as she processed the conversation.

After eating her healthy meal, she went to her hut, changed

out of her clothes and wrapped herself in a gauze towel. She slipped on her flip flops and headed down the path for a bath at the pool. Relaxing in the heat of the water as it caressed her skin, her thoughts drifted to her lost life, so far away. Shaking the heavy thoughts aside for fear of losing herself to depression, she knew that it would take changing her heart into stone to keep going on a day-to-day basis without falling into a mental pit. A quokin bobbed through the water on the opposite side of the pond.

She watched the water dragon for a moment and then focused on the next day and hoped she would learn many new experiences. She would get to see the terrain firsthand instead of seeing it in the motion pictures that Adrum had projected in her mind. Finishing her bath, she left the warm water and draped the soft material of the gauze towel around her body and strolled along the path to seek the privacy of her hut.

Lost in thought as she walked down the deserted path, D'laine was startled by a rustling sound from the dense foliage up ahead on the side of the pathway. Stopping to listen, her pounding heart made it difficult to hear anything else. The noise stopped and she tentatively moved forward a few steps only to hear it again. She was so scared she expected her knees to begin knocking. A few silent moments passed and then the rustling noise became louder. Finally, the intruder broke through the underbrush and stepped onto the path.

A short, stocky mruck, with crusty looking brown skin, stood several feet in front of her. It had a short, little snout, like an elephant, and little pig ears perched atop an ugly face with lidless eyes that stared back at her. It raised its snout, sniffing the air; its decision made in an instant—the four solid legs, each with a split hoof of a foot, went into motion as it charged forward.

Yelping in fright, D'laine turned and ran back down the

path toward the pool, her mind sifting through layers of information that she had learned. Mruck's took to water like hippos so she couldn't run into the water. It was impossible to leap into a tree; none of the branches were low enough for her to grab to hoist herself out of reach of the beast. Making an instant decision, she would head into the forest, thinking that the dense woodland would at least slow down the animal.

Turning to her right, she plowed into the punishing thicket and ran as best as she could, leaping over ground obstacles. She saw a tree base with a long narrow opening and she rushed to it. Turning sideways she jammed herself into the opening.

The mruck lunged through the underbrush and D'laine barely had time to pull her gauze covering into the hole. The mruck grabbed the end of the gauze and shook it.

Scared to death, she had a tug of war with the animal. Suddenly two large borjos swarmed the mruck. She saw the Kudaja warriors quickly retrieve bows, but not arrows. They aimed the bows at the animal and the bows glowed an eerie blue where a string should have been. She watched as the warriors pinched the glowing string and pulled back. An energy wave hit the animal and the mruck went down.

The borjos hovered in front of her as she squeezed out of the tree, securing the gauze around her. One of the warriors removed his helmet. He bumped his chest with his fist.

"So, we meet again," he said. "You are safe now, but you need to learn how to protect yourself. There are many dangers in the forest."

He was a tiny replica of the Ciertrons, but wore forest clothing similar to the fabled Robin Hood of Sherwood Forest. A handsome face with brilliant blue eyes and shocking black hair that fell in his face and down to his shoulders, he dipped his head respectfully.

"Thank you so much! I'm glad you were in the area and could help me," she said, stammering.

"Herish of the Cember Forest, at your service," he said with a fist to his chest. He smiled wickedly. "You knocked me down and flung me a whole day away from my home the first time we met."

"Oh! That was an accident. I'm glad you are okay. Thank you so much for saving me, Herish," she babbled. "I'm D'laine of... of the Egrom village." She blushed, not knowing exactly if that was an accurate statement or if she should have mentioned Earth.

"What kind of a weapon is that?" she asked, pointing to the bow.

He held the bow out in front of her. "You've never seen a wyre before?"

She shrugged. "It's like a bow where I come from, but we use a string to propel arrows, which are a wooden shaft with a metal point on one end and feathers on the other end. Yours doesn't have the string or the arrows."

"What you described is an ancient form of this weapon that our ancestors used many years ago. The wyre is an energy weapon. When you pinch, and pull here, it releases an energy arrow that can either stun or kill," he explained.

She watched as he demonstrated the weapon. "That is incredible."

Herish appraised her scantily covered form. "Perhaps we will meet again."

She stared hard at the warrior for a moment then left the Kudaja. Returning to the path, she ran back to the village, anxious for the solitude of her own space. She ran as fast as she could to escape the tiny warrior's eyes on her.

Ghury and Adrum sat by the fire and watched as D'laine ran into her hut.

"The Kudaja have aligned themselves with D'laine," Adrum said.

"A very unusual precedent," Ghury said.

Once inside her mushroom house, D'laine poured water in a bowl and dipped a piece of the cloth into the water. She wiped smudges off her arms and legs.

"Oh my god! I hope he didn't see me naked!" D'laine balked. Her face turned beet red just thinking about her bathing at the pool.

A few scrapes and scratches were present, but nothing serious. Changing into fresh clothing she went to bed, exhausted from the terrifying ordeal. She was contemplating the tiny warrior, Herish, grateful for him and his friend saving her from the mruck.

The next few days were filled with learning the ways of the Egroms. No film could have taught her the instincts she seemed to have developed overnight. Suddenly, she became aware of keen senses, detecting if something was not right.

"Where were these hidden things when I needed them just a few days ago?" she said as she came across several mrucks and learned how to avoid them by staying downwind. They were dependent upon their trunk for sniffing out prey since they couldn't see very well.

"Your abilities will form and present themselves to you little by little," her Egrom guide said. "It is quite possible those abilities have blossomed just now in your being."

Energized beyond her most fit experience on Earth, D'laine

marveled at the dynamic surge of vitality that she seemed to have developed overnight. Though she travelled for many miles on foot each day, she never seemed to tire. She knew that if she were back on Earth, she would have dropped with exhaustion from all the activity in the heat and humidity.

In the greater Houston area and all the way out to Katy, a car was essential to get from one point to another unless you lived in downtown Houston near a bus or train line. When she returned home, D'laine knew she would be in excellent physical shape.

Along with her new feelings, she seemed to be mending physically. A tooth that she had lost from the car accident was coming back and she wondered what her dentist would say about that. From observing her reflection in the drinking pond, she noticed that her hair was getting thicker and had grown incredibly fast, reaching almost to the middle of her back. It was much lighter, taking on a platinum color.

Making several crude tests, she knew that her hearing was much more acute. She could hear hosks milling around on their silent spider legs across the sponge ground cover. Another thing that amazed her was her vision. Now she could see things at distances that normally would be impossible, and she sensed that her vision was better than any other human being on Earth, but not yet comparable to the Egroms.

The ugly marks caused by the accident, had vanished that first day of healing. For the past five years, the scars across her thighs had been a constant reminder of that fateful day. This place seemed to have a purging effect on her, and she was thankful for what she had now, and wished that her family were here to share these wonders, especially Brian. Her thoughts forever drifted to her brothers, her father, and her best friends so far away.

Plagued with wondering how her family was coping, she

hoped that Rosa and Eric were still caring for them. If it weren't for her family and friends, she would never want to leave this place. Her dad was such a good father and had endured so much pain and heartache in such a short period of time. She had wished many times for a larger family of cousins, aunts and uncles, but she didn't know anyone on her mother's side. Her maternal grandparents had passed on before the accident, and her mom had been an only child. D'laine wasn't sure why her mother never kept in touch with aunts, uncles or cousins.

On her Dad's side, family was only blurred faces without names, as most lived on different continents and moved often with their energy-related jobs.

What would this terrible experience do to her father, she wondered. Losing his wife was bad enough. Why did this have to happen to her! Before getting overly emotional, she banished the anguished thoughts from her mind. Trying not to think of these things very often, she had trained her mind to think that survival was the only thing she needed to focus on. With some difficulty, she soon learned to construct a barrier to hold her private thoughts away from the Egroms, testing it often and trying to improve upon it.

Every once in a while, something would slip by to the unprotected side of the barrier. The first attempt had been crude. She had mentally built a wall, brick by brick, which was tedious and seemed to take forever and gave her a headache. Deciding she couldn't take all day building a wall in that manner, she projected the whole wall at once to keep her private thoughts on one side and her public thoughts on the other side. The real secret was keeping track of what side she was on during her alone thought-time.

To ease her pain, Ghury had taken her back to the spot that marked her entry to his world. She was happy to see her circle of crystals and rocks were still in the pile she created so long ago. The wonders of these creatures, she thought, as she remembered that first instance. With a wave of one of his powerful arms, he showed her that no hidden doorway hovered magically in the area.

"You see, there is nothing here now," Ghury said. "Try."

D'laine waved her arm in front of her. Nothing happened. "What does this prove?" she asked. Since she couldn't see anything but the sky in front of her, D'laine was not convinced of the portals.

"Come with me. We will find an active portal."

To demonstrate a clearer understanding, they walked across the field to another portal site. D'laine noticed that crystals were plentiful on the ground. Ghury had the sentry reveal the hidden doorway to another place in time.

The sentry waved his arm. Strange life forms passed through swirling misty clouds—unfamiliar life forms, at that. D'laine sucked in her breath and stepped back. She didn't know where they were from or where they were going and she didn't want to find out.

"Your powers will prevent you from being sucked into a portal," Ghury said.

"Powers?" she said.

"They are there, inside you, waiting to be used. You will know when the time is right," he said. "Try now."

D'laine waved her arm in front of her.

Nothing.

Ghury tapped her forehead. "Concentrate."

D'laine tried again. Her brows furrowed in concentration. A minor disturbance appeared in front of her; a different place appeared.

"I did it!" she gurgled in amazement and stared as the visual slowly dissipated and the portal closed. Looking through a gypsy's crystal ball would be the only true comparison.

Ghury sighed with relief. "Progress."

"Ghury, do you think these powers can heal my brother?"

"Healing is only one of the many great accomplishments you can achieve if you put your mind to work," he said. He tapped her forehead. "It's all in there."

In an instant, she knew that her being there on Thol was no accident. Whether she picked up a stray thought from Ghury or the sentry, she couldn't tell. But, she did know that destiny's road had been clearly paved when she stood at the open minivan on the smoldering parking lot, when the clouds sucked her up and dumped her on Thol's turf. She wanted the missing puzzle pieces of exactly why she was here.

D'LAINE PRACTICED EVERY DAY AT HER HEAPED STONES and crystals in the field, waving her arm slowly, expecting something—anything—to appear. Even though she took baby side steps to find the precise place to stand, and tried waving her arm within inches of the previous place—nothing. She concentrated so hard she gave herself a headache. There was nothing she wanted more than to see something familiar appear before her. After several unsuccessful days, D'laine sat beside her rock pile, her chin in her hands, disgusted with herself.

"What am I doing wrong? Why am I so drained?" she said.

She stood. She pulled in a deep breath, closed her eyes, released the tension and just let herself be. After a moment, she waved her arm in front of her. When she opened her eyes, a foggy mist appeared in front of her. No creatures were present, but she could not see through the mist. She was shocked and amazed.

"Oh my god! I did it!" Her face practically cracked from her huge smile. She didn't see the white form rushing toward her as she took a step forward. "Brian, Jamie... daddy—I'm coming home!"

The roaring in her ears drowned out the warning call behind her. She disappeared into toxic vapors.

The world she stepped into wasn't Earth. An intense heat radiated from the red skies to the pits of boiling, molten rocks all around her. She clutched her throat and couldn't catch her breath. Her skin started to blister, her tongue swelled and her eyes bulged in their sockets. She turned, waving her arms frantically searching for the doorway.

A large white shape appeared beside her. She reached out to the illusion as her knees buckled. Ghury enfolded her in his arms and stepped back into Thol.

D'laine struggled to breathe as Ghury laid her on the ground. The skin on her forehead, cheeks and chin had burnt and peeled in huge patches. Any area of her body that was unprotected by her suit had started to fry. The tips of her hair were singed and smelled burnt.

In between coughing and gasping for more air, the hysterics built until all she could do was cry.

"You're not quite prepared for these journeys," Ghury said.

"I thought it was just foggy. I'll never do that again," she croaked out.

"An ammonia nitrate atmosphere. Not likely to sustain life for more than thirty seconds," he said. "Shall I help you practice?"

"I think I've had enough for one day, thanks," D'laine proclaimed in a raspy voice. She was totally drained of energy.

WEEKS PASSED INTO MONTHS. MANY THINGS WERE taught to her, and she used more of her mind than she thought was possible. D'laine spent every day with her mentors practicing her survival skills, learning all she could about the terrain of the Cember Forest and beyond. She had success and failures with physical tasks, like lighting fires with the stones, some healing techniques, and identifying birds and animals.

A grophie caterpillar stung her and she suffered purple spots and insane itching until Adrum showed her how to make the antidote. It tasted horrible, but she drank it down. D'laine struggled not to scratch her arms, head and face until the potion kicked in and stopped the itchy, crawling feeling.

All the while through her training, she had dealt with the guilt of her family and friends left behind. Through all the lessons she had learned over the months, nothing alleviated the pain she felt in not being able to get home.

Ghury and D'laine sat at the table in Ghury's mushroom house.

"Do you think I'm ready to go on a short journey?" she asked.

"The mother bird never pushes the chick from the nest until she knows the chick is prepared," Ghury said. "I think you are ready to fly, don't you?"

D'laine's face lit up with a wide smile. She stood and exited the mushroom house. She walked through the forest to the pond and sat on the moss at the pond's edge. Tomorrow she would be going out on her own, the ultimate test. The quokin bobbed to the surface. It approached the edge and stared at her. She reached her hand out to the creature. It rubbed its face against her fingertips. Then it turned and dove below the surface. She felt peaceful once again.

A borjo buzzed into her view and landed on a flat black rock at the edge of the pond. A warrior jumped down, removed his helmet and D'laine recognized Herish.

"Hello, D'laine," Herish said. "I see the quokin likes to spend time with you."

"Yes, we are old friends," she said.

"You know what they say, don't you?" he asked.

"Yes, I have heard it before," she said, and laughed.

"A quokin's touch brings true love," Herish stated.

They were silent for a moment, both embarrassed at the folklore Herish brought up. He busied himself with the borjo reins while she stared across the pond.

"I'll be leaving here at sun's rise," she blurted out as she turned to face Herish.

"Leaving? Where will you go?" Herish asked. He seemed unsettled that she was leaving.

D'laine chuckled. "If this were the continent of Australia, back in the land where I come from, I would say I was going on a 'walk-about'. I'm going to do some exploring."

"How long will you be gone?" Herish asked.

"Not long," she said. "Most likely a couple of weeks."

"Be safe," Herish said. He hopped back on the borjo and they were gone in an instant.

"What the heck is wrong with him?" D'laine asked out loud.

When it was time to go to bed, she wondered if she would be able to sleep since she was excited about the forthcoming adventure. She could go anywhere now, feeling confident that she could take care of herself if danger presented itself.

Pulling secrets out of her mind, D'laine longed to see Ebscalon! She wanted to be near those people; they were so like her. As much as she had grown to love the Egroms, she needed to be among her own kind. Humans, who had a normal language and traits she could understand. There was another reason for wanting to go to the city, a reason that she refused to think about, but it kept surfacing and she couldn't keep it hidden.

The boy she had seen in the first lesson with Adrum; the very same one who had been in her nightmares for so long. Pushing him aside in her mind, he kept returning, disturbing her. There was an unknown bond between them that frightened her, and she didn't know why it existed and where it would take her. A couple of months ago she had mentally released Connor from the status as her boyfriend. It wasn't fair to keep him on hold. She hoped that he could release her and move on, to find another girlfriend without guilt.

Trying self-hypnosis, she told herself repeatedly that she mustn't think of her dream companion; she couldn't get involved with anyone here, least of all him. How could she be infatuated over this boy—she didn't even know him! This type of behavior and thinking was not like her at all. What was this world doing to her? She didn't know anything about his people. Were they even humans, she wondered? Then there was Herish. He was so handsome, but he was what—maybe four or five inches tall. If she kissed him, she'd most likely accidentally end up sucking his head into her mouth! The thought made her grimace.

Snuggling down in her bed, she pushed all thoughts aside so she could catch some sleep, wanting to be fresh in the morning—alert. That night D'laine slept deeply as if a burden had finally been lifted. The excitement of the adventure was too much for sleep to hold her for any length of time though, and the dreams hadn't helped either. She had drifted in and out of several skits centered around the mysterious Ciertron boy.

However, when morning arrived, she woke feeling refreshed and eager for the adventure to come. She was confident in her ability to survive. She was not uneasy, as she had been taught well. Adrum had shown her many movie lessons over the past few months which had expanded upon the complex training she experienced. The Egroms made sure that she could take care of herself.

She slipped a knife in her thigh pocket, gathered two lighting stones and her crystals in a pouch, along with a water flask, and slung them over her shoulder. At the last minute, she crossed the room, grabbed her dead phone out of her purse and shoved it in her pouch.

"What's the point?" D'laine asked herself. She shook her head.

She had her senses to protect her by knowing that if something were out of place she could detect it and take action, as well as a great deal of common sense to guide her. Initially, her plan was to leave before the morning meal; she felt that she could be self-sufficient and get her own fare on her journey.

She took a moment to look around her house; she stared at her purse in the corner, near the nest, then exited the hut without a backward glance.

# CHAPTER TWENTY-FOUR

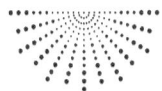

*T*he phone rang as Lee removed the thermometer from Brian's ear. Rosa walked into the dining room, where Brian rested in bed, with her hand over the mouthpiece of the portable house phone.

"It's the Houston newspaper," she whispered.

Lee blew out a puff of air as he reached for the phone and hurried out of the room. He headed to his home office and shut the door. "Lee Jackson."

He listened. "I don't know what the point would be, you know everything I do." He listened some more, contemplated then made a decision. "Okay. I'll agree to an interview, but no cameras. My family can't be disturbed any more than we already have been."

The call ended with "Two o'clock tomorrow, then."

Al Jordan arrived promptly at Lee's house at 2:00, alone. Rosa answered the door, looked him over and invited him inside. She escorted him to Lee's office, tapped on the opened doorframe and waved him in.

Lee sat at his desk, his laptop open. He closed the lid as Al entered the office. He stood and stretched his hand across the desk.

"Thank you for taking the time to see me, Mr. Jackson," Al said. "I know this is a trying time for you and your family, so I will try to be as brief as possible. If I overstay my appointment, just tell me to leave."

"That sounds fair. Have a seat," Lee said.

Al sat, pulled a lined tablet and pen out of his soft bag and crossed his legs. Rosa came to the doorway.

"Can I get you some iced tea?" She looked from Al to Lee.

"That would be great, Rosa," Lee said. "Tea, Al?"

"I never refuse iced tea! Thanks." He turned his focus to Lee. "Would you be okay with me recording this? I don't write that fast and I can't remember everything." He removed a recorder the size of a thumb drive out of his bag and held it up to show Lee.

"Huh," Lee said. "I've never seen a recorder that small before."

"This is the best tool I've ever owned, aside from my laptop," Al said. He demonstrated. "You remove this end cap and stick the USB into your computer and upload the wave file. Then all I have to do is listen and transcribe the interview."

"I can see where that would be handy in your line of work. Sure, I don't mind," Lee said.

Rosa entered and set two cork coasters then two glasses of tea on the desk.

"Thank you," Al and Lee said.

Al slid the switch on the recorder. He spoke into the device. "This is an interview with Lee Jackson regarding the disappearance of his daughter, D'laine." Al placed the recorder on the edge of Lee's desk. He took a sip of tea.

"I recently spoke with Dr. Ben Joplin over at Rice University about this incident. Dr. Joplin is with the physics department and he's brought in a couple of scientists from Whitting Institute out in California to help with the investigation," Al said.

"I figured since you worked at NASA, maybe you had some inkling of what really happened," Al said. He watched Lee, trying to see if there were any flinching or other almost invisible facial tics he could read.

Lee tented his fingers. "Everyone seems to think if you work at NASA, you know where the spaceships and aliens are hiding. That's all wishful thinking, Al. I'm in the mechanical field – rocket propulsion, things like that."

"But surely, you've read about Many Worlds Interpretation, worm holes and those types of things?" Al asked, almost pleading.

"What are you getting at?" Lee asked.

"Just look at the circumstances, Mr. Jackson," Al said. "I watched that kid's video fifty times and it's like your daughter was rolled out in the fog. To me that adds up to her going through a worm hole, or a portal to another world!"

Lee stared at the overexcited reporter in front of him. He huffed out a sigh. "I won't lie to you, Al. Those things have crossed my mind. I just don't know what to do about it. It's not like I can go there and bring her back when I don't know where "there" is, or even how to get there."

# CHAPTER TWENTY-FIVE

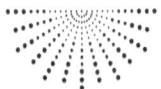

*S*tarting out toward the pool to wash, D'laine planned to fill the flask at the cold spring nearby and catch a meal of roots that were similar to sweet turnips enjoyed by the Egroms, and berries that were a cross between blueberries and blackberries. She promised herself that she would gather some to store in the pouch so she wouldn't have to make as many stops to eat.

After she finished cleaning up, she walked to the spring and filled her flask then she returned to the Egrom village. D'laine joined the Elders at the breakfast fire. Nods were exchanged.

"You are prepared?" Adrum asked.

"Yes," she said.

"Remember to look inside for the answers," Ghury said.

"I will," D'laine said.

Ghury held up one hand. D'laine placed her hand against his, and then grabbed him in a hug.

"Thank you for taking care of me," she said. "I know it wasn't easy because I was so stressed out." She blushed at the memories of her first week. Then she turned and left the elders, and the village behind.

The elders studied each other.

"Human affection is a very confusing emotion," Drusta said.

The Egroms nodded.

IN THE SOLITUDE OF HER TRAVELS, HER THOUGHTS WENT back to Brian, Jamie and her father, the accident that stole her mother from them, and conjured up a boy who had followed her through torturous dreams. He was a fantasy young man that any young girl would want, with an animal fierceness; you knew he could take care of himself with physical force alone just by his stance. Through all those nightmares he had been her faithful dream visitor. What shocked her was that she now knew he was real, and close by, and in some way, her life was linked to his.

The first week of living on Thol she thought for sure she was back in a coma and had traveled to this land in mind only. But she knew that her normal dreams were never like this. Keen senses told her that she was not lost in her mind, that this was happening in real time and her life was mapped out on a plat. She couldn't even guess how this had come to be, but she knew it was a force beyond her knowledge.

She was sure her father was trying to dissect the event, but what could he do? Without the portal alignment between the two worlds, neither side could move an inch.

Now, as she walked, she heard chirping and clicking noises as she passed Egrom sentries. Having learned the language through the translator and then Adrum's teaching, she responded to each in return.

"Have a safe journey," an Egrom called.

"Be safe while you protect Thol," she responded.

She had a special place in her heart for them. They were sensitive, intelligent and held powers that would make anyone from her Earth reel in shock at what they could do.

A few weeks back, D'laine had talked with Ghury about her body's rejuvenating process. The only information he told her was that she had the power to do many things, mostly unknown to her, but with time she would learn them all. It irritated her sometimes when he talked in riddles, giving part of the answer and leaving her to guess the rest. Everything was a mystery for her to eventually unravel and find the answers on her own.

As she trekked across the moss, a dozen borjos swarmed overhead then hovered in front of her. Herish and his platoon fisted their chests in greeting.

"Hello, D'laine," he said. "How is your journey?"

"Hi Herish. What are you and your team doing out here?" she asked.

"Just checking the outer perimeters of the Cember Forest," he said.

D'laine turned and looked back. The forest was far behind her. "Seems a little out of the way, don't you think?"

Herish's face turned red. There were some jostling and rude comments from his platoon. He looked over his shoulder and scowled at them.

"I just wanted to make sure you were okay," he admitted.

"Commander, we should get back to our patrol," one warrior said.

D'laine smiled, keeping her laughter in check. "You'd better go. I'm quite okay on my own."

Herish scowled. He and his platoon took off toward the forest.

D'laine giggled.

As the two suns set on her first day of travel, D'laine stopped at a small oasis. She pulled a sheet of gauze material from her pack and spread it in a protective curve at the base of a gigantic agrin tree. She placed her back against the tree, slid her knife within hands reach and drew the gauze over her. Sleep overtook her instantly.

She awoke to another brilliant day. After she folded the gauze sheet and placed it in her pack, she refilled her flask at the pond and then sank to the moss-covered ground. D'laine rummaged in her pack and pulled out two crystals. She crossed her legs and rested her hands on her knees so that the crystals were exposed to the bright sunlight. She inhaled deeply and closed her eyes.

"I pray to the Spirit and the Universe for they are one. I pray for inner peace and guidance. I pray to be reunited with my family." She sat quietly, picturing her father in her mind. "Daddy, I miss you so much. I'm okay, but I want to come home."

She took a deep breath and focused her intention. She repeated this for Brenda and Rachel. She did not include Connor. She thought that would be cruel.

After an hour in silent meditation, she opened her eyes and stretched her arms over her head, refreshed. She stood and performed yoga stretches.

Lee swung his legs out of the bed. A thought, loud and clear, popped into his head and he heard D'laine's voice as if she had called on her cellphone.

"D'laine! Are you there? Can you hear me? How can I help you get home?"

He waited and waited, but all he retrieved was stony silence. He sat in shock for a minute, not sure what to do. His cellphone rang.

"D'laine?" he asked in a panicky voice.

Brenda was crying hysterically, trying to explain her message from D'laine. Then Rachel called.

A WEEK OF UNEVENTFUL DAYS HAD ELAPSED, SPENT IN leisurely walking across the sponge, taking in the beauty of the land. D'laine had covered miles and miles and had come to an area where the sponge was changing from the bluish silver to a deep purple hue.

"Look at this color," D'laine said. She squatted and brushed her hand across the ground cover. "I wish my phone worked. This is one picture I'd like to have."

Furry hosks were abundant and she enjoyed watching them scurrying in circles, coming and going. Choosing a vacant spot to sit for a rest, she scooped up a male hosk, sat him in her lap and grabbed a handful of the sponge for him to munch. They were soft cuddly creatures who didn't mind the attention as long as they had food. It had been quite some time since she had heard any of the Egroms, so she decided she must be out of Ghury's district. She wondered if she would come across another village of Egroms soon and if they would contact her.

Forming a list in her mind, she wanted to see the desert, the mountains, and the Valley of the Wailing Winds that she had seen in her lessons. She wanted to experience as much as she could because one day, the portal with her world would align and she would have decisions to make.

Difficult decisions.

The serenity was broken by piercing squeals on both sides

of her in the far distance, approaching quickly. Jumping to her feet, she dropped the hosk to the ground. The noise was getting closer and she recognized the source.

Diwal dogs!

Scanning the area, she knew that she had to find shelter quickly. They were fierce beasts the size of a Rottweiler, gray with long snouts. Their four powerful legs ended on armadillo-type feet with thick, strong claws that churned up the ground as they swiftly sprinted across the moss. The only hair on their bodies was in the form of little tufts on their cheeks and the top of their heads. The rest of their body was as smooth as a snake, with a tail barbed on the end, like the Plotals. She spotted two of them; she then heard another approaching from behind.

Without a plan, she ran at a speed that amazed her. Running seemed to be the only defense, but she knew she could never outrun them to reach the forest at least a mile away. Carnivorous, diwals stripped their prey to the bone in minutes, as if they were land piranhas. She was losing distance fast.

With the creature's only a hundred yards away and bounding toward their next meal, her heart pounded furiously. She tripped and thought she was done for, but she jumped to her feet, turned to face them and thought of Ghury's parting statement.

*You can do anything with your mind. It is the most powerful tool that you possess and you must learn to use it; trust your judgment and instinct.*

Concentrating, she touched her temples with shaking fingers. She focused all of her will while she held one hand out in front of her, palm facing outward.

"STOP!" she commanded, using The Voice. She held onto her focus tightly.

The diwals stopped dead in their tracks as if someone had

yanked them to a standstill. D'laine turned her hand, palm down, and lowered it a foot. "*DOWN!*"

The diwals dropped to their bellies.

She stared at the dogs in amazement. "Holy mackerel! This is something else!"

The pack alpha inched forward on its belly.

"What do you think you're doing?" she asked in a normal voice.

The diwal stopped and stared at D'laine. She stared it down, and then made a decision. "You, come here," she said.

The pack alpha stood and trotted to her, head down, submissive.

"*SIT.*" She posed her hand as a slant.

The dog sat.

The other two diwals' teeth chattered threateningly, but they didn't move. D'laine pointed at them. "Stop that right now!"

They retracted their triple-layered teeth and sat, eyes darting from their pack leader to D'laine.

She reached out and scratched the tufts of hair on the pack alpha's head. Its legs gave out and it collapsed to the ground.

"Wow! I'll bet you've never been touched by human hands, have you? You probably don't know how love can transform you, do you?"

She continued to scratch the tufts of hair and then scratched under its chin. Its teeth made a low chattering sound that seemed to relay its pleasure.

"Can I trust you guys not to attack me?"

She stood. The diwals stood. The alpha approached and sniffed her. She patted its rump. "How about if I call you Pup?"

Pup wagged his tail.

D'laine bent down and looked at the underside of the other two diwals trying to determine gender. She pointed to each as she named them. "I'll call you Scooby, and you're Chatter because you just won't quit with those teeth." As if on cue, Chatter clacked his teeth at her.

"Do you want to come with me on my journey? I could use the company." She trotted off. Looking over her shoulder. "Pup, Scooby, Chatter—come!"

She urged them forward with a wave of her hand. They bounded forward and ran with her across the field, Pup, the alpha, at her side.

D'laine was exhilarated running with the diwals. They had a bad reputation and she was convinced that with human companionship and love, they could be pretty close to regular domestic dogs.

Time crept by. Uncertain as to how long they had been traveling, she shaded her eyes with one hand and glanced up at the sky to check the position of the two suns.

"Maybe an hour or more of daylight? What do you guys think?" she said as she glanced at the dogs.

They wagged their tails.

Off in the distance, she saw a glimmer of water and a copse of trees.

"Come on. Let's go to that oasis. We can have a rest in the shade," she said. She headed in that direction with the dogs romping at her sides.

# CHAPTER TWENTY-SIX

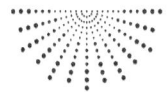

*a*s they approached the oasis, D'laine stared in awe at the water. It was a huge lake. She couldn't even see the far shoreline. The spongy moss and the sparkling sand met several feet from the water's edge. The turquoise water and the shore coral were an invitation not to be denied. D'laine deposited all her belongings, with the exception of her hip pouch that contained her large crystal, under a tree and flopped down. She patted the moss.

"Come on. It's time for rest and relaxation."

Pup, Scooby and Chatter sat down around her. She took turns patting them, scratching their heads and chins, and rubbing their bellies. Taking a drink from her water sack she relaxed in the moment. Chatter's teeth clacked up a storm.

"You're a talkative little doggie, aren't you," she said as she patted the top of his head.

That's when she saw a crestrider in the distance. Within minutes it whizzed past her overhead. D'laine jumped to her feet and headed to an open area. She waved. She recognized it as a one-man flyer from Adrum's teachings. She was amazed as she tracked its path in the sky.

"Oh, wow! What technology! If daddy could only see this!"

The aircraft circled the oasis, causing the diwals to jump to their feet. They stayed by D'laine in a protective cluster, barking up at the ship. Then, just like a helicopter, the crestrider hovered overhead, but unlike the helicopter, it only made a soft purring noise that was hardly noticeable and without the whipping wind.

Trakon leaned over the side of the ship. He took in the scene, shocked at what he saw. A young woman in warrior's clothes. Her long, wavy hair like sunshine over her shoulders and down her back. The deadly diwal dogs at her side appeared tame. *How could that be?*

Looking up at the amazing ship, D'laine saw an escalator staircase unfold toward the ground. The pilot started to descend the stairs when the ship sputtered. He ran back up to the controls. The command panel was flashing every known warning light and dials spun out of control.

"Not now!" Trakon could not contain his annoyance as the ship failed. He pressed a button on the control panel.

"Engage!" he said firmly.

Nothing happened. He ran to one of the solar collectors and kicked the side panel. The ship sputtered. Power returned momentarily and the ship wobbly rose several feet.

D'laine moved back toward the trees, coaxing the dogs to follow her. The ship appeared to stabilize as it rose higher, then it flew in a wide circle. As it approached the oasis from behind the trees it sputtered and dropped several feet, then fizzled out completely.

"Oh no!" she squealed.

D'laine and the dogs ran from the shelter of the trees to the water's edge. She waved her arms frantically trying to direct the pilot.

"The trees! Get away from the trees!"

The ship hurtled through the trees and crash landed, skidding through moss and sand until it halted a foot from the water.

D'laine ran toward the ship. "Hello? Hello? Are you okay?"

She grabbed the edge of the wing and hauled herself up. She carefully walked over the layered crystals, feeling tiny stings and shocks through her boots. "Yikes! Yikes!"

D'laine jumped down to the deck and saw the man on the floor, out cold. She approached him, threw her hand over her heart and sucked in her breath.

"My dream prince!"

She was rooted to the spot as she stared at him, her mind racing with ten thousand thoughts all jumbled together. It was one thing to see him so clearly in her dreams, and even in Adrum's projections in her head. It was nearly shattering to her heart to have him in front of her, hurt and out cold.

D'laine came out of her fog and observed his physical damage. There was an angry red spot and growing bump on his forehead where he must have smashed his head when the ship crashed. She noticed a spot of blood on the deck near his head.

She kneeled at his side and carefully lifted his head. She ran one hand across the back of his head; when she drew her hand back it was covered with blood.

"Oh, no!"

Scratching, scraping and grunts were coming from the ground. D'laine rushed over to the edge of the ship and looked down. Pup and his pack were jumping at the ship, wanting to get onboard.

"No! Go lie down!"

The dogs whined up at her.

"Pup, not now. Go hunt or play." She pointed away from the ship and watched as the dogs trotted away.

D'laine leaned against the railing as her mind whirled. She was shocked and amazed at being within several feet of the one person who troubled her dreams for so long. It seemed easier to accept the Egroms and that part of her journey to Thol. This new development had her teetering on the brink of questioning not just her beliefs, but physics, and science in general as she had come to understand its principles through her studies, as well as metaphysics and more esoteric beliefs.

This man in front of her was real. Her heart hammered in her chest and blood rushed in her ears.

"It's real. It's all so real. How can this be?" D'laine's thoughts spun out of control.

D'laine crossed the floor of the ship and sank to her knees beside the man. "What do I do? I don't know what to do."

She opened the pouch at her hip and dug out her crystal. She stared at the crystal in her hands while the litany of Ghury's words blasted through her brain. "Here goes, Ghury. Trial by fire."

D'laine took a deep breath. She clutched the crystal in her left hand and placed her right hand on the bump on the man's forehead. She closed her eyes and whispered. "Spirit. Universe. Guides and Angels. Help me heal this man."

She felt a transference of heat and energy jump from the crystal to her right hand. It tingled against his skin. And then the tingling stopped. She removed her hand, opened her eyes and the bump was gone.

"It worked! I can heal!" she exclaimed.

He groaned and moved his head slightly. His eyes opened and found her face. He sucked in a loud breath then his face transformed into disbelief.

"You!" he exclaimed. He muttered a strangled "wha...?"

and his face went through several displays of astonishment as he stared back at her.

His mind reeled. The girl in his dreams was right beside him. She was real. He couldn't make any sense of it. *This is impossible*, he thought.

"You have a head injury," D'laine explained. "I healed the bruise on your forehead, but you have a gash that's bleeding on the back of your head that I need to take care of. Can you sit up?"

Trakon could not take his eyes off her face. "I think so."

D'laine helped him sit up. "Are you dizzy?"

He shook his head then grabbed his head. "Yes, I guess I am."

"Just sit here for a minute. I'm going to look at your injury." She parted his hair where it was wet with blood. "You have a nasty gash. Sit still and I'll work on it."

Trakon pointed. "If you open that panel I have a sonicate box and a light healer."

"I won't need your tools," she said. She showed him her crystal. "This is what I use. It's different than the crystals on your ship."

"If you say so," he said somewhat sarcastically. "How does that work? What do you do?"

"If you'd stay still and be quiet, I will heal you!" She grasped the crystal and placed her right hand on the back of his head. She closed her eyes and she felt the energy building. It felt as if the blood was moving through his hair and going back into his wound.

"What are you doing to me?" Trakon jerked his head away and grabbed the back of his head.

D'laine growled in anger. "Stop it! Sit still so I can finish the process."

"It feels strange, like... like something was moving through my hair," he stammered.

"It was. I was restoring you," D'laine said, using Ghury's words. "Now let me finish!"

She gathered herself together, breathed in a couple of deep breaths and placed her hand back on his head. The energy jumped through her fingers and the flesh on his head knitted back together. Once the tingling stopped she removed her hands. If it weren't for the blood on the deck, no one would ever know he had been injured.

Trakon stood up. He poked the back of his head several times then he looked down and spotted the blood on the deck. "That must have been some head banger."

He rubbed the back of his head again, allowing himself to accept what just occurred.

"What are you doing out here by yourself?" Trakon asked.

D'laine snorted. "I might ask you the same thing. You're quite a way from Ebscalon."

"You know my city?" Trakon asked, confused.

D'laine shrugged. "I've never been there, but I've seen pictures."

Trakon stared at her, perplexed. "Pictures?" He shook his head. "Where do you come from? There's nothing around here for miles and miles as far as I know."

"I'm from a small village five days away in the Cember Forest," D'laine said.

"A village? Who are your people?" Trakon asked. "We haven't charted any villages out there."

"The Egroms are my adoptive family."

"Egroms? They've either been extinct for centuries, or are most likely the folklore of our primitive relatives." Trakon snorted, shaking his head. He looked at her skeptically.

"Maybe you should tell Ghury that because they are very

much alive and well," she snipped. "If they hadn't cared for me I would never have survived on my own. They are private creatures with a great responsibility."

Trakon gave a little snort and a shake of his head.

"Who is this Ghury?" Trakon asked.

"He's the Egrom leader, an elder."

Trakon stared at her silently, keeping his face arranged in a passive mode.

"What's your name?" she asked.

He tilted his head slightly then shook off his confusion from her comments. He stood a little taller. "I am Trakon, son of Jor-Dan and Kitry, the rulers of Ebscalon."

"You're a prince?" D'laine asked, in awe. She held out her hand to him.

Trakon grasped her forearm. She awkwardly grasped his forearm and they stood in an uncomfortable, momentary silence.

Following his lead, she straightened her shoulders and announced, "I am D'laine Jackson, daughter of Lee, the celebrated scientist of NASA, and Lori, nice to meet you." Her face clouded. "My mother passed on."

She stepped away from him but kept him in her line of sight, incredulous that he was there, in the flesh, not in the dream.

Trakon observed her somber mood change. "You are young to be without your mother. Was her death due to war?"

D'laine was startled by his question. "War? No... no, she was killed in an automobile accident."

She saw his brows raise in question. She tapped a finger against her lip. "Automobiles are a mechanical version of your ship, but they have round tires and roll on the ground on paved roadways and highways."

"Why would you want to roll on the ground? The air is a

much more efficient means of travel. Those roadways must require maintenance. We only have to keep a vigilant eye out for buildings, flying creatures and tall trees that the sensors may not pick up. How many of these automobiles travel along your roadways and highways?"

"Millions," D'laine explained knowing how ridiculous it sounded.

"I can't understand how you get anywhere with all those automobiles," Trakon said, dismayed.

"Exactly!" D'laine said. "Our roadways are so clogged with traffic. If a car breaks down, or if there is an accident, traffic is backed up for hours because people are stuck in their vehicles on the road in back of whatever happened. And the roads themselves are a hazard with pot holes that cause problems, like flat tires."

Trakon shook his head, mystified. He went to the ship's controls and pressed several buttons. "Commander one, come in." He bent and listened. "Commander one, this is a distress call."

Trakon pressed a small button on his wrist band. D'laine watched and looked at her own wrist and saw a button in the same place on her cuff.

"Commander one—can you hear me? My ship is disabled. Tracking is on."

"Will they send someone?" D'laine asked.

"If they pick up the signal. The crystal collectors shouldn't have drained so quickly, it's still sunny outside. I'm not sure if there's enough juice for the tracking signal." He looked over the side of the ship to the ground. "I'd better check for damage."

Trakon jumped to the ground.

D'laine followed.

The dogs rushed from the trees, their teeth clacking to mesmerize their new prey.

Trakon pulled his laser pistol from the holster on his hip. D'laine grabbed his hand before he could pull the trigger.

"Down!" D'laine commanded the diwal dogs with The Voice and one hand outstretched.

The dogs dropped to their bellies, their heads dipped low.

"How did you tame these savage beasts?" Trakon asked, shocked. He kept his distance, his laser pistol at the ready, and all of his focus on the dogs.

"Uh... animals like me," D'laine stammered. "You need to let them scent you so you're accepted."

Trakon balked. He took a step backwards. "You do know they can strip your flesh to the bone in minutes, right?"

"Not when they're with me. Stay very still." She motioned the dogs forward. "Come."

Pup led his pack forward. Chatter's teeth clacked riotously.

"Hold your hand out," D'laine said.

Trakon's face went through several changes. D'laine grabbed his hand and held it so Pup and the dogs could sniff him. She tapped Chatter's nose. "Stop that racket!"

Chatter's head dipped and he quieted his teeth as he sniffed Trakon. He gave him a little lick.

D'laine thought Trakon was going to faint at Chatter's little display of acceptance. "See how easy that was. You're no longer considered a meal."

Trakon scowled. It wasn't easy to be one-upped by a woman. "Where were you going out here all by yourself... with the dogs?"

"I wasn't going anywhere in particular. This was my first journey out alone—a test of my survival skills," D'laine said. She cleared her throat. "What are you doing out here?"

"Testing the GSB and crystal collectors from an upgrade and trying to see if there are problems," Trakon explained.

"What's a GSB?" she asked.

"Gravitational Synchronizing Beam. It works with the crystal collectors," he explained.

"Did the GSB fail?" D'laine asked.

Trakon shrugged. "Seemed to be running smooth until I arrived here." Trakon spread his arms to the wide-open spaces. "I'm not sure what happened, but the controls just stopped working."

"I thought you just upgraded. Did you go through QA/QC and test runs?" D'laine asked

"The collectors appear to be drained," Trakon said. "What is that Q thing? We did several test runs. Everything went smooth."

"Quality Assurance and Quality Control," D'laine said. "You don't have a back-up battery?"

"No," Trakon said through clenched teeth. "My mother warned me to have a backup. I'll never hear the end of this."

D'laine smirked. It didn't make any difference what world she was on, mothers seemed to get their point across one way or the other.

Trakon and D'laine walked around the entire ship. The nose of the aircraft was buried in at least six feet of moss and sand where it skidded to a stop.

D'laine bit her lip. "I may have caused the power failure."

"What do you mean?" Trakon asked, squinting.

D'laine walked over to the wing that was tilted low, due to the ship being encased in the moss and sand. "Remember I told you my crystal is different from yours? My crystal is called a quartz crystal, from my Earth. I don't know what yours are, but they are opposing forces."

She stretched her hand several inches above the crystal-ladened wing. Trakon watched as she lowered her hand, inch by inch. When her hand was about ten inches over the crystals, sparks rapid-fired in all directions.

"I'm not sure how I could cause you to crash since you were so high in the sky, but I know it has something to do with me and some sort of energy field," D'laine said.

Trakon looked to the horizon. Only one sun was in the sky. "We need to build a fire before sunsfall."

They gathered firewood in silence and D'laine expertly made a fire while Trakon circled the disabled ship, a scowl on his face.

Hidden from her direct view, Trakon tracked where she sat stoking the fire. Questions kept speeding through his mind. He wanted to run his fingers through her golden wavy hair that cascaded almost to her waist. He had never seen golden tanned skin. It looked so soft and smooth, free of any blemishes.

Because of her skin and hair coloring, he knew that she was not one of his people, nor was she of any other race of Thol that he was familiar with. Putting the confusing thoughts aside, Trakon shook his head so he could focus on the problem at hand, but quickly realized it was futile.

Darkness shrouded them like ink, with only a flicker of light from the fire. Trakon gave up at the ship and joined D'laine by the fire.

"I can't do anything until morning," he grumbled.

"At least we have water and a fire," she said.

Trakon thought for a moment. "Would you like to visit my city?" Trakon asked.

"Yes. Ebscalon is on my list to see," D'laine said.

He looked at the dogs. "Are they coming with you?"

She glanced affectionately at the pack. "No, they belong in the wild. People aren't ready to believe they can be wonderful companions."

"We may have to devise some type of shield between you and the power source," Trakon said.

They shared the offerings from their pouches. D'laine

longed for a bath in the pond. She was much too aware of her companion; he was hard to ignore. Their eyes kept meeting, each looking swiftly away in embarrassment, as if they each knew the thoughts that passed about the other. As the moments crept by, she found it difficult to keep the barrier up in her mind, and her private thoughts to herself.

Discovering his barrier, she knew that he was keeping his feelings guarded, as she could not read any thoughts from him. Her brain was in overdrive.

*Why was he here in this time, in this place?*

*Why not on Earth?*

*What do I know of him as a person, of his life or his way of living?*

*Did he have a girlfriend back in his city?*

*Did he feel the magnetism drawing them to each other?*

D'laine had a revelation: she and Trakon seemed to be the pieces of a mysterious puzzle that fit neatly into place, waiting for the whole picture to be formed. The thought alarmed her.

# CHAPTER TWENTY-SEVEN

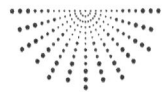

The buzzing of the alarm jarred Stanley awake. The strange room jolted his senses into gear, clearing the cobwebs out of his head. He bashed the button and stopped the annoying noise. He felt around and grabbed his glasses off the bedside table and looked at the clock. He sprung out of the bed.

"Victor! Victor, wake up. It's 8:00, Dr. Joplin will be here in an hour," Stanley called across the hall.

No answer.

Stanley smiled mischievously. He grabbed his duffel bag and proceeded to dump the contents on the messy bed. Amid the pile of wrinkled clothing, his trumpet tumbled out of the bag. He grabbed the instrument and tiptoed across the hall to the side of Victor's bed. He blasted one long note.

Victor jumped.

"Okay! Just give me five more minutes," Victor slurred, as he buried his head under the pillow.

A knock sounded on the door, and Stanley, in superhero pajamas, opened it to find Dr. Joplin holding up a bag as he stood on the doorstep.

"We're running a little late," Stanley explained as he swept his hands toward his pajamas.

"No, I'm early. I forgot what time I said I'd be by, and I figured you could use some breakfast," Dr. Joplin apologized.

Victor staggered past, on the way to the bathroom and raised his hand in greeting.

Dr. Joplin and Stanley chuckled.

"He's not a morning person," Stanley said.

By nine o'clock they poured into the car. Dr. Joplin explained that they would have a car at their disposal and an up-to-date map of the city in addition to GPS so they could easily find their way around. At the lab, they gathered up equipment and headed out to the SUV to go to the site to begin uncovering facts.

Well prepared, Victor's gear included his iPhone, a clipboard, paper, pens, and a calculator. He always used the voice recorder function which helped keep track of Stanley's thoughts, but the hands-on jotting notes was his backup system. He had learned from experience about mechanical failures.

Stanley, on the other hand, supervised the handling of the camera and other pieces of scientific equipment needed for the expedition. They had a discussion before they left for the site.

"Make sure you pack a microphone we can clip to Stanley," Victor said. "He typically does a lot of pacing and spouting off data. We have to capture his thoughts because I don't know anyone who can keep up with him, and we don't want to lose this information. You'll see."

Mark grabbed the required equipment and stuffed it in his pants pocket. "All set. We've got a good system."

The group piled into the SUV after storing the equipment in the back. Dr. Joplin chauffeured Stanley, Victor, and Mark, one of the techs, through the busy streets, avoiding heavily congested areas. The secret was to take the West Park Toll

Road to Grand Parkway until they arrived at I-10. They made it to the site just under an hour and discovered that the place was relatively quiet for ten thirty in the morning.

"Good thing it's not busy here right now," Victor said as he got out of the SUV.

"Give it another hour and the parking lot will be full with lunchtime shoppers," Dr. Joplin said.

"What's all that stuff?" Stanley asked as he approached the shrine to D'laine's disappearance.

Just like the shrine at Lee's house, this one contained dozens of items.

"We should contact Mr. Jackson," Stanley said. "He might want some of these cards and things."

"You're right. I'll contact him," Dr. Joplin said. "We'll have to move them out of the way."

"Why don't we just take them to him?" Victor asked. "Since we have to move them, let's just load them in the car."

"Yeah. We need to get those clothes, remember?" Stanley said.

They all pitched in and loaded the cards, candles, stuffed animals and flowers onto the floor of the third back seat area in the SUV.

"We'll have a little peace and quiet to make notes, look things over, get in a few shots, and take measurements before the crowd gathers at noon," Dr. Joplin said.

All that held the public out were four wooden barricades, and the flimsy plastic police tape. The security guard that was to be on duty was nowhere to be found. A short, stocky man got out of a car clutching a black metal oblong box. He rushed over to the group.

Dr. Joplin groaned. Mark snickered on the side. "It was bound to happen," Mark said, snorting a laugh.

"We're busy here, Dupree," Dr. Joplin said, anger flaring.

Dupree ignored Dr. Joplin and approached Stanley and Victor. "Clarence Dupree, inventor," he said in a strong Cajun accent.

Victor, Stanley and Dupree shook hands. Victor made the introductions. "Victor Bennett and Stanley Daigle from Whitting Institute out in California."

Stanley pointed to the box. "What's in the box?" Stanley asked.

"It's an invention of mine that you might find useful, even though some people don't seem to think so," Dupree said, looking haughtily at Dr. Joplin with accusing eyes.

"What's it do?" Stanley asked.

"It picks up spectral images," Dupree explained. "It's very accurate, I've tested it out at several locations with a high content of spectral activity."

"Oh," Stanley said, meekly. "We might need your help before our investigation is over, but right now, we're just going to make notes, take a few pictures and look around to see if there's any visible evidence."

This seemed to satisfy Dupree, who slapped his pockets and retrieved business cards that he handed to Stanley and Victor. They ended with a hearty handshake. The inventor snubbed Dr. Joplin and Mark, turned and left.

"Why did you tell that man we might need him?" Dr. Joplin asked, incredulous.

"It was a lot easier than telling him he was a nut-case. Has anyone checked out the box? What's it do?" Stanley asked, his curiosity getting the better of him.

"Mr. Dupree has a habit of dropping in at the lab on a regular basis with his wonderful boxes that come in all sizes, shapes and colors," Mark explained.

"Did you recognize the one he was carrying?" Victor asked.

"Oh yes. This particular box is an obsolete idea of a camera, nothing more. It was so crudely made, the man was lucky that it picked up anything, let alone spectral images," Dr. Joplin huffed.

"Who checked it out?" Stanley asked.

"Rod Tyson, one of our techs. He's a camera bug and knows everything there is to know about cameras, film, techniques—you name it," Dr. Joplin explained proudly.

"Yeah, but that's just a hobbyist. What about a real scientific investigation?" Stanley suggested. "Has anyone REALLY checked it out? You know it just may be useful under the right conditions."

"Well, no... ," Dr. Joplin said. "You've got a valid point. Rod is, after all, just a hobbyist as you pointed out. We all scoff at Dupree every time he comes around and I guess that's not fair. I'll have someone contact him when we get back."

Satisfied with the change of attitude toward the inventor, they got down to business.

"Let's set up here," Stanley directed Mark.

They uncrated the camera and equipment. Stanley scanned the area and then took pictures from every angle, even getting down on the ground, flat on his stomach, to scan again and take a couple of shots directly across the top of the graveled surface.

He scanned and took shots down into the center of the roped off area, several shots across the parking lot, and one shot of a landscaped green area in the same proximity.

"What are you doing? This isn't a study of flowers and shrubs, you know," Victor growled at Stanley.

"Look, mister know it all, these doorways may drift. We need to see if there are any variables, or "waves" within ten to twenty feet," Stanley sputtered angry words as he stood up to Victor. He continued scanning.

"Looks like a hot spot. Cooler to the left, tapering off to the right," Stanley said. The microphone clipped to his collar captured the information in the recorder in his pocket.

Mark measured the distance and scribbled notes.

"Can you detect any imagery?" Dr. Joplin asked.

"Nope, nothing. Just the change. Want to take a peek?" Stanley asked.

"Yeah. I've never had the opportunity to use one of these things," Dr. Joplin confessed. "I've only seen one at a trade show."

"Just like a video camera, except about a hundred twenty-five thousand dollars more," Stanley joked as he transferred the equipment to Dr. Joplin. "You ready?"

"Uh-huh," Dr. Joplin muttered.

"Okay, look through here and squeeze this trigger. If you see something you want to take a picture of, push this button," Stanley explained.

Dr. Joplin followed Stanley's instructions then looked through the lens.

"I see what you mean. I wonder what's there that we can't see?" Dr. Joplin asked.

"Could be anything. Could be what we're looking for or it might be a fluke," Victor said.

They finished their work, packed the equipment into the SUV and piled inside the vehicle. Back at the university, Stanley went directly to the computer lab to see what the camera had captured. The first thing he did was create a new folder titled "Jackson Disappearance." Then he flipped out the USB attachment on the camera and stuck it into a port on the computer. Within minutes, dozens of JPEG images were uploaded to the folder on the computer.

So far, he could see nothing out of the norm, but he had not finished looking over all of the pictures he uploaded. He noticed that the lower left corner was fuzzy in a couple of pictures. Checking the lens on the camera to see if it were smudged or had a fingerprint, he examined it closely and didn't find anything on the glass.

"Something's not right," he said to himself.

Taking another look at the picture, he found that it was not blurry in any other place, just that corner. He continued with his work and finished looking at each frame. The picture of the landscaping had a fuzzy area also.

"What in the world?" he said out loud as he studied the pictures closely.

The aura on the picture of the shrubs showed an emptiness that he couldn't describe. Leaving the lab, Stanley wandered around searching for Victor and Dr. Joplin. He saw Mark and hurried to catch up with him.

"Hey, have you seen Victor?" he asked.

"Yeah, he's in Dr. Joplin's office," Mark directed, pointing down the hall.

Stanley hurried down the hall to Dr. Joplin's office.

"Did you get something?" Victor asked, excited.

"Come and take a look and tell me what you think," Stanley suggested.

Putting their notes aside, the two men followed Stanley back to the computer lab.

"Hmm," Victor said, rubbing his chin.

Victor stared at the pictures and asked Stanley about both that showed the distortion.

Like a weakened dam, Stanley couldn't contain himself for a minute more, and burst out with explanations.

"I wanted to see if you thought they were unusual," he began. "They mean something, that's for sure. I've got to get back there and map out the exact location and look into the matter. I want to take more direct shots at both areas, compare the shots and see what shows up. It's all we've got to go on, but I think the aura means something. I can speculate about what it is, but I want more conclusive evidence," Stanley said in a sputter of excitement.

"I want to have Clovis run them through the computer. Oh, and let's take some pictures with the anti-negative filter," Dr. Joplin added.

Agreeing with Dr. Joplin's suggestions, Stanley applied the filter to the sensa-scan, grabbed a tape measure and note pad, and he and Mark headed out the door.

Dr. Joplin and Victor returned to Dr. Joplin's office.

"Has anyone asked the family or witnesses if we could get their clothes?" Victor asked.

"No, I'll contact them right away," Dr. Joplin said.

"I think maybe something will appear on the clothing since they had been so close to the event. I don't know what the aura means, but I do know that it's a significant finding," Victor stated.

STANLEY AND MARK WENT BACK OUT TO KATY MILLS Mall to take more pictures, measure distances and move the barricades around to make the area more accessible to his investigation.

Returning to the lab with his booty, Stanley came back scratching like a dog infested with fleas. Fire ants. A Houston hazard. Taking pity on him, Mark showed him where the first aid kit was and gave him a soothing cream to stop the nonstop itching. His work was too important to be interrupted by scratching every ten seconds while trying to get the pictures uploaded and studied. As Stanley removed his shoes and socks and pulled up a pant leg, he found an ant and squashed it.

The anti-negative filter showed just what he had expected. The distortion *was* something. It was solid and hollow at the same time. That meant it wasn't just a dirt spot on the camera lens. There was something there that human eyes could not detect. He wanted to experiment more. The picture from the site showed a large area surrounded by the aura.

He opened the computer lab door and hollered.

"Someone, call Dr. Joplin and Victor and tell them to come down here and look at the new pictures," he demanded.

Stanley slammed the door shut again. In less than five minutes, Dr. Joplin and Victor joined him.

"Stan, why don't you text me, or use this phone," Victor said as he pointed to the desk phone.

Dr. Joplin grabbed a sticky note pad and a fine point marker and wrote down his office extension and cell number. "Here you go."

Stanley looked at the note and the phone. "Oh, okay, will do."

The chilly room went deathly quiet while the scientists viewed the JPEGs from every available angle, then an excited chatter took over the calm in the room. Stanley was the first to talk.

"It's a wormhole. An entrance into a quantum world! See, it happens all the time; people are pulled through, that's why there are so many people on "vanished" lists," he stated.

Victor looked at Stanley and thought for a while.

"How do we know that's what it is? Why are there two spots?" Victor asked.

Stanley theorized on Victor's questions. "This one is just left over residue. Man, are we lucky that this thing drifted off! Evidently Miss Jackson went through the middle of it," Stanley explained. "It's a good thing she wasn't holding hands with her brothers or her father because they'd be right there with her."

Stanley gazed off into space, a romantic expression on his face. "Gee, I wonder where she is and what it's like there? I don't believe in that crap about mirror worlds. I think this place would be exotic."

# CHAPTER TWENTY-EIGHT

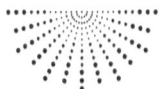

*M*orning came and D'laine awoke to find Trakon and the dogs gone and the fire burnt out. Alarmed, she jumped to her feet and looked around the campsite. The sponge still held his imprint, and the crestrider was still there, so he couldn't have gone far, she thought. Picking up the gauze that had covered her during the night, she headed over to the lake, the sunlight warm on her body.

A bounce in her step depicted her high spirits as she walked to the edge of the water. She bent down and tested the temperature of the lake with her hand. It was a little cooler than she would have liked for bathing, but pleasing to the touch. She wasn't going to hesitate since she hadn't had a chance to bathe the previous day.

Slipping out of her clothing, D'laine stepped into the water and let the coolness envelope her.

"I'd give anything for a bar of soap," she said.

She hurried with her bath, quickly got out of the water, wrapped herself in the gauze and went back to the camp to get dressed. Trakon still hadn't returned.

"Oh my God! I hope the dogs didn't kill him!" She almost had a complete meltdown thinking of the carnage.

D'laine placed her fingers at her temples to see if she could pick up any trace of him. There were no distant thoughts in the quiet of her mind.

Calling out to him telepathically didn't elicit a response either, but since she had not communicated with him telepathically yesterday, she didn't know if his people had that skill. Worried, she didn't know what to do. She paced frantically. She had no idea what direction he had taken, and decided to wait a little longer before she started searching for him.

In the next moment, she sensed someone approaching in the distance. She unsheathed her knife from her thigh. Looking hard, she couldn't tell if it was him, so she called out to him silently.

"Trakon?"

He responded tersely in her head. "I'm coming. I'm coming! Why are you mad?"

The dogs bounded into camp and greeted her with licks, clacking teeth and jumping, so similar to normal canines.

D'laine replaced her knife, patted each dog then faced Trakon and bristled. "Why didn't you answer me earlier? I was worried. We're out here in the middle of nowhere and you disappeared without a word."

A long silence followed. Then a meek response. "Oh. Sorry, I didn't think about it like that."

Seeing that he carried an animal about the size of a rabbit, she couldn't guess what it was.

Trakon held up the prize hoping to appease her after his blunder.

"Our morning meal," he exclaimed. "I was lucky to find a nest of sidels."

"I'm surprised the dogs let you catch that," D'laine said.

"They went off hunting, and when they returned I had to yell at them to keep away from our food. It was a very touchy moment." Trakon shivered.

She frowned. "I've never eaten any meat here. The Egroms eat only roots and vegetables that they use in soups and stews, and they eat a lot of berries," she told him as he approached the camp.

His eyes wandered over her body, caressing as they travelled along her curves. She held her breath as she took in his smoldering expression.

"The meat is quite tasty when it's cooked. I'm sure you'll like it," he said, noticing her damp hair. "Was the water warm enough to bathe in?"

She released her breath, his words breaking the tension between them.

"It's not really what I'm used to, but it will do for now," she said, her mind drifting to the warm springs that she had bathed in when she had lived with the Egroms.

"Would you make a fire while I prepare the meat?" Trakon took out his knife and began to skin the animal, a task that took only a few minutes. He cut the skin into three pieces and threw them to the dogs.

D'laine could tell that he was an accomplished hunter, and she was happy that he fed the dogs.

He walked towards the pool to wash the fresh game, the dogs on his heels. Trakon turned to the pack, pointed his finger away and yelled. "Go!"

Pup looked from Trakon to the game. Chatter clacked his teeth like castanets. Scooby sat and waited for instructions from his pack leader. After a short standoff, Pup led the pack to the trees and Trakon washed the game.

When Trakon returned to the camp D'laine had a fire burning. He grabbed a thin branch and made a point on one end to use as a skewer, then he located two forked branches, cut each to the same length, and placed the skewer holding the meat, over the fire.

D'laine dried her hair with the help of the gauze and the heat of the suns. Trakon assessed her from afar. "Does everyone have your coloring where you come from?"

She studied him silently. "No, we all have different skin tones and hair coloring."

"Really?" he asked, surprised.

"There are people with skin lighter than mine that we call white, different shades of brown from tan to very dark that we call black. The original native people have a reddish color skin, and there are people with a yellowish skin, but I don't think anyone has your skin coloring."

"Huh," he said.

"And we all have different colored hair. Mine is called blonde, but there are different shades of blonde. Plus, there's hair color like yours, then brown, red, white and gray, all in varying shades."

"That's interesting. We all have the same color hair." He stared at her hair. "Our elder's hair turns white as their years advance."

"I guess it's a genetic thing," she said.

The meat had quite a good taste, her appetite was enormous and she ate heartily. Walking down to the lake together they washed their hands, using the sponge for towels, then they headed back to the ship.

TRAKON, FILTHY AND SWEATY, WAS IN AN UGLY MOOD AS he dug the dirt away from the nose of the ship with a hand-held digging tool.

D'laine circled the ship, lost in thought. She approached Trakon. "I'd like to try an experiment."

Trakon grunted at her as he continued to mindlessly dig.

"Ghury told me there were many things I could do with my mind if I focused on the problem at hand." Not getting any response from him she placed her hands on her hips. "Hey, I'm talking to you!"

"Look, it's going to take a while for me to dig the ship out," he snapped at her.

D'laine fought to keep her temper under control. "Will you stop for one minute and move back?"

Trakon glanced at her, anger boiling to the surface. "I don't have time to play this game."

"Fine! Suit yourself, but don't tell me I didn't warn you!" D'laine placed her fingers at her temple, and stared at the ship. Dirt and moss exploded away from the ship taking Trakon with it. He tumbled to the ground splattered with moss and sand.

He wiped his face and spit debris out of his mouth. Trakon looked at the ground then turned to stare at her in wonder. There was a trench several feet wide around the entire ship.

"Don't say I didn't try to warn you," she said.

He stalked off toward the water and walked into the lake for several feet then dove in. When he emerged to the surface, he scrubbed his face, hair and arms, still spitting and then blowing sand out of his nose. After a few minutes Trakon left the water and returned to the camp. He picked up D'laine's damp gauze and dried his face.

He stared at her in amazement tinged with anger. He eventually capitulated. His face softened. "Thanks. That saved me a lot of time."

She stared him down. "And a lot of negative energy." She thought that maybe she had offended him, or bruised his ego by clearing the dirt and moss away. She wasn't sure what the roles of women were in his society.

He returned to the ship and climbed aboard. He hopped down in a moment with a peculiar shaped key in his hand. He walked over to the front of the ship and ducked under the nose, inserted the key and made a quarter of a turn. The pressure-sealed doors opened slowly.

D'laine watched from the sidelines. "Can you fix it?"

"I built it!"

She got in his face. "Look, can you just put your ego aside for a minute? Let's start this conversation over. Can. You. Fix. It?"

Trakon became quiet, then huffed in exasperation. "I don't know. The solar collectors should not have failed. I'm not sure what I can use for a shield, if you're right about your energy field."

He walked to the side of the ship and climbed aboard. He stood at the control panel and checked every switch, knob and button.

D'laine walked under the nose and studied the mechanics of the ship, touching things as she observed the layout of the system.

Trakon jumped to the ground and approached the front of the ship. "Don't touch anything!"

"Afraid I might fix it?" D'laine quipped.

"Not likely."

D'laine's eyes slitted in anger. "You are the most exasperating boy I have ever met!"

He got in her face. "I'm not a boy. I'm a man!"

She could not let it go. "You have no idea what my skills are. Are you the type of guy who thinks women are only good for one thing?"

Trakon smirked. "What exactly do you know about Crestriders?"

D'laine smirked back at him. "My father has been building space ships for over twenty years. I repair our personal vehicles." She prodded at the gears and wiggled the wiring. "While your mechanical system is different than what I've built, or worked on, it must be similar in function so I should be able to help you get this thing in the air."

D'laine turned her back to Trakon and continued to explore under the nose of the ship at the open doors.

"I assume you use VTOL," she said.

"What's VTOL?" he asked.

"Vertical Take Off and Landing."

"Oh. Yes," Trakon said, his face coloring slightly.

"And something like SEP – solar electric propulsion, but you use crystals to convert the sun's rays into energy, instead of traditional solar panels."

Trakon stared at D'laine. He marveled at her intelligence and his awe was written on his face.

"Show me the ship's controls. Then I want to trace the crystal solar collectors source to the power. I think that's where the shield needs to go," she said. Her brain was busy putting schematics together so she could understand this system and determine how to protect the power from her crystals and her own energy source.

They spent the next hour exploring the system and tracing wires. They found the specific component that was being overcharged.

D'laine looked it over. "I think I have something that would work."

She dug through her bags and pouches and pulled out her cellphone. She pried her fancy hard case away from the back of the cellphone.

"What tools do you have with you?" D'laine asked Trakon. She showed him her cellphone. "I want to take this metal panel off without damaging the system."

Trakon looked the cellphone over. "I have something that could cut around the edges without causing any harm." He climbed up onto the deck. He returned with a tool that looked like a manual envelope opener.

"May I?" he asked.

D'laine handed over the phone. Trakon slid the tool through a small square opening on the metal panel and commenced to slide it around the edges. The metal fell into the phone. He lifted it out and handed it to D'laine. She looked it over then held it up to the small rectangular component in the ship.

Trakon stood beside her. "I can bend this metal into a little cover."

"That might work," D'laine said.

An hour later, Trakon stood on the ship at the controls.

"Try it now," D'laine called out.

Trakon moved a lever. The ship hummed to life, sputtered, then quit.

"Wait a minute," she hollered. "We need something to secure the cover in place. It keeps falling."

Trakon jumped down beside her holding a tool bag. "I don't have everything I need, but we can improvise."

He dug through the bag and pulled out a tube. "This requires heat for a solid seal." He smeared the goop around the bottom of the metal shield.

"See if you can find a small twig. We can use the lighting stones to heat the twig. I think it may work," Trakon said.

"You know what? I think I have a better method," D'laine said. She pulled out a tiny eyeglass repair kit that contained a small magnifying glass. "You can use this glass and the sunlight to direct a beam of light that will heat and seal that thing."

She showed Trakon how to align the glass with one of the suns. It worked. Smoke rose from the goopy substance. After he heated all edges he held the metal in place and handed her the glass.

"I think this will do the trick," Trakon said. After a few minutes, he wiggled the metal and it held, secure.

"Go try to start the ship," she said.

Trakon climbed aboard and went to the controls; the ship hummed to life and rose several inches off the ground. He pressed a button and the escalator descended to the ground.

"Hold it there. How do I close the doors?"

He ran down the stairs, showed her a button just inside the compartment, pressed it and the doors slowly closed. He looked her square in the eyes. "You fixed it!" He smiled, locked the doors and removed the key.

D'laine moved over to the fire circle. She emptied her water pouch on the fire then kicked sand over the smoldering embers.

The ship settled two feet off the ground, the crystals sparkling as they caught the rays of the two suns. Trakon started gathering his provisions.

"Do you still want to come to Ebscalon with me, or continue on your journey?" Trakon tried to hide a hopeful expression, but didn't quite succeed.

"I'd like to see where you live," D'laine said. "I have never experienced an actual city here, so it would be nice to explore."

"Let's go then." He bounded up the escalator.

D'laine kneeled and patted the dogs. She looked deeply into Pup's eyes. "Remember."

Pup looked adoringly at D'laine.

D'laine patted him one more time then stood. "Until our

paths cross again, know that I love you." She walked to the escalator.

Trakon looked overboard. He pressed a button and the escalator reversed. D'laine walked up a couple of stairs. She turned her head and saw Pup fly through the air to come aboard. He was hanging on the bottom stair by his claws. She carefully turned around and reached out to him.

"No. You have to stay with your pack," she said. She rubbed his head. He whined, but finally let go and dropped to the ground.

"Oh, I'll miss you, too," she whispered.

D'laine turned around and jogged up a couple of stairs. Trakon pulled a lever making the vehicle rise rapidly out of reach of the dogs.

The little jolt of the ship's rise caught D'laine off guard. She slid down a couple of stairs and precariously balanced on the bottom step as the vessel made a slight arc.

"Trakon!" She screamed as she was flung backwards off the escalator.

As she went airborne, D'laine flapped her arms out in front of her and managed to connect with the bottom stair as the ship dipped. Her scraped and bloody hands clung to the metal while the craft leveled out then she tried to swing one of her knees up onto the bottom stair.

The diwals barked and whined as the ship rose in the air. Pup leapt and ran in circles followed by his pack.

Trakon looked overboard. "D'laine! Hold on!" He ran down the stairs, grabbed one of her arms until he had a firm grip of her, and hauled her aboard.

"I'm so sorry," he stammered. He noticed her hands first then glanced down and saw the torn material and her bloody leg. "You're hurt!" He swept her up in his arms.

"Aacckkk! What are you doing? Put me down!" D'laine

demanded. She pounded on his chest and squirmed to get out of his arms.

Trakon hurried back up the stairs. When he reached the deck, he set her on her feet then folded down a bench.

"Why don't you sit here." He turned to the ships controls and steered the ship around in the direction that he had come from. He decreased the speed and placed the ship on autopilot then turned his focus on D'laine.

He opened a cabinet that was partially hidden in a side panel under the railing and removed a box. He approached D'laine, set the box on the floor and pulled down a bench under the railing.

Trakon looked at both of her hands. "Only surface scrapes." He then focused on her bloody leg. He lifted her foot and rested it on his thigh and subconsciously caressed her calf.

D'laine bent and slapped one of his hands. "What do you think you're doing?" She was a smidgen away from decking him.

"I'm going to show you how our healing tools work," he said.

"Make sure that's all you do," she said, huffy.

He opened the box and removed a small pouch and a couple of small jeweled boxes. He grabbed a water flask that was hanging from a hook and poured water over her hands. He dug into the box and removed a piece of gauze, wet it and gently dabbed at the broken skin.

"Yikes! That's sore," she said.

"I'm sorry. I don't want you to get an infection," he said.

Trakon pressed the dot on her boot and the dot on the edge of her pant leg. They both deflated. He rolled up the pant leg and exposed her bruised shin.

D'laine sucked her breath in with a hiss and her eyes

welled with tears. A lump was already forming on her shin and the skin was an angry red.

Trakon caressed the bruise with his other hand.

"What are you doing?" D'laine snapped.

"I...I'm only examining the wound," Trakon stuttered, embarrassed. He poured water over the wound then picked up one of the boxes and pressed a sequence of jeweled buttons. A low hum emitted from the box as he held it a couple of inches above the leg wound and moved it back and forth.

"Hold your hands palms up, please," he said.

D'laine flipped her bloody hands over and rested them on her thighs.

After a few minutes, he repeated the process on her hands. Then he set that box aside and picked up the other one. He pressed a series of buttons and a bright blue light emerged. As he moved the box over the bruised skin the light changed colors and the broken skin healed.

D'laine stared at the transformation happening on her body. "This technology is amazing!"

Trakon couldn't believe her naiveté. "You have never seen a sonicate box or a light healer?"

D'laine shook her head as she first examined her hands. Then she rubbed her hand across the healed skin on her leg. She poked and prodded, but there wasn't any bruising to cause discomfort.

"No. Where I'm from medicine is still in the stone age. Doctors don't heal; all they do is prescribe pills to eliminate the symptoms, and perform surgery to cut diseased things out of the body if they don't have a pill to cure them."

Trakon stared at her. "My people should train them. Healing tools are available for everyone. Where exactly are you from?"

"Not from here," D'laine said.

Trakon put the tools away then returned to the ship controls. He guided the ship across the sky. "You're not one of my people, or from a neighboring city. I have never seen a light-haired person in my lifetime."

D'laine rolled her pant leg down and pressed the tiny button that inflated the material to the shape of her leg. Then she inflated her boot. The tear in the material suddenly wove itself closed; there was nothing visible to suggest the fabric had been damaged. It was seamless and perfectly blended with the whole suit.

"Wow. This is so incredible," D'laine said in complete wonderment. "This place is so far beyond where I come from."

Trakon was stymied by her statements. She didn't make any sense to him at all. "How can that be? Your healing with that crystal is far superior to the tools we have."

"That may be so, but only with me being here in your world. Where I come from I'm a normal person with no special abilities at all. We have airplanes, and rockets that go to the moon, but nothing as advanced as your crestriders."

TRAKON AND D'LAINE STOOD AT THE CONTROLS. THE SHIP hummed softly as it glided through the air.

"So far everything seems to be operating the right way," he said. "The shield must be deflecting your energy."

"Watch out!" She jumped back and ducked as a large winged creature flew within inches of the ship.

Trakon grabbed the controls and barely missed a collision with the orich. The thrust jolted D'laine and she collided with him. Her forehead bashed his lips.

"I'm so sorry!" she said and reached out a hand to touch his lips, but stopped herself and touched her forehead instead. "Your lips are swelling."

"You have a bump on your forehead," he said.

They giggled. The moment lengthened as they stood face-to-face in the open sky. "Are you all right?" Trakon asked.

"Barely," she said, breathless.

Their glance lingered. Her eyes pulled away as she followed the orich's flight pattern. It had a large body like a turkey, but the wide wingspan of an eagle.

Trakon turned back to the controls, as conflicting thoughts and feelings tormented him. As the crestrider glided through the sky, D'laine and Trakon were lost in private thoughts for several minutes. D'laine looked over the side of the ship. The moss changed to a gold color.

The walls in his mind wavered for a moment.

*...so beautiful...* D'laine heard. She looked at him then swiftly turned away to hide her surprise at his declaration and her brightly flushed face.

Suddenly, three borjos flew around the crestrider. They alighted on the railing. Herish dismounted from his ride and removed his helmet.

Trakon set the ship to hover mode settling just a couple of feet off the ground.

"Herish! What are you doing here?" D'laine asked surprised.

Herish hit his chest with his fist and glanced rudely at Trakon. He smiled at D'laine. "My platoon hunted down a sick og that was on a rampage, and I was worried about you."

Trakon looked from Herish to D'laine, suspicious.

"What happened? Did he hit you?" Herish asked as he saw her forehead. He glared at Trakon, ready to fight.

"You little..." Trakon took a fighting stance, his hand on the hilt of his laser pistol.

D'laine stepped between them. "Knock it off you two! Herish, we had a slight accident, that's all. Trakon, pick on someone your own size."

"You don't know the Kudaja," Trakon said. "All is not what it seems with them."

Herish snorted.

"And I know nothing about you either," D'laine said trying to neutralize the tension between the two men.

She swung her attention to Herish. "How did you find me? You're so far from your territory."

Herish looked Trakon up and down, full of loathing. "I followed your angry thoughts about this prince of Ebscalon."

"Everything is fine, Kudaja," Trakon growled at Herish. "Take your borjos and go home."

"You don't have to be rude, Trakon," D'laine huffed. "Herish came a long way to make sure I was okay."

Trakon snorted. "That's not the way I see it."

"Whatever!" D'laine spat. "Why don't I just continue on my way without either of you!"

D'laine grabbed her bags and water skin from a hook then jumped over the side of the ship and landed softly on her feet. Trakon scrambled after her and Herish jumped on his borjo.

"No, please don't go. You wanted to see the city," Trakon begged.

Herish's borjo swarmed around her and hovered. He swallowed then glanced at Trakon and back to D'laine. "Go to the city with him. You will be safe there. You should not be out here by yourself."

Trakon appraised the Kudaja, relaxing his features slightly.

"We have to continue to the east to visit another Kudaja community," Herish said.

D'laine smiled at him. "Thanks for everything, Herish. I appreciate you wanting to keep me safe."

Herish hit his chest with his fist, his eyes glued to hers. He whistled sharply to his team and they were off.

D'laine and Trakon climbed aboard the ship and resumed their trip.

THEY TRAVELLED FOR HOURS, FILLED WITH A combination of silence, discussions, and sharing. Much was to be learned about Thol while zooming through the sky. D'laine saw new sights and new forms of life that she had only seen in Adrum's moving pictures.

As the ship glided through the air, they passed a wild herd of pakows in a field that was partially fenced.

"Wait! Can we get closer to the pakows?"

"You've never seen a pakow?" Trakon asked, somewhat amazed.

"Only from a distance." She recalled the pakows that the Plotals rode.

Trakon maneuvered the ship into a U-turn and flew over the herd. Some of the pakows didn't appear to be interested in the ship at all. Others stampeded away which reminded her of a herd of buffalos. He explained that the pen below was where they put the wild pakows to be tamed. He landed the ship and they ran down the escalator. D'laine climbed the fence and watched the pakows.

"These pakows seem to be partially tame, otherwise they would not approach the pens," he explained.

"They're so huge."

Trakon glanced curiously at D'laine as she hung over the edge of the rail.

"Would you like to go for a quick ride?" Trakon asked.

"Can we?" she asked, excited over the prospect of riding one of the huge beasts.

"I will show you how to handle your mount. They respond readily and are not normally intimidated by any other animals, including the diwal dogs," he told her. "There are not many augugal's or ogs in this area, and those will only attack a pakow if they are either starving or mad from disease."

Trakon beckoned to one of the men that attended the animals, and asked to have two of the beasts brought outside of the fence. The climb down from her perch was more difficult than the trip up, the fence being quite high to discourage the animals from attempting a breakout.

A bull was picked for Trakon, a cow for D'laine.

"You can communicate with the beast either verbally or telepathically," he explained to her. "They know simple things such as come, go, stop, and stay. You can also direct them with the pressure of your knees against their sides."

The first lesson was to show her how to get the beast to lower its giant form to allow a rider to mount. All it took was a sharp rap on one of the forelegs, and the beast bent down to accommodate the rider.

"Why do you have to hit it?" D'laine asked.

"That's what they know." Trakon mounted his pakow by climbing on the beast's bent knee and pulled himself up to the sturdy back of the animal.

"Typically, we would have a saddle and harness, but I figured this would be okay. We'll go slow."

D'laine whispered into the beast's ear and stroked the side of its face. The pakow kneeled down to accommodate her.

"Good girl!" D'laine patted her ride. "I'm going to call you Lulu. Do you like that name?"

The pakow rubbed its large head against her chest.

Trakon watched what she did and how the pakow cow responded.

"Huh," he said. "That's odd."

He didn't know what she said to make the pakow kneel, he only knew that something odd had just happened. He never saw a pakow submit like that before.

She climbed up the pakow's leg and settled herself. She watched as Trakon rapped his mount twice. The beast stood up on all six legs. D'laine followed his actions and was reminded of what she assumed would be like the rocking motion of a camel getting up to a standing position.

They set off. D'laine clung to the long hair on the beast's neck, afraid of falling off her mount. It seemed strange feeling so much movement underneath her as the six legs of the pakow moved in a steady rhythm over the turf. The beasts moved gracefully side-by-side giving an easy ride.

After a twenty-minute jaunt, they returned to the pens and dismounted.

"That was fun!" D'laine said.

"I'm glad you liked it," Trakon said. He turned to the man in charge. "Would you deliver this cow to the holding pen at the palace?"

"Lulu," D'laine said.

Trakon appeared perplexed.

"Her name is Lulu," D'laine said.

They climbed aboard the crestrider and continued toward Ebscalon.

# CHAPTER TWENTY-NINE

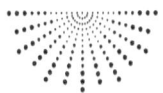

The city of Ebscalon appeared on the horizon as Trakon's crestrider closed the distance.

Trakon pointed. "There's Ebscalon, my home."

Another crestrider approached from the city. It raised a colorful banner. Trakon hit a button and raised his banner that showed the crest of the royal family for safe entry into the boundary of the city. The banner flapped in the wind as they soared toward the other ship.

They were fast approaching the city and D'laine saw that it was much larger than what she had imagined and more beautiful than a storybook picture.

"It's so beautiful," D'laine said, breathless.

Crestriders glided silently around the city walls, banners flew on the households in a wild array of colors, and roofs sparkled. People bustled about.

When their vessel was spotted, people saluted him as was customary, with a fist pressed to the chest.

"It's so different from the cities where I come from." D'laine took it all in.

Trakon watched her, curious about where she came from for all of this to be so strange to her. People saluted Trakon. He steered the ship to a landing pad near the open courtyard and settled it a foot off the ground. A guard came to the ship and saluted Trakon. He noticed the damage to the front of the ship.

"What happened?" The guard asked as he slid his hand over the gouges and scrapes on the crestrider. "We were about to send a search party." He looked from Trakon to D'laine, in silent question.

Trakon ignored the unspoken question. "Major power failure. Take the ship to the hangar. I'll work on it later."

The guard saluted and climbed aboard the ship.

Trakon and D'laine hopped down to the ground. Trakon grasped her hand and led her across the courtyard. She pulled her hand away from his and glared at him. He smiled back at her mischievously.

Her golden skin and light-colored hair aroused questions. People stared at her, displaying curiosity and acceptance.

"You will be the source of excitement for a while, but don't let it worry you. They have never seen anyone with your coloring. My people are very friendly and will accept you," Trakon said, trying to ease her anxiety.

"Accept me? What does that even mean? I'm just a visitor," she said. Bells and whistles were clanging in her head at the suspicious meaning.

D'laine stared at the people in return. She noticed that everyone had dark hair just as she saw in Adrum's movie. It was going to be difficult for her to live in a world where telepathy was so common and used as one of the main modes of communication. It was disconcerting because she couldn't tell if what she heard was out loud, or a tremendous number of voices in her head.

The buildings were of a sandstone material, as she had

imagined when she first saw them through Adrum's teaching. They approached the largest, most ornate building. They entered the palace through an open, arched entrance. Glassless windows with a faint grid work of blue light beams, let in the bright sunlight.

"Why don't you have something covering the windows? Aren't you afraid of thieves or bad weather?" she asked, confused.

"No crime exists in the city," he explained. "As for the weather, the rain is absorbed so quickly, it's never is a problem."

Floating globes of light illuminated murals on the walls. The scenes were a reflection of the hustle and bustle of the city that she saw upon arriving. The floors were crafted of colorful mosaics.

D'laine stared in wonder. "It's all so beautiful."

Trakon and D'laine passed several open doors, then entered a large salon filled with people. As people noticed D'laine, the chatter in the room slowly eased up. Everyone stared at D'laine and whispered, out loud and silently. Her ears filled with a roar of conversations.

In passing, D'laine overheard Trakon's name and "future wife" as people stared at her. She tugged his arm. "They think I'm your future wife!" she whispered.

Trakon looked at her in apology, stunned. "Oh, no!" He noticed people racing from the room. "They're going to spread that false rumor!"

Both he and D'laine appeared very worried.

At that moment, a noble woman turned her gaze from the group of people she had been talking with and noticed Trakon and D'laine. She rushed forward and embraced Trakon, but her eyebrows were raised in question as she stared at D'laine.

"Where have you been?" the woman asked, scolding him.

"Mother, you worry too much," he told her.

A remarkably beautiful woman, his mother wore a garment that D'laine thought was like a sari that Hindu women of Earth wore, in hues of yellow, brown and cream colors, which went well with her flawless skin. Her black hair was piled into a loose chignon on top of her head; her face had delicate features of refinement without pinpointing her age.

"I seriously doubt that. When you have your own children, you will know what worry is all about," she said knowingly. "Why didn't you check in with your father or your crew? Everyone was concerned!" Her eyes darted from Trakon to D'laine.

"Problems developed with the ship," he explained.

She looked smug. "I hate to say 'I told you so' but I warned you about a backup system."

Trakon rolled his eyes at his mother.

"Don't you roll your eyes at me, young man. Just because I'm your mother doesn't mean I am a brainless fool," she said.

"I seriously doubt if anyone would consider you a fool, mother," he said.

D'laine covered her mouth with her hand. She could hardly contain a laugh.

Trakon's mother swung her attention to D'laine. "Are you going to introduce me to your companion, or are you going to continue being rude?" she asked.

Trakon fidgeted under his mother's intense glare. "Mother, may I present D'laine, daughter of Lori and Lee Jackson of NASA? D'laine, this is my mother, Kitry."

"How nice to meet you," D'laine said trying to control a huge smile.

"Welcome, D'laine." Kitry appeared curious as she took in D'laine's blonde hair and tanned skin. "Where do you hail from?" She touched D'laine's hair lightly.

"She is a traveler, Mother. We crossed paths on the plain," Trakon explained.

D'laine glared at Trakon. "I have a mouth," D'laine said, coloring slightly. She turned to Kitry. "I was traveling with a small pack of diwals. I tamed them and they were accompanying me."

Kitry assessed that statement. "Diwals are capable of stripping the meat off your bones in moments. You were lucky that Trakon rescued you when he did."

"He didn't rescue me." D'laine saw the futility of the discussion.

Trakon gave a little snort. "You're the one with the mouth."

D'laine glared at him.

"Where is Jor-Dan?" Kitry scanned the room. "Trakon, we must find your father. He was about to send a search party for you."

Trakon winked at D'laine. "I've already alerted the guard, Mother. They know I have returned."

D'laine nudged Trakon. She had questions.

Kitry hooked her hands through Trakon and D'laine arms and marched them out of the salon; people stared after them and the roar of conversation resumed. They walked briskly down the corridor, turned the corner and approached two huge ornate carved doors in the most beautiful wood that D'laine had ever seen. Kitry freed her arms, swung the doors open and marched in with the small procession, determination clearly etched on her face.

They came upon a man that would be a clear vision of what Trakon would look like in years to come. The resemblance between father and son was unmistakable as D'laine looked from one to the other. He was standing beside a carved table with several seated men.

"We must concentrate our efforts to find our lost technology," Jor-Dan said.

"Jor-Dan! We have a guest!"

Turning, with a little smile on his face to greet his wife, Jor-Dan appraised D'laine. "Ah, my dear wife. What is it that cannot wait until we finish this meeting?"

"You spend too much time in meetings!" Kitry exclaimed, winking at the men seated around the table.

They chuckled.

Jor-Dan excused himself from his meeting and came forward. The men saluted and left the room.

"Trakon! Where have you been?" Jor-Dan showed mild irritation when he focused on his son.

D'laine noticed that his voice had a deep, husky timbre, like his son's.

"Crystal collectors failed," Trakon said. "Tracking failed and my communicator was dead."

"Where were you?" Jor-Dan asked. "Those systems should not have failed, especially your communicator."

"I kept to a southern flight pattern when I left my crew," Trakon said. "I'm not sure if the region has a name."

Jor-Dan sighed.

"I was five days west of the Cember Forest when we met," D'laine said looking from Jor-Dan to Kitry then to Trakon. She blushed.

"The Cember Forest?" Jor-Dan asked. "What would you be doing out there?" Not waiting for an answer, he scrutinized Trakon and D'laine. "Who is your lovely companion?"

Looking from one to the other, he waited for the answer. Taking one of D'laine's hands in his own, Jor-Dan smiled with great pleasure. "You are lovely, my dear."

D'laine was mortified. She felt her face burn from the attention.

Kitry glowed with happiness as she appraised D'laine. "Trakon has not told me where he has found this fair beauty on his travels, but Jor-Dan, this is D'laine. She comes from fine breeding."

Jor-Dan glanced from D'laine to Trakon, then Kitry. "She can give him strong sons to carry on his heritage."

Trakon and D'laine revolted.

"Wait, Mother... Father! D'laine is a traveler."

D'laine turned to leave the room. "Oh my god! If you'll excuse me I think I'll be leaving now."

Kitry placed her hand on D'laine's shoulder. "Why child, whatever is the matter? You two are perfect for each other."

Kitry and Jor-Dan beamed happily at Trakon and D'laine.

"We're total strangers. I have no desire to marry your son," D'laine exclaimed.

"Nor I," Trakon announced, furious at being ambushed by his parents.

"When did you meet?" Kitry asked.

"Yesterday in the field," D'laine said.

"You spent the night together?" Kitry asked.

Trakon and D'laine looked horrified at the implication. "Nothing happened!" they each exclaimed.

"The ship was disabled," Trakon said.

"I was just exploring the area," D'laine said.

"Do you like each other?" Kitry asked.

Jor-Dan had a difficult time keeping a straight face as Kitry steered the conversation with matchmaking in mind.

"He's pigheaded, bossy, impatient, and doesn't think a woman can do anything!" she said.

"Really?" Kitry asked. She tsk-tsked at Trakon.

Trakon and D'laine faced off in the heat of the moment.

"Pigheaded?" Trakon fumed.

Kitry and Jor-Dan watched the exchange with interest.

D'laine smiled sweetly. "If I were in the market for a husband, which I'm not because I am much too young to even consider marriage, you'd be the last boy I'd choose. My husband would appreciate not only my mechanical abilities, but my many other talents I'm just now learning about."

Trakon's temper flared. "My future wife wouldn't have her head filled with fantasies about Egroms."

Jor-Dan raised a hand. "What is this about Egroms?"

"Don't ask, father." Trakon fumed.

"Enough of this. Let's retire to my apartment and you can tell us your story. With skin and hair of your coloring, I cannot imagine where you are from. I feel that a mystery lies here waiting to be unfolded," Kitry whispered to the others.

THE AIRY, BRIGHT APARTMENT WAS VERY LARGE, consisting of several rooms: a sleeping chamber with a huge bed draped in pastel gauzes, a sitting room with a divan, several lighting globes floating along the walls, and other small pieces of furniture. Another room contained something that looked like a loom and a stool, and a table piled with several skeins of some type of brightly colored yarn or silk. The private room beyond this one was where the group settled. It was comfortable to look at, containing several divans and chairs, flowers in bowls on low tables, and magnificent pictures on the walls by great artists from another era.

"This is beautiful," D'laine said. "The Egroms live a very spartan life. They don't have homes like this."

A member of the staff brought in a large flask and four goblets. Grabbing the flask, Jor-Dan filled their glasses.

Directing D'laine to a divan in soft hues of lavender, Kitry sat down opposite her. D'laine looked at the goblet curiously.

"This is called kahl," Trakon explained. "It's sweet and may be very potent for you, so drink slowly."

Sipping the kahl, which was thick and tasted sweet like a berry mixture, D'laine thought it must be equivalent to wine. Kitry organized the seating by placing Trakon and D'laine beside each other.

D'laine knew it was going to be difficult to explain her unique story. It sounded so unbelievable, even to her own ears, but she was living proof that the portals existed and accidents did happen.

"Where are you from and why haven't we seen people like you before?" was the first question from Kitry.

"There are no Tholians that look like you," Jor-Dan said. "And I have travelled far and wide."

D'laine hesitated. She gave Trakon a "look". "You most likely will never see anyone else like me. I'm from a different place in time, parallel to your world and I think my being here was a 'contrived' accident."

She went on to explain the circumstances as they had happened to her, including the dangerous encounter with the Plotals, and all that she had experienced up to the point when she and Trakon met. Sitting spellbound by her story, Kitry and Jor-Dan were mesmerized as D'laine told of her life with the Egroms, how they had taken her in and educated her.

"I don't really know anything about your people, just a basic knowledge of your existence. The Egroms didn't teach me details so I don't know the everyday ways of your people. I was so overjoyed to know there were other beings like myself here. I thought I would never hear another verbal word again that could at least compare to my language," she confided. "I've learned the Egrom language, and yours, but I don't know anything beyond that. Without the translator, the Egrom language is quite complicated to learn. I was so afraid that I would never have a race that I could call my own."

"There are many legends of the creatures that you speak of, but no one in this century has seen them, so we don't know anything other than what the legends have told us," Jor-Dan said. "We were told of creatures with vast powers that could stop the suns from shining and darkness from falling."

"I think that's an exaggeration," D'laine said. She smiled and explained that she was very fond of the creatures. They would have a special place in her heart always. She projected a picture of Ghury in their minds and told a tale that described the depth of their intelligence. She marveled at the knowledge they had, their learning system that had taught her so much, and their compassion for anything that breathed life.

"The Egroms educated me in the basic skills of survival here."

Jor-Dan and Kitry were captivated. Trakon snorted.

"Where are your weapons if you're so well prepared?" Trakon nudged the knife on her thigh.

D'laine smacked his hand. "Not all weapons are physical, Mr. Know-It-All. Are you forgetting how your ship was dug out of the dirt and moss when you crashed it at the oasis, or do you think that was a dream?"

Trakon grimaced.

Jor-Dan and Kitry seemed amused at the tug of wills between Trakon and D'laine.

"And that filthy Kudaja even rescued you from a mruck!" Trakon said.

"How do you know Herish rescued me? That's none of your business," D'laine said.

"I read his thoughts and they were pretty interesting," Trakon said.

Jor-dan turned to Trakon. "She will have to be protected at

all costs. Jakla Bosakin would pay a high price to have her and force her to use her powers for his own benefit. We will have to make sure the city is prepared and plan an escape route in case something should happen. And what about any children you might have? Will your future unborn have these powers, or be normal beings like their father? We need to think of them also!"

D'laine appeared shocked at the conversation. "I don't even know you people! I just met your son twenty-four hours ago!" She noticed the questioning looks. "Yesterday. We met yesterday. One day! On my world, that's twenty-four hours."

A rebellious expression crossed Trakon's face. "We are not having children! D'laine is only stopping to experience a Tholian city!"

Kitry waved their protests aside. "What life have you left behind in this other world? Did you have these powers there?"

Three pairs of eyes watched D'laine with interest. "I have two younger brothers and my father. I am sure they would be like me, because back home I was an ordinary person."

"I would never call you ordinary," Trakon said.

"You fixed the ship?" Jor-Dan asked.

"She's brilliant," Trakon said.

"I'm just mechanically inclined," D'laine said. "My father is the one who is brilliant."

Kitry got up and sat beside D'laine and put her hand on her shoulder. "Our people were told of you many thousands of years ago. The prophecy states that someone would come from another place, with great powers, skin like gold, and would be a great warrior." She turned to Jor-Dan. "They never told us it would be a woman! I feel that much has been lost in the legend and we should try to find the original scrolls to see what was actually written."

Jor-Dan was lost in thought. "I'll speak with the Visionary."

*So much like the tablets that were handed down to Moses,*

D'laine thought. She was sure that this had no bearing on her, she was not a warrior, and her powers were not, in her opinion, what someone would consider great compared to the Egroms. She could understand the parting of the sea, but she did not compare what she had done up to this point, as anything as great as the biblical tale.

Trakon sat deep in thought.

"Why didn't the Egroms tell me that?" D'laine asked, deeply puzzled.

Trakon pondered this. "They know something we don't know."

Feeling a strong sense of family with these people, D'laine felt a contentment she had not felt since her mystic journey to Thol began.

A knock on the door broke their line of thought as a man entered.

"The evening meal is ready to be served," he said.

Kitry nodded her approval and the man left.

"A full stomach always makes problems less troublesome," Kitry said.

They all stood, Kitry putting her hand through the crook of D'laine's arm and led the way out of the room, with the men following. Everyone seemed to be lost in their own private thoughts as they left the apartment and walked down the corridor.

The large room which had been filled with people when she and Trakon had arrived at the palace was now empty.

# CHAPTER THIRTY

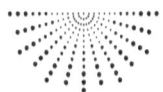

*S*tanley studied new pictures on a monitor in the computer lab. One picture appeared to have a defined hollow spot. Another showed a large area surrounded by a haze. He smiled as he picked up the phone.

"Dr. Joplin! Victor!" Stanley shouted. "Yes, yes, yes."

Moments later, Dr. Joplin and Victor burst through the door. They approached Stanley, both brimming with excitement. Dr. Joplin placed his hand on Stanley's shoulder. "What do you have?"

Stanley stood. "Grab a chair."

Dr. Joplin slid into Stanley's chair and Victor dragged a chair to the table. Dr. Joplin studied the pictures. "Will you look at that?"

Victor got nose-close to the monitor and squinted. He used the magnifier feature until the picture distorted then he reduced the magnification several times. He tapped the monitor.

"See this? There seems to be a pinpoint here. Like a hole in the air or sky."

Stanley and Dr. Joplin glanced at the picture on the monitor.

"Yes, I see what you're talking about," Dr. Joplin said. "Print out a clear copy of this and let's take a look."

Victor clicked and sent the picture to the color printer.

LEE AND THE BOYS SAT AROUND THE KITCHEN TABLE while Rosa stood nearby.

"I'm going to have to return to work tomorrow. I can't take much more time off unless I take a leave of absence, and I don't want to do that."

"You've spent way too much time sitting here worrying. Everyone needs to get back to living," Rosa said.

Lee sighed deeply. "I know. It's just difficult to think this is normal living when D'laine's not here."

Brian was lackluster sitting across from Lee. He kept quiet, withdrawn. Jamie squirmed in his chair. "You should hang out with your friends, daddy. Maybe you'll feel better."

Lee rubbed Jamie's head. "Good advice, son."

# CHAPTER THIRTY-ONE

*A*s the last sun set, Jakla and a war party approached the remote village of Mer. He silently instructed his warriors to surround the village so they could attack from all sides. He wanted to capture as many Mers as possible.

They moved in with stealth. When the troops were in place, Jakla bellowed a war cry that was repeated from around the perimeter of the village.

The sky lit up as men and warrior women of Mer fought with lasers and light swords. Women in sari dresses and children fled to a special building for cover. A lone Mer warrior fled out of the gates on a pakow, unnoticed in the confusion of the attack.

KITRY GUIDED D'LAINE TO THE DINING SALON WHILE Trakon and Jor-Dan followed. They walked through the open, ornate doors into the large salon. The floating lights kept the room aglow as the suns set. Four globes hovered over the table and reminded D'laine of the dining room back at her father's house.

A large, oblong, dark wood table with high-backed, ornate chairs dominated the large room. The plates were of the finest bone china, or of some equivalent, which reminded D'laine of mica. The goblets sparkled like diamonds, and she wondered what they were made of. *Crushed crystals?* She didn't know. The utensils were similar to silverware used on Earth, but not silver or gold. *Mother of pearl?* D'laine wasn't sure, but she recognized forks, knives and spoons.

A homey, but elegant atmosphere prevailed. D'laine was seated to the left of Kitry, across from Trakon, with Jor-Dan opposite his wife. The servants brought platters of food and offered each dish to them. She didn't know what was being offered and Trakon sensed her confusion and explained each dish.

"This is roast sidel, like we had this morning, but prepared much better," Trakon said with humor as he pointed. "That's braised par, and you most likely recognize the vegetables."

D'laine knew she liked sidel, which was similar to rabbit, and the steamed vegetables of several varieties, and the sweet kahl to drink. "I'll try a little of each."

The food was delicious and she ate with a hearty appetite while they discussed the schedule for the following day. Each had their own area of expertise.

Jor-Dan grabbed a hunk of bread. "Tomorrow, Kitry will familiarize you with the palace, and I will introduce you to the council."

Jor-Dan and Kitry appeared to be elated as they watched the interaction between their son and D'laine.

"That's not necessary. I really can't stay long. I'd like to see the city and how you live, then I'll continue my exploration of the countryside," D'laine explained. She concentrated on the dishes the staff presented.

"Where will you go? You have no home, no family here," Kitry said, somewhat shocked.

"The Egroms are my family now." D'laine sampled the food. "I plan to see the different regions of Thol."

"Nonsense. Stay for a visit. Trakon will show you the city," Jor-Dan said.

Trakon stared at his parents in wonderment. "Father, I have other plans."

"How could you? You've just returned!" Kitry said.

"I have a lot of work to do on the ships, and my communicator failed," Trakon said.

Jor-dan snorted. "Trakon, a few hours won't make any difference. We haven't flown ships after sunsdown in years."

Trakon glared at his parents' attempt to make arrangements.

Jor-Dan and Kitry smiled in secret conspiracy.

D'laine tried to suppress a yawn.

"You're tired. Let me show you to your quarters," Kitry said.

D'laine did a double-take. "Are you serious? I have quarters? I just got here!"

"My staff are quick to make preparations for visitors," Kitry said as she pushed her chair back.

D'laine stood up.

A guard entered and saluted. "Your Highness, my Queen. I apologize for interrupting your meal."

"What is it?" Jor-Dan asked.

"A messenger from Mer," the guard said.

"Show him in," Jor-Dan said.

The guard stood aside and the messenger entered, his metal battle helmet in hand, and his black hair shaggy and long. He saluted.

D'laine noticed that Mers differed from Ciertrons. Their features were dominated by a square jaw and a forehead that jutted out slightly, almost like Neanderthals, but not quite that pronounced.

"Mer is under attack by Plotals," the messenger announced. "We need your help."

Trakon and Jor-Dan jumped to their feet.

"Is this Jakla Bosakin's doing?" Jor-Dan asked.

"Yes," the messenger said.

"Is he the Plotal leader?" D'laine asked.

"Yes. Jakla is a blood-thirsty warmonger. He lusts for violence and power," Kitry said.

"How many in the war party?" Jor-Dan barked out.

"At least five hundred," the messenger said.

"They're looking for slaves then," Jor-Dan said.

Trakon strode around the table. "Prepare pakows," he ordered the guard. "We have to act immediately."

"I agree," Jor-Dan said.

The guard and messenger hurried out of the room.

D'laine stood. "I'm coming with you!"

Kitry stood. "Shouldn't you rest?"

"I forbid you to come!" Trakon bellowed. He looked formidable as his eyes pierced D'laine's, and his nose flared.

D'laine stared down Trakon, disbelief clearly on her face. "You what?"

"It's too dangerous for you to join the battle," Trakon all but shouted.

D'laine turned to Jor-Dan for support. "I'm the warrior, remember?" Her fury was barely under control.

Jor-Dan and Trakon had a tense stand-off. "D'laine will ride with us," Jor-Dan said. "She will be protected."

"She has no experience with a war party and we can't protect her if there's fighting going on all around us." Trakon's voice boomed out at his father, challenging Jor-Dan.

"She rides with us!" Jor-Dan declared.

Trakon stormed out of the room.

Kitry approached D'laine and put her arm across D'laine's shoulders in a motherly fashion. "Don't worry, he'll come around."

D'laine flinched. She looked at Kitry questioning her statement. "But I don't want him to come around."

Kitry stood back and appraised D'laine. "Not even a little?"

Jor-Dan joined Kitry, kissed her cheek and whispered: "Trouble maker."

Kitry winked at him and whispered in his ear. "I know a match when I see one."

Jor-Dan turned to D'laine. "Let's ride."

D'laine fumed as she followed Jor-Dan from the room.

Kitry smiled and turned in the opposite direction.

TRAKON SAT ATOP A SADDLED PAKOW. THE MESSENGER from Mer waited patiently on his mount beside Trakon.

Jor-Dan and D'laine emerged from the palace. D'laine noticed that Trakon's uniform looked different and he wore a battle helmet, but she knew he hadn't had time to change clothes.

Jor-Dan stopped and instructed D'laine. "Press this button on your cuff."

D'laine watched as he pressed the button and his suit did a complete metamorphosis from head to toe encasing him with a metal-like covering that snapped into place in one-inch strips. It sounded like the snapping of two halves of a deck of cards being shuffled.

She pressed her own cuff and was encased with the strong material. Her head was encased with the same type of battle helmet as Trakon and Jor-Dan's, leaving her eyes and mouth visible, and with a slat across her nose. "Oh! That's interesting."

D'laine watched as Jor-Dan slapped the pakow on the front knee, and the beast kneeled. He climbed up the bent leg and settled into the saddle. She stood before Lulu, her pakow. Lulu lowered her head and sniffed her. D'laine whispered in her ear and she knelt down. D'laine climbed up the animal's leg, grabbed the saddle horn and swiveled into the seat as the lumbering beast stood.

Trakon smoldered as he watched her. It seemed that animals only wanted to please her.

Jor-Dan and the Mer warrior took the lead positions with Trakon slightly behind his father, to the right. D'laine was to Jor-Dan's left. Jor-Dan inclined his head to Trakon. They thundered out of the city gates at a fast pace.

D'laine hung onto the saddle horn trying to get accustomed to the gait of her ride. With six legs, the pace was not like riding a horse back home. It was like a rumbling forward thrust and so unusual to adapt to, but she settled into the motion after a few minutes.

Just outside the gates D'laine saw the waiting war party. Several hundred warriors mounted on pakows fell in behind their king and prince. D'laine remembered how the ground vibrated when Jakla had arrived in the field. She could not imagine what it felt like with this many creatures galloping across the moss.

Nightly shadows crossed the landscape as the party raced toward the fight. The Village of Mer was similar to Ebscalon, but on a much smaller scale. Jor-Dan halted his party a quarter of a mile out and appraised the situation. Laser weapons flashed and neon glowing light swords streaked through the darkness as the battle unfolded before them. The demolished city gates leaned perilously.

Jor-Dan instructed his commanders. "Take parties around both sides and enter through the back gate." He then instructed Trakon and D'laine. "We take the front."

"She isn't armed," Trakon balked.

Jor-Dan offered her his laser.

"I don't need one," D'laine said.

"Are you sure?" Jor-Dan asked.

"Positive," D'laine said.

Trakon held his fury in check.

The parties split up. Jor-Dan led his party. They rode full forward through the front gates. Plotals and Mer warriors fought everywhere. Jor-Dan, Trakon and the warriors engaged in battle with Plotals, mindful of the barbed tails. D'laine watched the action from atop Lulu.

She had never seen anything like it before in her life, since war had not been experienced in the US since the Civil War. And never with these advanced weapons. She felt like she was in a science fiction movie. The Plotals were much more hideous up close than she had imagined, with their alligator-like scales that looked to be spotted with dirt, and deadly looking fangs in their large mouths with a pig-type snout. They were huge! Three or four feet taller than the Ciertrons, they looked very impressive on the backs of their huge rides.

A mounted Plotal warrior charged D'laine. Trakon eliminated his quarry and turned to find D'laine amid the battle. The Plotal fired his laser at her. She jerked her hand up in front of her and the laser beam absorbed into her palm. Without thought, she pointed a finger at the Plotal warrior and a lightning bolt exploded at the warrior and stunned him. He fell to the ground.

Not fully digesting what had just occurred, she realized that something amazing had happened. D'laine stared at her hand in awe and turned to Trakon. His mouth hung open. He finally acknowledged her strange capabilities, feeling confident that she could take care of herself. He nodded to her then turned his thoughts back to the battle and fell into combat with another Plotal.

Jakla Bosakin slashed his way through the throng of Mer and Ciertron warriors to the front. He caught a glimpse of D'laine, raised his long snout and inhaled deeply. He recognized her scent from the field. He bellowed and charged.

D'laine turned at the sound to see Jakla's approach. She held her hands out in front of her and spread them to the sides. A faint purple energy shield engulfed her and Lulu.

Jakla rode up alongside D'laine and slashed with his laser. The force-field shocked him and protected her. His laser weapon went flying through the air. She maneuvered Lulu with pressure from her knees and feet to keep Jakla in sight.

Enraged, Jakla turned his pakow and rode back around. He pulled a gun-type weapon from his holster and shot a plasma blast at D'laine. Again, the shield protected her and shocked him.

Trakon and Jor-Dan pursued Jakla. They fought fiercely. Jakla blasted Jor-Dan. He fell back on the pakow and tumbled off and hit the ground. Trakon and his warriors raged on with an attack. D'laine rode to Jor-Dan and jumped down. She expanded the force-field to encompass Jor-Dan.

Jakla surveyed the battlefield and noticed the tide changed against him.

"Fall back!" Jakla took one last blast at Trakon, missing him then turned his beast, and he and the remaining Plotals galloped out of the village at high speed without captured slaves.

Ciertron and Mer warriors made chase then returned to the village. Felled warriors from all sides littered the ground and pakows roamed aimlessly. Trakon returned to where D'laine and Jor-Dan were on the ground. He jumped off his pakow and rushed to his father.

"Father!" Trakon reached out to Jor-Dan.

"Wait!" D'laine thrust out her hand, but not fast enough.

The force-field shocked Trakon. He was flung back and skidded along the ground. He shook his head, dazed.

"Let's try this again." D'laine held out one hand and the force-field collapsed into her palm and was absorbed into her body.

Trakon rubbed his hand where the force-field had enveloped it. "Why did I get shocked?"

"Because I didn't invite you in," D'laine explained.

Trakon pondered that. He took in his father's bloody chest. "Father, can you ride?"

Jor-Dan struggled to sit up. "Yes. Help me onto my pakow."

Trakon and a soldier supported Jor-Dan. D'laine made Jor-Dan's pakow lie down while Trakon and the soldier settled Jor-Dan in the saddle.

"We'll double up," Trakon told his father as he mounted the animal behind Jor-Dan. "I want to make sure you don't fall off and make that wound worse."

The Mer Commander approached. He and Trakon grasped each other's forearms. "Thank you for coming to our aid."

"When the crystal collectors are working properly, I'll return and help you with the upgrades to your ships," Trakon said.

"We thank you!" The Mer commander approached Jor-Dan. "Shall I summon our healer?"

Jor-Dan grasped the Commander's arm. "It's just a surface wound. We'll return to Ebscalon now."

The Mer Commander retreated.

"Take over, son," Jor-Dan said.

Trakon raised his laser in the air. "Home."

The War Party assembled at the gate. Wounded warriors rode double with others. Dead warriors lay across the backs of pakows as the war party headed home.

Trakon and D'laine entered the palace followed by two warriors who supported Jor-Dan. The group entered one of the first rooms off the hallway, and the warriors placed Jor-Dan on a lounge chair. He reclined back and let out a deep breath.

Trakon went in search of his mother. They returned momentarily. Kitry rushed into the room and stopped in her tracks when she saw Jor-Dan on the lounge, covered in blood. She clutched her chest then rushed to him and knelt by his side.

"Jor-Dan!" Kitry cried out.

D'laine pressed the button on her cuff to restore her outfit to its former suit, but nothing happened. She tapped Trakon on the arm. "How do I make my uniform return to normal?"

"Press here," he said and showed her the second button on his suit. He pressed and the battle helmet, nose guard and battle material collapsed inside itself with soft clacking sounds.

"Oh!" D'laine followed suit. She was amazed that her suit felt so light and couldn't figure out how the hidden armor didn't weigh her down.

"Send for the Visionary!" Kitry commanded one of the guards.

Jor-dan tried to calm his wife. "Looks worse than it is."

Kitry harrumphed. "I'll be the judge of that." She pressed his suit deflating button. "Trakon, help me lower your father's uniform."

Trakon and Kitry eased Jor-Dan's arms out of the material. The large plasma blast on his chest was red, raw and almost glowing. D'laine looked it over.

"I think I may be able to help with this," she said.

Trakon hovered at his father's side. "Let her assist you, father."

Jor-Dan appraised D'laine. "Give it a try."

D'laine knelt opposite Kitry. She dug a crystal out of her pouch, closed her eyes then took three deep breaths in and out. Then she opened her eyes and placed a hand inches above Jor-Dan's chest wound. The crystal glowed in her other hand. Her lips moved in silent prayer.

The Visionary entered the room silently and stopped. The room became very quiet as everyone watched. After a long moment, D'laine jerked. She moved her hand. Jor-Dan's wound visibly closed as everyone watched—the skin completely restored itself with no signs of the wound.

Everyone exclaimed, except the Visionary. He studied those present in the room then his voice rang out. "And there will come one to be among us who will save us from destruction."

Everyone focused on D'laine. She stared at the Visionary, a little frightened of his prophecy. His eyes sparkled as he gazed upon her. Then he quietly slipped out of the room.

"That was a strange experience. I actually felt my skin knitting back together," Jor-Dan said, awed.

Trakon was unusually quiet as he watched D'laine with renewed interest.

Kitry patted her husband's hand. "I have never seen tissue repair itself quite like that before." She turned to D'laine. "Thank you, again. My family is my whole world."

"I'm glad I could help." D'laine blushed a deep pink, self-conscious of the attention to her new skills. If it weren't for Ghury and Adrum, and all those hours of training and coaxing her to get into her head and find the latent powers, she would not have been able to do anything remarkable. As it was, she discovered she could defend herself and heal others. It was a lot for her to digest.

Jor-Dan sat up and swung his legs off the chaise and stood. He wobbled slightly and Trakon jumped to steady him. "Careful, father!"

"You need to rest for several hours while the healing process completes. Blood vessels are being repaired under your skin," D'laine explained. "I went through a similar situation and it is very disconcerting until the restoration is complete."

Trakon and a guard helped Jor-Dan to the master suite. Kitry and D'laine followed them down the wide, well-lit corridor that turned several times. They finally came to the sector that held the family's apartments, and rooms that had been prepared for her. They stopped in front of huge double doors.

"These are your rooms. Twum will see to your needs. My suite is down the hall and around the corner," Kitry said and tilted her head in the direction where Trakon, the guard and Jor-Dan disappeared.

They embraced. "Thank you again for healing my husband. I am indebted to you," Kitry said.

"Oh, I'm so glad I could help, but don't feel..." D'laine stammered.

Kitry laid her hand on D'laine's arm. "You healed the ruler of Ebscalon. Every single one of us is grateful and in your debt." She patted D'laine's hand and hurried away after her husband.

D'laine stood in front of the huge doors to her apartment and watched Kitry disappear around the corner. Moments later, Trakon came down the hallway and joined her.

"My rooms are directly across the hall. If you should need anything, I will be close by," Trakon said, as he opened the door for her and escorted her inside the suite.

She stepped into the room and pulled in a breath. "It's beautiful! Thank you for this wonderful hospitality. It's been such a long time since I have experienced such luxuries."

D'laine scanned the room, appreciating the beauty. The sleeping chamber was lit by soft light from the floating globes. At the rear of the spacious room was a vast bed draped with colorful sheer material. The room was predominantly decorated in greens and blues and gauze of muted tones of rust, cream and peach hung from the high stately ceilings. The small divan, close by, was covered with emerald green material and adorned with cobalt blue throw pillows. Scenic tapestries hung on the walls.

"My father's house where I grew up is a very comfortable two-story house and I loved my bedroom, but this is like a fairy-tale bedroom!"

"I'll let you get settled in then," he told her. "Until tomorrow." He turned and left her suite, closing the door quietly behind him.

She heard Trakon's door close across the hall—he was so close!

Crossing the room to the dais, D'laine climbed onto the bed. Such comfort! She had forgotten what it felt like to sleep on a real bed. Lying down, she surveyed the room. The tapestries on the walls were magnificent, showing scenes of everyday life in the city, the colors blending in with the harmony of the room.

A tap sounded on her door, and Twum, a young woman in her early twenties, entered the room. She wore a flowing gown like Kitry's, and her dark hair hung loosely around her face and shoulders. She bowed her head respectfully.

"Hello, my princess..."

D'laine slid off the bed, and her mouth dropped open. "I'm not a princess. Are you Twum?"

"Yes," Twum said. "Are you not the prince's intended?"

"Intended?" D'laine's head spun. "Who said I was his intended?"

"That is all everyone is talking about. The prince brought home his intended and the people are excited for the long-awaited ceremony."

"Oh! That's a huge misunderstanding. I'm just a visitor. We just met..." D'laine shut her mouth to stop stammering like a fool. She felt her face heat and knew she must be bright red right about then.

"Tomorrow they will be talking nonstop about the warrior princess who saved our king!" Twum beamed with excitement. She walked to a door along the wall. "There are clean clothes in the chamber."

D'laine appeared confused. "Chamber?"

Twum approached the door, pressed a button, and the door opened. D'laine peeked inside. A glassed-in compartment with several buttons and LEDs on a panel housed several outfits—some like her warrior outfit, and some like Kitry and Twum's clothing.

"This is the restorative chamber. You press this button to have access to your clothing, and to place things you have already worn inside," Twum explained as she pressed the button. A soft hissing of air sounded then a panel door opened. Twum entered the closet.

She chose a knee-length wispy gown and handed the outfit to D'laine. "This will be very comfortable for sleeping," Twum said.

D'laine accepted the gown. "Oh, thank you."

Twum headed to the door. "After you freshen up, place your suit in the chamber and it will be restored."

D'laine appraised the chamber. "Does the chamber clean and mend the clothes?"

"Yes. It continuously filters the air, and all organisms that deteriorate, or cause material to break down are destroyed," Twum explained.

D'laine stared at the closet in awe. She shut the closet's outer door.

"Is there anything else that you need?" Twum asked.

D'laine looked around the room. "Just sleep."

Twum understood and touched the light globes. The lights dimmed. "Sleep well." Twum swept through the double doors.

Another room was beyond the bedroom and D'laine headed in that direction to explore its contents. Reeling in pleasure, she stepped into the room that contained a sunken pool holding steamy water, large enough for a whole family to soak.

Exploring, she discovered large jars around the edge that contained unfamiliar soaps and oils.

"Soap! Shampoo! There is a god!" D'laine exclaimed.

There were thick towels on benches within reach of the pool. The whole room shimmered in a soft white with varying accents of blues, greens and yellows in the mosaics of the pool.

She sat on one of the benches and removed her boots, then stood up and pressed the buttons to deflate the suit. She pushed the sleeves off her shoulders and wiggled out. Then she walked down the stairs of the pool. The delicious water felt like tender caresses on her skin. She found a bathing sponge near one of the jars and poured creamy soap onto it and rubbed her skin. Dipping under the water to wet her hair, she then poured a generous amount of the soapy liquid into her palm and scrubbed her head.

It had been ages since she had the pleasure of a real shampoo and it felt luxurious. Ducking her head under the surface to be sure the soap was thoroughly rinsed, she immediately giggled thinking of Kestrum, who used to get so distressed every time she did that. She felt totally refreshed and swam the length of the pool and back again, before she left the comforting warmth of the water for the silky feel of the gauze towel she wrapped around her body. She looked into the pool for a drain. Seeing none, she knew she had better ask someone how the pool worked.

In the corner of the room, a floating globe cast its soft shadow over an accompanying table and bench. Wandering over to the table, she discovered a comb made out of an unknown material, similar to glass or plastic, but she didn't think these people used toxic plastic. The comb was smoky brown in color with flecks of gold floating in the material. She sat down on the low bench in front of the table and was surprised to see an oval mirror on the wall.

She sat transfixed, staring at her reflection, somewhat startled at what she saw. Even without a trace of makeup, fresh out of a bath, she looked soft and glowing. Her skin was a warm golden tone, her eyes a liquid sea green and her lips were a natural peach color. Her hair had bleached-out to a soft platinum and was wavier and longer than she had ever worn. *How long have I been gone?*

Yes, she had changed unknowingly and dramatically and was surprised at what she saw. Picking up the comb, she sorted through the tangles of her hair, then took some gauze and toweled it dryer. She retrieved the gown and slipped it over her head and marveled at the silky material against her skin. She grabbed her dirty clothes and left the bath. She placed the boots on a wooden rack on the floor of the restorative chamber, hung the armor suit and headed to the bed. She touched the globes as Twum demonstrated, and sank into the comfort of the huge bed.

"Goodnight Brian. Goodnight Jamie. Goodnight, daddy," D'laine whispered as she looked toward the window and lapsed into sleep.

# CHAPTER THIRTY-TWO

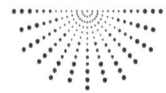

*T*he night passed in total comfort. Morning was upon her and it seemed as though she had just put her head to the pillow only moments ago. Someone had opened the shutters that had closed out the night. A knock sounded at the door as D'laine lay in the comfort of the huge bed.

"Come in," she said, scooting up to a sitting position.

Twum came into the room carrying several pieces of clothing. She smiled to D'laine. "Good morning, princess. The queen sent these for your consideration." She placed the clothes on a divan.

"Oh!" D'laine said.

"Have you become familiar with everything here?" Twum asked.

"I'm learning something new all the time," D'laine said. "How does the bath work? I didn't know what to do after my bath."

Twum covered her mouth with her hand. "Oh! I forgot to explain the bathing pool function. Not to worry. The water is continuously circulated and all contaminants are removed. The water level and temperature are constant."

"That's wonderful! I worried for nothing," D'laine said. "Have I overslept?"

"No, the Queen Lady has just risen. Do you need help dressing?" Twum asked.

"Oh, no. I'll be okay. Thanks anyway," D'laine said.

Twum left the apartment.

Getting out of bed, D'laine curiously looked over the clothing Kitry had sent. There were several outfits like the one she had arrived in and two of the draping silks that Kitry had worn. She changed clothes, slipping into another outfit like what she had worn, saving the more formal outfits for official occasions. She hung the other outfits in the chamber. There was no way for her to tell what time it was, but her stomach was telling her it was time to eat.

D'laine left her apartment and retraced her steps down corridors until she came to the room they had dined in last night. She found Kitry just getting started on her morning meal. The majordomo pulled out a chair for her and then tele-pathically called to one of the servants who brought a tray of breads and fruits. Another approached with a dish of fluffy eggs. Someone else brought a pitcher and filled her goblet with a yellow nectar. There was enough food for an army.

"You look enchanting. The people will fall in love with you instantly," Kitry told her.

D'laine couldn't keep her lips buttoned. "Twum said the people think I'm Trakon's intended, but that's not true. We only just met and we—I—am too young to get married, and I would never get married without my family present."

She felt her face burn with her embarrassment, but didn't know what else she could say to make Kitry and Jor-Dan understand the mix-up.

Kitry studied D'laine's face. "Perhaps it isn't a mix-up. There is a possibility that your being here and meeting my son is part of the prophecy."

D'laine bit her lip. She had to put this discussion out of her head, so she focused on her food.

Curious about this different life, D'laine asked Kitry about the status of the people who worked in the palace. "Are the workers in the palace slaves, or indentured servants?"

"We don't believe in slavery. These are the people of our city that have dedicated their lives to their king and queen. They are never treated unkindly and are never over-taxed. My personal staff are my best friends and I trust them beyond a shadow of a doubt. We can talk about any subject, and I will listen to their troubles and offer advice if they ask for it," Kitry explained. "I can understand your reason for asking though. There is a vast difference between the palace staff and the slaves of the Plotals. Those poor beasts of burden would be better off dead. They don't live long."

Trakon and Jor-Dan entered the room. Trakon sat beside D'laine. "I'm going to show you around the city when you're ready."

When they finished their meal, they left the palace, stepping out into the sunny courtyard.

TRAKON DECIDED TO TAKE D'LAINE TO THE MARKET square so she could see what the everyday life of the people was like. Ciertrons stopped and stared at the golden beauty at the side of their prince. It was obvious they approved of his choice.

Their thoughts wafted across to her.

*"What a gracious creature, with the beauty of her soul showing through her bright shining aura."*

*"Our prince can't go wrong with this tiny, beautiful girl."*

*"I would be proud to be her subject."*

*"I will be devoted to her."*

"Why does everyone think we are getting married?" D'laine asked, alarmed. "Twum said I was your intended, but I told her that was a mistake. But I can hear everyone else saying the same thing!"

"Once my parents get something in their heads they are formidable. No matter what, the citizens of Ebscalon will be very protective of you because you are different, and they will feel responsible in protecting you from things that you will not be accustomed to."

"How can I convince your parents that my main goal is to get back home to my father and brothers, and to go to college and start my education?"

Trakon grimaced ever so slightly, but straightened his face to a noncommittal expression. D'laine noticed the change, but kept quiet thinking he wasn't so disinterested in her as she thought. How could she even think of a boyfriend here, never mind a husband!

Yes, he was so good looking she could hardly keep her eyes off him, but they were practically strangers and knew nothing about each other. No intimate secrets, concerns, hopes, loves— nothing at all. D'laine kept her mouth closed and her confusion to herself.

"It will take time getting used to all these new things, but I will make an effort," she said.

They left the courtyard and he took her about the city, showing her the marketplace where people displayed their wares. The market was like a gigantic bazaar with tents and booths and all manner of goods to be purchased or traded.

D'laine was surprised when she saw the different peoples of Thol.

In addition to the humans, there were other creatures buying and selling goods. It reminded her of the bar scene in Star Wars. She learned that bartering was popular, and sepiks (copper-like coins) were one of the forms of money used to purchase items.

People saluted Trakon and stared at D'laine. Children played in the courtyard and alleyways. Most of the women were dressed in the draping gown that Kitry wore and D'laine wondered if she were dressed correctly.

"Why do most of the women wear those gowns like your mother?" D'laine asked. "Should I have worn something like that? Do I look alright?"

"Your type of clothing is suitable for you as it's worn by women that have been trained as warriors who guard and defend the nurseries. The women who wear the gowns are more domestic in nature, but that doesn't mean that they wouldn't protect their city and families if we were attacked by an enemy. They would protect the children and the nurseries with their dying breath," he explained.

"Oh, do the children stay there during the day when their mothers are busy?" D'laine asked thinking about the common day care concept of her Earth, and being uncertain of what he was actually trying to explain.

Trakon scrunched his face in thought. "We have communal centers where the eggs are hatched."

Her head jerked at that statement. D'laine was deep in thought as they continued their tour. There were children playing in the streets and one little boy, about two, ran right into her and fell backwards onto his bottom.

D'laine knelt and tried to help him up. "Are you okay?"

The boy jumped to his feet and his little hand went to his

chest in recognition of his prince. "Forgive me, my prince, Warrior Princess. I should have been paying more attention." The boy backed away several feet, turned and ran back to his playmates.

D'laine appeared surprised. "That little boy sure speaks well for a two-year old. My brothers barely made sense at that age."

Trakon thought for a moment. "Life here is not the same as what you are used to. From what you have told me, we die in the same ways, under some of the same circumstances, but we are not brought into the world in the same manner as the children of your world."

He hesitated. "The child you just saw was not as old as you thought. On your world, yes. Here, no. Your people have live births, as do most of the animal species and other races here on Thol. My race conceives in the same way that your race does, but that is the end of any similarity."

D'laine listened quietly while her mind spun out of control.

Trakon frowned as he turned toward her and placed his hands on her shoulders.

"We look the same on the outside, but our internal structures are different. The woman's body has a similar type of system that a woman of your world has, but when the eggs are fertilized, they travel down the tubes to the womb where they rest for sixty days, then pass through the body."

D'laine kept her mouth shut. Her head pounded. They started walking away from the market.

Trakon explained the process in detail. "The woman then takes the egg and carefully transports it to a resting chamber in the communal center where it will sit, cushioned on soft material and be kept warm from the heat of the suns. It will grow over a period of three years, the shell enlarging and the child maturing as time passes. The eggs are guarded very closely and each mother knows when her egg will be ready to hatch."

Stopping for a moment, he checked D'laine's response to what he was telling her. He could clearly see that she was overloaded with information. Her face had a stern look as she stood still, digesting what he had told her.

"The child emerges from the shell a perfect Tholian, with the intelligence equal to a grown man. He still needs to be taught fundamentals and manners, but most of the training has been genetically transferred to him and he is ready to take his place in society."

D'laine was rolling things around in her head. "What a way to start life!"

"The boy you saw just now hatched a week earlier and was practicing strategies with his fellow youngmen," Trakon said.

D'laine's mind reeled with the information. She had never heard of such a thing!

"And to think my mother was in labor for at least six hours with each of us when she could have just squatted and laid an egg!" D'laine shook her head in total disbelief. "I can't believe it. You're serious, right?"

Trakon gave her a look that told her he was serious. "You have changed; adapted to Thol. I'm sure that if you were to return to your world you wouldn't change back."

D'laine dismissed his speech with a wave of her hand. "Some things have changed, but I doubt if that has." She gazed after the children, lost in thought. "My body is different! We come from two different worlds, each with its own evolution. We have mixed marriages between different ethnic groups, but we all have children in the same way. The only difference between ethnicities is a cultural difference, skin color or religious differences. We don't have internal differences!"

"You have changed; you have adapted. From what you told

me, even Ghury suggested that. You just didn't realize what the meaning of his words were at the time, but you have become one of us now."

"Maybe so, but we don't have to worry about it now. I'm a long way from having that type of relationship with anyone," she stated.

Not willing to listen anymore, she saw that he was pleading for her to understand, and accept the life that was destined for her.

She truly missed the wisdom and guidance of the Egroms, but knew that this city was where she belonged. Adrum had armed her with knowledge, but not enough.

"Why would the Egroms leave out these details? I think that information was intentionally hidden, but I can't understand why. Don't you think it would have been better to have me totally prepared?" D'laine asked.

"It doesn't make any sense why they would hide that from you," Trakon said.

Everything would come together eventually, but she wanted to know the answers right now, not some time in the future when the Egroms felt it was the right time for her to know the missing information.

*How did they evolve?*

*Why were the Egroms more intellectually advanced than any of the other races here, or from her world?*

*Where had they come from and how had their powers developed?*

*Why were they such a secret race, thought of as only a legend?*

The questions gnawed at her. Where were the answers?

A civilized species, they were primitive at the same time, with skills beyond humankind's abilities. She was sure that they were capable of much more than what they had shown her;

such a mystery surrounded their existence. She felt certain that the few wonders that she had seen were just simple lessons for her entertainment, compared to what they were capable of doing.

What she couldn't understand was why the isolation from the Ciertrons and other human-type people? Why just this whispered wonderment of fable where they were concerned? What was being gained by this seclusion? Didn't they realize how they could improve life for others?

She knew they were capable of traveling through the portals that they guarded—Ghury had rescued her, after all. They could improve other worlds and bring people together to share in the wealth of knowledge that her people and others would prize so highly.

Leaving those thoughts behind, she thought of the Ciertrons. She was gaining knowledge every day, but there was still so much to learn. They were so like her and yet so vastly different. Their life had evolved beyond what her own people had achieved, but she didn't see anything of commerce here except for the marketplace.

Had they evolved beyond the business and industrial conglomeration that her world was struggling with? Did they have political strife here among their own people? It was all so confusing, with the different classes of people; the differences between the common man and royalty—she wasn't sure if there were any differences. Was there just one royal family? Were there others? Did the people vote on who held the position, and for how long, or were these people of royal birth? There was much to learn.

D'laine thought of Trakon. How strange that they were drawn to each other like a magnet and steel, the force being so powerful that she was sure neither one of them had a chance to reject the thought. It was as if someone, or something were guiding them towards a planned future that was beyond their control. It had been instantaneous from the moment she had seen his image in her dreams, and then in Adrum's projected vision. She guessed that at that moment, the thought had been planted in Trakon's mind, too.

This brought her to haunting thoughts of home, and a wave of sorrow crashed down around her. She wanted to know what was happening.

Were her brothers alright?

What about her father?

He had been through so much pain and agony in the past; how was he reacting to this situation?

Did anyone really know what had happened to her?

Had anyone else been dragged into this land, or perhaps thrown into another barbaric place? Maybe they were dead. Deciding to stick to the belief that they had stayed behind on Earth, she wondered what her father thought of all of this. She was sure his scientific mind was agitated.

"I just can't comprehend what you told me and I do not think it is possible for one of my species to change the whole process of our evolution."

They turned to head back to the palace when there was a commotion at the front gates. Warriors yelled and shot their laser pistols. People were running and screaming.

Then D'laine heard barking. "Oh no! The dogs! Tell them to stop shooting!"

Trakon took off running with D'laine beside him.

"Stop shooting! They're the princess's dogs!

The warriors didn't stop. D'laine held out her hand and the laser pistols were yanked away from the warriors and landed at her feet.

Trakon looked from the weapons to D'laine and out toward the warriors.

Pup led Scooby and Chatter to D'laine. She dropped to her knees. The dogs were all over her, whining and licking her. People looked out of their hiding places shocked at what they saw.

Jor-Dan rushed over, laser pistol in hand. He stopped and took in the scene in front of him. D'laine was rubbing the dogs' bellies. Chatter licked Trakon as he ruffled his tufts of hair on his head.

"How could this be?" Jor-Dan asked.

The Visionary approached him. "Anyone who can tame these savage beasts is all powerful."

D'laine looked up at them. "Animals like me."

"They're here now. What are we going to do with them?" Trakon asked. "How can we be sure they won't slaughter everyone?"

"They didn't attack the guards, and they didn't run after everyone who was running away, so I'd say they're going to be okay. I'm just afraid people will shoot them," D'laine said.

Trakon walked over to his father with Chatter on his heels. Jor-Dan looked at the dog in distaste.

"How did this happen?" Jor-Dan asked.

Trakon scratched Chatter on the head. "Father, all I can tell you is that all animals are like her children. They love her and seem to change their nature when they are around her."

Jor-Dan summoned a palace guard. "Tell cook he has three more mouths to cook for. I suppose if they're fed, they will be safe around people."

They returned to the palace with the dogs at their side. Trakon led her back to her quarters. Twum must have been aware of their approach because she was waiting for them when they arrived at the doorway to D'laine's apartment.

Twum screeched when she saw the dogs.

"Calm down, they're tame," Trakon said.

Scooby sniffed Twum's toes. The young woman practically fainted. Trakon sat her in a chair until she recovered.

"I think they should sleep in here with me at night so they don't get into trouble," D'laine said.

"They may want to hunt at night," Trakon said. "Maybe they should sleep out in the hallway"

"That makes sense," D'laine said. "They can come and go as they please. Are you okay, Twum?"

Twum swallowed hard and nodded. "Is there anything I can help you with?"

"The Princess would like to rest for the time being. See that she isn't disturbed, " Trakon said as they went through the door into the inner room, and sat on one of the divans, looking out the window, beyond the city.

"I guess they will want to stay with you for now," Trakon said.

D'laine punched his arm. "Why did you call me that? You know it's not true!"

He shrugged. "Look, the entire city, and most likely beyond, recognizes you as a princess, thanks to my conniving parents. There's no point in trying to convince an entire population of anything else."

She glared at him. "My father would set them straight if he were here."

"How about if I come back later?" He stood and sauntered to the door. "If you get bored, I'll be at the hangar."

Chatter stood. He followed Trakon.

Trakon looked down at the dog. "I guess I have a dog now." He grinned.

When the door clicked shut, she let out a loud sigh. "This is crazy." She scrunched down on the divan and pouted while Pup and Scooby flopped down on the floor.

# CHAPTER THIRTY-THREE

$\mathcal{T}$he apartment was quiet, giving D'laine the needed serenity to collect her thoughts. Everything was happening much too quickly for her to digest. Was it weeks, months or years since she had left her world? Confused, she was having difficulty keeping track of time since that day, so long ago, that she found herself on the moss in the meadow. Her main cause of confusion was due to the drastic change from day to night in this existence; she couldn't gage how long each day was compared to Earth time.

Rising from the divan, she crossed the room and lay down on the vast bed, gathering some of the silky material around her. She studied the texture of the fabric in wonderment. Soft as silk, but woven like gauze bandage, the material did not have the characteristics of either. Shimmering with brilliance, it was a solid color one minute, a whole rainbow of colors the next minute. It was the most beautiful material she had ever seen, and she was sure there was nothing of comparable worth on Earth. In the silence of her chambers, D'laine reflected on the new life that she had stepped into since her arrival to Thol.

From the humble surroundings of the Egroms, to the lively city of Ebscalon, the contrast was vast. After several minutes of trying to de-stress from all these thoughts, she drifted off to sleep.

THE DOGS BARKING CRAZILY JERKED HER AWAKE. SHE SAT up, getting her bearings. The dogs were at the windows barking. Finally wide awake, a loud disturbance involving shouting and explosions jolted her into action. Jumping out of bed she raced to the window and was alarmed at the sight. People were running in every direction. Leaning further out of the window, she saw a lot of activity down by the main entrance to the city.

Stretching to see more clearly, she glimpsed several pakows and wondered what in the world they were doing inside the gates. They were never allowed beyond those heavy gates; the beasts were too big to be lumbering around loose. Something was not right. Guards ran in every direction. Then she noticed the Plotals! A sinking feeling overcame her. The city was being attacked!

D'laine held her hand out and made Pup and Scooby lie down.

"This is no place for dogs. You could get shot by either side. Stay!" she commanded as she got up and left the room shutting the door behind her.

She raced from the room to the main salon which was deserted. From there, she retraced her footsteps back to Jor-Dan's quarters and found his manservant, Mayaar.

"What's happened?" D'laine kept control of her panic.

"I don't know where the king is, everything happened so fast," Mayaar exclaimed.

The man bordered on hysteria and could not provide any

information. Looking inside her mind, she found the answer. Placing her fingers to his temple, she thought soothing thoughts.

"Be calm. Tell me what happened," she projected into his mind.

He became tranquil and began telling D'laine what had happened.

"The outer sentries sent word that the Plotals had been spotted on the outer edges of Ebscalon. A massive army with many thousands of men and beasts. There wasn't time for our leaders to make formal plans. They are scattered throughout the city," he said as if in a trance.

"Go find shelter," D'laine planted in his mind.

D'laine left the building, running to the courtyard. She observed the action, staring at the ongoing battle. People were fighting everywhere with laser swords and plasma blasters. On the walls surrounding the city, in the streets—everywhere. There were several Plotal warriors close-by in battle with Ciertrons.

Coming out of her daze, she discovered a Plotal warrior approaching on a pakow at a fast pace and she sidestepped his beast, just missing being run over by inches. The warrior aimed his laser at her.

He jumped down from his beast to face her, laser in hand, ready to finish her off. His angry thoughts were transmitted to her. He didn't like being beaten. Turning the tables on him, she held out her hand and pointed to him. A stream of energy unknown to any human or creature, hit him and he immediately fell over, dead.

She stood silently over the dead warrior, feet apart, breathing ragged rasps of air into her lungs. She looked down and stared at her palms in astonishment, still not used to her new abilities. Suddenly, she felt different, stronger. A feeling of enormous power came over her, as if her brain was expanding to the very walls of her skull. The commotion around her pulled her thoughts back to the present. The beast stood where its rider left it, and she knew it wouldn't damage anything. It would most likely wander around until it found something to eat.

She left the dead warrior where he lay and scanned the area for familiar faces. There was no sight of Trakon or Jor-Dan. Making her way further into the city to see what was happening there, she noticed that there were no women or children and she assumed they were under lock and key in the nursery.

D'laine ran through the streets, darting around crowds of fighting Ciertrons and Plotals, and ran right into an ornate Plotal. She knew by instinct that this was the fiend Jakla Bosakin. Shuddering from the sudden confrontation, he was more formidable up close than she had anticipated.

His eyes lit up when he saw her. "The prized golden girl! Mine for the taking!"

Not anticipating his move, she was caught unprepared as he stunned her with his laser. As if atoms exploded inside her, she felt her senses being caught in limbo, suspended. Helpless, she fell to the ground and discovered that she could still hear but she couldn't move to defend herself, or even speak. The only thing that seemed possible was to blink, but that wasn't any help at all.

D'laine knew her thoughts hadn't projected as she called out telepathically to Trakon. Jakla picked her up in his cold scaly hands and threw her over his shoulder. He summoned his pakow, mounted and left the inner city as fast as he could. Knowing the opportunity might not arise this easily ever again, he was not going to lose his prize by hanging around to witness the outcome of the battle, and in his haste, he ran down a Ciertron and one of his own men that fought in his path.

The Golden Girl. Daydreams ran through his mind; he had heard stories about her powers and she was now his. He would be all-powerful! He would conquer all! He would force the girl to use her powers for his benefit, or he would torture her. A maniacal laugh rumbled up through his body and shook the air.

"COVER THE EAST WALL AND FIND OUR WEAKEST SPOT!" Trakon shouted to his men as he assessed each situation of the battle. Chatter stood by his side looking ferocious.

Trakon sensed something wrong and stopped suddenly. He looked toward the palace and hurried to search for D'laine. He and Chatter bounded down the hallways and threw open the door to her suite and found the dogs on the floor. Pup jumped to his feet.

Chatter romped into the room and the dogs acted like they had been away from each other for a week. Trakon held out his hand to the dogs.

"Stay!" he commanded as he shut the door behind him.

He backtracked until he reached the nursery chamber where his mother and the other women and children were. Pressing the hidden control button, the wall opened for his passage through to the prized chamber. He quickly scanned the room and discovered that D'laine was not among the women. The room was alive with activity, his mother barking-out orders to protect the future generation.

Without stopping to talk with his mother, he left the chamber and climbed higher in the palace and looked out a window from one of the turrets. A scene caught his attention, constricting his throat. A pakow charging out of the city carried

Jakla Bosakin. On the back of the beast was D'laine, in a limp heap.

Fear filled his chest until he thought he was frozen to the spot. Snapping out of his immobility, he quickly leapt into action. He raced out of the small room, retracing his steps down the stairs and corridors, out into the courtyard. He searched for a pakow and spotted a stray beast wandering about. Making his way toward it, he avoided groups of fighting Plotals and Ciertrons and almost reached the beast when a Plotal turned from its dead quarry and faced him, laser sword in hand, red with the blood from his latest victim.

Trakon drew his laser and faced his tall opponent. The fight commenced. Ruthless in battle, the Plotals used their brute strength and their impressive height to their advantage, as well as their mighty barbed tails.

Suddenly a swarm of borjos arrived carrying Kudaja warriors. Herish aimed his wyre and struck the Plotal Trakon was battling. As the Plotal lurched from Herish's strike, he swung his heavy tail around and knocked Trakon off his feet. As Trakon fell to the ground, the massive tail came around once more striking a blow at his head, knocking him unconscious.

Herish finished off the Plotal. He steered his borjo over to Trakon where Ciertron warriors rallied around their prince.

"Is he alive?" Herish called out.

"Just a nasty head wound, but he's out," a Ciertron warrior said.

The number of Plotal warriors left in the city was limited now, being either killed, captured, or escaped. Prisoners would be few and the dead would have to be carried off later. Without their leader, the Plotals fought without tactics and became careless, bloodthirsty fools.

Herish followed the Ciertron warriors as they carefully carried Trakon to the palace and placed him on one of the divans in a sitting room. Herish landed the borjo on a table and dismounted. He watched from his perch on the table.

"Go find Jor-Dan! Bring the Visionary!" one of the Ciertron guards barked out.

Two runners sped out of the palace and went in two different directions. Loud, running footsteps approached the small group crouched over Trakon. The group pressed their fists to their chests as their King entered the room. They enclosed him in their circle.

"I don't think his wound is near fatal, Sire," one of the men offered. "A Kudaja warrior killed the Plotal that attacked our prince."

"The Kudaja are here in the city?" Jor-Dan asked, surprised.

"Aye, Sire," the Ciertron said. "The warrior is here." He pointed to Herish on the table.

Jor-Dan turned and saw Herish. "Thank you for joining in the fight. Why are you here though? The Kudaja aren't known to socialize with Ciertrons."

Herish hit his chest in respect for Jor-Dan. "Herish of the Cember Forest, King Jor-Dan. We were returning from a distant village and heard the fighting. I wanted to make sure D'laine was safe."

Jor-Dan looked at Herish quizzically. "You know my son's intended, the princess D'laine?"

Herish balked. "Intended? I know nothing of any pending nuptials, but I do know D'laine from her life in the Cember Forest with the Egroms."

"I see," Jor-Dan said, not too happy. Looking around, there was no sign of D'laine. He bent over Trakon.

"I can see the tail marks on his head and face," Jor-Dan said. He looked at his guards. "Have you sent for the Visionary?"

"Yes, Sire. He should be here soon," a young guard said.

"Stay with him until I return. I need to find the Princess," Jor-Dan said, then went in search of D'laine.

Jor-Dan found the three dogs, but not D'laine. He shut the dogs in the room and went in search of his wife on the off-chance that D'laine had gone to the nursery to protect the children and eggs.

Kitry was relieved to see her husband. "Jor-Dan! What is happening?"

She lived in constant fear that battle would eventually kill him, but had kept her fears deeply hidden. Trying to keep a straight face, she went to him and hugged him tightly, grateful that he had been spared once again.

Tight lipped, Jor-Dan looked around the room. Fear clutched his heart. "Where's D'laine?" he asked, with a flat expression.

"I thought she was with you or Trakon!" Kitry exclaimed. Panic touched her face.

"Trakon is down," Jor-Dan said.

"Oh no! How bad?" Kitry asked.

Jor-Dan grasped her arms. "We need to find D'laine first. Trakon will live! He was struck in the head by a Plotal tail. A Kudaja warrior killed the Plotal."

"The Kudaja are here?" Kitry asked, surprised.

Jor-Dan sighed. "Yes."

Kitry pulled her senses together. She called out specific orders and left the chamber with Jor-Dan.

They hurried down the corridors together. Kitry entered the sitting room while Jor-Dan continued and left the palace. When he came to the courtyard, Jor-Dan hailed one of his warriors.

"Have you seen the Princess?" he asked.

"No Sire! Not since before the attack earlier in the day," the warrior said.

"Go and check with the guards. See if anyone has seen her," Jor-Dan commanded.

The warrior hurried away.

Jor-Dan was worried. He called to her telepathically. No response returned to him. He returned to the palace and checked on Trakon. Trakon remained unconscious on the low sofa. The old Visionary hovered over him, tending to his wounds.

"He will have a severe headache when he regains consciousness. It will be important for him to stay calm and not overtax himself for at least two or more completed days," the Visionary explained to Jor-Dan. He stood, bowed his head to Kitry and left.

Kitry knelt beside Trakon and brushed the hair off his forehead; worry lines creased her face.

The warrior from the courtyard entered the room and saluted Jor-Dan. "Sire, there have been no reports of the Princess," he said.

Kitry and Jor-Dan exchanged worried glances.

"Find the Captain of the Guard. Tell him to gather the army. I'm certain that Jakla has kidnapped Princess D'laine!" Jor-Dan directed.

The warrior quickly left the palace to pass on the information so the preparations could be arranged.

"Trakon?" Jor-Dan called out softly.

Slowly, Trakon moved his head from side-to-side, and finally opened his eyes. The dizziness of his head injury forced them closed again. In that scattered second, Jor-Dan picked up a wild thought from his son. He saw Jakla leaving the city on the huge pakow with D'laine thrown over the back of the beast.

Jor-Dan turned to Kitry. "I was afraid this would happen. Jakla has her." He stood and kissed his wife.

"Bosakin has D'laine?" Herish shouted. "The Kudaja will find her!" He jumped on his borjo and was gone in a flash.

"Take the dogs!" Kitry exclaimed. "They will track her."

Jor-Dan rushed to D'laine's apartment and opened the door. "Come!" he said.

The dogs followed him back to the room where Trakon was, still out cold. Chatter rushed to Trakon, his teeth clacking while he whined. He sniffed Trakon from head to toe.

"We must leave now, while the tracks are fairly fresh, or we may never find them. Try to detain Trakon if he wakes. Tell him everything is being taken care of and I will return with D'laine if it takes a lifetime."

Jor-Dan patted his leg. "Come," he said to the dogs.

Pup and Scooby were ready to go. Chatter would not leave Trakon's side.

Jor-Dan nodded. "Protective and loyal. Make sure the dog eats."

The remaining warriors joined the king and the two dogs as they left the room. As he reached the courtyard, he was briefed by one of his men. Scouts had been sent in search of the tribe.

Not much time had elapsed and the Plotals were on pakows. Though they were surefooted creatures, they could only go so fast and the crestriders would catch up with them quickly and quietly.

Jor-Dan knelt in front of Pup. "Find D'laine!"

Pup seemed to understand. He and Scooby shot out of the city on Jakla Bosakin's trail.

Jor-Dan and his entourage continued to the large hangar and disappeared inside. A loud hydraulic sound emanated and the roof of the building opened. The silent mothership emerged and momentarily hovered over the building. Jor-Dan stood on the bridge with some of his men surrounding him.

"Follow the dogs!" He instructed the pilot.

As the ship moved forward, the cleanup activity was visible on the ground. Crews gathered the dead enemy from the skirmish to be disposed of outside the gates. Pakows were led out to the pens. Dead Ciertron warriors would have a proper, honorable burial.

As the ship progressed across the sky, they were joined by several smaller scout ships. They left the city in a southerly direction, moving at a moderate pace. They saw a band of warriors on pakows behind the dogs.

"Those dogs will find her," a warrior said. "They are loyal."

With only three more hours of daylight, they would have to either hurry and find the tribe, or make camp for the night and continue their search in the morning.

Because D'laine was in danger, Jor-Dan pressed onward; he didn't know the capacity of her powers and was sure that she didn't either. Trakon's brief image indicated that she was incapacitated. It worried him to think what Jakla could do to her, not knowing if she was even capable of defending herself.

A passionate believer in justice, honor and commitment, he would kill any man or beast that harmed her, no matter what it took. She was the future; premonition told him so.

# CHAPTER THIRTY-FOUR

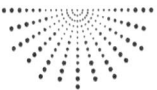

*T*he thundering beast finally came to a stop. Inside D'laine's head, a cranium explosion brewed from the sound of many feet beating the ground at the fast pace. Paralyzed from the laser, she couldn't do anything until she had her senses about her again; all self-protection had disintegrated with the blast. The laser had attacked her muscles and nerves; she still had her wits about her, but she couldn't make her body move. Confused, she couldn't understand why the first laser hadn't hurt her, unless it had something to do with her hand capturing the blast. This attack caught her off guard. Maybe her system required an intense focus, she wondered? She would have to figure this out for future battles. D'laine already made up her mind that this would never happen to her again. She would not allow her powers to betray her.

Jakla jumped down from his beast and hauled his captive down. When he discovered she could not stand on her own, he let her drop to the ground, still clamping her arm in a vise-like grip that cut off the circulation in her arm. His cold, clammy skin made her think of slimy night crawlers, or snakes.

From Adrum's movies, she knew that the Plotals loved to be cruel, and D'laine was not going to give them the satisfaction of seeing her suffer. It was bad enough that she couldn't defend herself, but they didn't know they were not dealing with a Ciertron. They were faced with a mortal from a different world; someone equipped to stand ground and face them. If only she could prove herself now!

The Plotal warlord daydreamed, his ego soaring. The stories he had heard of this Golden Girl from his well-paid spies were fantastic, but unproven. The business about her skin and hair coloring was another matter. He could only assume that her coloring was different from the Ciertrons because she was either a throwback, or perhaps from another tribe on the other side of Thol that he hadn't discovered yet. Or, this was a trick of some sort where a dye had been used to bleach out her true coloring. Seeing no reason for a trap, he dismissed that possibility as improbable.

Darkness would be approaching rapidly, and as soon as the night ink draped everything in total blackness, she knew a rescue would be unlikely. Looking around as far as her gaze would let her, she saw the pakows on the outskirts of the camp tethered to a line. The Plotals assembled colorful tents. Fascinated, she was reminded of hot air balloons; they were so big.

Jakla turned his attention back to his prize. "Do not try to escape. There is no place for you to run," he said. He turned and walked toward one of his lieutenants.

D'laine tried to speak and was alarmed. All that emerged was a gurgling sound. Had her vocal cords been damaged by the weapon? She couldn't even talk. Tears pooled; she was thankful that her captors were not close enough to witness her shame and weakness. Jakla busily ordered preparations for the night: guards were posted, firewood was gathered.

He left his men and walked toward his prisoner and

stopped beside her. D'laine looked up at his huge form from her position on the ground and felt like a helpless bug about to be squashed. He nudged her with his blood-stained black boot. She could not move, much less scream out her hatred to him. He looked down at her and grunted.

"So, you do have a weakness! YAARRAH!" He bellowed the Plotal victory cry as she lay humiliated in her helplessness.

She wondered how long the paralysis would linger.

TIME PASSED AGONIZINGLY SLOW AS SHE LAY IN A TWISTED heap on the ground. Darkness cloaked the night. Guards paced along the perimeter of the encampment keeping their eyes and ears alert for any sign of an approaching foe. Jakla discussed strategy with his lieutenant.

"The Ciertrons will come for her. We should have kept moving. We'll break camp before the first light of morning and join with the larger army."

Jakla walked back to D'laine. Looking down at her limp body, he sneered; he had the upper hand, she couldn't do anything.

"When we join the main army, there will be too many Plotals for the Ciertrons to fight. You are mine now!" he said, ending with a snort.

He nudged her again with his blood-spattered boot, enjoying his position. After several moments, he turned away and headed for a tent.

A warrior approached with medieval-like shackles dangling from his fist. Kneeling, he grabbed one wrist, then the other, closing the shackles tightly on her extremities. Wincing with pain, she damned herself for showing weakness, but didn't utter a sound. He opened his water pouch and grabbed her by the hair and poured water down her throat as she opened her mouth in protest. As she began sputtering and choking from the deluge, he must have felt satisfied that she had enough to last her through the night. Corking his pouch, he sauntered away to stand guard nearby.

Alone again, D'laine's body twitched. She suddenly realized that the effects of the laser must be wearing off. Slowly she regained her strength. It wouldn't be long, she thought. Jakla would pay for this barbaric treatment. She couldn't stand the thought of these brutes taking others captive. By Plotal standards, she was being treated like royalty; she couldn't even believe they had given her water. Commanding all of her strength, she tried moving her legs. They finally obeyed. Lying quietly, D'laine rubbed a welt on her wrist and looked about.

Off to the side, a creature hung by its arms from two tall lances. As she studied it, she recognized it to be a Safri, one of the lesser tribes of Thol, but nonetheless, an intelligent creature just the same. Looking for a sign of life, she detected a slow pulse; he was barely alive. She felt that she had to help him. They were friendly with the Ciertrons and traded with them. She remembered seeing Safris at the market.

Strange creatures to look at, being neither man nor beast, Safris were slight of build and covered with brown fur. Their pointed ears were at the sides of their head. Their forehead was topped with short, stubby horns. Their backs sported underdeveloped wings at the shoulder blades, feet were hoofed like horses, which allowed them to walk upright, or run with a speed on all fours that defied man. And their hands had three large fingers at the end of a large palm. A nagging thought in her memory rose to the surface and D'laine was reminded of Pan, the god from Greek mythology.

With Jakla down for the night, D'laine thought that she might be able to escape if she could collect her senses. Not trying to be a hero, she formed a plan. Gazing at the Safri, she called out to him telepathically.

"Ssshh," she whispered in his mind. "I am nearby and will try to help you."

The Safri stirred.

"Over here, in the shadows. Can you see me now?" she coaxed.

He responded slowly, opening his eyes and jerking his head in her direction. "Save yourself. You can do nothing for Bok-Tor," he whispered, practically lifeless.

"Don't give up so easily," D'laine told him. "Stay alert!"

Jakla stepped out of his tent to give one last order and was surprised to see D'laine sitting. Crossing the distance quickly, he grabbed her shackled wrist and dragged her to her feet, inspecting her. She felt like gagging as his cold clammy skin touched hers, especially now that she knew his intentions. Not knowing that she was playing helpless, he dragged her across the encampment to a group of young Plotal warriors.

Such ugly creatures, their evil looks reflected their love of inflicting pain on others as they sneered with pleasure at D'laine's treatment.

Jakla gripped her wrist in a vise-like hold.

"Who are you and where do you come from?" he demanded.

About to sputter off a string of insults, D'laine was alarmed when her voice failed her. All that emerged were raspy sounds that hurt her throat. Clutching her neck in pain, she tried swallowing away the horrible feeling inside her.

"Do you dare to defy ME, Jakla the Mighty Warrior?" he boomed.

D'laine looked up at him and spoke in a steady, but raspy voice which commanded authority. "Why did you kidnap me if you didn't know who I was? Do you always make such rash decisions? Those are not qualities of a born leader!"

Jakla bellowed his rage.

"If you try to harm me, you will only harm yourself," she warned as she made eye contact with each of them.

Humored by this statement, the young warriors laughed and snapped their long snouts fiendishly in her direction.

Jakla released her wrist, dropping D'laine to the ground. "You'd better cooperate, or you'll get the same treatment as the Safri. Now, tell me what region of Thol you are from!" he demanded.

She refused to answer him, looking him directly in the eye, defiant. Intruding on the private side of his mind, she read his furious thoughts .... *will not put up with such insolence in front of my men. She will not make me look like a fool!*

He drew a barbed stick from the holster at his side and snapped it on her thigh.

Shock numbed her mind. D'laine looked down and saw the blood seeping through her uniform. Where had her powers fled to, she thought, frightened. Terrified, she realized that she couldn't help the Safri and she couldn't even protect herself.

"Think about that!" Jakla boomed as he kicked her aside and turned to his men who boosted his warrior ego. The young Plotal warriors howled and jeered.

In the privacy of her mind, D'laine let loose of the tremendous pain with an internal scream. Having no defenses to protect herself, she would, at best, have to wait for someone to rescue her. Would she survive?

D'laine flinched. A muscle spasm? Clearing her throat, she tried speaking out loud, softly, so no one would hear her. Her voice had finally returned to normal and she felt overwhelming joy. She wondered if her powers had returned as well.

With an evil sneer on his ugly face, Jakla gripped the

barbed stick. Instantly, she knew she was in trouble. He raised it over his head to strike her. Concentrating all her power, the weapon halted in midair, inches from her shoulder. A vortex of power filled her as Jakla discovered that he couldn't release his hold on the stick either. She rose to her feet, keeping the stick and Jakla locked in a tight grip.

"How does that feel?" she asked him.

Beads of sweat stood out on his scaly forehead; he was clearly worried.

The power consumed her, filling her body with a tingling force. In that instant, she knew that she was stronger than she had ever been in her entire life and there was little to hold her back. D'laine knew the dangers of being reckless and she could not afford to let the power get out of control. She would use her power wisely.

At her suggestion the iron bands dropped from her wrists.

The young warriors muttered loudly.

"Grab this insolent girl! Punish her!" Jakla roared with rage. With all his might, he found that he still could not release his hand from the stick.

As his men approached her, she shook her head and pointed at them giving them one warning. "You should not try to harm me. You think I'm a stupid girl? How mistaken you are! This kind of behavior is not acceptable, and you will have to suffer the consequences."

They stopped to listen to her, then rushed in for the kill.

Like a magician, D'laine drew a line with an outstretched hand. She suggested a power field and when the warriors approached it, an electric force repelled them. They howled in agony.

Trapped, Jakla bayed his rage as his men screamed in pain. He watched in humiliation as his men were being beaten by a mere girl with strange powers.

"Stun her! Stun her!" he commanded.

D'laine drew a circle around herself and pointed her finger in an up and down motion. Now she was protected horizontally and vertically. The shield hugged her form like an ethereal skin. They could not reach her unless they broke through the electric force, and the force would kill them if they tried to be so brave. She was safe from them and their deadly lasers which would be their only hope of salvation.

D'laine darted towards the Safri who had watched the events in amazement. A mere look at his bonds released him. Carefully, she drew him into her circle and put her arm around his body, supporting him.

"Don't worry, I'll take you to my people; we'll take care of you," she told the frail creature.

"You have saved Bok-Tor from a fate worse than death," he said. He gazed at her with adoration.

D'laine extended her hand and drew a circle around the group of Plotals, covering all of them. The aura that circled her disappeared and she helped Bok-Tor toward a pakow. They approached the beast and D'laine reached out and put her hand on its front leg. She spoke gently to the beast and patted him, trying to coax the animal to lower its form to the ground so they could mount.

Pup and Scooby rushed into the camp followed by Ciertron warriors with Jor-Dan in the lead. A swarm of borjos accompanied the Ciertrons.

"I knew someone would come!" she cried.

"We are thankful that the dogs found you and led us here," Jor-Dan said.

Pup and Scooby lunged at Jakla and the Plotals behind the force field. The shocks of energy jolted the dogs but they were determined to get at the prey.

D'laine called to them, but the dogs would not relent. She walked over and grabbed Pup by the scruff.

"Stop!" she commanded.

Pup whined as he looked from her to the Plotals.

Jakla and his warriors watched in disbelief as she patted the dogs on their rumps.

She looked at Jakla. "Don't shoot while you are detained. The laser shots will bounce back and kill you."

D'laine urged the dogs back over to Jor-Dan and Bok-Tor. Looking around, she expected to see Trakon. Fear gripped her as Jor-Dan came to her side, a serious look on his face.

He read her thoughts and immediately set her at ease.

"He has had but a mere accident, there is nothing to worry about," he said.

Herish hovered on his borjo beside D'laine and Jor-Dan. "You are safe with the Ciertrons," he said. "We will be off now. I'll see you tomorrow." He hit his chest and he and his tiny warriors took off into the night.

Jor-Dan watched the Kudaja fly off. When they were out of sight he turned to D'laine, a concerned look on his face. "I would not encourage that one."

D'laine waved off his warning. "Herish is harmless. We're just friends."

Jor-Dan shook his head. "You are wrong in that assumption."

D'laine looked quizzically at Jor-Dan. "I don't understand why you and Trakon are so concerned about a tiny warrior."

"All is not what it seems with the Kudaja," Jor-Dan said.

"That's what Trakon said. What does that mean?" she asked.

"The Kudaja males have their own agenda," he said, and left it at that. "How long will your powers hold the Plotals?"

"I don't really know the extent of these powers yet. It's all too new to me," she said. "I wish I could explain it. I simply went with my instinct."

Jor-Dan summoned two of his men to carry the Safri, then he drew her toward the fire. "I witnessed what you did and I feel that we could have stayed home. Will they be released if you leave the campsite?" he asked, perplexed.

D'laine shrugged.

"Jakla doesn't have his full army with him, so I'm sure he won't try anything foolish. He'll wait until the time is right, you can be sure of that. Come, let us return to our camp, we are not far away," he told her.

Helpless inside the force field and not daring to reach out and touch the deadly barrier, Jakla sneered at them.

"I will be back with tens of thousands of warriors and we will destroy Ebscalon! Now that I know your weakness, you can be sure that I will find a way to get to you, D'laine!" he screamed.

She faced the Plotal. "Once a weakness is discovered, Jakla, it is no longer a threat."

D'laine knew he would be after revenge and would hunt high and low over the surface of Thol for a way to overcome her. She dreaded the day when he discovered the secret to her powers—something she didn't even know. If he could find the source, he would use it to defeat her.

# CHAPTER THIRTY-FIVE

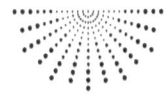

*T*hey walked out of the Plotal encampment towards the Ciertron camp about a half mile away with the dogs bounding ahead of them. A peculiar feeling overcame her; D'laine was certain that the Plotals were free of the barrier that held them. Entering the camp, she crossed the small distance to the fire where Bok-Tor lay in a pathetic heap, weak from starvation and scarred from beatings. She knelt down beside him. The dogs checked out the Safri then plopped down beside D'laine.

"Where do you hail from, fair one," Bok-Tor asked D'laine. "I have travelled the whole surface of Thol and I have never seen a skin color or hair such as yours, and only the magical Egroms have such powers!"

Surprised by his statement, D'laine and Jor-Dan exchanged glances across the top of his head.

"Oh, come on, when did you ever see an Egrom?" she teased.

"My grandfather had spotted one once on the edge of a great forest in a little-known region," he said, smiling weakly.

"Do you think that was just a story?" she asked.

"Perhaps some of the details have changed a little, but it has been handed down from my grandfather to my own father and then to me, and it sounds real enough for me. Dag-Ra-Bo, my grandfather, had seen an Egrom subdue an augugal. You know how quick, cunning, and dangerous they are when confronted. One bite and a mature augugal can take a pakow's leg right off," he explained, breathless. "My grandfather was very careful to describe exactly what happened."

She knew of the creature he mentioned. D'laine had seen one in Adrum's teachings. An augugal was similar to a giant hard-shelled turtle, but not the slow poke of Earth.

Seeing that the story was getting them nowhere, D'laine changed the subject. "How did Jakla capture you?"

"I had been traveling by myself and they just came upon me. There was no place to hide. Jakla Bosakin was heading specifically for Ebscalon. All he talked about was the Golden Girl of Ebscalon," Bok-Tor explained.

D'laine enjoyed the conversation with Bok-Tor, a very congenial creature, even if he was a little long winded. Deciding that it was time to do something about his condition, she realized that he must be concealing his pain. From the looks of it, the Plotals had whipped him severely. He was scarred and had open wounds that needed attention. Leaning over him, D'laine diagnosed the extent of the bruises and wounds.

Jor-Dan watched her, curious to see how she would handle the situation. He knew she had healed him, but she had never tried to heal anyone since then. This would be a test.

D'laine held a crystal and placed one hand gently near the worst of the wounds. She focused her intentions. The fur-covered skin felt warm beneath her fingers and then her fingers began to tingle. Not sure how long it would take, she waited a few more minutes. Satisfied with her intuition, she removed her hand from Bok-Tor's fur. The wounds were gone. The fur showed no traces of the clotted, matted mess that had been there just moments before the healing.

"Amazing!" Jor-Dan and Bok-Tor boomed at the same time.

"I felt your healing powers working!" Bok-Tor exclaimed. "I am your servant." He bowed his head humbly.

"I have these fantastic powers to heal people, and I use them when I can. You should never commit yourself, like a slave, to someone just because you're thankful. I never would have left you behind, Bok-Tor. Why don't you just be my friend and advisor?" she asked him.

Jor-Dan was in deep thought as D'laine continued with her task of healing the remaining bruises and lacerations.

D'laine nodded to Jor-Dan. "He will need sufficient food and drink to help with the healing."

She knew that he had most likely not eaten very much since his capture. They talked for a few minutes, then D'laine left Bok-Tor when his food arrived.

She walked a few feet away from the fire and sat down under a tree, resting her back against the smooth trunk. As she rested her eyes, Jor-Dan approached her with two bowls of stew and sat down beside her. He handed her a bowl.

"Keep your energy up," Jor-Dan said.

They ate in companionable silence, each buried in their own private thoughts, barring the other from intrusion. Moments passed and D'laine sat bolt upright.

Jor-Dan jumped to his feet, laser in hand. "Is someone approaching the camp?" he asked.

She held up her hand, silencing him. He noticed her lips moving, and a slight movement of her head as if she were talking to someone. He waited patiently, knowing she would speak when she was ready. He looked out into the darkness, scanning the shadows.

D'laine smiled as she turned to Jor-Dan. "An Egrom sentry greeted me. I don't know what they are doing so far away from home. Listen! Do you hear those soft noises? Those are the friendly greetings of the Egroms. I sent a message to Ghury, telling him of my plan to stay at Ebscalon. Somehow, I felt that he already knew of my decision, as if he had a map of my future."

"I have heard those noises in the past but it has been a long time since my last encounter. I wonder what reason they have for being so secretive. Surely, they know us by now, because it is obvious that they have been watching us closely, even following us into battles," Jor-Dan said.

Clearly confused, she could offer him no explanation. There was a reason for everything, and D'laine was sure that in good time the answers would be told. Stifling a yawn, she told Jor-Dan that she needed to get some sleep. Calling to one of the guards, he asked the man to bring a sleeping pad. It looked like an exercise mat made from layers of the gauze. It was large enough to fold over to use half as a cover. The dogs curled up on the moss, close by. She bid everyone goodnight and made herself comfortable, falling off to sleep almost immediately.

Powered by stress, D'laine awoke before dawn and not alone. Pup had managed to crawl into her sleeping mat during the night.

"Are you comfortable?" she asked the dog. Pup licked her on the nose like Buffy would. "You're so much like my doggie back home."

The soldiers bustled about, making preparations to leave. Scouts would soon be sent out in one-man ships as it became light enough to make sure there were no surprises on the way home. D'laine approached Jor-Dan as he was pointing to the west and talking to an officer.

"We'll be leaving soon," he informed D'laine knowing she was anxious to return to the city.

Not knowing the full extent of Trakon's injuries worried her. A dozen scenes flashed in her mind throughout the night, each worse than the previous one. Exhausted, she barely ate the morning meal and then she checked on Bok-Tor. She happily discovered that he was in much better condition, eating twice the normal amount for a healthy Safri, making up for all the meals that he had been refused during his captivity. She smiled as she saw the warriors tossing bits of food to the dogs. Pup and Scooby seemed pretty adept at catching the food in the air. D'laine was relieved when the men started boarding the ships.

Fully aware of her state of mind, Jor-Dan led D'laine and the dogs to the mother ship and helped them aboard. Large enough to hold up to a thousand warriors, supplies and pakows, the ship stood seven decks high. Jor-Dan explained the layout of the huge vessel.

"The bottom deck contains the penned animals, the next deck stores provisions—food and equipment, the following four decks house the men, and the top deck holds the superstructure," Jor-Dan told her.

Fascinated with the size of the craft, she giddily thought of the ship in one of her favorite movies, *Close Encounters of the Third Kind*, when the giant mother ship landed at Devils Tower in Wyoming.

They embarked from the silent, open elevator onto the top deck. D'laine had the dogs lie down so they wouldn't be in the way.

A navigator was stationed off-center, in a tower. All along the edge of the ship were glowing disks, approximately five feet in diameter. D'laine asked what they were.

"Those are our power collectors. The ship runs on energy processed by the suns," Jor-Dan explained. "As you know, the newer ships use the crystal collectors." He pointed out large hooks on the deck and explained that they were for securing the one-man flyers. Walking across the deck, they entered another elevator and rode up to the top of the tower.

"You can see forever from here," she said, romanticizing. She walked around the small room and peered at the instruments and asked the navigator questions. As she gazed ahead with impatience, Jor-Dan approached her side.

"It won't be long before we reach Ebscalon. Trakon is okay."

The landscape passed quickly as the giant ship returned home. The purple spongy moss covered the ground like a thick carpet. They traveled way too fast for her to notice hosks wandering about on the surface. The furry little creatures never failed to entertain her; she was obsessed with them. The only things they passed were two diwal dogs, probably scouts for a pack.

As they approached the outskirts of Ebscalon, they passed the field where the pakow pens were located. The scenery could not hold her attention any longer; she tried to control her anxiety and squirming. The distance closed rapidly and they would soon be inside the city walls. The pilot navigated the mother ship over the walls and buildings until they approached a huge, flat building, where he landed the vehicle.

A crewman stepped out of the lower deck and ran across the roof to the side of the building. Never having been up on top of the buildings before, D'laine didn't know where they would descend. There weren't any visible stairs or ladders visible that led to the street level.

"How do we get to the ground?" she asked.

"Just wait and see how it's done," Jor-Dan said chuckling.

She watched as the crewman pushed a hidden button. Immediately, a barely discernible hydraulic mechanism engaged and the whole roof structure started sinking slowly. The ship was slowly lowered to its hangar, keeping out of view, and a rooftop slid into place. Clangs indicated the roof was latched securely.

"No other city of Thol owns war ships of this size," Jor-Dan explained. "We keep the location as secretive as possible for fear of sabotage."

"This is truly amazing," D'laine said, as she looked around. She noticed several other large, flat-roofed buildings and determined the other mother ships were housed there.

In an unfamiliar section of the city, Jor-Dan guided D'laine down alleys and around buildings until they came to the courtyard that led to the palace.

Chatter stood on hind legs looking out a window, barking. Pup and Scooby barked a return greeting and rushed into the palace.

He knew she was as anxious as he was to check on Trakon's wellbeing. Entering the palace, they briskly walked down the long corridor to the main salon, where D'laine was delighted to see Trakon sitting, his head bandaged, and a group of advisors and his mother close by.

Regardless of his concussion, Trakon jumped up and sprinted across the room to D'laine and enfolded her in a hug. "You're safe!" He wobbled slightly.

She hugged him back then drew away. "You should not be up with a head injury. Back in my world that is called a concussion and it calls for complete bed rest."

He led her to the table and they sat. "I'm sorry I could not rescue you."

"Rescue? She didn't need any of us! The dogs found her at the plotal campsite, but she already had Jakla secured. All we did was carry her and the Safri back to the city!" Jor-Dan exclaimed.

Everyone was all agog to hear of the adventure of her capture and rescue. Boisterous in his account of the victory, D'laine let Jor-Dan have the floor.

"What Safri?" Quark Zerfre, one of Jor-Dan's advisors, asked. He could hardly contain his questions he was so excited. "Where is he?"

They all looked about and could not see anything of Bok-Tor.

"I know we brought him back with us, where did he go?" Jor-Dan asked D'laine.

"The last time I saw him, he was on the ship," she explained, confused. "I assumed some of the men would bring him along."

Preparing to dispatch one of the guards to the ship with a message, Jor-Dan stopped short as an assembly of guards accompanying the skinny Safri entered the room.

"Sire! Where do you wish us to bunk the Safri?" the lead guard asked, bringing his fist to his chest in respect.

"Leave him here; we will prepare a place for him later," Jor-Dan said.

The guards saluted their king, turned, and left the room. Instantly, the room of people converged around Bok-Tor, firing words at him from all directions.

"Let's not devour our guest," Jor-Dan bellowed over the racket, pushing his way toward Bok-Tor. "The Safri has suffered the brutality of the Plotals and is still weak. Now, let me make introductions."

Greetings aside, the council questioned Bok-Tor about the Plotals.

"What direction did the main body of warriors take when they disbanded after the raid on Ebscalon?"

"What plans did they talk about once they had the Princess?"

Questions flew around the room and doing his best, Bok-Tor calmly answered as many as he could. The discussions were lengthy but went by quickly. Interrupting the loud chatter, the majordomo entered the room and announced the evening meal which put a halt to the activity in the room. Disbanding, the family and Bok-Tor wandered to the dining chamber, and others took their leave to return to their homes.

D'laine studied Bok-Tor at dinner. He had been presented a bowl of mush, and ate like a horse with a feedbag. She assumed his three fingers were not knuckled, and his eating ability was that of an animal.

She called out silently to Trakon, explaining her need to talk to him and Jor-Dan in private. Knowing Jor-Dan's discretion, she was confident that he would find a way to end their evening meal without arousing curiosity.

Feigning exhaustion after the meal, D'laine left the dining salon and went to her apartment. Ten minutes later, Trakon and Jor-Dan knocked at her door, then entered. "What's wrong?" Trakon asked, worry shadowing his eyes. "Why the secret meeting?"

She led them to a group of chairs arranged in a close cluster. They reluctantly sat down, both men brooding over her strange behavior.

"Are you comfortable?" she asked.

"Yes," they said.

She could see their impatience.

D'laine reached out and placed one hand on Jor-Dan's temple and the other on Trakon's temple. Silently, she instructed Jor-Dan to place one of his hands on her left temple, and Trakon was to place his hand on her right temple.

"Your minds are locked with mine and all others are locked out. No one will be able to read our thoughts and I think this precaution is necessary. I'm sure you will both feel the same when I tell you what actually took place yesterday. I couldn't tell you any of this last night or today, Jor-Dan, and I didn't want to seem too anxious to get the two of you alone for fear that I would alert someone," she explained.

"Jakla has a spy in the city. I don't know if there is just one, or a dozen spies, and I don't know how we could detect who it is."

Jor-Dan and Trakon both looked stricken with that knowledge. Trakon jumped to his feet, ready to take action. He was furious.

"Who could possibly turn traitor?" Trakon bellowed.

"Sit down so we can reconnect and discuss this before you bring the guards running with your noise!" Jor-Dan boomed to his son, grabbing one of Trakon's arms and pulling him back to the chair.

They quickly rejoined.

"When I find out who the traitor is he'll wish he had been captured by the Plotals! D'laine, you must keep a protective shield around you at all times until we catch the infidel!" Jor-Dan said.

"I couldn't tell you for fear that someone would hear. Who do you trust the most? Is there anyone you are suspicious of?" she asked.

"I don't know, but it must be someone close by, and that pains me. We must set a trap," Jor-Dan said.

"Tell us everything," Trakon begged.

THEY EACH SUFFERED SEPARATE, RESTLESS NIGHTS. AFTER breakfast, they searched for a small room to be used as a secret meeting place. Discovering the perfect place off a back corridor, D'laine stood in the center of the small room, having the others wait out in the hall. She held her hands out then moved them up and down as she turned around in a circle.

"No one has been in this room for many years. I feel that it will be a safe place to meet. What I suggest is that you bring whomever you are going to make the secret plans with to this room so I can feel their energy. If their energy feels pure, I will lock your minds together, ensuring your privacy. This will have to be done each time you meet. I can't see any other way of getting around the problem," she explained.

"An excellent plan," Jor-Dan agreed. "I will make arrangements and we will meet back here later today."

They left the room and closed the door behind them.

*Come to me* sounded in D'laine's head. She was startled. She looked all about.

*Come to the temple.*

Slipping out of the palace, D'laine headed to the Visionary's temple with Pup. She entered the building, unsure of the protocol. She looked around in stunned silence at the beautiful interior. She stopped at a large open doorway and made Pup lie down.

Silently, the Visionary beckoned her to join him. She walked across the entrance into the room with a glass dome. The Visionary was sitting cross-legged on a mat.

"Sit across from me," the Visionary instructed D'laine.

D'laine sank to the floor, sitting crossed-legged.

"Place your hands upward to absorb the energy from the universe," he instructed.

She rested her hands on her thighs, palms turned upward.

"Now close your eyes and silence your mind."

Sitting quietly, she commanded the fuss and worry into

nothingness. As her mind settled down in the silence, the voice of the holy man eased into her mind.

"Although you come from another world, your powers descend directly from the universe. Do you feel the connection?" he asked.

"I don't know," she said, confused by his words.

"Many worlds seek your gift; you will have many challenges. Each day will be a lesson. Pay attention to your visions and keep your powers closely guarded until you have command of them; that will come in time. This world is a higher grade in your schooling. Earth taught you resilience, that was the lesson to be learned there. Thol offers many lessons and you have done well. You have a true, bonded link with the Egroms that will span the dimensions; remember this always. At night, before you retire, sit by a window and meditate. Knowledge will flow through you from the higher order."

Feeling bright light shining on her, D'laine opened her eyes. They were bathed in light from an unknown source which faded slowly as she acknowledged it. Sensing that the session with the Visionary was over, D'laine stood, silently staring in wonder at the man who sat before her. Quietly, she turned and left the temple with Pup at her side.

# CHAPTER THIRTY-SIX

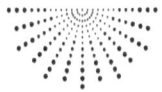

*T*he next day, D'laine spent time with Kitry learning about the murals throughout the palace. D'laine had noticed that some of the murals showed current styles, but others showed a different city with people wearing very different clothing.

"These are scenes from before the Great War of Taylon. A much simpler time," Kitry said.

As they wandered down hallways, the peace was disturbed by a loud commotion outside with people screaming and running.

"Are we being attacked again?" D'laine asked. Her heart thumped loudly in her chest.

They rushed to a window and looked out. D'laine was shocked to see what she thought was a full-sized dragon landing in the courtyard. A familiar warrior jumped to the ground.

Kitry sucked in a deep breath. "You should go to your room and stay there until I send for you!" She pushed D'laine in that direction.

"Why? What's going on?" D'laine asked, refusing to budge. "That looks like Herish, but it can't be."

Trakon approached the courtyard running at a breakneck speed with Chatter keeping pace. His face was a mask of anger. He grabbed Herish by the arm and swung him away from the palace. Chatter jumped toward Herish's throat.

"Chatter, no!" Trakon commanded. "Go. This is my fight."

Chatter slinked off to the sidelines near some warriors, but his teeth clacked non-stop. The dog could barely control the natural thirst for killing.

D'laine ran down the long hallways with Pup and Scooby until she came to the palace entryway. Trakon and Herish were in the midst of a fist fight.

"What are you doing?" She screamed at them. "Stop it this instant!"

Pup and Scooby joined Chatter. The warriors and guards backed away from the dogs. They were in a frenzy.

D'laine recognized the strain. "Go hunt!" The dogs slunk away then raced through the gates and disappeared.

Guards formed a loose circle around the combatants. Kitry and Jor-Dan ran toward the fracas.

Trakon roared at Herish, his jealousy unleashed. "Tell her! Tell her, you freak of nature! Tell her you can only stay that size long enough to mate with her, then you will revert back to the insect that you are!"

D'laine stared at them, her mouth hanging open. "Herish— is that true?"

Herish swung at Trakon, furious. He clipped his jaw. Trakon staggered backwards.

"Answer me, Herish! Are you here to try to seduce me, or something?" D'laine asked. Her neck and face bore splotches of red from her anger.

Herish stood tall and faced her. "I have every right to present myself for your hand."

Trakon was enraged. He grabbed Herish by the back of his jacket, swung him around and slammed his fist into Herish's eye.

"You have no right! You would only be a husband for one night," Trakon bellowed at Herish. He turned to D'laine. "He had you fooled with his helpfulness and friendship, but what he really wanted was a chance to mate with you and pray for a full-sized Kudaja half-breed."

Shocked to her core, D'laine turned away and walked into the palace. Kitry went after her.

Herish shoved Trakon hard. He jumped on his borjo and they flew into the air, stirring up dust and making the banners atop the palace and buildings flap in the wind. Within moments they were a speck on the horizon.

Jor-Dan approached Trakon. He signaled for the guards to disperse.

"I was afraid of this," Jor-Dan said. He placed a hand on Trakon's back. "But now that she knows, everything will be fine."

They walked to the palace.

"It's not fine! He'll be back in his true form filling her head with who knows what," Trakon growled.

"It seems to me that you are more interested in making a match with D'laine than you insisted before," Jor-Dan said. He stopped and faced Trakon. "If that is where your heart lies then perhaps you should make your intentions known."

Trakon appeared startled, letting the words sink in. He stayed behind, his mind racing, as Jor-Dan walked into the palace.

☀ ☀

D'LAINE PACED FURIOUSLY IN HER ROOMS AS KITRY tapped on the door and entered.

"I'm such a fool," D'laine said. "I thought he was my friend."

Kitry took her hand and made her stop pacing. "The Kudaja males will stop at nothing to ensnare a normal Tholian female. You are not to blame—you are new to this world and don't know all of its secrets."

D'laine sat on a divan and sobbed. "I can't believe he deceived me like that. Why didn't you tell me sooner?"

Kitry sat beside her. "It did seem like he was your friend. I think that was his true intention until Jor-Dan told him you were Trakon's intended. I'm sure that caused the Kudaja to act irrationally."

D'laine looked up through tears. "But I'm not Trakon's intended! If my father were here he would put a stop to that talk!"

AFTER D'LAINE BECAME CALM, KITRY LEFT TO ATTEND TO business. D'laine sat curled on a divan. She thought of the times that Herish had been around. They seemed so innocent. He had been so thoughtful and friendly. Never did she feel there was an underlying agenda. It made her sad to think he had been using her for such an ugly purpose.

A tap sounded on her door. She looked up as the door opened a few inches and Trakon stuck his head through. "Can I come in, or are you mad at me?"

She got up and went to the door and opened it wide. "Come on in."

They walked over to the divan and sat.

"I'm sorry," Trakon said. "I know I embarrassed you for springing that on you so publicly."

D'laine felt her face, neck and ears burning. She knew she'd have huge red blotches on her neck. "Someone should have explained this to me."

"I didn't think about it, or maybe I did, but I was blinded by jealousy," Trakon admitted.

"Jealousy?" she blurted out. "How could you be jealous of someone who was five inches tall? And what do you mean by jealous? Do I suddenly mean more to you than just a traveler new to Thol? I don't understand, Trakon."

Trakon studied her. He took a little breath and exhaled through his nose. "I admit I'm more than a little confused with my feelings. My parents have tried to match me to someone for a long time, but I have never even been attracted to the princesses they've paraded in front of me. They're such idiots—only interested in their social standing, how they look and how they are perceived, and what they can benefit from a marriage."

"Until you came along I thought I'd be a bachelor for many completed paths," he said.

D'laine listened raptly. "So, now you are contemplating your future? And you think I'm different than those girls?"

Trakon glowered at her. "Think? There's no thinking involved, D'laine. You are a warrior, highly intelligent, you possess mechanical skills that surely surpass my own, and you are unique with your powers. I've never seen you get all gooey about your clothes or your looks."

He took her hand in his. "I want to plan a future with you, if you will have me."

D'laine stared at Trakon for a moment. The only sound in the room was their breathing. "I told your mother that if my father were here, he would put a stop to all this talk about marriage. I'm one year—completed path—younger than you. I like you, but I hardly know you."

Trakon stood. "Then it looks like we need to spend more time together so we can get to know each other." He smiled widely.

D'laine stood. She slugged him in the arm.

"Ow!" he said, rubbing his arm. "What was that for?"

"Don't ever embarrass me like that again!"

THE DAYS FLEW BY WITH MANY LESSONS REGARDING LIFE in the city and getting to know the people. Taking D'laine and the three dogs about, Trakon showed her things that she had overlooked since his last tour. Long discussions with Jor-Dan and the council also took place, as well as sittings with Kitry.

The council met once a week. Discovering this was similar to governmental meetings back home, D'laine's political education increased. Each member had his own responsibility and reported to Jor-Dan.

Security was under the direction of Hal-sa-Bin; Quark Zerfre headed the fleet; Dannin kept track of the livestock, food supplies, water and the hosk gathering. Trakon involved himself with many positions of great importance, but his number one expertise was the ships. Amazed at how he could keep up with everything, D'laine found that his information was accurate every time. He commanded respect by all and was considered a great leader after his father.

Tucked away in the little room, Hal-sa-Bin had several private meetings with Jor-Dan, Trakon and D'laine. A trap was set and they hoped the traitor would take the bait. It pained Jor-Dan to think that a Ciertron would change sides to the Plotals for material gains. Their city was peaceful, their people happy. He wondered how this person could have strayed from good.

Jor-Dan headed the tribunal to sentence Ja-Toy-Anic and Laoife, his mother. The wiry Ciertron was like a rat of the back streets and alleys of Ebscalon. He reeked of kahl and his body stunk. Laoife had lost all her radiance and appeared haggard. She hung her head in shame beside her son.

"What did you gain for your traitorous behavior?" Hal-sa-Bin asked the prisoner.

Ja-Toy-Anic sneered at Hal-sa-Bin, Jor-Dan and the tribunal. "What have you ever done for me? You live in your fancy palaces and houses while my mother and I live in poverty!"

"There is no poverty in Ebscalon!" Jor-Dan bellowed. "I have been over every inch of this city and my people are all well cared for through their own commerce and relationships with each other."

"My mother and I live in a tiny hut and scavenge food and clothing," Ja-Toy-Anic said.

A guard leaned in and whispered in Hal-sa-Bin's ear.

"It appears that you and your mother sleep until the day is nearly gone then you drink throughout the night from the well-meaning patrons of the communal meeting places," Hal-sa-Bin said. "Perhaps if you put an effort into making a good life for yourselves, like all the other Ciertrons, you wouldn't have had to take payment from Plotals and betray your own people."

"We will contemplate your sentences," Jor-Dan said.

The members of the tribunal filed out of the room. They hastily entered a smaller room on the other side of the large hallway.

"Mother and son require a harsh punishment, but I don't see what good will come of that," Hal-sa-Bin said.

"They should be pulled back into society with wage-earning positions and responsibilities," one of the tribunal members said.

The group thought among themselves.

"What work tasks should they be assigned?" someone asked.

"Laoife had been a cook at one time. Perhaps she could work in the palace where she could be monitored closely," another member said.

Jor-Dan and Hal-sa-Bin considered the suggestion.

"What about the son?" Jor-Dan asked. "He is young and requires a skill."

"The army would be good for him," Hal-sa-Bin said. "It will give him discipline, and he will find pride for his city once again. I would suggest strict supervision and monitoring for one entire year, at which time we will reconvene and hear from the mother's workmates, the boy's commander, and people in the community," Hal-sa-Bin said. "If they make a full recovery and have turned their lives around, it would benefit the community if we are forgiving."

# CHAPTER THIRTY-SEVEN

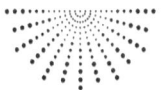

*S*tanley, Victor and Dr. Joplin sat at a table in the lab covered with research magazines, stacks of letters, government reports, tablets and laptops.

"What do they think, we're stupid? Look at all these reports. Where did all these people disappear to?" Stanley complained.

"They have warehouses full of bound reports stashed away someplace," Dr. Joplin said.

"We just need to find them," Victor said.

"I think we need to do some serious experimenting," Stanley said, as he scribbled on a lined yellow tablet.

Dr. Joplin drummed his fingers on the table. "What do you have in mind?"

"I want to try going through the portal," Stanley said.

Victor shot out of his seat. "Are you crazy?" He paced around the table.

"Without a body going and returning, we don't have any physical proof, just conjecture," Stanley said.

"Let's think about this for a minute," Victor said.

☀ ☀

THE SCIENTIFIC TEAM GATHERED AT THE CORDONED-OFF area in the parking lot at Katy Mills Mall at eight-thirty Monday morning. It must not have been a peak shopping time because the parking lot near the site was almost empty. Traffic zoomed down Interstate 10 between Houston and Katy, and further west.

Dr. Joplin tied a digital movie camera with heavy twine and reinforced it with duct tape. "Are we ready to start this experiment?" Dr. Joplin asked. "Shoppers will be filling up the lot soon, then the lunch crowd will be swarming up and down the sidewalk after that."

"Yeah, we've got motion sensors set up and three cameras," Victor said.

Dr. Joplin pressed the record button on the video camera and set the camera on the ground.

Victor used a hockey stick and pushed the camera across the ground while Dr. Joplin held the twine.

The front two inches of the camera disappeared.

"Look at that!" Stanley took pictures from all angles and sides with the sensa scan camera as he and Dr. Joplin circled the area. Dr. Joplin did his part taking pictures with a hand-held digital camera. They kept a wide berth of the actual space where the video camera vanished.

"It looks like it's chopped off. Keep pushing, slowly," Dr. Joplin said. "Stanley, we'd better get back over to Victor's side because we don't know if this push will affect time and space."

Victor pushed the camera slowly, and more disappeared. "Is this dangerous? Do I have to worry about getting sucked in there?"

Stanley paused. "That's a possibility. Maybe we'd better rethink this."

THE CAMERA INCHED ACROSS THE DARK GROUND AND bumped into a robot's foot. The robot examined the camera with white light, then shot it with a short burst of laser.

The robot scanned the immediate area to no avail. He turned and marched off.

ZANDAL SAT IN THE LARGE, WAR-TORN BUILDING ON HIS opulent dais that was made from materials confiscated from the inhabitants of the planet. The walls were lined with robots, ten deep, silently waiting for a command.

A robot marched into the room and stopped before Zandal, his LED lights blinking.

Zandal scanned the robot. "Report."

"A foreign object has entered Zan," the Robot said in an electronic voice.

"Where is this object?" Zan asked. His LEDs flashed.

"It is destroyed," the robot said.

Zandal stood. "Show me." Zandal and the robot turned and marched from the room. One section of the robots against the wall followed them.

The robots marched from the building in formation. The reporting robot stopped before the charred ground. "There." The robot beamed a light on the blackened ground.

Zandal's eyes glowed and a beam streaked down to the ground and traced the shape of the camera, string and portal. The beam scanned the ground and stopped.

"Find and eliminate the infiltrator," Zandal commanded.

VICTOR PULLED ON THE TWINE. THE CAMERA CAME BACK, smoldering. "Holy shit!"

"Get away from there!" Stanley shrieked, in a panic.

Victor pulled the camera across the ground.

Stanley took pictures of the area from every angle. "There has to be something that will show up on the sensa scan camera."

"Put that thing in something, but don't touch it! We need to find out exactly what happened," Dr. Joplin instructed. He was totally rattled.

Stanley ran over to the SUV. He returned with a metal storage box. Victor hauled the camera by the twine and Stanley lifted the box under it. Victor dropped the twine in the box and Stanley closed the lid.

"Man, oh man oh man." Stanley panicked.

They gathered up all the equipment and shoved it in the SUV and drove out of the parking lot, tires squealing.

Lost in thought with the fear they just experienced, they rode back to the university in silence. They knew they had their work cut out for them. It all depended on what today's discoveries led them to. If just a fragment of evidence existed on the film or audio, the experiment would be labeled successful and they could get on with more sophisticated experiments. So many "ifs" existed that frustration built inside all of them.

SEVERAL PEOPLE WERE STILL IN THE LAB WHEN THEY returned, and Dr. Joplin claimed priority over another experiment being run on the super computer. Much was to be done and they began preparing for the series of tests.

Victor pulled on fireproof gloves and lifted the camera and

twine out of the box. He measured the string and made a note. Stanley headed for the computer lab.

"I hope we didn't open Pandora's box," Dr. Joplin said. He paced nervously.

Stanley stopped in his tracks. "Maybe we'd better have the military in on this."

Stanley, Dr. Joplin and Victor made eye contact. They were silent in thought for a moment.

"Nah." Victor wrote on a tablet. "This isn't Terminator. Everyone stay calm."

Stanley stared at Victor then entered the small computer lab.

Victor trashed the twine and duct tape and made notes.

Dr. Joplin sat with his chin in his hand, lost in thought as he stared at the waste basket. Reaching down, he picked up the twine and duct tape as if he had never seen such things before in his life.

"We're not even paying attention to what we're doing!" He paced with his chin in his hand, and stared into the floor. Suddenly, his mouth dropped open.

"Clovis!" Dr. Joplin called out, spinning in the direction of the other room where the technician worked. "Come out here for a minute, will you?"

The six-foot-ten lanky technician sauntered through the door.

"Clo, I want you and Victor to put these things under the most powerful microscope you've got back there and see if you can pick out anything. We pushed it along the ground and it disappeared, so it must have picked up something from the ground on the other side, a piece of grass, sand, something foreign that stuck. Find something and try to identify it. I want you to take the camera apart and check the exterior for grit or any other substance, but I think you'll come up with something in that duct tape or the twine.

Things have a tendency to stick to duct tape and there has to be something from the other side that stuck to it." Dr. Joplin barked.

"You're getting carried away Dr. Joplin. We'll take care of things in here," Clovis said.

"I know when I'm not wanted, so I'll leave you guys alone before I change my mind again," Dr. Joplin said, a little sheepish grin on his face.

He knew he would turn into a basket case if he stayed there much longer, wanting results that would take hours. He had to stay out of the way least he bungled matters during the discovery process.

Dr. Joplin left the lab and went into his office, closed the door, and settled down at his desk. He picked up a pencil and began doodling on a piece of paper. Then he started forming lists of items. He listed tests, equipment, people working on projects. Disgusted with himself for being so keyed up, he threw down the pencil, picked up the office phone, and placed a call. Waiting patiently for the connection to go through, he silently counted the rings. On the fourth ring, the phone was answered.

"Joe?" he asked. "This is Ben Joplin in Houston. Oh, quite well, Joe, that's what I'm calling about."

He went on to explain in detail, what had happened to date, not concealing his excitement about what had happened with the camera.

"I know I'm calling a bit prematurely; I should be waiting for the test results or the pictures, but I wanted to check with you about getting Victor and Stanley on a long-term loan if you can spare them. This project will be going on for a while, I think, and I don't want to get them involved any further until I have your permission to keep them here for the duration of this thing," Dr. Joplin relayed.

Dr. Paxton's voice squawked excitedly through the receiver.

"I don't know how long," Dr. Joplin said. "It all depends on what we uncover from the video and audio and the packaging, if there is any evidence at all on the duct tape or twine, which I think there will be. Yes, I know, but do you think you can swing it?"

Listening, he automatically bounced his head continuously to what he heard, making affirmative sounds and finally said his good-byes. He picked up the pencil and began tapping the eraser on the desk pad, a bundle of nerves. Unable to sit still a moment longer, he went back to the lab.

"Looks like we'll be here for a while, anyone want pizza?" Dr. Joplin asked.

"Extra cheese," Victor said.

"How can you eat at a time like this?" Stanley slammed the computer lab door shut. He sat bent over a photo with a powerful electron magnetic spectrograph.

With all the votes in, Dr. Joplin retreated to his office and called the nearest pizza place.

Forty minutes later three large pizzas arrived at the lab. Everyone stopped working to pull out wallets to collect money for the feast.

"Put your wallets away, I'm treating!" Dr. Joplin announced, paying the teenager who balanced the boxes with one hand and a knee. Victor retrieved the pizza boxes so the boy could negotiate the money without making a mess. He headed toward the conference table. Dr. Joplin was in a generous mood and told the boy to keep the change. Beaming from ear-to-ear, the delivery boy left the lab, and the crew sat at the long tables digging into the feast.

"Where's Stanley?" Clovis asked, mouth stuffed.

"I thought it was awfully quiet in here," Victor said with a snicker.

Dr. Joplin crossed the room and opened the door to the computer lab. "Pizza's here."

It was eerily quiet. Dr. Joplin entered the computer lab. There stood Stanley, lost in thought.

"What have you got?" Dr. Joplin asked.

"Look at this, Dr. Joplin," Stanley said while pointing to a spot with a pen.

One picture showed the camera half gone. The missing half showed a wavering spot like a fun house mirror. Stanley then pointed to a spot on the next picture with a pen. The twine seemed to be suspended in the air; the camera was completely through the portal. The time sequence on the film had captured when the camera had been pushed into the other dimension.

Dr. Joplin let out a loud whoop of happiness as he slapped Stanley on the back. Victor and Clovis ducked in the door and joined them at the computer.

"What's going on?" Victor bent and looked at the pictures displayed across the monitor. "These are really great photos, Stanley."

Clovis leaned over and examined the pictures. He tapped the time stamp on a couple of pictures. "Did you delete some pictures in the sequence?"

Stanley stared at the time stamps Clovis pointed out. "No, everything's there."

"You're missing 12 minutes," Clovis said.

"Impossible," Victor said. He went through the entire sequence of pictures. "This doesn't make sense at all."

Stanley looked up and stared into space. "Yeah, it does. There's obviously a time difference moving from Earth into this other world."

The room became silent as several pairs of eyes made contact with each other.

"Let's get back out there and see if we can find the center where the gravity pulls the strongest! Come on, let's get the others in here!" Victor said.

"Stop!" Dr. Joplin shouted. "It's already dark outside. Eat your pizza and we'll get started in the morning."

"I knew something like this would happen!" Stanley boasted, his face radiant with smiles as Dr. Joplin went to the door to call the others. "Let me find a little more," Stanley whispered to himself.

He was hungry for the unknown which would fill him with more knowledge once he pried every bit of information to pieces and put it back together again, as only his mind could do. As he leaned into the pictures on the screen, his mind was busy making plans for the next experiment.

Stanley swiveled his chair and faced Dr. Joplin and Victor. "What the hell zapped that camera?"

They stared at the pictures. "I'm not sure I want to know," Dr. Joplin said.

"Has to be some sort of a security system, don't you think?" Victor asked.

They left the computer room and dove into the luke warm pizza.

Lee sat in his office at NASAs Johnson Space Center, highly focused on his computer, brows knitted as his eyes scanned the folder names on the screen in front of him. A celebrated career and top security clearances made this particular task much easier.

Now that he was back at work, he could think clearly and

put his years of skills to work. He had recalled a fuzzy conversation with one of his bosses a couple of decades ago, early in his career. It was thought at the time that he would be working on what everyone jokingly referred to as the *John Carter of Mars* phenomenon. The *Edgar Rice Burroughs* character had somehow been transported from Earth to Mars in a dream state without a vehicle.

He scrolled through the list until he came to a folder dated 1952. He clicked on it. It was password protected. He entered his password and a multitude of files and folders scrolled past at an alarming rate. He perused the sub folders until he found what he was searching for: Gregory Claymore dated 6-12-52.

Lee clicked on the folder. There was one document file in an ancient program. He would have to convert it so he could read it in Word. He pulled up a program and clicked and clacked. The whole process took several minutes. He opened the file and saved it as a current Word document. It was filled with programming code junk.

He ran another program to remove all the extraneous dots, squares and symbols that looked like hieroglyphics. Now he could read the file.

Gregory Claymore was a well-documented case of not just a missing person, but his disappearance was too much like D'laine's for Lee to not connect the dots. Claymore had disappeared from San Diego, California on the beach, with hundreds of people present. His wife and children never saw him again.

Lee printed the 125-page document (double-sided) then he commenced to read, make pencil tics at the edge where significant information caught his attention, and highlighted the facts. A couple of hours later, notes scribbled on the pages, he made a color copy, stuffed it in a manila envelope and headed out the door.

He arrived at Rice University and texted Dr. Joplin to find out where, exactly his offices were located. His phone pinged an answer, he turned in the opposite direction from where he was faced after getting out of his car, and started walking.

Dr. Joplin and Victor waited for Lee outside in the heat. Dr. Joplin waved at Lee when he saw him in the distance. "Over here!"

Lee sped up his pace, reached out his hand and shook their hands. "Sorry for dropping by unannounced, but I went back to work and found something crucial that I wanted to share with you."

They went inside, walked down corridors and approached Dr. Joplin's offices and labs. Victor went in search of Stanley. Dr. Joplin escorted Lee to the conference room. When Victor and Stanley showed up, Lee asked that they shut the door.

With the room secured, they sat at the table. Lee kept hold of the envelope in front of him on the table. "I'm going to share a secret document with you. This is not to leave this room, and I will take it with me when I leave here, and destroy it. Understood?"

That got their attention. Victor, Stanley and Dr. Joplin exchanged looks.

"Okay, we understand. What do you have?" Dr. Joplin asked.

Lee opened the envelope and slid the pages across the table. Stanley read the top sheet and glanced up, a shocked look on his face. He snatched the pages and sped through them, front and back, while making sounds with his mouth. Victor and Dr. Joplin could not keep up with him, but they knew that with his retention, he would get it all.

When Stanley was finished, he pushed the pages over to Dr. Joplin and Victor. They started with the top sheet:

## Greg Claymore Government File

Subject: Gregory R. Claymore
Incident Date: 06-12-1952
Gregory Reginald Claymore
DOB: 07-04-1919
1551 Allen Street
San Diego, CA 92122
SS: xxx-xx-xxxx
SD Grammar School
SD Middle School / Junior High
San Diego Sr. High School
Enlisted in USN 1937 @ 18 YO
Assigned to mobile target/gunnery training ship Utah
(AG-16)

**Lavinia (Stone) Claymore** (subject's wife)
suffered heat exhaustion after witnessing her husband
disappear.

**Florentine Matthews (subject's sister)**
On Thursday, 06-12-1952 @ approximately 11:22 a.m.
PST, the family was having a picnic at Coronado
Beach, Coronado, California, San Diego County.
Sixteen family members and friends witnessed
Gregory R. Claymore vanish on the beach while partic-
ipating in a game of volleyball. Matthews and others
stated that one minute he was there, the next minute he
had vanished.

**Morty Mellingham** (friend) stated Greg (Gregory
R. Claymore) had possession of the ball. His arm was
raised to volley the ball when he disappeared. The ball

fell to the ground. Mellingham said they all called out for Greg (Gregory R. Claymore) but didn't receive a response. He vanished into thin air.

**Eugene Trusty** (maternal cousin) stated Greg (Gregory R. Claymore) was home on leave and due to return to his ship the next day (Friday, 06-13-1952). Trusty speculated the disappearance was due to being so close to Friday the 13th. Trusty reiterated Mellingham's statement.

**J.C. Feduccia** (friend) stated that Gregory R. Claymore had the ball and was ready to cast it over the net. He took one foot forward and disappeared into thin air. Feduccia stated more than once that his friend most likely stepped into another dimension.

### Update, 02-12-1975

Gregory R. Claymore returned to Coronado Beach, Coronado, California, San Diego County, at approximately 9:07 a.m. PST. Witnesses stated a man wearing a costume "appeared" on the beach in front of them. He appeared confused, and quickly walked off the beach in the direction of a neighborhood.

**Lavinia (Stone) (Claymore) Walters** contacted this office and stated her former husband knocked on her door. He was dressed strangely in a costume. She said she almost fainted when she saw him because he had not aged one day. He explained that he had been pulled into another dimension called Thol, and he just now learned how to return to Earth. She informed him she had him declared legally dead in 1964 and she remarried (Harrison Walters) in 1965. He left her house and she didn't expect to hear from him again.

STANLEY TEEPEED HIS FINGERS WHILE THINKING. "THE last entry was in 1975. It appears that Gregory Claymore returned to the exact same spot in San Diego. There were witnesses that saw him appear just as suddenly as he left the first time, and more than ten people who witnessed him vanish into thin air hours later."

"There was one interview and pictures captured by someone on the beach. Claymore said that he came from Thol, another dimension, which was nothing like our earth. He thought he was coming home for good, but didn't like what he saw," Lee said.

"What could have made him give up his family and life here the second time around?" Victor asked, dumbfounded.

"I don't know, but I'm going to find out," Stanley stated.

# CHAPTER THIRTY-EIGHT

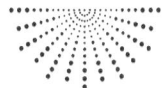

*M*oonlight twinkled through the window as Lee stood in the middle of D'laine's room in the dark. "Brian needs you. Where are you?"

Jamie, sock monkey in hand, shuffled into the room, rubbing his sleepy eyes with one hand. "What are you doing, daddy?"

"Just talking to your sister," Lee said. He rubbed Jamie's head affectionately.

"But she's not here," Jamie said.

"I know that, son, but her spirit is." Lee hugged Jamie. "Go back to bed."

Jamie shuffled off. Lee sat on the edge of the bed and turned on the light. He picked up a picture of Lori and stared at his dead wife. "I can't have lost her, honey. I was supposed to keep her safe, but I can't even get to her. I don't even know where she is, or if she's still alive."

Lee pulled in a deep breath. "Please look over our daughter, Lori. Keep her strong. Help guide her back home."

# CHAPTER THIRTY-NINE

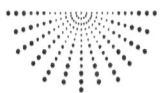

*D*'laine tossed and turned in her bed in the palace. She screamed as she sat bolt upright. Pup barked. Scooby blinked, looking around for danger.

The door burst open and Trakon and Chatter stormed in. Trakon was shirtless, tussled with sleep, with laser in hand. He sprinted to her bed and they embraced.

"Are you safe? What happened?" Trakon asked.

Kitry and Jor-Dan, light sword in hand, rushed into the room.

"What's wrong?" Kitry asked.

"Intruder?" Jor-Dan looked around the expansive room, checking behind tapestries on the wall, the bathing room, and the restorative chamber.

D'laine parted from Trakon. "I'm sorry to wake everyone. I had a terrible, terrible nightmare."

Kitry approached D'laine and comforted her with an arm around her shoulders. "What is troubling you?"

D'laine stammered out an explanation. "Robots, man-like

machines from this war-torn place were everywhere. Death and destruction all across Thol."

Trakon tried to comfort her. "It was just a dream."

D'laine became adamant. "No. I had a dream about this same robot in my homeland. You, Ghury and Jakla were also in the dream, and guess what? I've met you and Ghury. Jakla was the second being I came into contact with after the Egroms. So, no, this isn't just a nightmare. It's a vision or something."

Kitry walked to a window and gazed across the horizon. "All is peaceful here. You have had many experiences in a short period of time. Rest."

D'laine hugged the covers to her.

"You are well-protected here," Jor-Dan said. "And the dogs will never let anything threatening get close to you."

"Dogs are no match for these machines," D'laine explained. "They would kill the dogs.

"We will be on high alert for any suspicious activity," Jor-Dan said.

"Let's get some sleep," Kitry said. "This is a discussion for tomorrow."

Kitry, Jor-Dan and Trakon left the room. Moments later, a tap sounded at the door.

D'laine got off the bed and went to the door and opened it.

Trakon stood in the doorway. "I want you to tell me everything."

She stood aside and Trakon entered. They walked over to a sofa and sat. D'laine went into great details of the nightmares back home and this current nightmare.

"I can practically feel the static of this energy in the air," she said. "Something is building up. A terrible thing is going to happen."

☀ ☀

The Visionary stood at the glass dome in his temple. He waved a hand over the glass and the bleak landscape of Zan appeared.

Thousands of robots were gathered at the portal entrance where the five robots attempted to break through the portal barrier.

The Visionary left the temple immediately.

Jakla's shadow was visible on the large tent canvas. He paced within, unable to sleep. The tent flap swung open and Jakla emerged, restless. He paced by the fire, kicked some embers then raised his snout to the air and inhaled deeply. The pod on the end of his tail opened and closed. He watched the pakows sway in their sleep, then he grunted and returned to his tent.

In a futuristic factory in Zan, tattered human slaves polished new robots as they emerged from liquid molds. Some slaves tested robot reflexes and others checked light beams and functions in the new robots. Completed robots stood en masse in a large room.

A loud knock shattered the silence in Jor-Dan and Kitry's bedroom. A soft light illuminated the room as Jor-Dan stumbled to the large door. He swung the door open to the Visionary.

"A bad thing is happening," the Visionary said.

Jor-Dan beckoned him into the room. Kitry tied a robe around her and joined Jor-Dan and the Visionary.

"D'laine had a nightmare. Are these things related?" Jor-Dan asked.

"Was her dream of man-formed machines in another place?" the Visionary asked.

Kitry clutched her robe tighter. "She said they were here, on Thol."

The Visionary paced. "A premonition. I saw these things in the glass. Many thousands of them. They are coming."

"What can we do?" Kitry asked.

Jor-dan wrapped his arm around her shoulders. "Prepare."

TRAKON, JOR-DAN AND D'LAINE STOOD AROUND A WORK surface and studied plans beside a one-man ship as workers tinkered on one of the ships close by.

"The way solar energy works on my world is by using photovoltaic (PV) cells, which are these little squares on solar panels. They're made from crystalline silicon," D'laine said.

"What do your people use for energy storage?" Trakon asked.

D'laine pondered a moment. "This was not my father's area of expertise, so I'm not that familiar with solar. I do remember reading that developers use a battery bank which is a back-up system. I wish I knew more."

"I feel it is something so simple. But I can't see it," Trakon said.

"We should start tracing everything back to the point of origin," Jor-Dan said. "There is probably a break we overlooked, or a problem with the exchanger."

"We had to shield the power exchanger from D'laine's crystals and her unique energy field," Trakon said. "Maybe there's something to that."

D'laine looked the ship over. "One-man crestriders aren't warships. How will they do in battle?"

"You've seen our motherships. They can transport thousands of men, pakows and supplies," Jor-Dan explained. "And the smaller ships help defend the ground troops because they are very fast."

Thud.

A one-man ship sank to the ground. They all looked on, exasperated.

"In the daytime only! If someone strikes at night, you have to rely solely on pakows," D'laine said belligerently.

"Those animals are swift and sure-footed," Trakon said.

D'laine scoffs. "Primitive!"

Trakon became defensive. "Most of our technology was destroyed in the Great War of Taylon."

"What happened to all the records?" D'laine asked.

"The land was decimated. Our cities in ruin. Whole populations destroyed. It has taken years to rebuild to what we have today," Jor-Dan explained with a wave of his arm.

"Atlantis all over again," D'laine exclaimed.

Jor-Dan and Trakon didn't understand the reference.

D'laine met their stares. "I'd give anything for my father right about now."

# CHAPTER FORTY

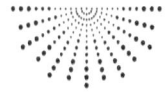

*S*tanley and Victor sat in the living room with Lee and the boys, a paper sack by their feet.

"I'll bet she's with those monsters and that boy," Brian said.

"What monsters? What boy?" Victor asked, chuckling.

Lee contemplated. He explained D'laine's nightmares. Stanley and Victor leaned forward in their chairs.

"By any chance did she draw any of them?" Stanley asked in a hopeful voice.

Jamie sprung off the sofa and bounded up the stairs. He returned in a few minutes with a drawing tablet.

"What's that?" Lee asked. He held his hand out and Jamie reluctantly handed over the tablet. Lee flipped it open and saw sketch after sketch of the four players in D'laine's nightmares. He turned to Jamie. "Where'd you get this?"

Jamie squirmed, biting his fingernail. He spoke very softly. "In D'laine's room. She hid it behind her dresser."

Lee stared hard at Jamie. "We'll talk about you poking around where you don't belong later, young man. For now, I'm glad you did, but…" He cleared his throat and handed the tablet to Victor. "This looks like the four beings she saw every night. The boy—she thought he was a prince, the white creature was helpful, the alligator man and the robot scared her."

Victor and Stanley huddled over the tablet. Every page was dated and as they flipped the pages the drawings took on more depth of character. Stanley noticed the gap between the dates.

"It looks like she stopped drawing them for a couple of years," he said.

"The dreams just quit almost four years ago," Lee said. "I don't understand why they started up again."

Victor and Stanley kept flipping slowly through the pages until the drawings stopped, the day before D'laine disappeared. On the very last page she had drawn an additional picture: herself in an outfit similar to the nightmare boy's clothing.

"Did you see this last drawing?" Stanley asked. He held out the tablet to Lee. "She's in the drawing. I think this means something. It could be a connection to her disappearance."

Lee looked at the picture of D'laine. "She told me that the alligator creature called her by name. That was the very last dream. What could this mean? Is this some sort of a prophecy we don't understand?"

Lee, Victor and Stanley contemplated in silence.

"Can we take this tablet so we can scan in the pictures?" Victor asked. "I think there's something here."

"Sure," Lee said. "Just be careful with them. I'd like to keep them close."

"I promise to take good care of them and return them as soon as they are scanned. I want to study the progression," Victor said. "Her drawings became so clear in the last week before she disappeared. Also, would you be able to email or text me any conversations you can remember about these dreams? I'd like to be able to have a bigger picture of all of the events leading up to when she vanished."

Stanley appeared dreamy-eyed. "I'd give anything to be with her. Maybe even find and talk to Greg Claymore."

"He was in his 30s when he disappeared the first time, he's probably dead by now," Lee said.

"Will D'laine ever come home?" Brian asked.

Stanley sighed deeply. "We just don't know. This is the closest we've ever come to an experience like this. Your sister's dreams, and these drawings are a huge missing piece of the puzzle."

Jamie hopped off the sofa and walked over to Stanley. He put his arm across Stanley's shoulder. "If you see my sister, would you tell her I miss her?"

Stanley swallowed hard. He one-arm hugged Jamie. "You bet."

"Come on, let's get back to the lab," Victor said. He clutched the drawing tablet and thrust the sack of clothes at Stanley and they left the house.

BACK AT THE LAB, VICTOR HANDED THE BAG OF CLOTHES to Clovis. He and Stanley went to Dr. Joplin's office, tablet in hand.

"You'll want to look at this," Victor said. "Let's go to the conference table."

"You definitely sparked my curiosity," Dr. Joplin said. He got up and followed Victor and Stanley out of the room.

They sat at the conference table with the drawing tablet open in front of them.

"Wow!" Dr. Joplin said. He carefully studied each page. When he came to the time gap he asked them about it and Stanley explained the situation.

Dr. Joplin kept flipping pages. When he arrived at the very

last page, he stared in disbelief. "This is almost photo quality. The details of each being is so realistic." The picture of D'laine sent a shiver down his spine.

"Mr. Jackson thinks this must be some type of prophecy," Victor said.

Dr. Joplin swallowed loudly.

"That could be, but there are too many pieces missing on our end, and I don't know how we can close the gap."

Stanley drummed his fingers on the table. "I have a suggestion."

STANLEY, IN A BULLET-PROOF VEST, AND A MOTORCYCLE helmet, with a video camera strapped to his chest, wore a sturdy harness. A thick-gauged cable ran from the harness to the frame of the SUV. Stanley appeared anxious as Victor adjusted Stanley's vest.

"This is stupid! Not to mention risky as hell," Victor ranted.

Dr. Joplin walked to a tripod and turned on the camera. "Science is nothing without risk. Stanley is very brave to do this."

"There's a fine line between bravery and stupidity and we are about to cross over," Victor challenged. "You saw those drawings. Any one of those creatures could be on the other side."

"Well, we know the white one is friendly, according to what D'laine told her father," Dr. Joplin said.

"I don't feel so reassured," Victor grumbled. "You will be considered an invader to their world."

Stanley patted Victor on the back. "Victor, everything will be okay. What could possibly go wrong?"

Victor grumbled again. He pressed the record button on Stanley's video camera. "Let's get this over with."

Victor and Dr. Joplin stood back several feet. They donned gloves and grabbed the cable.

"Remember, if we see any trouble, we're pulling you back," Dr. Joplin said.

"Okay, okay." Stanley took a deep breath and stepped forward. He walked a few paces. Nothing. He turned and shrugged at Dr. Joplin and Victor. "We missed the opportunity. The doorway's gone already."

He sighed loudly and hung his head in failure. Dr. Joplin and Victor relaxed; they all pondered the situation. Stanley paced the roped off parking space.

"We'll never be able to..." Stanley's words warped off as the front half of him disappeared.

Dumbfounded, Victor and Dr. Joplin jumped into action.

"Holy shit! Hold the rope." Victor rushed to the other side of the parking place.

"Oh my God! Is he okay?" Dr. Joplin asked.

"It looks like he's been sliced in two!" Victor was in a complete panic. He came to his senses, pulled out his phone and clicked numerous pictures.

Dr. Joplin and Victor kept their focus on Stanley's back.

STANLEY SUCKED IN A BREATH AS HE REALIZED THE success of the experiment. The war-torn landscape of Zan spread before him, a desolate, barren wasteland. Structures, abandoned and ravished from a war these people obviously lost, were in the surrounding area. He saw a small group of dirty humans in rags scurrying from one shadow to another trying to keep invisible from their enemy.

An ominous robot marched heavily toward him. Stanley opened his mouth to scream. He flailed his arms to alert his teammates as he let loose the loudest, longest scream of his life. The Robot emitted a white light that engulfed him. The Robot walked backward with Stanley in tow.

THE BACK SIDE OF STANLEY'S ARMS FLAILED WILDLY. His body slowly moved forward into the portal.

Victor jumped into action. "Holy shit!"

Victor joined Dr. Joplin. They pulled the wire rope. They slid toward the portal. The rope strained against the SUV.

"Quick! Get in the SUV and move it! Don't go fast or we may hurt him!" Dr. Joplin was sliding forward, his heels dug into the ground, but not getting any traction on the blacktop.

Victor jumped into the driver's seat, started the SUV and threw the vehicle into reverse. The tires spun and smoked as the vehicle strained. The wire rope began to unravel.

Dr. Joplin freaked out. "The rope! We're going to lose him!"

THE HARNESS DUG INTO STANLEY'S SHOULDERS AND WAIST. His eyes shut tight as his body strained. "Oh God! I'm going to be pulled apart."

The Robot's feet dug into the dirt, and it slowly moved toward the portal. The beam generator on its chest bent outward and snapped out of the robot's chest.

Stanley shot backwards out of the portal, trailing a scream. He landed on the parking lot tumbling head over heels.

Victor threw the SUV into park and jumped out. He ran over to Stanley.

A burst of white light followed and dissipated short of him. The beam generator skidded across the parking lot creating sparks and sizzling sounds. Dr. Joplin came out of his paralyzed stupor, grabbed a metal bucket and ran after it.

"What the heck is this thing?"

The beam generator came to a halt by a tire on a pickup truck. Dr. Joplin used the bucket to scoop it up and ran back to the site. He wiped sweat from his forehead as he joined Victor and a traumatized Stanley.

Victor removed the harness from Stanley's sore chest. He placed the harness in a plastic bin. He lifted Stanley's T-shirt and examined the deep welts in his skin where the tug of war between the robot and the SUV had taken its toll.

"We'll get you fixed-up back at the lab, Stan," Victor said.

For once in his life Stanley didn't comment. He just sat on the edge of the opened SUV cargo area and stared into space.

Dr. Joplin placed the bucket on the ground. "Don't know what this is, but we're going to dissect it and find out what it does."

"Beam generator," Stanley said. "From the robot." With that, he got up, walked to the back seat, opened the door and flopped down.

Dr. Joplin and Victor stared at each other, both filled with trepidation. They gathered up their equipment and left the scene.

STANLEY, WRAPPED IN A BLANKET, SIPPED COFFEE AT A table in the lab surrounded by Victor, Dr. Joplin, Clovis and Mark. The beam generator smoldered in the metal bucket with hot mats under it on the table.

"Thank God nothing happened to you!" Victor said. He raked his hands through his hair, his emotions wild. "You could have been killed by that thing, or torn apart. This was the stupidest thing we have ever done, all in the name of science!"

Dr. Joplin stood and placed his hands-on Victor's shoulders. "Look, I realize this was a very risky experiment, but everything turned out alright. Stanley's here in one piece. We have this beam generator to study and we're going to get to the bottom of this disappearance. If anything, this goes way beyond the 1952 disappearance. We have physical evidence in our hands."

Stanley threw the blanket off and jumped up. "What if I've caused some ripple effect in this doorway? What if those robots come here?"

"Do you feel up to talking about this now? Exactly what did you see?" Dr. Joplin asked.

Stanley sat slouched in his chair. He stared down at the table. "Terminator. Robots have taken over this place. Humans being hunted. D'laine's picture was down to a tee as to what these things look like. I hope to never see another robot for as long as I live."

"Let's upload the film," Victor said.

# CHAPTER FORTY-ONE

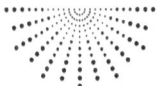

*Z*andal sent a beam of light across the desolate landscape. Robots marched from all directions and joined him at the portal.

AN EGROM SENTRY FELT A DISTURBANCE. HE WAVED HIS hands in front of him and a portal materialized. He was face-to-face with a robot. He quickly waved his hand again and the portal and robot vanished. He made a series of loud clicks and chirps which were relayed across the field. Within moments, a dozen Egroms joined him at the site and stood guard, hands up in front of them reinforcing the portal to create stability.

The Elders and Ghury sat around the fire in the village. They all became suddenly alert as a silent message was relayed.

"Great danger is on the horizon. A portal has become unstable," Ghury said.

There was much conversation around the fire.

"We must send for D'laine at once," Adrum said.

Ghury shook his head, sadly. "Her powers are immature."

Drusta shook his head, adamant. "She has had time to assert herself and grow into her powers. I think you underestimate our young warrior. She is needed. Send for her."

A WAVY VERTICAL LINE SHIMMERED ON THE LANDSCAPE AS the portal burst open. Zandal moved his forces through the portal leaving four sentry robots to guard the portal doorway at Zan.

Within seconds, Egroms appeared at the portal doorway on Thol. And within a split second, they lay dead as the Robots marched through the portal.

D'LAINE, TRAKON, JOR-DAN, KITRY AND THE VISIONARY gathered around the glass dome in the Visionary temple. They watched as thousands of Robots blackened the field.

"Trakon, send messengers to all the neighboring kingdoms, and gather the armies," Jor-Dan said.

"We are vastly outnumbered," Trakon said.

"The Plotals must help the Egroms," D'laine urged.

The Visionary agreed. Trakon and Jor-Dan looked at her as if she had lost her mind.

"Have you gone temporarily insane?" Trakon asked.

The scene in the globe showed hundreds of Egroms emerging from the Cember Forest.

D'laine pointed. "Not only are these my adopted people, but they are the ancient guardians of Thol. We can't let them be slaughtered without summoning all the help we can gather. We're being invaded by a formidable foe that threatens our very existence. Not only Thol, but all the sharing of places; my world too. They must be stopped!"

The field was black and white with robots and Egroms in battle. Egrom energy blasted and robot laser fire engulfed the field in a lightening-like storm.

JAKLA AND HIS ARMY ATTACKED THE CITY OF CARADON. A Caradon soldier escaped and flew away from the battle, heading toward Ebscalon.

D'LAINE, TRAKON, JOR-DAN AND THE VISIONARY STOOD AT the glass dome.

"We must convince Jakla to join in this fight—there won't be any more battles if we wait much longer," D'laine said.

Trakon shook his head.

The Caradon Crestrider landed at the Ebscalon landing pad and the soldier jumped down.

Several Ciertron guards approached him.

"Caradon is under attack!" the Caradon soldier announced.

The Ciertrons ushered the soldier to the palace. One guard ran to the temple.

"Lock up the dogs," Trakon said.

THE ROOFS SLID OPEN ON THE HANGARS. SEVERAL HUGE motherships slowly emerged followed by a fleet of smaller crestriders. The entire fleet slowly moved across the city sky to

357

the outskirts of the city walls and hovered over the immense animal pens.

A beam from each ship shone down on the pens. The pakows disappeared from the pens. Then the ships shot across the sky and disappeared.

The motherships hovered over the besieged city of Caradon. D'laine, Trakon, Jor-Dan, and soldiers, mounted on the beasts, became engulfed in bright white light and disappeared from the ship's surface.

Mounted Ciertrons appeared in the midst of the fighting on the surface. They made their way through the throng of fighting warriors and plotals to find Jakla, fighting mightily with two Caradonions.

D'laine, in the lead, held out her hand in front of her, clutching one of her crystals. She charged through the masses of fighting soldiers and engulfed Jakla in a force field, immobilizing him with his arm raised to strike his opponent. He bellowed in rage as he could not move.

"D'laine! I vow to harness this power of yours!" Jakla yelled.

Fighting warriors from all sides noticed the Plotal leader in a frozen state. The fighting slowly ceased. D'laine motioned for Trakon and Jor-Dan to stay back. She approached Jakla on Lulu.

"Thol is being invaded. We need your help," D'laine said.

Jakla struggled to strike out.

D'laine rode into his force-field. She touched his forehead to share a vision. Robots and Egroms in battle were reflected in Jakla's eyes. His expression changed to confusion.

"What is this I see?" Jakla demanded.

"An invading force from another place. They must be stopped before they reach our cities... your encampments," D'laine explained.

"What is this species?" Jakla asked.

"Intelligent machines called robots. These seem quite evolved and have a single purpose," D'laine explained.

"What is their purpose?" Jakla asked.

"War, destruction, enslavement," D'laine said.

"Why should I help you? I could use these machines to conquer Thol," Jakla said.

"They're not looking for a partnership. They will kill all leaders and enslave the remaining population," D'laine said.

Jakla pondered momentarily. D'laine held out her hand and absorbed the energy field. Jakla fell to the ground. He looked up at D'laine.

"I would rather die than fight at the side of my enemy," Jakla said.

"Don't worry, you will get that chance. Do nothing to save your people and you will die," D'laine said. She looked at Jor-Dan. He stepped forward.

Jakla got to his feet.

"Jakla, the Great War of Taylon left Thol in ruins, but we had the ability to recover. These machines would prevent that. Do you want your peoples' sons and daughters enslaved?" Jor-Dan asked. He stretched his arm out toward the masses around them.

"I understand your hatred. Every nation on Thol has treated the Plotals as savage creatures. Unworthy of kinship," Jor-Dan said. He hung his head in shame.

"For generations, we've tried to be friends with your people. Fighting with you because you forced us," Jor-Dan said. He faced the battlefield and addressed the warriors.

"From this day forth the Ciertron people will live beside and among the Plotals in peace," Jor-Dan said. He turned and met Jakla's gaze. "As equals. Fight with us today or not, the struggle between us is over. But, if you should attack us, we will retaliate at full force."

Jor-Dan walked away.

Jakla's eyes bore into D'laine. "Jor-Dan cannot be trusted."

"Do you really believe that? We are going to fight the invaders. You can fight with us or get in line to be destroyed next," D'laine said.

Jakla walked toward Trakon.

Trakon slowly wrapped his hand around the hilt of his laser sword as Jakla approached. He glanced at his father in the distance. Jor-Dan moved his head ever so slightly. Trakon drew in a breath and released his hand from the weapon.

Jakla stood directly in front of Trakon. He pulled in a loud sniff. "Together then." Jakla extended his arm.

Trakon grasped Jakla's arm. "Together."

D'laine felt a tingle in her head. She zoned out for a moment. Trakon noticed her vacant look.

"D'laine? Are you alright?" Trakon asked as he quickly crossed the space that separated them, Jakla and Jor-Dan not far behind.

A scene played in her head. She saw the robots slaughtering the Egroms. Then she saw Ghury look to the sky. She heard *D'laine, help us.*

D'laine's knees buckled. Trakon caught her before she hit the ground.

"Ghury!" D'laine screamed. She was filled with terror from her vision. She focused on Trakon. "There's no time to spare!"

Jakla pointed to two plotal warriors. To one he said, "Return to camp. Gather the reserve party and ride hard." To the other he said, "Gather the main army. Join forces. I will await you at the battlefield."

Jor-Dan placed his hand on Jakla's arm. "Wait. Crestriders are much faster."

Jor-Dan pressed his chest communicator. "Take these two Plotal warriors to their encampments to gather their army." He pressed his communicator again. "Follow the crestriders. Upload the Plotal army and their mounts. Head to the field!" He turned to the two Plotal warriors. "Tell your armies to mount their pakows. You will all be beamed up to the motherships."

Jakla turned to his warriors. He watched as the two Plotals were beamed up to the crestriders. They shot across the sky with two motherships close behind.

The remaining mass at Caradon were beamed up to a mothership.

THOUSANDS OF ROBOTS THUNDERED ACROSS THE landscape. Egroms, ten deep in their path, blasted them with an energy wave. A few Robots fell, but not many. Robots fired lasers at the Egroms. Some Egroms fell. Some evaporated.

The Motherships carrying the Ciertron, Plotal and Caradon warriors arrived first. The mixed army beamed down behind the Egrom lines. The Egroms parted to allow the warriors access to the enemy. Other Tholian nations arrived in ships and on the ground and joined in the battle. Full scale war erupted as warriors thundered forward astride pakows. More Plotals were beamed down from the two motherships and joined the fight. More Egroms charged from the Cember Forest and from across the plain.

A black shadow on the moss and in the sky moved from the Cember Forest. Tens of thousands of Kudaja warriors swarmed across the field, or flew on their borjos. Their deafening chatter leading the way.

Combat was fierce. Many more warriors fell than Robots.

Jakla and Trakon fought back-to-back on pakows with D'laine close by.

"Go for the eyes. Then the control panel on the chests," D'laine commanded.

Jakla took a direct hit in the chest from a robot. He toppled from his pakow. D'laine jumped from Lulu and ran to his aid. Trakon, Plotals and Ciertrons close by defended them. D'laine knelt at Jakla's side. His breath came in ragged wheezes. He grasped her forearm.

"You must conquer these things and save Thol," Jakla said.

"Yes. With your help," D'laine said.

Jakla shook his head. He succumbed to the moment. "No, my time has passed." He closed his eyes to welcome death.

"Not today." D'laine rubbed her hands together. A bright energy glowed around her hands. She touched Jakla's chest. His body jerked, then settled. A moment later, she removed her hands.

Surprised, Jakla opened his eyes and raised up to an elbow. He stared at her hard. He grasped her forearm. She awkwardly grasped his much larger personage.

"You have spared my life. Why?"

"We all want the same things: peace, love and family. Besides, today we need all able-bodied warriors we can get," D'laine said.

Together they stood and joined the fight.

An energy wave shimmered in the distance. The portal to Earth wavered. D'laine stopped in mid battle. An awareness crossed her face, then overwhelming happiness. Ghury was suddenly at her side. He faced her.

"You are D'laine, a warrior of Thol," Ghury said. "This is your duty—your responsibility."

D'laine looked shocked. "I need to go home!"

Trakon and Jor-Dan joined D'laine and Ghury.

"You have the power to stop all of this," Ghury said, sweeping two arms wide.

"No, I don't! They're invincible. My brothers and my father need me. I must go now—before it's too late." She turned to leave. Trakon grabbed her arm.

"You can stop this. Don't leave. We need you," Trakon said.

D'laine hesitated.

Trakon gazed at her with love-filled adoration. "I need you." He touched her shoulder.

"You must force them back to where they came from and seal the portal," Ghury explained.

D'laine hesitated. She glanced toward the portal to Earth with fierce longing.

# CHAPTER FORTY-TWO

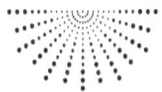

*L*ee stood in D'laine's room by a shelf full of crystals, holding one. "Trust your instincts. I know you're okay."

The crystal in his hands glowed brightly. Lee stared at it, astonished.

"Roosssaaa!" He yelled. "Rosa!"

Footsteps thundered up the stairs and Rosa burst into the room, clutching her chest.

"What happened? Is Brian okay? What are you doing in here, Lee?" Rosa asked, highly agitated.

He held the glowing crystal out toward her. "Look!"

Rosa stared at the crystal, astonished. She made the sign of the cross. "What does it mean?"

Lee stared at her with just as much surprise. "I don't know. This is a simple quartz crystal."

"But they don't glow!" Rosa said.

"This has to do with D'laine. It's some kind of a message or something," he said.

"Will it stop glowing if I hold it?" Rosa asked.

Lee shrugged. "I don't know. Here." He passed the crystal to her.

Rosa stared at the crystal in her hands. It wasn't glowing. "Huh. Here, let's see if it was a fluke, or if something funny is going on."

She handed the crystal back to Lee. It glowed in his hands.

"It has to be a sign. Of what, I don't have a clue, but it gives me hope that my little girl is alive and I'll see her again one day."

# CHAPTER FORTY-THREE

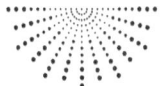

*J*or-Dan grasped D'laine's shoulder. "If we don't stop them here, your Earth is next."

The crystal on her necklace glowed. She grasped it. D'laine stood on Lulu's saddle on her pakow. D'laine shouted. "Send the Egroms to the front!"

D'laine rode her pakow to the front. She jumped down. D'laine and the Egroms joined together to employ a vast energy field. The robots stumbled backwards.

After several moments, D'laine weakened. The energy field lost strength and the robots advanced. The battle erupted full force. D'laine and Ghury faced each other.

"We need more strength, more energy," D'laine said, exhausted.

"You must bring forth all your knowledge. All your power," Ghury said. He tapped her forehead.

As D'laine tried to regain her strength, she spied a large crystal on the ground. She reached for it. Sparks flew. She snatched her hand away. At that moment, she became quiet.

"Spirit, Universe—I need your help, your strength. Give me courage!"

She closed her eyes for a moment, then opened them. She grasped the crystal and stood. A swirling vortex of energy engulfed her. She used The Voice. "*Stand aside.*"

Trakon, Jor-Dan and Jakla barked orders to fall back. The Egroms and Kudaja fell back.

D'laine held the crystal out in front of her. A force field engulfed the robots, their energy sucked into the crystal. Robots fell lifeless to the ground. D'laine moved forward—slow and struggling at first. Then gaining power as she charged forward in a run. She threw the crystal into the portal to Zan. A lightning storm appeared in the portal. The slit on the landscape sealed. Everything was quiet. Plotals, Ciertrons, Egroms, Kudaja and Caradonions stood in absolute silence for tender moments. Then they erupted in celebration.

D'laine and Ghury nodded to each other. She and Jor-Dan hugged. D'laine and Jakla grasped arms then D'laine pulled Jakla into a hug, which confused him.

Trakon grabbed her away from Jakla. They melted into a kiss. She pulled back. "I have to go."

Trakon pulled her close. She eased out of his grasp. "Don't make it any harder. I have to go home," D'laine said.

Trakon pulled her to him. "Please, please don't go." He kissed her tenderly.

"The time closes," Ghury urged.

D'laine tugged herself free from Trakon. She sprinted across the field toward the quivering portal. She turned and waved, then disappeared.

Only a handful of the group understood what happened, and those were semi shell-shocked as they witnessed her crossing over to her home world. A murmur among the troops started as a low whisper. Within moments a roar of celebration at defeating their formidable foe ruptured the air.

Neither the leaders, nor the Egroms joined in the jubilation. They fully understood their great loss.

Jakla grasped Trakon's shoulder. "D'laine is a great warrior. Duty bound. You must respect her wish and carry on."

Trakon walked off through the mass of warriors, numb.

# CHAPTER FORTY-FOUR

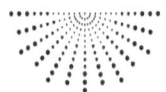

*S*tanley pointed a Geiger counter-type device around the parking place which was no longer roped off or barricaded. A wave of energy shook the ground and Stanley lost his footing. He slammed to the blacktop while the ground continued to shake.

"Earthquake!" Stanley made it to his feet again, albeit unsteadily.

D'laine emerged through the portal and crashed into Stanley. They fell to the ground in a heap. After a moment, Stanley recovered his senses and scrambled to his feet. He looked at D'laine and the sudden realization of who she was and what just happened hit him full force. "Holy shit!"

D'laine glanced around, a little dazed, then stood. "Sorry."

Stanley rushed forward. "D'laine Jackson?"

D'laine stared at Stanley strangely. "This is Earth?"

Stanley's face exploded into a smile. "Yes! You're home!" He stared at her warrior's outfit. "Wow. I can't wait to hear what happened, and how you finally were able to come home."

She tented her nose and mouth with her hands then tried

desperately to hold back the tears. "I never thought I would hear a human speak English ever again! Yes, I'm D'laine."

Stanley steered her toward the SUV. "You're a little conspicuous."

D'laine touched his arm. "My brother, Brian..."

Stanley opened the passenger door and helped her inside. "He's very ill." Stanley retrieved his equipment, tossed it into the back of the SUV then climbed into the drivers' seat.

D'laine placed her hand on Stanley's arm. "Will you take me to him?"

"You bet, but we have to make one stop first," Stanley said. He hastily drove out of the parking lot, merged onto the Katy Freeway and blended into the traffic.

Dr. Joplin and Victor poured over stacks of data. "What's taking Stanley so long?" Dr. Joplin asked.

Victor discarded a piece of paper onto a pile on the table. "Should have had the Chinese food delivered."

The door slammed open.

"It's about time. We're starving," Dr. Joplin said, quite annoyed.

Stanley, overly hyper, rushed into the office. "Grab the camera. Hurry!"

Victor and Dr. Joplin jumped up.

"The robots?" Dr. Joplin asked.

Victor appeared angry. "You didn't do anything stupid, did you?" They rushed to the lab.

D'laine paced in the deserted lab.

Dr. Joplin and Victor dashed into the lab, following Stanley.

Victor stopped in his tracks. "Oh, my God. Oh. My. God."

Dr. Joplin did a double take. "Miss Jackson?"

Stanley grabbed memory cards and stuffed them in his pockets. He swung the digital camera strap around his neck.

D'laine turned and faced them. "You must be Dr. Joplin and Victor."

Stanley became impatient. "Introductions are over. Grab the camera stuff."

"Where are we going?" Dr. Joplin asked.

"My Dad's house," D'laine said.

Victor grabbed the video camera as they headed for the door.

THE SUV PULLED UP IN LEE'S DRIVEWAY. D'LAINE practically leapt from the moving car. Stanley, Victor and Dr. Joplin followed after retrieving their equipment. D'laine sprinted to the house and tried the door handle.

Locked.

She rang the doorbell once, twice. Stanley bounded up to the door and pounded loudly.

Lee finally opened the door. He sucked in his breath and grabbed D'laine in a bear hug, tears spilling down his face. "You're home!"

"Daddy... oh, daddy!"

They hugged and cried on the doorstep. Buffy joined the group at the door. She whined and wailed, her tail wagging nonstop. She jumped on D'laine.

The group moved into the house. D'laine hugged Buffy. "Buffy! I didn't think I'd see you again, girl."

Another door slammed shut upstairs and footsteps pounded down the stairs. Jamie entered the room. He squealed at the sight of D'laine and ran to her.

"D'laine!"

D'laine scooped him up in her arms and showered him with kisses. "Hey, sport. Look how you've grown!" She put him down.

"Did you see Harry Potter, or Captain Kirk, D'laine?" Jamie asks.

She ruffled his hair. "No, but I know someone you'd really like."

D'laine turned to her father. "Brian?"

Lee sighed and shook his head, filled with sadness. "It's not good, honey. The doctor doesn't think he's going to make it."

D'laine sprinted up the stairs followed by everyone else. Buffy bounded ahead of the group and ran into Brian's room. Brian slept in the room amid monitoring machines lit up with LED lights. Soft beeps sounded in the stillness. D'laine approached the bed and sat on the edge. She fluffed his hair. He stirred and woke. Buffy jumped on the bed and lay beside Brian, panting and whining. Lee and Jamie stood close by while Stanley, Victor and Dr. Joplin stood on the other side of the bed.

"Look who's here, Brian," Lee said.

Brian stirred then woke fully. He reached out a weak hand toward D'laine. She grasped his hand. "D'laine? Am I in heaven?"

"No, you're still in bed, but not for long."

D'laine pulled her crystal out of her pouch. A soft glow emitted from the rock. Dr. Joplin hoisted the camera and recorded.

Stanley whispered into a recorder. "She's holding a quartz crystal and it is producing a light."

Victor yanked the recorder from Stanley and whispered into it. "The crystal glows."

Stanley shrugged.

D'laine placed her hands on Brian's chest. The glow spread across Brian's chest. "Brian, tomorrow you'll be able to run and play just like all the other kids."

Brian sighed. "I didn't get a new heart, D'laine."

The glow sank into Brian's chest and disappeared. D'laine leaned forward and kissed him on the cheek. "You don't need one anymore."

Brian took a deep breath. "I feel stronger!"

D'laine got up and held out her hand to him. "Come on, it's time you got out of that bed."

Brian swung the covers back and stood. "Daddy, look!" He turned to D'laine. "This is the first time I've been out of bed in a couple of months!"

D'laine turned to Lee. "Daddy..."

Buffy sprung off the bed. Lee held up his hand. "You're not leaving without us."

She smiled wide. "That's what I hoped you'd say. We've got to hurry."

Dr. Joplin stopped recording. "What's going on?"

D'laine led the group out of the room. Victor, Dr. Joplin and Stanley tagged along. Buffy romped before the group, down the stairs to the foyer. They all gathered by the front door, including Buffy.

D'laine looked to Victor, Stanley and Dr. Joplin. "Will you drive us to the mall?"

Victor's brows furrowed. "You want to go shopping?"

Stanley got in Victor's face. "No, you simpleton. She wants to take her family back to where she just came from."

Victor appeared shocked. "You can't do that."

Lee gave Victor an arrogant look. "Why not? I'm her father and I approve."

Victor thought about it, then shrugged. "I guess you can."

Jamie pulled on D'laine's outfit. "Are we coming with you, D'laine?"

"You sure are. Wait 'til you see what school is like," she said, excited.

She opened the door and they all left the house and piled into the vehicle.

THE SUV STOPPED AND PARKED NEAR THE FORMERLY roped-off space. Everyone emerged from the car, including Buffy. D'laine gathered her family around her. "Everyone hold hands."

Stanley approached D'laine. "Take me with you... please."

D'laine thought a moment. "What do you know about solar power, quartz or silicon crystals?"

Stanley brightened. "I worked on a couple of solar projects with Lockheed and NASA."

D'laine grabbed his hand. "Hope you don't mind traveling light."

Stanley gave the thumbs up to Victor and Dr. Joplin. "This is REAL science at its best!"

Victor put his hands on Stanley's shoulders. "Are you sure?"

Stanley removed the lanyard with his badge, the camera and the recorder, and put the cords over Victor's head. No longer fretful, no longer whining. He was in full control of his emotions as he grasped Victor's hand. "I've never been more sure of anything in my whole life."

Dr. Joplin tried to balance his conflict, but understood the once in a lifetime opportunity for the scientist in front of him. "I'll expect a full report!"

"That's a deal," Stanley said.

Buffy joined the family. D'laine dropped to her knees. She rubbed and hugged the dog. "Buffy, you have to stay here."

Victor approached D'laine and Buffy. "I'll take care of her."

D'laine teared up. "Thanks." D'laine stood. She grabbed Brian and Jamie's hands. "Daddy, hold Brian's hand. Stanley, hold Jamie's hand. Don't anyone let go!"

D'laine turned her head to Victor and Dr. Joplin. "We have to go. Thank you for your help. I'll never forget your kindness."

Buffy lunged to join D'laine. Victor held her by the collar. "You have to stay here, Buffy."

Buffy whined, inconsolable.

D'laine urged the group forward, and within a tick of a second, they disappeared with a blast of white light.

# CHAPTER FORTY-FIVE

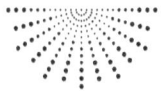

*T*he somber war party cleared the field of wounded and dead. Rows of disabled robots littered the ground. Zandal's immense form set him apart from the others. Jakla watched his warriors gather their dead and place them on pakows.

Jor-Dan consoled Trakon. "She may return one day, son."

Trakon escaped Jor-Dan's company and walked away. "Not now, father."

Ghury approached Jor-Dan. "His wound will heal with time."

A loud blast and a wave of energy shook the ground. D'laine and the group stumbled into Thol.

Trakon turned and ran toward D'laine.

Jamie stared up at Ghury. "Wow, a Wookie!"

Ghury grumbled.

Trakon and D'laine embraced.

Brian touched a Plotal Warrior. "Wow, an alligator man!" Brian exclaimed.

The Plotal snapped his snout at Brian.

Brian snatched his hand away and backed up toward his father.

Stanley spotted the robots and rushed over to them. "I hope they're dead! I wish I brought some tools with me." Then he saw a ship gliding through the air. "If only Victor and Dr. Joplin could see this!"

Lee and Jor-Dan grasped arms and approved each other.

"Welcome," Jor-Dan said.

"I think I'm going to like this place," Lee said.

D'laine and Trakon stood arm-in-arm. "This is going to be real interesting," D'laine said.

# CHAPTER FORTY-SIX

*D*arren sat stunned, holding onto the picture of the four images. Victor appeared to be dreamy. Buffy jumped on the bed and snuggled into Victor's side.

"Was that the last time you ever saw Stanley, Dad?" Darren asked.

"Yup. I will never forget D'laine Jackson," Victor said. He rested a hand on Buffy. "D'laine restored me before she left earth—that's why I'll never need glasses again."

"How did you get this picture, Dad?" Darren asked.

"It was the last picture she drew—where she was in the picture," Victor said.

"Can I have a copy of the picture? I promise to keep it hidden." Darren pleaded.

"Sure. I'm pretty sure your mother knows this picture will be a discussion eventually, but it would be best if you didn't flaunt it."

Darren sat thinking. "Wow, Dad. Don't you wish you could have gone, too?"

Victor laughed. "No, my place is here, son. And besides, if I had gone to Thol you know what that means, don't you?"

"I would have been history, right?" Darren asked.

Victor rubbed Darren on the head. "Right."

They got off the bed and left the room with Buffy bounding around them.

*The End?*

# Creatures of Thol
© 2020 by Dawn Greenfield Ireland

### Ghury
### Egrom elder of the Cember Forest Tribe

### Jakla Bosakin
### Plotal Commander

### Diwal Dog

### Borjo

# MAP OF THOL

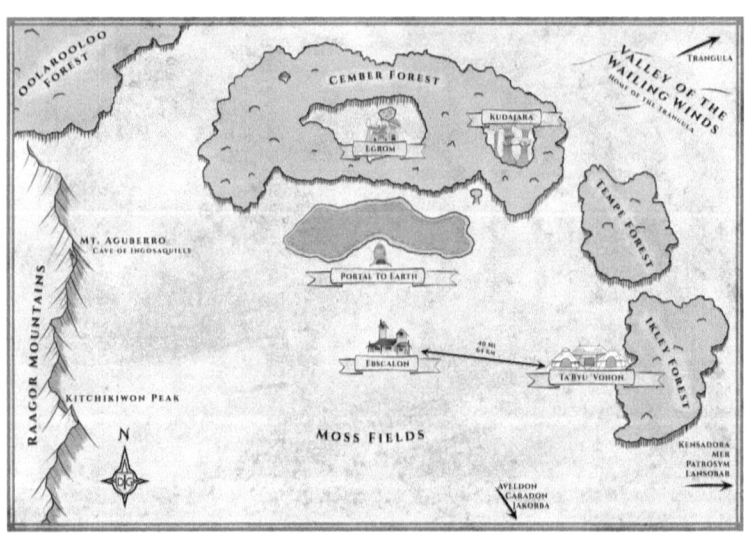

# WANT MORE THOL? CHECK OUT BOOK 2, GIFTS FROM THOL

Here's what's going on in Thol in book 2.

D'laine is happy that her family is settling in and getting used to their new surroundings. She knows that Thol changes people from Earth who cross over.

Lee and Jamie discover their gifts. Brian doesn't seem to have any innate gift, and it makes him feel left out. On the other hand, big-brained Stanley Daigle has the Egroms keeping their distance because he almost drained Adrum's brain during their first lesson together.

Lee and Stanley are on a quest to find Greg Claymore. They seek help from the Egroms. They find Greg on the other side of Thol living with the Oolarooloo people who are great healers. At first Greg refuses to talk to Lee or Stanley. He wants nothing to do with his former Earth.

Victor, left behind on Earth, is frantic. His wife is terminally ill and he knows D'laine can heal her. He writes a note and goes to where Claymore disappeared on the beach. He places the piece of paper in the area and uses an advanced camera to see the energy flickers. He slides the paper over there and it disappears.

Buffy leaps through the portal. Victor couldn't stop her.

Pup rescues her from a diwal attack. Pup leads Buffy to the palace. The Ciertrons don't know what to make of the earth dog. Pup and Buffy become inseparable friends.

In Thol, D'laine wakes and sits instantly. The piece of paper flies through the air to her hand. She reads it and sends a mental message straight to Victor telling him she will come and help.

D'laine, Trakon and Stanley, bearing gifts, walk through the portal to earth. But will they be able to return to Thol? Will D'laine and Trakon get back in time to fulfill their marriage vows? Or, will they be stuck in a place that Trakon despises due to the noise, traffic, and pollution?

**The adventure continues**

**Book 2 ~ Gifts From Thol**
**Book 3 ~ Love of Thol**
**Book 4 ~ King of Thol**
**Book 5 ~ Earth Calling Thol**

# Prophecy of Thol: A Glossary

## Characters

| | |
|---|---|
| Absadul | One of the Egrom village elders. |
| Adrum | One of the Egrom village elders, he is tasked specifically with teaching D'laine the history of Thol. |
| Akubel | An ancient Egrom leader from long ago who received a prophecy. |
| Al Jordan | A junior staff member at Houston Daily News looking to make his big break, and a science fiction fan at heart. |
| Anderson Cooper | Reporting on CNN from Katy Mills Mall. |
| Ben Joplin | The 62-year-old head of Rice University's physics department. |
| Bensol | One of the Egrom village elders tasked with helping and training D'laine to realize her destiny. |
| Bok-Tor | A Safri prisoner D'laine saves from the Plotals. |
| Brenda | D'laine's childhood friend since 3rd grade. |
| Brian Jackson | D'laine's younger brother; at 10 years old, he plays in the Little League, but a sudden health complication might put a stop to it all. |
| Bruce Miller | Witness in parking lot at Katy Mills Mall. |
| Buffy | The Jackson family's tan and white Pit bull. |
| Clovis | Six-foot-ten lanky technician at Rice U. |
| Connor | Tall, dark-haired, and D'laine's boyfriend. |
| Dannin | One of Ebscalon's council members, he is in charge of livestock, food and water, and hosk gathering. |
| Darren Bennett | Victor Bennett's son; this 8-year-old is both space obsessed and loves a good story. |
| Ditol | One of the Egrom village elders tasked with helping and training D'laine to realize her destiny. |
| D'laine Jackson | Smart and resourceful, D'laine, 17, is in for more than she could have ever imagined when the mysterious dream that's haunted her since a tragic accident becomes reality. |
| Detective Ferguson | Investigates D'laine's disappearance at Katy Mills Mall parking lot. |

| | |
|---|---|
| Drs Vickers and Reynolds | Texas Children's Hospital. |
| Drusta | One of the Egrom village elders tasked with helping and training D'laine to realize her destiny. |
| Clarence Dupree | An inventor defensive about his achievements; he comes up with a device to pick up spectral images. |
| Ekal | One of the Visionary's only two disciples. |
| Eric Villarreal | Rosa's husband; a ranch hand of the Jacksons. |
| Fox News Crew | 2 men in Fox van who video the police investigation at Katy Mills Mall. |
| Ghury | The leader of the Egrom village elders, Ghury becomes D'laine's mentor and guide for the path that lays ahead. |
| Hal-sa-Bin | A member of the Ebscalon council; he is in charge of security. |
| Herish | A Kudaja warrior of Cember Forest and D'laine's first friend on Thol. |
| Jakla Bosakin | The vicious Comander of the Plotal army, he is bent on capturing D'laine and using her powers to plunder all of Thol. |
| Jamie Jackson | At only 6 years old, he's D'laine's youngest brother. |
| Ja-Toy-Anic | Despite being a citizen of Ebscalon, his loyalties may lie elsewhere. |
| Jimmy Shoemaker | Young man who used his phone to video D'laine's disappearance. |
| Joey | D'laine's childhood friend since 3rd grade. |
| Dr. Joseph Paxton | Victor and Stanley's boss at Whitting Institute, LA., world renowned scientist. |
| Jor-dan | The King of Ebscalon, 66, doesn't shy from being both venerable ruler and fearless warrior. |
| Jubulon | The ruler of Aveldon. |
| Kestrum | A female Egrom who guides D'laine through getting adjusted to Thol; the two quickly become fast friends. |
| Kitry | The motherly Queen of Ebscalon (60), always looking to make those under her care as comfortable as possible. |

## Characters, *Continued*

| | |
|---|---|
| Laoife | Mother to Ja-Toy-Anic, she shares both his leanings and vices. |
| Lee Jackson | Father of D'laine, Brian, and Jamie, this 46-year-old NASA scientist's faith is tested when his eldest mysteriously vanishes. |
| Lori Jackson | Lee Jackson's late wife, and the victim to a tragic accident. |
| Majordomo | In charge of the dining salon in the palace. |
| Mark | Victor and Stanley's tech assistant. |
| Mayaar | Jor-Dan's manservant. |
| Mitch Lowenhaupt | Lee Jackson's NASA boss. |
| Police | Gary Davidson, |
| Quark Zerfre | One of Jor-Dan's advisors, he heads Ebscalon's crestrider fleet. |
| Rachel | D'laine's childhood friend since 3rd grade. |
| Rettu | The second disciple of the Visionary. |
| Rosa Villarreal | The Jackson family's housekeeper. |
| Stanley Daigle | Victor Bennett's old friend and fellow physicist, this genius's enthusiasm with the alternate dimension theory is unmatched. |
| Swezek | One of the Egrom village elders tasked with helping and training D'laine to realize her destiny. |
| The Visionary | Both healer and spiritual guide, the old Ciertron man is one of only three inhabiting Ebscalon's sacred temple, waiting for something. Or someone. |
| Trabet | One of the Egrom village elders tasked with helping and training D'laine to realize her destiny. |
| Trakon | The Prince of Ebscalon (18) has refused all his suitors so far in favor of his love for a mysterious dream girl. Trakon has many roles in the kingdom including working on the crestrider ships. |
| Trudy Weatherford | Witness in parking lot at Katy Mills Mall. |
| Twum | D'laine's handmaiden assigned to her during her stay at Ebscalon's palace. |
| Victor Bennett | An accomplished physicist and best friends with Stanley Daigle, he's one of few who found out what happened to D'laine Jackson. |
| Youndon | The ruler of Lansobar. |
| Zandal | The cruel leader of the robotics forces of Zan, he aims to conquer all who stand in his way; and an unknown anomaly might provide just that opportunity. |

# Locations & Places

| | |
|---|---|
| Caradon | A city-kingdom, and home to the Caradonians. |
| Cember Forest | Home to the Egroms and Kudaja, this giant, colorful forest is filled with massive, unknown flora and fauna. |
| Ebscalon | A Ciertron city of diamond-like roofs and colorful banners rebuilt in the wake of a devastating war, its name means "knowledge". |
| Raagor Mountains | A large mountain range home to the Raagor Ice people. |
| The Visionary's Temple | The sacred Ciertron temple is set in the middle of Ebscalon. |
| Thol | An alternate Earth, Thol is the third planet in orbit; but this is where similarities end, with two suns, four large moons, vibrant landscapes, and a plethora of unique creatures and races. |
| Valley of Wailing Winds | Located on the opposite side of Thol. |
| Zan | Another alternate Earth, this world has been reduced to a barren wasteland by its robotic inhabitants, humans made into slaves and prey. |

# Races

| | |
|---|---|
| Caradonions | Tholian humans similar to Ciertrons, but less technologically advanced. |
| Ciertrons | Most resembling Earth's humans, but with bronzed skin and dark hair. Ciertrons are a technologically advanced society, defenders of justice who value honor despite their constant conflicts with Plotals. |
| Egroms | A wise, ancient race possessing wonderous abilities. The long-lived Egroms have since faded into myth and legend, isolating themselves in the Cember Forest while they continue to carry out their self-appointed duties. |
| Kudaja | Described as tiny peoples who inhabit the Cember Forest, the Kudaja ride borjos as their mounts and wield wyres. Despite their stature, they possess a significant ability. |
| Mer | A very similar race to the Ciertrons, Mers only differ by their square jaws and pronounced foreheads. |
| Plotals | Tall reptilian bipeds that appear both human and alligator with the addition of hidden barbs on the ends of their tails. Their society was destroyed by the Great War of Taylon, leaving the survivors to live a nomadic life of plundering and slavery across Thol. |
| Raagor | Living in the mountain range of their namesake, the Raagor Ice People wear little clothing, exposing their hairless, blue-veined pale skin without fear of the cold. A touch by a Raagor is death. |
| Safri | An intelligent race of Thol, the Safri have friendly relations with the Ciertrons and trade with them. Their appearance resembles a blend of human and goat, with little horns, pointed ears, and cloven hooves; the small wings and three-fingered hands being an exception. |

# Creatures

| | |
|---|---|
| Augugal | A large spiked, hard-shelled animal, augugals are capable of blending into their environment, but these herbivores will prove to be both quick and dangerous when threatened. |
| Borjo | Resembling small dragons unable to breathe fire, the dragonfly-like borjo are used as mounts by the Kudaja. Some borjos have unique abilities. |
| Diwal dog | Roaming the sponge plains, diwal dogs are widely considered vicious carnivores, capable of stripping their prey in seconds with their layered, razor-sharp teeth. However, some find the gray-skinned, tufted canines to be misunderstood creatures. |
| Floff | Despite its cute, wide-eyed appearance and fluffy limbs, this is a carnivore that hunts on the wing. |
| Gagu | Brightly colored feathers cover most of this flying creature, with its clawed membrane wings being the exception. |
| Grophie caterpillar | Living in the Cember Forest, its sting results in itchy purple spots that must be soothed with an Egrom antidote. |
| Hosk | This spider-creature's palm-sized, fluffy body varies in color, and contrasts its black legs and eyes. Living in colonies, it produces plenty of silken webbing from the moss-like sponges of the plains; a material widely used by all the races of Thol. |
| Lulu | A female pakow that becomes D'laine's mount. |
| Mruck | Appearing a mishmash of creatures with its lidless eyes, long trunk, split hooves, and short ears, mrucks are surprisingly edible and enjoy water. |
| Og | Large, lumbering animals that live on the sponge plains. |
| Orich | A large flying creature with a heavily built body and broad wings. |
| Pakow | The epitome of gentle giants, pakows are bulky, wooly beasts with six legs, wide faces, and compound eyes. They are used by several races as mounts, transportation, and labor. |
| Par | A type of scarlet-winged bird. |
| Quokin | This draconic creature makes its home in water, recognizable by its green-tipped black scales and curious personality. It is said a person touched by a quokin will find their true love. |
| Saber-toothed chun | Large, saber-toothed creatures that inhabit the Raagor mountains; they are used by the Raagor people as mounts. |
| Sidel | A rabbit-sized creature that lives on the sponge plains; its meat is an easy source of food. |

# Measurements

| | |
|---|---|
| Complete path | A Tholian year |
| Full turn | A Tholian day |
| Keld | A Tholian month |
| Chack | A Tholian hour |
| Dunct | A Tholian moment |
| Notch | A Tholian week |
| Sepiks | Copper coins used by Tholians as currency. |

# Technology

| | |
|---|---|
| Crestriders | Flying ships invented by the Ciertrons for travel and city-wide defense against intruders. |
| GSB | Short for "gravitational synchronizing beam," crestriders use it to enable flight and store solar energy in crystal cells. |
| Light healer | A Ciertron invention that uses a beam of light to heal injuries. |
| Restorative chamber/Smart Closet | A glassed-in multi-purpose chamber serving as wardrobe, that restores and mysteriously cleans clothing. |
| Sonicate box | A Ciertron invention used to assess injuries. |
| Translator | A small metal clip placed behind the ear which then settles into the flesh and serves as an automatic language translator. |
| Wyre | Bows used by the Kudaja; they form an arrow made of pure energy when the glowing string is drawn. Arrows can be set to either stun or kill. |

# Miscellaneous

| | |
|---|---|
| Agrin trees | These gigantic trees produce large amounts of sap, which is tapped and blended with hosk webbing to create many durable items like footwear, clothing, banners, and crestriders. |
| Board Game | Played with markers, octagonal dice, and dowels. Similar to Cribbage and Chinese checkers |
| Silvery leather armor | A Tholian type of clothing made from breathable fabric and worn by its warriors. |
| Kahl | A thick, sweet alcoholic drink consumed by Tholians. |
| Lantern-wick plant | The exact name of this plant is unknown. It grows in large clusters among shaded areas of the Cember Forest, and its thick, oily blue stalks are used in lanterns due to their slow-burning nature. |
| Lightning stones | A special type of rock that produces a purple flame when gently tapped against itself. |
| Sari | Similar to the Earth clothing; worn by domestic women of Thol. |
| The Great War of Taylon | A lengthy Tholian-Plotal war that left all sides decimated. |
| The Voice | A mysterious ability that allows one to control others with verbal commands. |

# A NOTE FROM THE AUTHOR

If you discover a missing element that should be included in the
Glossary, please let me know at
dawn@degreenfield.com

# ABOUT THE AUTHOR

D.E. Greenfield, aka Dawn Greenfield Ireland, is the award-winning author of 22 published novels which consists of 5 series: cozy mystery, sci fi/fantasy, billionaire shapeshifters, and dystopian. There's also a stand-alone sci-fi romantic adventure, 7 nonfiction books (1 hardcover), and she adapted 4 of her screenplays into book format. She also has created over 50 themed notebooks.

Two of her screenplays were optioned, and she worked on a screenwriter-for-hire project. Dawn has a certificate from the Professional Program in Screenwriting from UCLA (2002) and with ScreenwritingU.

D.E. Greenfield's business, Artistic Origins, has been around since 1995. Besides writing, she coaches writers, edits, formats and publishes clients' books.

Her former day job as an award-winning technical writer played a major role in her fiction writing. She is detailed-oriented, the organizational queen of the known universe, and never misses a deadline.

☀ ☀

## Actions Appreciated

**Please leave a review on** the website where you bought the book. Reviews help authors get recognized, get the word out and sell more books. I will love you forever if you leave a review!

**HINT:** don't regurgitate the synopsis for your review. Just tell people what you liked, didn't like – that's what people want – your opinion.

http://degreenfield.com

f  facebook.com/dawn.ireland.18

X  x.com/dawnireland

⊙  instagram.com/dawngreenfieldIreland

in  linkedin.com/in/dawnireland

g  goodreads.com/dawnireland